CUPID'S COMPASS

THE SOULMATE SEEKERS SERIES – BOOK ONE

ASHLEY WEISS

First Edition: June 2023

For more information contact:

Ashley Weiss

www.ashleyweisswrites.ca

ISBN 978-1-7389347-1-3 (hardcover)

ISBN 978-1-7389347-0-6 (paperback)

ISBN 978-1-7389347-2-0 (e-book)

Note from the Author:

For my beloved readers whose hearts have been through the wringer at some point or another, this is a warning. This story explores both the light and dark sides of relationships. I have done my best to approach the bits of heavy content with as much grace and love as humanly possible, whilst not downplaying the effect trauma can have.

Potential triggers include sexual assault, suicidal thoughts, death of loved ones, a religious cult, self-harm off page, homophobia, and emotional abuse.

These stories are acts of fiction, but yours is not. If you have lost a loved one, my heart is with you. If you have considered leaving this earth, I'm grateful you haven't. If you are plagued with anxiety, PTSD, or other mental health struggles, I stand with you—and for you when you can't. This is for the people who aren't okay.

I see you, and the world wouldn't be the same without you.

May this book make your heart swell through the trials of love and romance. Hope cannot be lost where there is love.

Ashley Weiss

CUPID'S
COMPASS

Merry Christmas

Ashley Weiss

DEDICATION

For sixteen-year-old me.
To the girl who had her entire future planned out, lived for romantic
subplots, and believed the best books were the ones you threw across the
room in horror—this one's for you.

PROLOGUE

The Arrival

There is no way to describe the moment a compass arrives. It is faster than a bolt of Jupiter's lightning and as imperceptible as time flickering from one minute to the next. And when Cupid's arrow strikes, there is no going back.

One second there is nothing but stillness—and then the force of nature bends.

Launching up in a tangle of sheets, the young girl with russet red curls gasped. Under the glow of her star projector, an icy and unfamiliar sensation pierced through her chest and prickled down her left arm. She shook her hand out, opening and closing her fist against the numbness. That's when she saw it for the first time.

Stumbling out of bed in a trance, her eyes fixed on her new wrist tattoo. The enchanted compass-clock rose in a stunning silver masterpiece, each detail sparkling against the dark, celestial base. Wisps of starlight danced luminous around its surface and a whispered, ethereal tune hummed as the magic took root.

It was the moment every child and adolescent waited for: the day the gods decided a mortal was mature enough to be linked to their perfect match. Well, not any god. As the sky was ruled by Jupiter and the Underworld was run by Pluto, every god had their own domain. And soulmate links were Cupid's.

In the seconds since the girl with wild curls shot awake, the initial burst of energy had already ebbed away and the soft light casting off her enchanted compass-clock had faded. She strained her eyes, desperate to imprint the quieting magic in her mind.

She was only eleven years old, and the adoration in her chest strained against everything she'd ever known. But this love was not for her soulmate. No, not yet.

She was in love with Cupid's magic.

The Meeting

A young woman with thin yellow hair stiffened as the train jostled and the distinct smell of sweat permeated the air. Her brain had hardly kicked into gear as dawn crept to morning when a sudden awareness settled over her.

I'm about to meet my soulmate.

A foreign tingling drew her attention to her left wrist, different from her tattoo's usual subtle flutters. The white disposable cup trembled in her hands and she tightened her grip despite the scalding tea inside. A quick glance at her compass tattoo confirmed what she already knew.

The hairs on her arms rose as the car approached its next stop. The heart-shaped arrowhead of her compass-clock took a dive to the left in time with the screeching halt, turning and pointing to the doors behind her. The clock on the display above her head flickered to 7:13 a.m.—the exact time her tattoo had promised she would meet her soulmate.

A cluster of people milled out of the car, and she twisted in her seat, leaning forward.

Is it weird if I stay seated? I should stand, right?

But the thoughts didn't translate to her body and she sat frozen. A new batch of people hustled on to avoid the slamming doors and her silver tattoo vibrated with the nearness of its link—her perfect match, destined by Cupid and the three Fates themselves.

How can anyone be ready for this?

Then it was as if time froze. Sharp dimples, bright blond curls, and a confident smile blurred the rest of the car to a hazy background. A buzz filled the commuting woman's ears and she barely registered as the cup slipped from her hands and splashed across the floor. Her lips parted in shock. Even the scalding water that dashed up the front of her pants wouldn't tear her gaze away from this long-awaited moment.

This is my person, my forever. Here, on a train, with me.

The Exception

Wide-eyed and breathless, the pale brunette reached out with shaking hands. The moment the doctor placed the tiny bundle in the new mother's arms, she felt the shift without looking.

Impossible.

She'd been seventeen when her tattoo first shimmered to life. Every faithful year since, it pointed to her husband no matter where he was in the world. But now the needles of her compass settled into a new position, and the timepiece quadrant of her tattoo changed to 9:18, mirroring the analog clock on the wall.

This can't be. It doesn't make any sense.

Of course, she had heard rumors of things like this happening before. Whispers of people who had a soulmate, only to have their needle change later in life. She never imagined it would happen to her, let alone from having a baby; it was unheard of. And yet her tattoo pulsed in its new place with a new time, affirming that everything she needed was right there in her arms.

Incomparable devotion and wholeness settled over her as the baby fussed. Emotions she once held only for her husband now pulsed through her body with fresh vigor. In an instant, she knew until the end of time that she would lay her life on the line for this tiny human. The newest love of her life, her baby girl. Tears spilled over her cheeks.

With exceptional tenderness, the woman with sweat-slicked hair brushed one of her tears from her baby's precious head. Her smile stretched in wonder as she could already make out her own features mixed with her husband's.

She didn't care that her compass changing made no logical sense; no one could ever take this happiness from her. The new mother closed her eyes and held her baby tight, rocking her as she hummed a soft tune. It was a song her mother had once sung to her as a child. She wondered how her own mother's love compared to her love at this moment. Then her thoughts led to how her husband's love for their baby would compare. An inkling of fear knotted deep in her rib cage, but she willed herself not to lose the purity of this moment. She kissed the tiny girl's head, trying not to think of what this could mean for their future.

ACT 1

NONA

Of the three sisters, Nona comes first
The celestial mother; the one who gives birth.
From her hands she weaves ultimate creation:
mankind, the humans; mortals of Terra Mater.
Each string a soul's essence, streaming with light,
Nona's hands forge the beginning of life.
—The Spinner of Fate

CHAPTER I

When her alarm chimed, Jaylynn's feet hit the floor in an instant. She dashed down the carpeted stairs to the kitchen, her red curls bouncing wild behind her.

"Mother, it happened! I got my compass!"

Her wide smile stretched across her freckled face as she sang and swung off the last stairway post. She twirled out into the small foyer, her arms in a triumphant arc. Upstairs, a door swung and crashed against the wall. Heavy feet tromped toward her, and Jaylynn glowed as her sister hit the landing with a crash.

"You got your compass?"

"Yes!" Jaylynn screeched. Nylah raced across the soft pink rug and scooped Jaylynn up in her arms.

"Oh, for the love of Cupid! I'm so happy for you!" Two years older than her, Nylah towered over Jaylynn's short frame. Her sister's red hair was cropped short to her ears, much to their mother's dismay, and her partially freckled face beamed with pride.

A flurry of movement broke up the girls as the rest of the Clare family rushed into the foyer. Natalie Clare was a short woman, barely five feet tall, with a pointed nose, bright freckles, and pinched lips. Her hand trembled against the handrail as the other clutched her fuzzy gray bathrobe.

"It can't be. Already?"

Natalie looked up at Jaylynn's father, whose hands clasped her shoulders. Richard Clare was in every way his wife's opposite. He was incredibly tall and sported a long, soft nose with spatters of muted orange freckles—a mirror image of Jaylynn's oval face.

With a Cheshire grin, Jaylynn held out her left arm, palm up.

Natalie swooned. "Oh, Jupiter Almighty."

Richard held their mother up and guided her to the kitchen table, where she buried her face in her hands.

Jaylynn's grin faltered. She looked at Nylah, confused, but her sibling shrugged. Richard poured a glass of water and set it on the table beside his wife, then wrapped an arm around Jaylynn and led her away. They walked back across the foyer, hardly catching Natalie's murmurs.

"She's only eleven years old! She can't possibly—a soulmate? At her age? No, she can't. What will the teachers think? The other parents? I can't possibly…"

Richard gently cupped Jaylynn's chin and drew her attention away from the kitchen. He offered a conspiratorial smile and her lips curved up to match his.

He brought Jaylynn into his office, a room she often got scolded for playing in. One wall was lined with dark bookshelves filled with thick, leather-bound books. Jaylynn found the yellow pages and swirling ink uninteresting, most being her father's religious texts, but she loved to run her fingers over their soft covers. A black and gold globe sat on a pedestal in one corner. It was Nylah's favorite part of the office, and she often spun it and pointed out all the places they would travel to one day. Behind Richard's oak desk stood a high-backed, antique armchair that made an excellent water slide for Jaylynn's dolls.

"It seems congratulations are in order." He playfully nudged her as he sat. "Will you show me?"

Jaylynn held her arm out, bearing her brand-new metallic tattoo with sudden, unexplained shame. She swore that the three ivory statues decorating her father's office glowered at her with their gold-painted eyes. She pressed her eyes shut as he took her hand in his palm.

"Ah, and so it is. Our little girl is growing up. How do you feel?"

Jaylynn shrugged. She wished she could take back her gleeful announcement and only have told Nylah.

Richard nodded. "I didn't feel that different either at first. Have you tried to read it yet?"

"No," she whispered.

"Would you like me to show you how?"

Jaylynn nodded, her heart fluttering with a new but softer excitement. Richard patted his knee and Jaylynn hopped up onto his lap. She held her left arm out alongside her father's to see their compasses side-by-side.

"Will mine always be so much smaller than yours?"

"Compasses are like your bones. They grow with you, so they always fit on the inside of your wrist perfectly."

"Oh."

"Okay, are you ready? The first thing to understand about Cupid's compass is that it has two layers. One that sits on top and one underneath." He grabbed two papers off his desk, one covered in writing, the other mostly blank. Jaylynn moved off the edge of his knee to between his warm arms as he worked.

From the drawer, he pulled out a pair of scissors and cut the papers into matching circles, then stacked them with the emptier one on top. "Like this. Except the top one doesn't cover the whole bottom." He took the first paper and cut out a big triangle, which he handed to Jaylynn. "Do you see how when I stack them now, the top paper has a window that shows a section of the bottom paper?"

Jaylynn nodded.

Her father grabbed a silver pen and pushed the tip through the middle of the papers, pinning them against the desk. "There. Now, do you see when I do this, I can spin the top piece? When the window moves, we can see different parts of the bottom layer."

Richard lifted the edge of the top paper. "This layer is your compass. Some of it is just decorative, like the lines of a normal compass, but here is the important part." After rifling through a drawer for a pencil, he sketched a pie-shaped cutout from the center of the circle. Then, with a light hand so the pencil barely grazed her skin, her father traced the same shape on her wrist tattoo. "This section is Cupid's bow."

The paper triangle in Jaylynn's hand fluttered to the ground, instantly forgotten. With her index finger, she traced over the swirls that decorated the arch of the bow. Her lips parted in surprise as she felt the subtle rise and fall of the floral linework.

Then her father pointed out the thick, steady line through the middle. "And this is Cupid's arrow."

Jaylynn marveled over the sparkling, heart-shaped diamond. It floated outside of the compass clock ring, glittering in magical promise. She ran her finger from the gem down the thick platinum shaft to the textured feathers at the end, which also stretched out past the circular border in a notched and drawn position.

Jaylynn whispered, "It's so beautiful."

"It is, isn't it? And if you move," he guided her arm back and forth, "the bow and arrow will move too. That's because it's a compass, but instead of pointing north, it points to your soulmate."

"And my soulmate will have the matching one?"

"Yep. They'll wake up with theirs today too."

An inexplicable flush crept up Jaylynn's neck. She swore that the ivory statue of Juno, the goddess of marriage, grew an inch taller in the corner.

"Then we have the second layer underneath the compass. This is the clock. Just like the papers, it can move too." He picked up the pen and pinned the pages again, pointing at the bottom sheet, turning the second piece of paper clockwise.

Jaylynn moved her arm to reveal a different section of the clock underneath. The chrome roman numerals were stark against the dark star-spattered base.

"Now, part of the magic is that the clock hands won't ever move. That's because they tell you the time you will meet your soulmate."

"They won't change even when we meet?"

"Nope." Richard's voice dropped with a hint of sorrow. "The only time someone's clock hands change is when their soulmate passes on to the Underworld."

"Oh."

He squeezed her shoulders. "But that's not important right now. Can you tell me what time your clock says?"

Jaylynn shuffled off his lap to stand by the tinted octagon window where morning light filtered in. She maneuvered her arm so she could see both clock hands, which were luckily close together. Jaylynn stared hard as she tried to remember the roman numerals she learned in school.

"Seven…" she mumbled. She turned as she counted down the clock. "Seven thirty-five?"

Her father stood and leaned over her shoulder. "I would say seven thirty-six. Do you see how the long hand is farther than the first notch?"

Jaylynn craned her neck as she scrutinized the clock hands.

"So, you will meet your soulmate at seven thirty-six. But you won't know if it will be in the morning or at night. Silly, hey?"

Jaylynn giggled in agreement.

"And then there's just one last piece. Did you notice anything funny about the clock numbers?"

Jaylynn frowned as she looked back down.

"Instead of a twelve, there's a capital *N*. This is because the clockface, a.k.a our bottom paper, always points north. So instead of the clock hands moving, the clockface does. Make sense?"

Jaylynn wasn't sure it did, but she nodded anyway. "What does this say?" she asked as she traced a finger along the outside rim.

"*Omnia vincit Amor: et nos cedamus Amori,*" Richard read out. "It means love conquers all, and so let us surrender ourselves to love."

The tight calligraphy was bunched together in a cramped cursive, hardly leaving a gap between one word and the next.

Jaylynn hopped back up onto the chair and swung her feet lightly. She stared down at her compass-clock. "Why is Mother so upset I got my compass?"

Richard ruffled her messy auburn curls. "She's not upset, darling, just surprised. I mean, Nylah is thirteen and doesn't even have hers yet. Your mother will come around."

Jaylynn knocked her toes together. "Does this mean my soulmate is going to come take me away?"

Richard knelt and took her chin in his hand so she would meet his eyes. "You don't need to worry about that yet. You can never know when they will come, but it could be years. All Cupid's compass does is confirm that you have a perfect match out there, ready for you. No one is taking you away."

Jaylynn pressed her lips together. She adored her compass. It was beautiful and magical and everything she'd dreamed, but it also unsettled her.

The kettle whistled, and a head of choppy red hair popped into the doorway.

"Are you guys going to sit in here all morning?" Nylah complained. "Or can the rest of us see your compass too?"

CHAPTER II

JAYLYNN

Disobeying their parents wasn't Jaylynn's preferred way to spend a summer weekend morning, but Nylah was impossible to say no to. As the girls wandered, subtle tingling drew Jaylynn's eyes from the sunny sky to her compass tattoo. Even after two weeks, she hadn't adjusted to the foreign silver marking or the flutters of movement that tickled her inside wrist.

Jaylynn sighed as Nylah tugged her sleeve and turned down an unfamiliar Toronto street. Nylah grinned a toothy, mischievous smile in return. Propped open on the cracked sidewalk stood a rustic sandwich board. The sign's white script was faded and chipped in places, but Jaylynn made out the words:

RIVER'S REVELATIONS.
Soulmate Sibyl & Fortune Teller
Compass, tarot, palm reading, and more!

The girls got lucky and caught the busy shop at a quiet time. Bells chimed as they crossed the threshold into the hazy boutique. Jaylynn tucked her russet curls behind her wide, red-hot ears. Billowing curtains draped the ceiling and walls, making the store look like a giant blanket fort—if people filled their blanket forts with candles, books, and dried flowers. Jaylynn's gaze flickered over the room with skepticism. She wove her fingers with her sister's.

"Nylah, are you sure this is a good idea?" Jaylynn dipped her chin as she whispered.

"It's fine, Jay. You trust me, don't you?" Nylah squeezed her hand. Jaylynn shrank into her sister's shadow as they walked in farther.

"I do. It's just, Mother said it's bad luck to get your compass read." Jaylynn's eyes darted to a dream catcher that glittered in the sunbeams.

Nylah trailed her fingers over a giant rock. The geode reached Jaylynn's chin. The back half was rounded rough gray, while the front sparkled in violet bursts of crystals.

"Jay, Mother's superstitious. The gods won't damn you because you want to know about your future soulmate. Trust me, this is going to be fun."

Jaylynn tightened her grip on her sister's hand as they moved farther into the boutique. Centered in the space was a short bronze table with three carved legs. Round, faded emerald cushions neatly circled the low table.

Nylah paused and took both of Jaylynn's hands. "This will be our little secret. No one has to know. Besides, don't you want to know what your soulmate is going to be like?"

Jaylynn didn't answer. Her hand got slippery in Nylah's when the shop owner came around the back corner. Jaylynn had been expecting the psychic to be an old, wrinkly woman with rotten teeth. She was shocked to see the radiant adult before them. Voluptuous raven-black curls framed her warm face and spilled over her slender shoulders. Her crisp arctic-blue eyes shone the brightest blue Jaylynn had ever seen. Perfectly placed freckles danced over the bridge of her nose, the exact opposite to the soft brown ones splattered all over Jaylynn's face and body. River looked more like a model than a fortune teller.

Bills and coins clattered on the bronze table as Nylah dumped their pooled allowance. She nudged Jaylynn to take a seat on the closest green cushion.

River moved slowly. Her ring-cluttered hand trailed over a column of books. "Welcome, young ones. Tell me what brings you in today." Her voice was deep and soothing.

Jaylynn took a nervous breath and brushed a loose curl back.

"I'm here to have my compass read." Her voice came out quiet, despite how often her mother scolded her for not speaking up.

River didn't seem to have a problem hearing her, though, and returned a warm smile.

"Well, dear, you've come to the right place." With the grace of a ballerina, River lowered herself to the cushion directly across the bronze table. "Let's see what we're working with."

Jaylynn held her left arm out across the round table. She could feel Nylah's hovering excitement. River's long, delicate fingers glittered in impossibly beautiful rings and gemstones. Jaylynn's immediate favorite was an opal teardrop, its iridescence caught in the trickle of sunlight. River traced her warm thumb across the cool metallic tattoo. Then the psychic closed her eyes and hovered her hand over Jaylynn's compass.

Almost immediately, River's brow furrowed. She gave herself a shake as she withdrew. Her speculative eyes rested on Jaylynn's pale and bland blue ones. Without turning, she reached behind herself and grabbed a nearby box of cards. The oracle deck was a midnight blue with tiny stars worn white on the corners. As River shuffled, she murmured a soft prayer.

"Janus, he who sees both past and present, shine your gaze upon us now. I offer my intention to be open to receive your wisdom and guidance. Show me only the truth. Let there be light. Let there be love. Your eternal servant, I will always remain."

Jaylynn shivered at River's mantra. Their parents exclusively prayed to the Capitoline Triad: the king, Jupiter; the queen, Juno; and the goddess of wisdom, Minerva. Though, of course, they respected Cupid as well. To hear River pray to one of the other lesser gods confirmed Jaylynn's suspicion: her parents would be furious if they found out what they were doing. Not that it was blasphemous to honor lesser gods, but her parents were Purists and insisted their daughters be the same.

Nylah had gone completely silent. In her peripheral vision, Jaylynn swore she saw the candles on the window's edge burn higher, though she didn't dare look away from River. Partly because she wanted to be sure she wasn't being cheated, but mostly because she felt like she was about to witness real magic again. River hummed as she laid out three cards faceup. Her warm smile slipped as she took in the cards.

"Perhaps, dear, you would like to reconsider knowing your future. I can give you a full refund and you can continue to live your life as you have up to this moment—looking ahead with bright eyes and a heart of innocence."

Curiosity and fear brimmed in Jaylynn's chest. How could she turn down knowing what the woman could see now?

"Jupiter Almighty! Is that the Death card? Is Jaylynn going to die before she meets her one true love?!" Nylah shrieked over her shoulder, startling Jaylynn further.

Of course, her sibling was right. There, lying faceup on the table, was a card named *Death*. At first glance, the card appeared to depict a knight upon a gallant steed, riding with a large flag overhead. But, upon closer inspection, it was a dead skeleton riding the horse. Jaylynn's stiff fingers traced over her cushion's edge.

"Please, Miss River… I-I really would like to know." Her voice was faint as her eyes stayed locked on the skeleton knight.

River let out an exasperated breath and resettled herself into the reading.

"Very well, little one. I will have you know that in tarot, not everything is as it seems. Often, the cards laid out represent the most likely path you are bound to take, but can be changed by your actions. Please take this reading as a possibility of what could come, instead of that which is set in stone."

The opal stone on River's hand glinted as she pushed the first card toward Jaylynn to inspect.

"Your anchor card seen here is the Fool. In our three-card spread he is your past. You can see he is shown walking toward a cliff, unknowing of the danger to come as he optimistically gazes above instead. Though it could be seen as a warning, the Fool isn't a bad card. He is cheerful, innocent, and unaware. Yes, of course your first card is the Fool…"

Jaylynn stared at River, transfixed as she spoke, doing her best to commit everything the woman said to memory. River no longer met Jaylynn's gaze as she was consumed by reading the cards.

"Your second card represents your present. As seen here, we have the Moon. You have unconscious psychic abilities that you are only beginning to embrace. I would expect you are finding your sensitivity to the world is heightened, and that your feelings and intuition are growing. This doesn't mean you will be a psychic in the future, just that you are developing a great awareness that many people live without. The Moon is a card of great wisdom, and it speaks profoundly of your soul's journey."

Though Jaylynn liked the picture of the moon with the animals looking up to it, she couldn't help but anticipate the last card's reading. River took a deep breath before turning to it.

"And finally, in your future, we have Death. Please don't be alarmed, child, as the Death card rarely translates to a physical death. It usually means the death of a cycle, and transformation for the better. Though I will admit, this card feels significant in your reading. You will have an event occur that will change your life path, and it will be painful beyond measure. I can't get a good feel on how far down the road this will happen... But when it comes, it will change everything."

River's husky voice drew out the last sentence, the words hanging in the incense-clouded air. Jaylynn couldn't breathe. The room felt like it might catch fire at any moment as the candles burned as bright as her cheeks. She pushed back from the table and whispered a polite but rash thank-you. Nylah scrambled back as Jaylynn made a beeline for the door.

"But you didn't tell us about her soulmate! This was supposed to be a love reading, not a death reading!" Nylah complained. "Will he be rich and handsome? Will they have children? When will they meet?"

River ignored Nylah's complaints. She made her way across the room to catch Jaylynn's shoulder before she could escape.

"Young one. I know this isn't what you want to hear, but for your sake… Forget your compass. There are greater journeys you will travel in this life, and that one will only bring you grief. I will be here when you choose to come back to me. Until then, stay safe, little one." Jaylynn couldn't bring herself to look back at the beautiful woman's bright blue eyes. Nylah brushed past River and took Jaylynn's hand. She pulled her out of the shop and back to the real world.

Nylah squeezed Jaylynn's arm as they walked in the summer sun. "It's going to be okay, Jay. Cupid will keep you safe and make sure you find your soulmate. He always does. Besides, that woman probably wasn't even a real psychic. I mean, did you hear her prattling on about Janus? Like the god of doors could know anything. I mean, Minerva at least is the goddess of wisdom. If she…"

Jaylynn tuned her sister out as Nylah continued with her reasons why River's reading was a lie. She stared down at her glittering compass, its clock sitting at 7:36. For the first time in the last two weeks, fear outweighed her love for it.

CHAPTER III

RENEE

"I just don't understand!" Kade fumed as he pushed his hands through his sandy blond hair. When they were fresh out of high school, Renee used to tease he would pull out all of his hair one day from stress, but that joke died as it became a reality. Sleepless nights and endless fights wore on them both, and their twenties were proving to be less glamorous with every passing year.

If Renee was being honest, it wasn't having a child that made things hard. It was that her compass had changed. Even the doctors were baffled. No one could explain the spontaneous change in her tattoo or why her compass now pointed to her little girl and read 9:18, the time she was born, instead of 8:29, the time when Renee and Kade first met. They were sent home to figure it out on their own and five years later, they were still struggling. Since buying their apartment in Mississauga, only an hour away from Toronto's bustling city center, Renee felt more isolated than ever.

Kade sat in his favorite gray armchair, his elbows digging into his knees. "How am I supposed to be fine with the fact that you love that child more than you love me? How am I supposed to love a woman who will always choose me second?"

She felt her heart closing off and a deep-seated desire to protect herself and Lacey blossomed in her chest. "*That* child is also *your* child, Kade, and she has a name." Her voice wavered. "How many times do I have to apologize before you'll forgive me? It's not like I had any choice in the matter!"

Renee caught her weak reflection in the glass door that led to the balcony as she turned away, trying to rein in her anger. Her beautiful, tanned skin from her parents' Mexican heritage had paled from the long Canadian winter. Her chestnut-brown hair fell out of her braid in feeble wisps. And even though the reflection was hazy, she knew if she looked closely, her honey-brown eyes would be washed-out and strained. It was as if her very essence was draining away.

She softened her fists, conscious that she shouldn't fight fire with fire. "This would be easier if I had you on my side instead of making me choose. I'm tired enough without you always trying to pick fights with me."

Kade's stare was flat. "Why is it every time I try to bring up how you're hurting me, you turn it around and make me out to be the bad guy?"

Renee crossed her arms with a huff. "I never said you were the problem. But now that you mention it, this *would* be a lot easier if you weren't so committed to playing the victim all the time."

Kade's jaw dropped. "Me? Playing the victim? Are you *kidding* me, Renee?"

"I already feel like an anomaly," she said, her voice rising to match his, "and then you start rubbing in my face how much of a freak I am and how much it hurts *you*." She could feel the heat building in her chest—anger begging to be lashed out.

"You think you're a freak? My own soulmate doesn't love me back!" He stood from his armchair, fists tight by his sides. Hostility rolled off his body in waves.

Renee didn't turn away from the challenge. Instead, she leaned into his chest and glared up at him. "Listen to yourself, Kade! You're acting like a child! We are *both* equally alone in this, but your behavior is what's tearing us apart!"

"You know, Renee, you can call me a child and continue pretending this is my fault if it makes you feel better. I would rather be a child with genuine emotions than a psycho who's obsessed with their child and happy to leave their marriage to crumble."

"For the love of Cupid! What is wrong with you?" Renee's prior attempts at not yelling washed down the drain. "You think name-calling is going to fix this? Do you think any of this" —she waved her arms in his direction— "is going to make me love you more?" Hot tears broke over her pinched face.

"Well, I don't know what else to do! I've tried being patient, I've tried being nice, I've tried telling you what I need. Nothing I do seems to make you happy anymore!" He took a shaky breath, then lowered his voice. "You don't give a damn about me. You don't have a care in the world other than Lacey."

As if on cue, Renee heard the telltale sound of scampering feet. Pain and guilt washed over her as she turned to call out to their daughter, but she knew the damage was already done.

"You know that's not true." Renee didn't turn to face him as she spoke. Her voice was raspy as she wiped away the trail of tears that carved down her sharp cheekbones. "I've told you before that I care. It's just that I'm exhausted, Kade. I'm tired and I'm scared, and I've never felt more alone." She rested her arm on the pale wall and leaned into it for support as her spirit sank.

His voice, as soft as hers, seeped with hurt. "You're only alone because I'm invisible to you. Nothing I do is ever right. The only time you acknowledge my existence anymore is to tell me how I could do better, how I could be more helpful, how I should try to bond with Lacey more. You treat me like I'm just another chore to complete."

Renee tried to catch her breath as his words slid like daggers through her ribs.

Kade's voice broke. "I don't even remember the last time I felt genuinely loved by you."

Renee's heart clenched tighter than a fist as she turned to face her husband. His head hung in defeat and his arms wrapped across his torso. "Kade. I've told you this before. My compass may have changed, but that doesn't mean I've stopped loving you. Why do you refuse to believe me?"

"Because I don't feel it. At least not half as much as I can feel you love her." He pointed down the hall to where Lacey's pink face peeked around a doorframe, her hazel eyes wide and shining. Her upturned nose mirrored Renee's, but their daughter had Kade's square cut chin. The quiver in Lacey's bottom lip promised tears.

Great, Renee thought. *Now I have three broken hearts to mend.*

She knew she had to settle things with Kade first, but she longed to take Lacey up in her arms. Holding her daughter always soothed her highs and lows, the way Kade used to when he was her soulmate and he held her tight. She grappled for the right words to say to be free of the conversation, but nothing new came to her. This fight had been the broken record of their home for years. How could she fix it this time? "You're being unfair. I am trying my hardest to love both of you, but this is exhausting. Kade, we can't go on like this."

"Maybe I should leave for a while, until we figure this out." Kade's voice was quiet, but his words hit her like a sonic boom. Her breath hitched.

"You… you would leave us?" she whispered.

He pushed his hair back and his usually stunning green eyes were red and swollen. "I just don't know what else to do. My world came alive when I found you, and it has melted away ever since your stupid compass changed." He took a shaky breath. "I feel like I need some space and maybe some help. I don't know. All I know is being here with you, seeing the way you look at her—the way you always look at her… You're breaking my heart, Renee. I think we need a break. We need time apart."

He started down the hall toward their bedroom, his head hung and feet heavy. Renee rushed to grab his hand. Lacey bolted to her room, her sobs echoing in the bare apartment. For once, Renee didn't go to her.

"Please, Kade, please don't leave. I know this is hard… I-I'll… I'll try harder. I'll try to be there for you more. Maybe all you need is more time with her and you'll grow to love her the way I do…" Fresh tears rushed over her cheeks. "Please don't walk away from this because it's hard. We can figure this out together."

He came to a stop, and she held his forearm tight in her hands. "Please. Don't give up on me."

Kade let out a heavy breath as he pulled his arm out of her grasp, shrugging her away. Renee's knees collapsed under her as another piece of her life crumbled out of her control.

CHAPTER IV

CHARITY

In Charity's dream, the scarlet sky blazed in vengeance. She couldn't be sure if she was flying or falling. Perhaps it was both. An eerie screech clawed at her eardrums and Charity instinctively covered her head as she tumbled in slow motion. Specks of black and brown rained around her, pelting her skin in a relentless fury. Charity's bottom lip trembled as she held back a cry.

Then her body shattered against Terra Mater and Charity couldn't stop the blood-curdling scream that escaped. Her spine splintered in agony, shooting white-hot fire down her arms and legs. But the sky wasn't done with her yet. Even with the wind knocked out of her lungs and her limbs quaking, Charity tried to reach up to shield her face from the aerial assault.

Make it stop.

But Terra Mater continued to turn beneath her crippled body. The rubble in the air rained down in a fury and battered her into the ground. The dirt that hit her upraised hands stung sharp as blades. No, not her hands. The hands raised in a desperate plea were tanned and masculine compared to her own delicate, pale ones.

Before Charity could make sense of the hands that weren't her own, her attention was torn back to the impossible pressure against her lungs. The soil clung moist and heavy now, weighing down on her body as it smothered her into silence.

Jupiter Almighty, am I being buried alive?

The blazing scarlet sky disappeared as her vision was covered over in black and her entire body succumbed to the weight of the world. When she was sure the pain couldn't get any worse, the tearing started. It was as if Pluto, the god of death himself, reached through her chest and wrapped his hands around her heart like a vise. Charity started screaming. She felt her soul being wrenched apart, stitch by stitch, unraveling as her spirit was pulled out of the darkness.

"No!" Charity shot up in her damp bedsheets, her heart thundering in the silence of her bedroom. "Please," she rasped, "please, no."

Blood pounded in her ears as she grappled with her surroundings, her eyes desperate to find the man who normally slept by her side. But there wasn't a head of tousled blond curls.

There were no strong, steady hands to soothe her. Luke wasn't there and hadn't been there for weeks, not since he'd been deployed to the front lines of the Roman Empire's war as they fought over their northern border.

She fell out of the bed as she rushed to the window, her soft hands spanning the dew-covered pane.

"You can't do this," she sobbed through the phlegm that lined her throat. The cloudy night sky gave no response. "You can't take him away from me!" Her hysteria thrummed in her very alive veins as her voice rose.

Charity pounded her fists on the glass. She screamed at the top of her lungs, "Give him back to me, you life-sucking, soul-damning demons!" A hollow ache carved deeper into her chest. All the warmth leached from her tall, willowy frame to the hardwood floors. Her knees gave out and she reached for the drape. She hit the ground ten times faster than she had in her slow-motion dream, the sheer fabric tearing and floating down over her.

The curtain that folded itself over her limp body did not offer any cover from the truth. Trembling, Charity held out her arm to confirm what she already knew. A weak light cast through the windowpane. Her right hand shook hard as she traced over the tattoo on her left forearm, and she knew it wasn't right. Where the edges should have risen and crested, her skin lay flat. The base that usually glittered like a night sky blackened, and all the metallic details dulled to a matte gray.

That was when she noticed the time. How many years had the

clock of her compass read 3:13? Without grabbing her phone, she already knew what the new time, 2:35, symbolized—the hour and the minute her husband died.

A fresh sob caught in the lump of her throat as her nails clawed at the changed, dead tattoo.

"It's not fair," she whimpered. "This isn't fair."

Charity curled in a tight ball. She wished she could tunnel through the cruel hardwood and meet her husband on his way to the Underworld. She dreamed of his full, warm lips pressing a kiss to her forehead. Charity could almost hear his voice.

Charity, he would say. *Charity, help me.*

She shook herself, her fingers clawing at her scalp. *No, that's not what I want him to say. Tell me you love me. Tell me you're okay.*

But Luke's voice was a steady whisper. *Help me, Charity. Help me.*

She was pulled back to reality as clammy fingers picked her clinging hair from her face. Charity risked a glance up and was met with big gray, glossy eyes. Nessie, her eleven-year-old daughter with puffy cheeks and sharp dimples, whispered in the dark, "Mom?"

Charity knew she should reach out. She knew she should take her girl in her arms. But her arms wouldn't move. Her mouth wouldn't open. Her whole body was still.

I can't do this without you, Luke. Please. Don't make me be a mother without you. Come back. Come back to me.

Nessie's lip quivered. "Mom, what's wrong?"

When Charity didn't respond, Nessie's trembling lip set firm.

Charity didn't hear her daughter's feet race down the hall. Instead, she curled up and a fresh wave of sobs surfaced as Luke's whispers danced on the night walls.

Then Nessie was back. The house phone shook as she punched at the buttons with clumsy thumbs, her full cheeks scarlet. A single tear carved down her heart-shaped face. Seeing her fearless child so shaken should have stirred Charity to feel something—to *do* something—but she felt nothing, only the undeniable emptiness inside.

Nessie curled up on the ground beside Charity, her knees tucked up with the phone pressed to her ear. Her lips moved in a blur as she cried into the phone, but Charity couldn't make out what she was saying. She couldn't hear anything. All she could see was her daughter, shaking under a head of blond hair.

Luke's curls. They're Luke's curls. Just like his dimples. How could she live to face this mini human who was a carbon copy of her husband?

Charity's eyes rolled back to darkness.

CHAPTER V

RENEE

"Mommy, why don't you love Daddy?"

Renee's heart skipped. Why was it that children never grew out of asking the most painful questions? She'd thought that by ten years old her daughter's curiosity would falter. Renee forced herself to shake off her surprise and put away the last of the laundry for the night.

"What makes you think I don't love your father?"

"All the girls at school say so. They laugh because your compass follows me. They say that you don't love Daddy and that our family is messed up. Is your compass broken?"

Renee's shoulders sank as she moved to sit on her child's bed. Lacey looked up at her with her ever-curious hazel eyes. Questions were often her way of stalling bedtime, but Renee felt the importance of the conversation.

"My compass isn't broken, little love. I just have an extra-big heart and an extra-lucky soul. I get to love two people instead of one. My compass points to you now, but it doesn't mean I love your father any less."

Lacey sat up taller. "But how do you know you love him?"

"Well, I just do. I can feel it in my heart. Just like you love us. You may not have a compass yet, but that doesn't mean you don't love people."

Lacey looked down at her bare arm, then reached out to touch Renee's. Renee smiled as her daughter's hand tickled her humming compass. It always vibrated a soft and soothing tone whenever Lacey touched her.

"Mommy, where do compasses come from?"

Renee sighed. Did all children insist on avoiding sleep?

"How about this: I'll tell you a story about compasses, but first you have to swear to the stars there's no more delaying bedtime after. When the story is over, there won't be any ifs, ands, or buts. No questions. Just you, with your eyes closed, sleeping. Okay?"

Lacey's eyes sparkled as she locked in their promise and snuggled deeper into her sheets. Renee sat with her back against the headboard, her daughter's body in the crook of her arm. Lacey's fingers continued to trace the outline of her tattoo.

"I'm pretty sure your lights should have been out already." Kade leaned on the doorframe, a smile tugging the corner of his lips.

Renee's heart swelled. She couldn't fathom how different their lives would have been if he hadn't come back. To her great relief, somehow their little family persevered. It was nothing like she imagined a normal family to be, but at least they were trying.

"Mommy is going to tell me a bedtime story, then I swore to the stars I would sleep. She's going to tell me about where compasses come from!"

Renee's face fell as she saw her husband's subtle flinch. He cleared his throat.

"Well, I'm sure Mommy can manage that." He crossed the room and planted a kiss on Lacey's forehead. "I'm going to make us lunch for tomorrow. Sleep tight, little worm."

"I love you, Daddy. Even if Mommy's compass doesn't."

Renee's heart sank. She knew her daughter didn't mean to make things hard, but sometimes her comments were sharp lashes across Renee's back.

Kade's expression darkened. "I love you too." He didn't make eye contact as he left the room. He turned out the overhead light, leaving Lacey's princess lights twinkling along the walls.

"Okay, missy. No more water or pee breaks. Time to keep that pinky promise." Renee tried to relax into the story, but her shoulders stayed rock solid. She closed her eyes and tried to let the comments go.

"Once, millennia ago, the Roman gods and goddesses blessed our world with their presence. Jupiter reigned the skies with his great lightning bolts, while Juno, his queen and wife, ruled by his side to oversee all marriages and unions. Minerva, the fierce goddess of wisdom and warcraft, led our people through times of conflict, and together the three gods formed the Capitoline Triad: conquerors of the stars and mortals. But they weren't the only forces to be reckoned with.

"One day, in a massive bed made of the softest clouds in the world, Venus, the goddess of love and beauty, delivered a beautiful baby boy. The god of love was born, and he was named Cupid. As he grew up, he spent his days flying through the clouds with his white feather wings and ruby-flushed cheeks. He would play all day with his favorite toy: an enchanted bow and arrow. Rumor said that being struck by one of these arrows would cause you to fall helplessly in love with the next person you saw."

Lacey's fingers stilled on Renee's forearm, her attention on the story growing.

"One day, Venus noticed a change in the mortals who roamed Terra Mater. A princess named Psyche had been proclaimed the most beautiful in all the land. Men from all over traveled to her kingdom to revel in her beauty, whispering that it was even greater than Venus's. As the goddess's temples were visited less and less, her jealousy of Psyche grew. Furious, she went to her son to beg for his help.

"'Cupid, my love, help me. Go to this mortal, Psyche, whose beauty is compared to mine. Find her and strike her with one of your arrows. Have her fall in love with a man who will whisk her away. Make it so the world forgets about her. Please, I cannot bear this insult any longer.'

"Cupid loved his mother like no other, so he took his bow and arrows and set out to soothe her fears. Flying through the clouds and down into the trees, he tracked down his mother's nemesis. He landed with inhuman grace and pulled his bowstring taut when a sudden breeze blew through the girl's hair. As Psyche stood to brush it away, Cupid saw her face for the first time. Stunned at the sight of her, he slipped and his notched arrow shot into his foot instead. His fate was sealed instantly, enchanting him to love her forever.

"He spent the rest of his day torn between going back to his mother and staying at Psyche's side. He was positive Venus would be furious, so he resolved she couldn't know what had happened. But when he considered abandoning Psyche, his heart ached. As the hours passed, he worked on a plan, one where he could keep both women in his life. Under the cover of night, he stole Psyche away, spiriting her in her sleep to a mountaintop temple. From here, she would no longer gather the attention of the mortal men and he could keep her to himself. He could also keep her hidden from his mother.

"He manifested a spectacular temple. He laced it with magic that would keep Psyche safe and would serve her every need. Anything she wanted would appear in a puff of magic—exotic fruits, beautiful tapestries, the sky was the limit. The secluded temple had the effect Cupid desired. When she woke, Psyche had never known such devotion and adoration, let alone witnessed magic, and her heart grew for the mysterious provider who worshipped her.

"Days passed before he came to her under the cover of night once again. Psyche begged to see his face to thank him properly for all the gifts, but he refused. Between his love for her and his fear of his mother, he was committed to keeping his mistake hidden from the world. He explained that the only way they could be together was under the cover of night, and that so long as she never saw his face, their budding love could continue.

"Hardly any time passed as Cupid's love for her magnified, and Psyche loved him back effortlessly. She didn't need to see his face to know that he was a god; no mortal could procure every one of her desires from thin air. So they cherished the time they had together, even if it was only in darkness, and their love stayed a secret from the world and the gods. Cupid spent his nights by Psyche's side, then would return to his mother's side every day.

"On her mountaintop, Psyche's days were long. She often caught herself gazing at the skies, wondering where her lover went. As the weeks and months passed, Psyche couldn't help but grow less satisfied with her temple and her gifts. Her heart ached for the sisters and friends she'd left behind. One night, as the candles went out, her lover landed softly by her side and she asked him if he could cure her loneliness. Cupid spent all the next day and late into the night trying to find a way to satisfy his love, when he was struck with a wonderful idea.

"He reached into the clouds and began creating a beautiful gift of love, magic, and stardust. Then he tethered it to one of his arrows and shot it down to her. From the window on her mountain peak, she watched the shining light grow brighter and larger than the sun, until she realized it was headed straight for her. Psyche held up her arm to shield her eyes as the arrow struck her hard, Cupid's unspoken love and longing flooding her senses. The immediate connection to his soul laced into her own, and tears of unimaginable happiness poured over her face. For all time, she could know exactly where Cupid was, and she would forever feel his love and soul woven deep within her own heart. And that is how compasses came to be."

Renee opened her eyes as she finished the legend and looked down to see Lacey's wide eyes staring back at her.

"Venus never caught them?"

"I don't know. But what I do know is that you made a promise." She stood from her daughter's small bed, her lower back aching in protest. "No more questions. Goodnight, Lacey."

A million thoughts flashed in Lacey's eyes, but she honored their promise.

"Yes, Mommy... I love you."

"I love you too, baby. Sleep tight."

CHAPTER VI

NESSIE

"Hey, Lacey! Does your mom sleep with you?" The older kid on the bus leaned over the seat across from Nessie. He peered down at the girl as she held her backpack tight.

Nessie hardly made out Lacey's gruff retort for the boy to shut up. Nessie's grip on her book bag tightened as the boy cackled over Lacey's shoulder.

The older boy turned to the kids in the back half of the bus. "Did you guys hear that? Lacey has sex with her mom!"

Cruel laughter rang through the bus as kids started yelling out more gross things, and Nessie shrank in her seat.

"Does your daddy watch when your mommy kisses you? I bet she kisses you on the mouth, you little freak."

Nessie felt bad for the girl in her class. She'd only known Lacey Baker for a couple months since they'd moved to Canada, hardly enough time for Nessie to get to know anyone. Overall, she liked their small home in Mississauga, west of the busy streets of Toronto and an hour north of the US border. She also liked her new school. Well, other than the bus rides.

Lacey stood up. Her face was bright red as she faced the taunting crowd. "I said shut up!"

I should do something. I need to say something. Even though her hands shook, Nessie forced herself to be brave and stand up. She grabbed her schoolbag and moved into the aisle, facing the tall seventh-grade boy in front of her. "Yeah, leave her alone."

The group of kids hooted and hollered as the boy grinned.

"What's up, McKenzie? You feeling left out? Or maybe you want to be friends with the creep because she's just as messed up as you are."

Another voice chimed in. "Two girls with messed-up moms. Betcha they'll be soulmates when they get their compasses!"

Lacey swung a clumsy fist over the back of her seat at the nearest boy. "I'd rather be with her than some dumb-dumb who picks on girls half his size!" The boy laughed as Lacey rained her fists down on his backpack.

The bus came to a hard stop and the bus driver stood up, stalking back to the commotion. "That is enough, young lady." He grabbed Lacey by the arm and pulled her to the steps of the bus. "I will not tolerate violence on my bus. You can walk from here and think

44

about what you've done."

Nessie's jaw dropped. "You won't tolerate violence, but you'll tolerate bullying?" She pulled her backpack on and trudged down the aisle behind Lacey. "I hope you don't like your job, because my mother will hear about this." She stormed off the bus with as much authority as a twelve-year-old could. Lacey glowered as she watched the bus pull away.

"Stupid bus driver. He should be fired." Nessie thought back to her empty threat, wishing there was more she could actually do about the situation. Nessie's mom wasn't exactly a fighter, though it seemed like Lacey was.

Lacey's clenched fists softened as the bus pulled away. "My mom's going to be so mad." She kicked a pebble, her feet scuffing the concrete as she followed its trail.

Nessie caught stride with her, not wanting to walk home alone. "I'm sorry those kids were so mean to you," she offered. Lacey didn't reply. "If it means anything to you, I don't think you're weird."

Lacey stopped and looked over, her hazel eyes glistening with almost tears. "You don't?"

Nessie reached out and squeezed her new friend's hand. "I don't."

They walked a block in silence, Lacey still kicking her pebble along.

"You know, you should come over to my house and hang out," Nessie suggested. "Maybe we could even have a sleepover."

Lacey's shoe scuffed the ground as she missed her pebble. "I'm not allowed to go to sleepovers."

Nessie scrunched her eyebrows. "Why not?"

"My mom says it isn't safe."

"Oh." Nessie ran through other ideas. "What if I came to your house for a sleepover? Would that be safe?"

Lacey looked up with a dash of hope on her face. "Maybe. But my mom would probably have to meet your mom first. She's really picky about who I hang out with."

Nessie shrugged. "Sure. We can walk by my house and grab my stuff, then I can tell my mom to drive us to your house. Then they can meet, and I can stay over. Deal?"

Lacey met Nessie's smile with a bright one of her own.

When the girls came up to Nessie's house, Charity was in the front yard gardening.

"Hey, Mom. I brought a friend over!" Nessie bounced on the balls of her feet, hopeful her mom would agree to their plan, though she rarely said no to Nessie's requests. "I was wondering if I could sleep over at her house."

Charity looked up from her pile of dirt at the two girls. Her gray-blond hair was pulled into a low, messy bun. Strands trailed down the sides of her neck, and she was wearing a cotton mint-green jumpsuit. The thin straps showed off the calligraphy on her shoulder, as well as her delicate frame. It was a typical way to find Nessie's mom: relaxed and a bit tousled.

"Of course, Ness. It's great that you're making friends."

Nessie beamed. "Could you drive us to her house?"

"I'm just in the apartments at the start of the subdivision!" Lacey added.

As Charity started to answer, Lacey's phone rang. She rummaged through the pockets of her backpack to grab it. Nessie stared.

"Wow, you have your own phone?"

Lacey shrugged. "My mom says I need it for emergencies." She answered the phone, turning away from Nessie and Charity.

Nessie couldn't make out the other side of the conversation, but it sounded like a lot of yelling.

"I'm sorry, Mom," Lacey pleaded. "I just went to a friend's house. I swear—"

The earpiece rattled on.

"Yes, Mom." Lacey hung up and turned back to Nessie, disappointed. "My mom should be here any minute. She's coming to get me. I don't think we're going to be allowed to have a sleepover."

Nessie smiled and took her new friend's hand. "It's okay, maybe next time. Do you need our address so your mom can find you?"

Lacey shook her head. "No. My mom will be able to find me."

"Oh, right." Nessie smacked her head. "I forgot your mom's compass points to you."

Lacey looked at her feet. "Oh, yeah. I guess that too. But she also has the find-my-phone app."

"Huh, weird. Is that for emergencies too?"

Lacey looked up from her shoes as a black SUV with tinted windows ripped into the subdivision. "Yeah, I guess so."

Lacey's mom stepped out of the car with a look of fury in her eyes. Nessie could see where Lacey got her temper from. The woman's sleek navy-blue suit jacket was tight and fitted, cuffed just below her elbows, and her tall stiletto heels were sharp as daggers. Nessie tried not to flinch as they rang against the sidewalk with every authoritative step.

"Lacey Baker, what in Minerva's name happened? You never get off the bus except for your stop! Did it even occur to you to call me? Did you think of how stressed out I would be when I saw the bus pull up and you weren't on it? You're lucky you ended up so close and I didn't have to drive across half the city to find you!" Lacey's mom's high-pitched voice rang across the yard. Nessie glanced sideways at her mom, unsure of what to do. Charity wiped her dirty hands on her jumpsuit and made her way toward the commotion.

"Oh, hello. You must be Nessie's friend's mom. I'm Charity. Charity McKenzie." Her mom spoke in her yoga teacher voice, soft and direct.

Lacey's mom hesitated to shake Charity's dirty hand.

"Renee Baker. Nice to meet you too." She rested a protective hand on Lacey's shoulder. "Sorry my daughter invited herself over. Kids these days, hey?" She faked a laugh.

Nessie tried not to scowl as she prepared to launch into a full account of what had happened. Before she could, Lacey shook her head. Nessie frowned but kept quiet.

"Oh, no. Don't be sorry. It was probably my kid's idea." Charity ruffled Nessie's blond hair, dusting it with bits of fresh dirt. "I'm surprised she hasn't brought friends by before, and I was excited for her to get some time with kids her own age for once."

Nessie blushed and pushed her mom's hand from her head.

Renee perked up. "Oh, you don't have other children?"

Charity's smile faltered. "Nope, it's only the two of us. If you ever want to come by for dinner, you're more than welcome. We could use more people around."

Renee offered a polite smile in return. "That would be nice, but perhaps another night. I left dinner on the stove, so we have to go back."

"Another night, then."

Lacey gave Nessie a wave before she was towed away to the SUV.

"See you on Monday," Nessie called, unsure if Lacey heard her as the door slammed closed.

CHAPTER VII

JAYLYNN

"I think I'm going to die."

Nylah's laughter chimed over the phone. Jaylynn walked through her puffs of breath left on the crisp autumn air as she made her way across the Vancouver University campus.

"Don't be dramatic. You're not going to die."

Through the phone, Jaylynn could hear the kettle in the background of her sibling's call. *Oh, what I would give for a hot cup of literally anything right now.*

"Nope. Definitely actively dying over here. You need to save me, Nylah, please. Convince Mom she needs to fly me home ASAP." Jaylynn's boots clicked against the cold stone walkway, the sound ringing through the night.

"As if," Nylah teased. "What would I even say? 'Oh, hey, Mom. I know it's been months since we last talked, but Jay wanted me to call you. I know you paid a fortune to fly her across the country, but she needs to come home because she'd rather hide in a hole than meet her soulmate.'"

Jaylynn huffed into the phone. "Come on, Nylah, there's got to be something you can do. I've only been here a week and I'm honestly convinced I'm going to puke every hour of every day. My compass literally won't stop spinning."

"Maybe you should stop evading the love of your life and go to classes like the good philosophy student Mom and Dad expect you to be," Nylah scoffed. "Minerva knows I'm not the angel child they wanted. They'll have a conniption if you refuse to follow their ideals too."

Jaylynn's freckled cheeks burned. She'd already skipped two classes because she couldn't bring herself to leave her dorm room. "I swear my soulmate is a crazy stalker! It's not my fault I can't go to classes. Every time he gets close, the world gets all slow-mo and the air stills, and I panic! Last time I literally didn't leave my room for an entire weekend. I thought I was going to starve to death."

She spied her private dorm building as she rounded the next block and it brought her a bit of ease. *At least I have a safe haven.*

"Jay, give it up! Your soulmate is on campus, and they're going to do anything to find you. It's only a matter of time. Why can't you be like most people and be excited? Do you want to end up like me? Twenty, still waiting on my soulmate, living all alone?"

Jaylynn rolled her eyes. "Girl—wait, no. Man? No, that's not right either." Nylah's forgiving laughter eased her conscience. "Listen, you know why I can't be excited. Impending tragedy? The worst event of my entire life ending in death, ring any bells?"

"Ugh, I can't believe you're still hung up on that. I wish I never…" Nylah's voice faded.

Jaylynn's stomach rolled with a fresh wave of nausea.

No. Oh, Cupid, please no. Not now—

Jaylynn tried to break into a run for the door that was only feet away, but before she could, she felt a hand grasp her jacket sleeve. Too polite to wrench her arm away, she forced herself to stop. She coughed once and cut Nylah off. "Nylah, I have to go." Before they could say goodbye, Jaylynn ended the call and slipped her phone into her mustard-yellow wool coat.

"You know, despite our souls being linked, you're a hard lady to track down." The man's deep voice echoed off the nearby walls into the night sky.

The door is literally right there. Just pull away and make a run for it.

Despite every instinct Jaylynn had to move away from her captor, her compass tugged her back. Ignoring it the past week had been unbearable, and every time her soulmate had drawn closer, it pulled even harder. How had she not noticed how close he'd gotten this time?

Damn Nylah, distracting me.

Jaylynn turned slowly to face her pursuer. The warm glow of the streetlight revealed the first glimpse of her destiny. Under a flat tweed hat, wrapped in a sharp, businesslike scarf, stood a short and full-figured man.

So much for him being tall, dark, and handsome. Damn you, Nylah.

"Hi." Her voice squeaked. *Jupiter Almighty, get it together,* she thought to herself.

"Hi." He sounded amused. Jaylynn forced a smile. "Sorry to interrupt your race back to your lair."

Jaylynn blushed as she backed toward the door. Relief flooded her core when he released his grasp.

"I-I," she stammered, grasping for her key fob, "I'm so sorry."

Before her soulmate could get out another word, she slammed the fob against the lock and threw herself through the lobby doors, fleeing into the warmth and pulling them closed behind her.

"Sorry!" she called through the glass, cringing at her own awkwardness, before turning to escape down the hall. With every step she took, the ground solidified under her feet. She slammed the door to her cramped room and sank to the floor.

For the love of Cupid, why am I like this? I'm such a blasted fool.

But the goddess of wisdom shared no answers. Jaylynn grabbed her phone and redialed Nylah's number.

"Seriously, Jay, talk about rude—"

"I just met him," she said, cutting off Nylah once again. "Well, kind of." Jaylynn hit her head against the door with a satisfactory knock. "I met him, and I ran."

"What?! Jaylynn Clare, you listen to me now. As your older sibling, I am telling you to hang up this phone right now and go back and apologize to that nice man! He does not deserve this!"

"I can't!" Jaylynn whined back. "I can't do this. As soon as he leaves, I swear I'm getting on a plane and coming home."

"You mean he hasn't left yet? Man, your soulmate must have a heart of gold and infinite patience. I would hate to be linked to you." Nylah scoffed.

"Ugh, yes, he's still there. I hate that I can literally feel my compass pulling me toward him. Curse you, Cupid!" Jaylynn glared at the ceiling before standing up. She walked over to the small square mirror that hung on her otherwise bare wall. Her freckle-covered cheeks were bright pink and her nose ran from the cold.

"Jaylynn, I will literally pull a Mom and disown you as my family if you do not go out there and apologize right now." There wasn't anything playful in Nylah's voice.

"I can't!" Jaylynn croaked. "I can't do this. I'm not like you, Nylah. I'm not brave, or beautiful, or strong. I'm cursed, and stupid, and I never should have come here." Tears brimmed in her sky-blue eyes as she turned away from the reflection of her frizzy red curls.

Nylah paused. "This isn't about the prediction, is it?"

Jaylynn sniffled. "Maybe. I don't know. Maybe not. I'm just not ready."

"Jay." Nylah's voice was soft. "I know you're afraid, but he probably is too. Meeting your soulmate is supposed to be the best moment of your life, and you've probably scared the living daylights out of him. Can you imagine how you would feel if your soulmate was actively avoiding you?"

Jaylynn let out a sigh as her thoughts traced back to the guy she'd slammed a door on.

"You deserve to be happy, Jay. The only thing standing in your way is you. Now, get your butt up and go say hello to the fine man waiting for you, or so help me I will fly over there and drag you out myself."

The corner of Jaylynn's mouth perked up at her sibling's threats. *Nylah's right. I can do this. I need to do this.*

"Okay, okay. I'm going. I'll call you back after. If I get kidnapped and die, I hope you remember that you're the one who told me to go out in the night to meet my stalker."

"GO. Stop your nattering. And wipe your nose. If you kiss, you don't want to cover him with snot."

"I will not be kissing a complete stranger!"

"Sure, whatever you say, sis. Get your butt out there. Love you, bye!" Nylah's cheerful tone cut off as the line dropped. Jaylynn put her phone back into her coat pocket. *He's your soulmate. He's not going to kill you. Now, go out there and apologize for being a dufus.*

She wiped her nose before stepping out and gazing back down the hall. There, outside the glass doors, her stalker leaned against the cement wall, his expression obscured by his hat's shadow. *Soulmate. Stop calling him a stalker, even though he kind of is.*

She collected herself and walked back down the hall to the entryway. As she opened the door, the man looked up.

Jaylynn swallowed the lump in her throat. "It's kind of cold. Would you like to come in?"

The man offered her a lopsided grin as he walked up to the door. Jaylynn stumbled a step back. The air got lighter again as her awareness of the ground beneath her feet evaporated. *Don't say something stupid. Act cool. You've got this.*

The man chuckled as he stepped into the light and took off his hat. "Does this mean you've stopped avoiding me?"

Jaylynn couldn't process what he was saying, as she was immediately distracted. A wave of sandalwood tinged the air as he stepped closer, his rich, earthy cologne permeating the lobby. She hadn't noticed he had a beard when they were outside, and how nicely it shaped his round face. Or how his light blue scarf drew out soft flecks in his imploring eyes, beckoning her to come closer. *Oh,* she thought to herself. *Oh, I was so wrong.* He was easily double her size, and incredibly handsome. Based on his impish grin, he was used to the attention.

"Elias," he said, holding out his hand to break the elongating silence.

Jaylynn blushed and took off her black leather glove, holding out her hand in return. "Sorry," was all she managed to say before her skin touched his. Nothing could have prepared her for the adrenaline rush that surged through her body. All the hairs on her arms and neck stood up at once and ecstasy pulsed through her nervous system, setting the world alight around her. Her lungs brimmed full with the purest air.

In an instant, Jaylynn felt like she had known this stranger forever. It was as if a piece of herself she'd never known was missing had settled into place. Every fear she'd ever had of this moment faded away as his chilly hand intertwined with hers. She wasn't sure who took the first step, but they stepped in closer to one another, faces inches apart.

Even in the perfect quiet, his eyes spoke a thousand words. *I see you. I see all of you.* Her body shuddered at the intimacy of holding his gaze. *I know,* she thought back at him, even though she felt foolish. People couldn't read minds.

"I-I don't even know your name"—Elias held her gaze as he spoke—"but somehow finding you feels like coming home."

But his hooded eyes said even more. *I love you already, and I will love you forever. I dare you to try and make me think otherwise.*

Jaylynn's free hand clenched as Elias lifted his other hand to brush one of her curls back. The shock of his contact was less intense this time, their other hands still clasped tight. A cooling sensation ran over her stunned body, coaxing her mind to clear.

The corner of his mouth perked up. "Not that I'm opposed to waiting for you, as I would wait for you forever, but I really would love to know your name. Or I'm going to assume your name is Sorry."

Jaylynn laughed an easy laugh, relaxing for the first time in ages. "Well, you've made that clear in the past week. And I am sorry, but my name is Jaylynn. Jaylynn Clare. But you can call me Jay."

"Jay, like a blue jay?" He smiled as his eyes flickered down to her lips before meeting her gaze again. "I have waited, for what feels like an eternity, to meet you."

Jaylynn's compass begged her to close the gap. Instead, she

whispered back, "Seven years isn't so bad."

He bit his lip and retorted, "Maybe not for you. But to think I've missed seven years of making you blush? Now, that's a true crime."

She felt her cheeks get hot again—or had they even stopped?

Elias's eyes drank her in. "You have the most stunning freckles." His voice was low and quiet as he leaned closer. "They're like stardust, rained from the heavens, kissing every perfect piece of you."

Jaylynn swallowed. "I... I didn't imagine you to be such a romantic." As soon as the words were out of her mouth, she wanted to slam her head against a wall. *Is that the best you can do?*

"I didn't imagine my soulmate would avoid me like the plague." His voice was teasing and hushed, like he was about to divulge a secret. "Tell me, Blue Jay, do you still wish you'd stayed hidden in your tower?"

She shook her head. No, she didn't want to hide anymore. Not now that she knew what she'd been missing. His stunning yet mysterious eyes stared back at her, their question undeniable. She leaned in for the kiss, not sparing a moment to think what Nylah might say.

His beard brushed her chin as his full lips met hers, sweet and soft. Jaylynn's head spun. She sank into his arms as her knees buckled. In Elias's embrace, Jaylynn could hardly think straight, but the quote from her philosophy text clicked.

Love is composed of a single soul inhabiting two bodies. Was it Aristotle? Or Plato? Jaylynn couldn't bring herself to care. She finally understood. She wanted to spend the rest of her life losing daylight staring into his gorgeous eyes, and every bit of starlight tracing the lines of his body with her hands. She wanted to drink him in forever.

"I..." she started. But even as the romantic notions swept her consciousness, they blurred as Elias pulled back to meet her gaze again. Her cheeks flushed.

His thumb traced her bottom lip where his lips had just been.

"I know," he whispered back.

CHAPTER VIII

Sebastian groaned as a heavy thump sounded against the wall between his bedroom and his parents. He wrapped a pillow around his head to muffle his mum's giggles. He knew there was no point in complaining; his parents wouldn't care. As far as they were concerned, what were rainy weekend mornings in London for, if not for making their two teenage children incredibly uncomfortable?

The grinding of the headboard against his wall broke him. Sebastian knew he had to get out before the moaning started. He rolled out of his bed and glared as his clock flickered to 7:10 a.m.

Total bollocks. His blackout shades let next to no light in, but Sebastian moved expertly in the near dark, sliding into his favorite gray sweats and yesterday's shirt. Hardly a minute passed before he slugged downstairs with the overnight bag he never unpacked and bailed out of the house.

Sebastian didn't bother leaving a note as to where he was going, and he didn't plan to send his parents a text either. He was confident they wouldn't care if he was gone. The early-summer rain pattered on the pavement before him, its gloom reflecting his own. Fortunately, Gareth only lived a block away and he was sure to be up.

Ugh, morning people.

When he finally stepped out of the rain into his best friend's house, mouthwatering smells of cinnamon and dough coated the air, and a familiar background of yelling and wrestling noises echoed down the hall. Elise Williams rounded the corner and Sebastian offered his best surprise-I'm-back smile.

"Sebastian Evans! Doesn't your mum tell you to comb your hair?" She fussed with the knotted mess of shaggy blond hair. "How can anyone see your handsome face with half of it covered?" Elise pushed back his hairline and beamed. Her rich black braids hung in perfect lines, framing the wide smile she'd passed on to all three of her boys. He always liked the way she took in his entire face without wincing at the splatter of bright pink scars cast down the right side of his temple and jaw. In the ten years they'd known one another, his childhood burns were likely as familiar to her as to himself.

"If I combed my hair, what else would you have to nag me over?"

Mrs. Williams patted his cheek. "Breakfast will be ready soon. Can you be a darling and tell Gareth to get off his Xbox?"

Sebastian felt the last layer of annoyance slide off his shoulders as he settled into his home away from home. Even when he didn't call ahead, Mrs. Williams always made enough food in case he came by, which was often. Before Sebastian could make his way up to his best friend's room, he found his knees clamped in a viselike grip. At nine years old, Gareth's youngest brother, Addi, had an impressive mass of black spiraling curls.

"I told Emmet you would come today. You always come over on weekends."

On cue, Addi's eleven-year-old brother, Emmet, came running into the room. "No, *I* said he would come. *You* said he wouldn't."

Sebastian smirked as he leaned down and wrapped his arm around Addi's waist. He laughed as the boy squealed. "And miss the chance to wrestle you scamps? Never."

Emmet came sailing into the equation, knocking Sebastian down. Instinctively, he cradled around Addi's head, careful to shield him from harm as they fell. The young boys clamored to pin down Sebastian's arms, and he laughed out loud as he strained against them.

"Boys." A deep voice cut through the laughter. Mr. Williams stood at the entryway with his arms crossed. "Your mum said to set the table, not to maul Sebastian. Off you go."

Addi and Emmet leaped up, their continued giggles ringing off the shallow ceiling as they rushed back to the kitchen, unlikely to fulfill their tasks anyway. Kenyon Williams offered Sebastian his warm, ebony hand, clasping tightly as he helped him up.

"How's the ankle doing?" Mr. Williams asked. Though Kenyon was often regarded as a serious businessman with his dark, assessing eyes and reluctance to laugh, Sebastian knew Gareth's father to be a kind and generous man. In reality, the whole Williams family was wonderful. They were the family Sebastian dreamed of, and luckily, they seemed to have no objections to taking him in whenever he needed an escape.

Sebastian waved him off. "A couple of days and it was nothing."

Not that my own parents have thought to ask.

Kenyon nodded, his face grave. "At least it was only rolled and not sprained, or worse."

Whatever amount of order the house had almost restored erupted once again when Gareth entered the room. Addi and Emmet ran back into the living room, tackling their tall, older brother. Sebastian didn't hesitate to join the fray, wrapping his arms around Addi once again to balance the teams. Not that two boys of sixteen against a nine-year-old and an eleven-year-old would ever be fair.

Elise's voice rang out over the wrestling boys, demanding order. "If this table isn't set in the next two minutes, not one of you will eat today. Understood?"

The three brothers clamored over one another to grab cutlery and plates, and Sebastian took the opportunity to sneak off to the loo. He glanced at the mirror briefly, doing his best to wrangle his stubborn hair for breakfast. Then he paused, the reflection somehow less familiar. It wasn't his scars, sea-green eyes, or dark eyebrows that brought him to a stop. Those were the same every day. Instead, it was the tiny glimmer of silver peeking out of his jacket sleeve. He hadn't taken off his coat when he'd come in, and now he was grateful he hadn't. His back thumped against the wall as he stumbled back.

Oh, no. Please no. He was only sixteen! He should still have time…

He pushed up his sleeve. There, on his left forearm, was the infamous compass tattoo. His jaw went slack as he took in the unfamiliar line work. He'd never looked at one closely before. Most people kept them covered for privacy. Well, usually. In school, when someone woke up with their marking, they often bore it with pride. Nothing could make you popular quite like a magical tattoo.

Damien Diaz had been the first in their class to get his compass-clock a couple of years ago, and he used every chance he could to flaunt his "maturity" over everyone in the beginning. Opposite to their rival, Gareth had been private when his compass appeared, and Sebastian was happy to give him space and privacy. He was grateful Gareth hadn't become annoying and never acted better than him for not having one.

But now Sebastian had his own.

He traced his fingers over the fresh lines engraved on his arm. It surprised him how the tattoo protruded up from his skin and that the metallic engraving was cool to the touch. It pulsed gently, almost humming. He took his time as he spun in a circle, watching the diamond arrowhead keep its mark.

"Sebastian!"

His head shot up. *No one can know.* He scrambled for a lie as he realized he couldn't get away with wearing his jacket through a meal without being rude, but he couldn't outright skip breakfast when he'd only just arrived.

He cleared his throat and called down the hall. "Gareth?"

Hardly a second passed before his broad-smiling friend poked around the corner. His hair was cut in a sharp fade, the top curls cropped neatly and out of his face.

"What's up, mate?"

Sebastian kept his left arm tucked behind himself.

"Do you have a jumper I can wear?"

Gareth didn't wait for whatever Sebastian's excuse might have been. He hurried down the hall and was back in a flash, throwing a black jumper at Sebastian's face. Sebastian sighed in relief as he took off his jacket and pulled the baggy jumper over his slim frame. Gareth's long limbs afforded Sebastian the exact cover he needed, as the sleeves came past his wrists.

Now to remember not to accidentally roll the sleeves up.

He made his way back to his hollering second family.

CHAPTER IX

BLAKE

Blake was already having a miserable day without her path being cluttered with lovesick morons. She tucked a strand of her thin, bleached hair behind her ear, wincing as her freshly stretched ears flared in objection. She should have known it was too soon to push them up another size. As she stalked across New York's most famous park, she glowered at the thought of how much it was going to cost her to leave the wretched city.

She eyed a nearby woman's handbag, weighing if she could successfully take it without a scene. Her thoughts of the potential cash faded away as she spied what she was looking for, though. Blake cut over to the nearby park bench, relieved something was finally going her way.

"Tatiana! Listen, I need—"

Blake was cut off as she was lifted off her feet. Tatiana's arms wrapped around her own, crushing her in a hug and filling her nostrils with the smell of weed. Tatiana flipped her dark, bouncing Latina curls out of the way as she leaned in to plant a kiss on Blake's impatient face.

"Stop it. I'm being serious. We need to talk, and I need your help."

Tatiana's face soured as she took in Blake's seriousness. "What's got you in such a tizzy today?" She released Blake and took a step back. Blake felt a twinge of guilt twist in her gut. *Just spit it out.*

Blake reached for Tatiana's hand and pulled her to sit on the park bench. "Listen. Don't freak out, okay?" She took a breath and braced herself for the truth she'd been so adamant about denying hours earlier. "I got my compass today."

Tatiana's face fell hard.

Ugh, I knew this wasn't going to go well.

Tatiana rose with her fists clenched, turning to leave. Before she could, Blake grabbed the sleeve of her baggy sweatshirt.

"Tatiana, come on. You know I don't believe in this garbage any more than you do. My parents are a testimony to how trash compasses are." She thought back to the other thing that had kicked off her terrible day: finding her mother in the bathtub, covered in her own vomit again. She shook her head and reached up to her girlfriend's face, begging her to meet her eyes. "Come on, you know I hate this. You have to help me."

Tatiana pushed Blake's hand away, crossing her arms over the thick gold chains that draped low from her neck "What do you want me to do, J.B.? It was bound to happen eventually."

Blake pulled her girlfriend's arms loose, conscious of how much she needed Tatiana's help. "You're not listening to me." Blake hated begging, but she took Tatiana's hands in her own. "I know you have people. Help me get rid of it. If nothing else, just cover it up. Please, Tatiana. I have the money and you know I don't want this."

Blake could see Tatiana's inner battle playing out on her face. The hurt, the hope, the swirl of overwhelming emotions.

"You're really set on this?" Tatiana's teeth played with her lip ring.

"You know I am." Blake wove her pale, thin hand into Tatiana's warm one, pulling her in for the kiss that she knew would fix everything. That was the thing about Tatiana: all she ever wanted was to be kissed and held. Even though Blake loathed public displays of affection, they were an easy way to win over her girlfriend's heart.

Tatiana sank into the kiss and held Blake tight. She did her best not to pull away.

"Okay. If you're sure." Without another word, Tatiana turned with sudden intention. She pulled Blake through the greenery of Central Park, weaving through the people crowding around Psyche's temple. As always, marble Psyche leaned forlorn against her marble pillar gazebo, her hand outstretched to the sky. Nearby, a group of people let out an audible chorus of awws as a man got down on one knee in front of his partner in the sacred gazebo.

Blake cursed under her breath in annoyance.

Tatiana's brow furrowed as she glanced back. "You know, it's not their fault. Just because they believe in something you don't, doesn't make them stupid."

Really? Stupid compass, strung-out mom, and a moody girlfriend? How much worse can this day get? Blake adjusted her backpack with her free hand, tearing her gaze from the proposal. "I just don't understand why they're convinced it's all real. Proposing in Psyche's temple doesn't guarantee a perfect marriage, any more than Cupid's Compass guarantees lifelong love." She thought about her dad, hours away on a beach somewhere with some dumb tramp. Blake glared at an innocent spectator.

Tatiana shrugged and continued to pull Blake along. Hand in hand, they left the park and moved into the busy streets. For the hundredth time that year, Blake considered leaving her mom. She imagined living with Tatiana in her trashy apartment with all her booze-hound roommates or getting a job and leaving her mom to her own problems. Idly, she wondered if her mom could manage without her.

Blocks of Manhattan passed before Tatiana came to an abrupt stop. Her grip on Blake's hand tightened, but she didn't meet her eyes.

"Listen, J.B. If you want to go in there and do this, I get it. But you should really think about it. You've got a soulmate out there somewhere. Even if you sever your half of the line, they could still come looking for you."

"I know," she said, "and I'll tell them to screw off if they do."

"You mean *when* they do?" Tatiana glowered.

"T, what did we say? You and me, screw the gods. You might not have your compass yet, but if it appeared, you'd still choose me, wouldn't you?" As expected, Tatiana's shoulders softened.

"I'm nineteen, J.B. If it was going to happen, it should have already. But of course I would choose you."

Blake's gut nagged in suspicion, but she ignored it. She pulled Tatiana's chin toward her own and planted a soft kiss on her warm lips. "I'll see you after, okay?" Tatiana nodded as she pulled away.

Here goes nothing.

Blake walked down the unfamiliar concrete stairway to a metal door and knocked. After a minute, the door opened, wafting a cloud of cigarette smoke into her face. A short woman with thick, muscular arms answered the door, tattoos and gleaming piercings marking her rich umber skin.

"You lost, kid?"

Blake fought the urge to roll her eyes. "No. I'm exactly where I need to be."

The woman snorted. "Why are you here?"

She shrugged. "A friend recommended you. She said you can make problems go away."

The busty woman leaned on the doorway, breaking into a silver-toothed smile. "Did they, now? How old are you?"

"Old enough," she replied. Blake prayed she looked as old as Tatiana believed she was. Though she didn't enjoy lying to her girlfriend, she was sure Tatiana wouldn't have been as into her if she'd known Blake was only sixteen.

"Okay, pip-squeak. If you say so," the woman replied, "but I'll have you know, I don't work with babies. If you're going to cry, you're out."

Blake nodded. "I understand."

CHAPTER X

RIVER

River startled at an unexpected knock as she stoked the fireplace. She hadn't seen any tell-tale headlights to warn her someone had arrived. She wiped the sweat that clung to her forehead and hung the curved iron poker on its stand.

River hesitated for a heartbeat before she opened her cabin door to the cool night. The fall breeze rustled the hem of her skirt against her bare ankles, a welcome respite from the heat. Outside stood a short, cloaked woman, her face obscured by a hanging hood. Her breath clouded in soft puffs.

Despite being alone in the woods late at night with a stranger standing at her door, River couldn't have explained the warmth in her gut upon seeing the petite silhouette. Trusting her instincts, she stepped aside and welcomed the huddled figure into her home. The lady stepped inside and pulled back her hood. Warm, auburn curls poured out over her shoulders. Rosy cheeks and curious eyes met hers in the warm light.

"You!" the girl exclaimed. "I hadn't imagined... Well, I don't know what I had imagined... I just, I don't know, I thought maybe..." The woman stumbled over her words as her brow furrowed in confusion.

"Ah," River said in relief. She recognized the once young girl, now grown. "Welcome, dear one. I'm sorry not to be whoever you were expecting. Alas, it is just me. Let me make us a pot of tea. I trust we have much to catch up on. Please, take a seat. You look like you're about to faint."

The small wood cabin's windows dripped with condensation as they fogged up from the moisture inside. A pot on the stove filled with herbs and essential oils bubbled, the smell of crushed rose petals caressing the cabin air. Though Re-Sparking Love Potions were one of her greatest sellers, River didn't care for their sickly sweet smell; she missed the usual musky incense that filled her home.

River moved to fill the kettle as her concoction on the stove foamed a soft pink. She took it off the heat, conscious the batch would be unfinished and ruined. Though she'd spent a lot of time brewing the new draft, she'd waited far longer for this visit. She'd wondered when the redheaded child would find her way back to her. She'd grown so much since that time, now a beautiful young woman. Her soul still shone bright, but her eyes… her eyes had changed. They no longer carried the innocence that River had once admired.

"Why would my compass lead me here?" the young woman whispered, holding the edges of her cloak tight against herself. Tears welled up in her eyes as she took a couple of trembling breaths, despite the undeniable warmth of the cabin. River yearned to take her hands and soothe her fears. Instead, she took to blending a medley to help the girl's mind settle, adding a dash of chamomile in hopes of calming her nerves.

"Drink," River said, when she placed the fresh, steaming mug into her hands. The girl looked at the cup with apprehension. "Fret not, I mean you no harm. It's just a tea to help you settle. Welcome to my home."

Home. It surprised her that this small reprieve was where she considered home now. Most of her life she'd yearned to be among the people, in the hustle and bustle of it all. Now she found herself embracing silence and solitude more often. She tired from the endless love stories that she'd witnessed in her psychic shop, mocking her own. She brushed the excess lavender bits that stuck to her dress as she looked around the single room.

There wasn't much furniture in the common area of her cabin. A small cot sat along one wall, with a pile of old, well-loved knit blankets folded on top. Pots and baskets hung from the ceiling along the kitchenette, and ruffled white curtains framed the many windows. By the fireplace, a deep, worn-green couch was buried in textured pillows, and the old, bronze table that once centered her shop embraced its new life as a coffee table.

River chose two of the largest pillows of the couch and placed them on the ground closer to the fire, then gestured for the girl to join her. The woman peered at her surroundings, eyeing the fireplace skeptically before finally settling on River.

"Are... are you a witch?"

"No, I am not a witch. I do not serve Hekate, the goddess of sorcery, but would consider myself a servant to all the gods. Otherwise, I am naught but a woman like you, taunted by a compass that promises love but only brings pain. I truly am sorry for your loss. If I could have changed your fate, I would have. I understand your loss and grief intimately."

The lady took a tentative sip of the tea, as if afraid it might taste dreadful.

"If you're not a witch, how is it you claim to know what happened with Elias? How can I believe you know what happened and yet didn't cause it yourself? How did you know I would come back to you one day? Did you enchant my compass?" Questions bubbled forth before the tea had its effect, bouncing from curious to accusatory. River sighed as she finished making her own tea and settled across from her interrogator.

"How about we start with something simpler? What is your name, young one?"

"You... you knew my future, and yet you don't know my name?" A giggle escaped her throat. "I go by Jaylynn. Is your real name

River?"

"It is my chosen name," she responded. River removed the deep green shawl from her shoulders as the cabin's heat increased. She considered closing the fireplace doors, but chose to wait until Jaylynn appeared more acclimatized.

"When you read my fortune as a child, what did you really see? What of my story do you actually know?" Jaylynn looked eager for information and truth, the previous anger that had laced her energy dispersed at last. River bowed her head and complied. The memory itself still felt fresh, even though it had been so long since they'd met.

"When you walked through my door that day, I didn't immediately know what misfortune would come. You had such a gentle and pure energy. I never imagined the skies would curse such a beautiful soul with such tragedy." River took a sip of her own tea, grateful for its calming influence. "I noticed your destiny felt both long and of great significance. But the heavy air that hung around your fate was undeniable. You would bear the weight others could not, and it would be because of the purity of your heart that you would survive it. When I read your cards, it confirmed all that I already knew. You would have the love for which many dream, but it would be followed by heart-wrenching tragedy. And that this exact tragedy would one day lead you back to me. I couldn't interpret the timeline or the details, and I wished I was wrong for your sake."

River stared at her tea, thinking back to the day. "The only other thing I was certain of that day, and am still certain of today, is that you and I are tied somehow. I couldn't say how, but our energies dance like old lovers from lives past."

Jaylynn looked perturbed at the statement. River couldn't help but chuckle. "Not that I believe we are sexual lovers in this lifetime. There are many types of love. The love of Agape, for instance— unconditional and selfless love. Seen in people such as Mother Teresa. Or that of you and your first lover: Eros, deeply passionate and burning with desire. I would guess the love between us will be Storge: familiar love. No physical or sexual attraction, but a strong bond of kinship."

"You know, for not having seen one another for almost a decade, you don't look much older," Jaylynn replied.

River's brow creased. "Has it really been that long? How old are you now?"

"I'm twenty." Jaylynn ran her finger around the rim of her steaming mug. "How old are you?"

River smiled as she brought her own mug to her lips. "Well, I certainly wish I was only twenty."

Silence filled the cabin as both women lost themselves in thought.

Is this girl the answer I've been waiting for? Have the skies finally answered my prayers? River mulled over the petite redhead's presence. Whatever they were to one another, River resolved she was prepared to see it through.

"Will you tell me the story?" River asked.

Jaylynn glanced up. River wondered if she was ready to know what great misfortune this beautiful girl had survived.

Jaylynn cleared her throat. "His name was Elias, and I met him when I was eighteen."

CHAPTER XI

JAYLYNN

Two years earlier

Jaylynn spun in a circle on the raised, carpeted platform in front of the three mirrors and basked in Nylah's delighted shriek. Even over video chat, Nylah's enthusiasm for the wedding dress was palpable.

"Oh, Jay! It's stunning! You look like a fairy princess!"

Jaylynn beamed at the camera propped on the stack of shoeboxes, then turned to the mirror. The dress did make her look stunning. Her only request had been to have a lightweight dress that she could dance the night away in, and the consignment store consultant had nailed it. Intricate white lace wrapped the sleeves of her arms and made up the conservative chest. The only skin that stood bare was the top of her back, where the lace scooped down before billowing out in soft, flowy skirts. As the consultant placed the lavish green flower tiara over Jaylynn's curls, Nylah shrieked again.

"What I would give to be with you in person right now!" Her sibling's forlorn voice drew Jaylynn back to the camera. Nylah's ringlet curls were cut in a short bob that traced the edges of their chin and choppy fringe bangs brushed the tops of their oversized, round-rimmed glasses. Jaylynn's blurry freckles and bland auburn waves paled next to Nylah's striking style, but the insecurity that surfaced washed away as she caught another glimmer of herself in the gown.

If Elias could find the beauty in me before, wait until he sees me in this.

Jaylynn smiled as the pieces of her fairy tale fell into place. "We'll be together soon. It's only a couple of months before Elias is finished his bachelor's degree and we'll be on our way back to Toronto for the wedding." She smiled at her reflection one last time, imprinting the image in her mind, before taking the ring of greenery off her head. She slipped back into the changeroom to take off her dress, placing the phone so it was facing the ceiling as she changed.

"So, have you told Mom you're not moving home?" Nylah asked.

Jaylynn sighed. "No. I already feel bad for dropping out of school and surprising them with a wedding in less than six months. Like, I know they can afford it, but I don't want to crush Mom's spirits by saying, 'Oh, by the way, thanks for paying for my wedding, but I actually plan on living across the country for the rest of my life now.'" Jaylynn shimmied back into her clothes, her hair coming alive with renewed static.

"Well, you need to tell her eventually. She's going to be devastated to lose both of her beloved children."

Jaylynn's phone chimed and Elias's name popped up over top of Nylah's face.

"I'll deal with that another time. Sorry, I've got to go. My fiancé is calling." She laughed at how weird the word felt in her mouth. "I'll call you back later. Love you!"

"Love you too."

Jaylynn's arm itched as she hauled the dress up to the front desk. Suddenly she worried that maybe the lace sleeves were a bad idea for her sensitive skin.

"Is there any way I can put this on hold? Just to think about it for the day?" The clerk nodded, and Jaylynn smiled as she handed off her fairy dress.

She picked up Elias's call as she pulled her winter boots on. "Hey, baby, sorry. I was just finishing up some wedding business. How's studying going?"

She broke out into the snowy street, scratching her arm through her mustard wool coat.

"Jay... My Blue Jay. Thank the stars you picked up."

Worry hummed in her chest at the panicked relief in his voice.

"Elias? What's wrong?" She pulled her scarf tight as she made her way back to the bus station.

"I hate making this call, but I had to—" He broke off in a ragged cough. "I had to hear your voice. I had to talk to you."

Jaylynn looked up at the oncoming bus but hesitated before boarding.

"Baby, what's happening? Where are you?"

He coughed harder. She pulled up her sleeve to look at her compass and confirm her suspicion. Though the campus had lovely libraries, Jaylynn knew that he was likely at his favorite bookshop, only a few blocks from where she was now. He'd always loved the privacy of the upstairs studying space, snuggled between endless piles of books. It was much more pleasant than the sterile environment at the university. Her arrow pointed true and based on the current pull, she was confident he was only minutes away. She started a brisk walk in his direction, trying to talk calmly as she navigated the icy sidewalk.

"Elias, please answer me. You're making me worry. Is something wrong? What's happening?"

Her compass throbbed in a way it hadn't before, burning where it usually felt cool.

"Jaylynn" —he cleared his throat—"you have been my greatest gift in this lifetime. I love you endlessly." Elias had always had a way with words, but there was a weight in his voice as he professed his love this time.

"And you know I love you too. Baby, please. Are you okay? You're freaking me out."

Urgency burned in her chest as she clutched her phone tight to her ear, picking up her pace.

"I… I don't know how much time is left. There was—"

Sirens wailed by, drowning out his voice.

"Elias? I didn't catch that."

He coughed. "Everything's going to be okay."

For the first time ever, Jaylynn didn't believe him. Her sweaty hand clamped tight on her phone as she broke into a full run. She let her compass guide her, following the magnetic pull that promised he wasn't much farther. The sound of her boots pounding over partially cleared snow was overtaken by the growing sirens. With a final turn, she saw where all the noise and commotion was coming from. The little two-story nook bookstore was alight, smoke billowing out from its roof. Firefighters and EMTs ran around as the police forced spectators back.

Bile burned the back of Jaylynn's throat. She stuffed a finger in one ear and held the phone to her other, trying desperately to hear over the disaster.

"ELIAS! Elias, sweet Venus, please tell me you're not in that building." A sob crept out as she cried into the phone, already knowing the truth. She could hear him crying too.

"I'm so sorry, baby. I wish—" He coughed so hard he sounded like he was choking.

"Elias, please. I need you. I need you to get out. You need to come home to me." Tears streamed down her face as she watched the firefighters wave people away from the building. "Please don't leave me alone in this world," she whispered.

"Jaylynn…" The line began to break up. "… aren't going to be able to get me… one of the shelves fell and… I would never leave you alone—"

"No. Please, no. I can't do this without you… Somebody help me, please!" she screamed as she pushed at the police line. "I need a firefighter! Please, help! My fiancé is still in there!" Her throat burned as she cried. Smoke filled her lungs, dry and heavy. She couldn't imagine what it was like in the thick of it.

"Officer!" she cried as she grabbed a nearby uniformed man's arm. "Officer, please! My fiancé is in that building. Please, you have to send someone in to get him."

The man's face filled with sorrow as he took her arms in his hands. "I'm sorry, ma'am. We have to pull out. The roof is about to go at any moment."

She cried as she held her phone tight to her ear, listening to Elias's heavy breathing.

"Jaylynn." His voice was so faint. "My Blue Jay." He coughed. "It's going to be okay. You're going to be okay. I promise." He paused, trying to catch his breath. "Everything happens for a reason, right?"

She cried even harder as she tried to pull out of the officer's grip. He held her tight as her compass burned, pulling her to the flaming building.

"Elias, oh, my sweet Elias. I love you. I love you so much. And I swear to the stars I'll love you from this lifetime into the next. I believe you and I were meant to be and the stars wouldn't have brought us together just to tear us apart—"

She choked on her words as the roof of the building collapsed, sending flames high into the blackening sky.

Jaylynn screamed. The officer wrapped his arms around her torso as she thrashed, desperate to join Elias, desperate not to be left behind.

CHAPTER XII

BLAKE

"You know, kid, you've got balls." The man sitting beside her smirked as he held Blake's left arm. "How long did it take them to mutilate this?"

Blake blushed as she looked down at the splattered mess of ink on her forearm. "A few hours, I think?"

"Did it hurt?" he asked. He ran his hand over Blake's disfigured compass to assess the damage.

She shrugged and suppressed the urge to pull away. Though it had been three years since she'd covered her compass, she'd never forgotten the pain and the puking that had come afterward. She also didn't want to fess up that it hadn't even worked in the end. She could still feel the blasted arrow spinning on her arm, even if she couldn't see it anymore. It was the biggest waste of five hundred dollars she'd ever spent.

"You know I can't fix this, right?" the tattoo artist said.

"I know," Blake sighed. "I was just thinking that if I got the rest of my arm tattooed, it wouldn't look as obvious."

"I've got you, kid." Sal was a heavyset man. He had tattoos crawling from his arms to his balding head. His hand was easily twice the size of her own and it was warm against her cold skin. He measured out her arm on draft paper, prepping her future sleeve.

"So what do you want? Daisies and daffodils?" His eyes twinkled as he teased her, and she smirked back.

"I think the only flowers I could pull off would be black roses, which was what that cover-up was supposed to be. So maybe I can't even pull that off."

Sal's laughter bellowed deep in his gut. "So skulls and guns?"

Blake perked up. "You know, maybe not outright death skulls, but I could go for a sugar-skull girl?"

She watched over Sal's shoulder as he sketched. He smiled as he outlined the figure of a woman, then wrapped her in black roses that would blend into the puddle on Blake's inner forearm.

"Any colors in particular that you'd like her to have? I'm thinking I'll keep her face makeup really bright and white to draw away from the compass. Then I could add some cobalt and royal blues to match the tones of your hair?"

Blake nodded, her thin lips plastered with a grin. "That would be perfect."

"And are we doing a full sleeve, or just the bottom half?"

Blake thought back to the Ziploc of cash she kept hidden at the community center. Though she'd been getting close to being able to afford a flight out of New York City and getting her own apartment, the thought of getting her entire arm tattooed was more tempting.

"What do you have in mind?" she asked. Deep down, she already knew she would love whatever he suggested.

Sal leaned back. "Hmmm," he mused. "You may be skinny, but I also get the sense that you're stronger than you look. Maybe a leopard or a lynx or something?"

Blake shook her head. "I'm not a cat person." She ran through animals in her mind that she might want to add to her sleeve. "What about a wolf?"

Sal broke into a toothy grin. "I can see some wolf in you. Let's do it."

After some sketching and paperwork, Sal spent the next few hours tattooing Blake's arm. She laughed more than she had in years. Sal had an easy way about him and was a brilliant conversationalist. It made the numbing hours of the needle fly by. Blake was relieved to discover that it didn't hurt nearly as bad as covering her compass had.

"Your artist, if you can call them that, probably went too deep. Honestly, I'd never take on that kind of project. You'd be doomed to fail."

"Do you like being a tattoo artist?" she asked, watching his careful hand as he drew out the texture of her wolf's fur.

"I love it. It's the best career I could have found. I get to be my own boss and I get to put my art out into the world without following anyone's rules. It's great."

"I used to draw a ton, but since I left home, I haven't had the time." Blake wondered how her waitressing job would feel about her new tattoo. *Well, they hired me with blue hair, stretched ears, and a mutilated compass. I can't imagine they'd say anything now.*

That caught Sal's interest. "How old were you when you moved out?"

"Sixteen." She was proud she'd gotten herself out of her toxic mother's grasp. It had taken her a couple of years of scrounging to make her life something more than dumpster diving, but it was worth the grind. She wasn't sure she'd ever gain weight back after her time on the streets, but her more recent waitressing job was helping. Bit by bit, her spine and ribs were less noticeable, and her life was shaping up to be better.

"And how old are you now?" he asked.

Blake smirked. "How old do you think I am?"

"I'd say early twenties, maybe? You've got those ageless eyes, though, so it's hard to tell."

Blake preferred when people thought she was older. For whatever reason, she wanted to tell Sal the truth, though. "I'm nineteen."

"Nineteen, hey? Are you going to college?"

She shook her head. "As if I could ever afford that, even if I had finished high school."

Sal paused as he switched out colors, choosing a bright cobalt blue for the jewels around the sugar-skull girl's eyes. "Have you ever thought about your future?"

"Not really. I never really think much further ahead than a few days. Make money, eat, sleep."

"What about your friends? Are they in school?"

Blake leaned back in her chair. "Nope. I'm not really close to anyone anymore. It's easier that way."

Leaving Tatiana had been a disaster Blake was not eager to relive. Her girlfriend had been so sure Blake wanted to leave to go find her soulmate. She refused to believe that she just needed space. Well, space was what she got. First, she was shut out by Tatiana. Then her roommates suggested she leave to make things less awkward. That, coupled with not being willing to go back to her mom's, made Blake's social life uneventful. She kept positive relationships with the people at the community center and at the diner, but that was mostly so she could keep a roof over her head.

"What about becoming a tattoo artist?" Sal asked.

"What?"

"Why don't you come work for me? We could start you up at the front to get the swing of things. I mean, you're pretty enough that you'll draw people in. Then once you've got your drawing portfolio fattened up, I could take you on as my apprentice."

Blake felt her cheeks flush as new possibilities flashed before her eyes. "You would do that for me?"

Sal stopped tattooing her arm and looked up. "Listen, kid. I've been where you are. I was lucky enough to have a helping hand pull me out of my rut. It would only be fair for me to do the same."

Blake smiled at the balding man, and her heart hammered in excitement. Who would have thought that by spending money, she could get an opportunity to make more? She thought back to her measly savings and how plump they would grow with a second income. It looked like she had found herself a new friend.

"I would love that."

CHAPTER XIII

KADE

Kade woke in a cold sweat to dark, rhythmic rap music echoing down the hallway. How their fifteen-year-old daughter slept to the same haunting melodies night after night was a mystery. The eerie sound gave him goosebumps.

Unexpected pain burned deep to his sternum and Kade winced as he sat up, clenching a fist over his racing heart. Heat licked up his spine as he turned, and his feet met the cool, laminate floor.

Jupiter Almighty, am I having a heart attack?

Careful not to wake Renee, he staggered upright and made his way to the ensuite bathroom. With a shaky hand, he closed the door as quietly as possible before flicking on the light. He clasped his head between his hands as the room spun and sank down to the floor.

Something was very wrong. Kade forced himself to take deep, measured breaths to calm the inexplicable panic that flooded his core. Then the oddest sensation caught his attention. He looked down at his forearm, unable to believe what he was seeing. His compass arrow was spinning steady, in a counterclockwise direction.

A shiver prompted the hairs on the back of Kade's neck to rise. He looked up at the door that divided him from Renee, curious if she would wake. When her compass changed all those years ago, it had felt like a bone-deep chill in his own body—an unignorable shock to his system. But no sound stirred on the other side of the door.

Kade looked back down. The tip of his gleaming arrowhead slowed. He sat frozen as it resettled itself in a different direction. Not where the thin bathroom door stood guard. Not where his wife slept in their double bed on the other side. Even as his nausea from the spinning settled, his heart pounded louder than Lacey's headphones.

What could this mean? Was this the sign he had been waiting for? Was it finally time for him to move on? The clarity of that thought was a jagged knife through his heart. If things hadn't already been hard enough in their family, his changed compass was about to make things a lot harder.

He sat on the bathroom floor and stared at his new compass. His clock hands had shifted, now pointing at 9:46. His whole adult life it had sat firm at 8:29, so to see it changed was baffling. Kade wondered if he was having a nightmare. He stood up and took a good look in the mirror. He didn't look different, though his receding hairline was worse. It had come to the point where he'd considered shaving his head. He gave himself a little shake and forced himself to return to bed, resolving that if his compasses new coordinates were still there in the morning, he would deal with it then.

He woke only a few hours later. His back ached in protest and his eyes burned under heavy lids. As he reached out to shut off his alarm, the nightmare came back to him in a flurry. He held out his left forearm.

So, it wasn't a dream. Kade was unsure if this was a blessing or about to ruin his life even further. Beside him, Renee hadn't stirred yet. He got up and chose a long-sleeved dress shirt for the day, despite the warming May weather.

As he made his morning coffee, a million questions raced through his brain. Should he tell Renee, or wait and see if she noticed? Should he call his therapist? Would this worsen Lacey's raging teenage temperament? Would she hate him for this? Would Renee? As the thoughts swirled in an uncontrolled flurry, he tried to suppress one agonizing question.

Who did his compass point to now?

Work was rough that day. Between his headache from not sleeping and the way his stomach turned every time he thought about leaving Renee, he was a mess. His boss wasn't the least bit impressed as he bumbled through his presentation. Thank the stars it was Friday. As he left the office, he snuck a peek at his compass. He could feel the gentle pull of it, drawing him east of the city.

He couldn't help himself as he got in his car and drove in the opposite direction of home. He was curious, and he rationalized he could tell Renee he had to stay late. Driving in rush hour traffic was its usual chaos, but he let his thoughts wander as he followed his compass. He refused to think about what he was doing. As he made his way into the heart of Toronto an hour later, he found himself driving down a street with endless stores. His compass arrow suddenly flipped from its forward-bound position to behind him, bringing a fresh bout of nausea. He shook himself out of the daze and pulled a U-turn to proceed back up the street.

As he scanned the sidewalk, his heart crept up his throat. A figure stood with her back turned to him, busying herself as she locked the door. The girl was petite and her red hair pulled up into an unruly bun. He couldn't see her face, but based on the way she was dressed, she had to be much younger than him. Her light blue skirt rippled in the wind, and her waist was accentuated by her tied-up white blouse. Shame gouged a gaping hole through his stomach as he looked back at the road and forced himself home. He felt sick and tears welled up at the thought of how his life was about to change.

Kade sat silently through dinner. To his great relief, neither of his family members asked why he was late. Lacey had her usual attitude when Renee asked about her day. He couldn't imagine dinners without her sassy commentary. Solemn, he got up from the table early and started cleaning. Though it was Lacey's chore, he was sure she wouldn't complain. He needed to keep his hands busy. Renee joined him soon after and dried the dishes at his side.

"You okay…?" she asked. Her voice was tentative, as if she was feeling out how dangerous the waters were.

Kade didn't know how to reply. "I… I think… I don't know."

"Hey." She took his chin and turned his face to hers. Her warm brown eyes were soft in the kitchen light. "Listen. I know things have been hard lately, and I know work has been rough. We've been fighting so much, but I hope you know I love you. I'm not sure what's going on, but it hurts my heart to see you like this."

Kade broke her gaze, and his shame burned deeper. Even after all this time, she still tried. The walls around his heart shuddered, threatening to collapse as she pulled him in and gave him a firm hug. They stood in the kitchen like that for a long time. Kade wondered how many more moments like this they had left.

Lacey came around the corner and raised her eyebrows. "Umm, sorry… I'll just leave. Thanks for doing the dishes, Dad." She dropped off her plate and scurried back out of the kitchen.

Renee looked up into his eyes. "You know you can talk to me, right?"

He nodded as he pulled her closer, resting his chin on her soft brown hair. As he breathed in her pomegranate shampoo, he wondered how to tell her he was going to leave.

ACT 2

DECUMA

From Nona's hands, Decuma casts the thread.
Each inch she adds, the more breaths before death.
The task falls on her, the Fate to decide
The span of mortal's life; tragedy, treasure, or pride.
She dictates men's misery and the lives they will lead,
and in so becomes the entity to which they plead.
—The Weaver of Fate

CHAPTER XIV

NYLAH

"**Sweet Mother Juno!** Could it be? Has my savior arrived?"

Across the counter, a tall, well-built man rolled his eyes and smirked. "I didn't realize you were in need of saving. You've always had that tough, I-don't-need-no-man vibe."

Nylah laughed, brushing their short, bright red curls back. "Well, you're not wrong. Minerva knows I could use an excuse to take a break, though." Nylah slung the drab black apron over the wooden gate.

On cue, the café manager's face soured in their direction. "Smoke break?" he asked, as if it wasn't obvious.

Nylah gave a cheeky grin and pushed up the bridge of their wide, circular glasses. Without missing a beat, Nylah slung their freckled arm around their friend's muscular one and slipped out into the alleyway. Contrary to the lovely Toronto street that the café faced, the back exit came out to a shaded and cramped path littered with trash cans.

"I never will understand why you started smoking."

The man leaned against the brick wall. His warm, russet skin beautifully offset the dirty backdrop. This was a view that Nylah had no problems with taking in. Between his dark, sharply groomed beard, and the white, crisp neckline of his tight shirt, Nylah's high school friend was as dazzling as his stud earrings.

"Why do I do anything, Jazz, if not to perpetually taunt my mother?"

As expected, Jazz rewarded the comment with another perfect smile, his white teeth flashing.

"Jupiter Almighty, can you stop being so—" Nylah flailed their hands as they looked for a word to capture him.

"Unbearably good-looking? The bane of your future soulmate's existence? A constant reminder of what you're missing out on?" He winked.

Nylah shoved his shoulder, which was a foot higher than the top of their own five-foot-one head. "Distracting. I was going to say distracting." Leaning against the brick wall, Nylah slipped the thin rolled paper tip between their pale lips and dug in the pocket of their faded scarlet overalls for a lighter.

"I can't apologize for what the Fates gave me." He shrugged his broad shoulders and Nylah's eyes lingered on the curve of his deltoids.

"Whatever. The Fates don't make you gorgeous. You have Venus to thank if anyone." Nylah sucked against the crisping edge of their habit, willing the nicotine to feed their craving.

"Psh, Venus is nothing without the Fates."

Nylah tilted the back of their head against the brick wall, closing their eyes. *Not this again.*

"Seriously, Nylah. You should come with me sometime and meet my new friends. I think you'd appreciate their take on the world after everything you've been through."

Smoke trickled through Nylah's nostrils as it escaped to the blue-skied day. "Your new friends that steal you away all the time?"

"If you came with me, you wouldn't have anything to complain about."

"If I came with you, Boots might get lonely." Nylah's split-faced black-and-white cat surely would object. She survived solely on a diet of pets and cuddles, and cried endlessly if she didn't get enough.

Jazz bumped Nylah's shoulder. "C'mon. What's it going to take for you to give these people a shot?"

Nylah ran through the list of things they wanted most and quickly settled on one. "Travel the UK and the Roman Empire in August with me."

Jazz's warm eyes twinkled at the offer. "Steep. I offer you new friendships for free, and you offer me a thousand-dollar bill?"

"It's not just a thousand-dollar bill. It's an adventure with your favorite person, scouring cities you know you want to go to. Not to mention a month-long escape." Nylah's wrist danced through the air as they listed the benefits to their plan.

Jazz coughed. "No way. I can commit to two weeks or as far as two thousand dollars will get me. And if Boots can't manage one night without you, how exactly is she going to survive this trip?"

"Obviously, Jay will take Boots," Nylah said, as if that wasn't already obvious. Overall, Jazz's offer was better than going on this trip alone, even if it meant getting acquainted with his new friends. "How about this: three weeks and you can choose the date we leave? I'll do all the research and make the trip as affordable as humanly possible."

Jazz shook his head. "Two weeks, and if you want to stay longer without me, you can. Not everyone has a job that lets them disappear whenever they feel like it."

Nylah sighed. "Fine. Two weeks. But this isn't conditional on me liking your friends. If I hate them, you still have to come with me."

Jazz grinned, gaining traction in a battle he'd been fighting for months. "Give them two or three tries. They can seem like a lot the first time you meet them, but I'm sure they'll grow on you."

Nylah knocked the edge of the burning cigarette to the ground. "Two tries. Two weeks."

"You drive a hard bargain, but how could I say no?" He wrapped his arm over Nylah's shoulders and squeezed.

Nylah sighed as Jazz's spiced, cardamom scent filled their nostrils anew. "Why couldn't we have been each other's soulmates?"

"Probably because we're both too headstrong for one another and you would kill me if we had to live together," Jazz offered.

Nylah smirked, thinking about Jazz's disastrous apartment. Both their places were cluttered, but where his furniture and floors were covered in endless clothes and dirty dishes, Nylah's walls were plastered with vintage art and plants. Well, those and cat hair, of course.

He continued, "And it would have been too easy. Too perfect. The world couldn't handle our combined queerness and beauty. The Fates know our high school hardly managed."

Nylah inhaled the last drag of their cigarette, regret filling their lungs as the tiny break before lunchtime madness ended. "You're full of yourself, you know."

Jazz coughed and laughed, withdrawing from the hug. "You encourage it."

"Whatever." Nylah gave his shoulder a playful shove. "I need to get back before my manager kills me. Do you want anything before you go?"

Jazz smiled, and before he could name it, Nylah interrupted. "Cortado. Of course. I'm not sure why I even ask." With dreams of traveling to the UK and down through the Roman Empire on the horizon, Nylah made their way back in and grabbed the plain black apron.

Nylah couldn't help but grin. How bad could meeting Jazz's new friends really be?

CHAPTER XV

NESSIE

Nessie laughed out loud as her phone lit up with the text from her overdramatic best friend.

LACEY <3: If you love me, you'll trade me parents.

NESS <3: HAHA. You couldn't handle it. My mom's curfews would break your soul.

She added a skull and laughing emoji before sending it off. The clock in the corner of the screen ticked to the next minute and Nessie sighed. Seven fifty. She only had ten more minutes as it was.

Nessie hated having her phone taken away every night. It made her feel like a child, despite her sixteenth birthday only being a couple of months away. No matter how good her arguments were, Charity held fast to this rule. Through some heavy negotiations, she managed to get the curfew extended on weekends, but during the week there was no wiggle room.

Her phone lit up again.

LACEY <3: My soul is already dead.

Nessie smirked as her phone dinged again.

LACEY <3: I basically inherit your 8:00 curfew by knowing you anyway, so trading would still be in my benefit.

Nessie typed away, conscious her time was short.

NESS <3: Our souls can be dead together, then. Remember with curfew also comes nightly meditations, morning yoga, and endless tofu. If your soul is dead, you can be sure my mom will try to bring it back to life.

She set her phone on her dresser as she looked over at her final exam study guide. Her phone lit up again as she picked up her pencil.

LACEY <3: NVM. You're right. I'd rather die. Have fun saving your soul haha BTW Good luck tomorrow and please text me when you're done! Love you!

Lacey's signature kissy face marked the end of the text. Nessie got up to take her phone downstairs, and on cue, she heard her mother call up the stairs.

"Ness. It's eight o'clock. Let's go."

Nessie sighed as she headed down to the main floor. Charity stood in their living room, going through her nightly stretches. Even at over forty, her mother's flexibility put many people to shame, but she worked hard for it. Unfortunately, having a yoga teacher for a mother did not guarantee super-bendy genes, and Nessie's hamstrings still threatened to rip with every downward dog she ever tried.

Charity's body was made for marathons, flat and lean. She didn't have a heavyset chest or generous hips and curves like Nessie. And while Charity's graying hair was thin and often pulled into a bun, Nessie kept her heavy yellow locks in a high ponytail to keep it out of her face. Otherwise, the only other physical difference between the mother-daughter pair was Nessie's heart-shaped face and dimples; she'd gotten those from her dad.

Charity looked up as Nessie's phone slid across the counter, the corners of her eyes creasing as she smirked. "You've just got to push it to the very last minute every single day, hey?"

Nessie smiled back. "Gotta keep you on your toes. Besides, how else can I survive high school? I've got to do double the socializing in the little screen time I have."

She would never admit out loud that the curfew had its benefits. Daily meditation reduced her stress a lot, which helped minimize her skin breakouts. It would have been too good if it also helped with her sleep problems.

"Well, consider me on my toes. Also, I grabbed this new supplement from the store today. It's supposed to help regulate your melatonin naturally, and I figured it would be worth a shot."

Nessie picked up the bottle of pills. Some days, Charity's pursuit of natural remedies and wellness was excessive. She knew her mother meant well, though, so she rarely complained.

"Thanks, Mom. I appreciate it."

Charity smiled as she moved into a deep lunge. "So, how are you feeling about your appointment tomorrow?"

The bottle of pills nearly slipped from Nessie's hands as her mind scrambled. "Hmmm?"

Charity's brow furrowed. "Your specialist appointment? The one you've been waiting months for? There must be something in the air if *I* remembered and you forgot."

Nessie coughed as she tried to act casual. She readjusted her ponytail. "Oh, yeah, no. I don't know how I forgot. I mean, it's not really a big deal. I'm sure it'll be good." *Stop rambling.* She turned her back to her mom as she pretended to read over the ingredients on the bottle.

Lacey often teased Nessie for being a terrible liar. Her lack of skill in being deceitful combined with Charity's incredible intuition meant she rarely got out of telling the truth.

"Well, remember to set your alarm. I know this exam break has let you sleep in more than usual, but it's an early one."

"Okay." She scurried back up to her bedroom, anxious to avoid talking about the appointment in depth. As soon as her door was closed, she sprawled on her puffy duvet. It wasn't that she didn't want to go to the doctor. She'd counted the days down with great eagerness.

Charity had reassured Nessie that if anyone could figure out why her compass was frozen, Dr. Cavanagh could. Though Nessie wouldn't admit it, sometimes she worried the reason her compass didn't move was because her mom's had been faded gray for four years. Perhaps broken compasses could be passed down through the generations, or maybe their family was outright cursed.

Nessie tried to settle into her nightly meditation. She hoped the routine would help settle her pounding heart from her white lie and flight up the stairs. Nessie tried to clear her mind of the appointment the next morning, but knew it was useless. Even if she managed to fall asleep at a reasonable time, too often she was woken by her mom's night terrors anyway.

Nessie sighed. *Stupid compasses.*

Their drive from Mississauga to downtown Toronto was long, despite the fact the cities basically blended together. Charity chattered on about setting positive intentions, but Nessie could hardly pay attention. The skin under her eyes swelled and her stomach turned with nerves. When they finally settled into the doctor's office, she was confident she was going to puke.

Dr. Cavanagh smiled when they entered the room and offered a firm handshake before leading them in.

"Good day, ladies. How may I be of service to you?" He sat behind his massive cherry oak desk. Nessie was grateful her mother did the talking. She gave the doctor their family history, including the story of her own compass.

Nessie's forehead glistened with sweat as she eyed a nearby plant pot as a potential emergency place to empty her stomach. She was minutes away from finding out what was wrong with her, and she wasn't sure she was ready to know. After giving his condolences, Dr. Cavanagh turned his attention to Nessie.

"Nessie, is it? May I look at your compass?" She nodded her head, afraid to speak. He was polite as he took her arm with icy but gentle hands. At first, he looked at it with her sitting facing his desk. Then he spun her chair in a 360-degree circle, taking notes as he went. He brought out a sharp tool with two prongs that met like a wishbone. She tried not to flinch as the cold metal touched her skin. He did all kinds of tests, always going back and jotting notes. He took the temperature of her forearm. He assessed if it changed with restricted blood flow. So many of the things he tried she couldn't make sense of. No matter how he moved her, though, the heart-shaped arrowhead pointed straight up her forearm. Only the clockface underneath rotated, with both hands planted firmly at the capital N. When he finally sat back in his chair, the specialist looked uneasy.

"Well, Nessie, your compass is alive and well, though I can't quite understand why it refuses to move. Honestly, I've never seen anything like it." He paused, rubbing his chin. "I'm going to conduct further research and reach out to some colleagues to see if they have any insights. I'll get back to you if I learn anything new. For now, all I can recommend is to hang tight and report back to me if anything changes."

Nessie bit her tongue as she fought back a flood of impending tears. She hadn't realized how much she'd expected to walk out of this appointment with a changed compass and a proper soulmate link. She offered the doctor a polite smile, excusing herself to the bathroom while her mother settled their appointment.

She made sure the door closed before letting the first sob escape.

CHAPTER XVI

LACEY

"Where exactly do you think you're off to, missy?" Renee's voice rang from the living room as Lacey turned the door handle. She huffed to a stop.

"I was just heading over to Nessie's. I'll be back before dinner, I promise!" she called back. Her mother's arm struck out over Lacey's shoulder and closed off her escape route.

"Oh, okay. So I guess studying before dinner isn't a thing today? All hail Queen Lacey, she who makes and breaks all the rules as she pleases!" Renee sang out.

Lacey rolled her eyes. "Come on, Mom! You know Ness isn't allowed people over after eight and by the time we finish dinner, I won't get to see her! I'll study after dinner, I swear."

"I know you, Lacey, and I know that if you don't study now, it won't get done at all. Back to your bedroom you go. Besides, you only have one exam left before school is out for the summer and then you'll get to see her all the time." Renee leaned against the front door to further seal her point. Her chestnut-brown hair was twisted back in a braid, and her honey-brown eyes were set on Lacey's. Renee wasn't tall, but she made up for her below-average height in firm posture and tightly crossed arms.

"Mom, Ness needs me! She hasn't answered my texts all day and I know something is wrong. Please, let me go just this once. It's important!" Lacey clasped her hands together. She would have gotten down on her knees if she thought it'd win her case.

"Not a chance. You need to be studying for your math final and you know it. I'm sure Ness will text you when she's ready. She's probably studying by herself. This is your last grade ten diploma, and I won't have you flunking out."

"You know, it's hard to believe you love me as much as you say you do. I swear all you ever try to do is ruin my life." Lacey glared daggers at her mom as she flipped her freshly dyed long black hair over her shoulder. As she stormed around the corner, she heard Renee yell not to slam the door. She slammed it anyway.

Lacey knew she would get in trouble for that later, but at the moment she didn't care. She tilted her head back to blink away tears of frustration.

Who studies math anyway?

Lacey shoved the last of her notes off her bed and took what little pleasure she could from the scattering equations.

In a dramatic slump, she collapsed to the ground in front of her full-length mirror and glared at her own reflection. She sank her head into her hands with an exasperated sigh before reaching for a tissue. She blotted away the tears that hovered on her lash line, then methodically began smoothing out her foundation. Wearing makeup had become an art for her, a method to hide her misery under a canvas of bronzer and mascara.

Look good, feel good.

Despite the Mexican heritage from her mother's side, Lacey hadn't gotten her mother's warm-toned skin. Instead, she ended up with a complexion closer to her dad's: Canadian pale with perpetually flushed cheeks. Instead of his sandy-blond hair or her mother's warm brunette tones, Lacey's natural hair was a muted color in between, not blond or brown. And she'd hated it until the day she dyed it.

Renee had warned her against dying her hair black. She insisted it wouldn't look natural and that she should add highlights instead. If anything, her mother's vocal dislike for her jet-black hair drove Lacey to love it more. She was obsessed with how sharp it looked, contrasting against her naturally full, cherry-tinted lips. She'd needed something more spirited, and black was the way to her heart.

As Lacey tried to recompose herself, a usual chorus of shouting hummed through the small apartment.

"You're driving her away!"

"Maybe if you didn't leave all the discipline to me all the time, our whole family would be more functional."

"You think parenting makes our family dysfunctional? It's you, Renee! You make this family dysfunctional. You and your stupid compass!"

Lacey rolled her eyes and started rummaging through her disaster of a room in search of her headphones. She tossed various black and neon concert T-shirts around with her feet, her scattered math pages adding to the wreckage.

Renee's voice rang through the hollow door. "You know, Kade, one day you need to see that it isn't my compass that you hate so much. It's yourself. Your jealousy is what poisons our family."

"Of course you pin this on me. It's exactly like the therapist said. You always paint yourself as the victim, when it's your compulsive micromanaging that is toxic."

Lacey threw the crumpled comforter off her bed.

"For the love of Cupid! Why are you set on tearing us apart?" Renee's voice teetered on the verge of screaming. Lacey winced, conscious everyone on their apartment floor could probably hear this fight.

"Because maybe Cupid was wrong!"

In the nook between her mattress and the headboard, a glint of rose gold caught Lacey's eye. She dove for her headphones.

"You think we shouldn't have been matched?" Renee's voice quivered.

Lacey's fingers wrapped around the headband. Her heart

hammered as she hesitated, unsure if she could bear to hear more.

Kade's voice, as soft as Renee's, seeped with hurt. "I think it's time we talked about getting a divorce."

Oh, Juno, please no, Lacey pleaded to the goddess of marriage.

"You can't run from this, Kade. You can divorce me and you can leave us, but at the end of the day your compass will always point to me. You will always come back to me."

Lacey slammed her headphones on and scampered back to her phone. Cursing the slow Bluetooth connection as she picked a playlist, she cranked the volume as high as it would go. One of her favorite rap songs roared through her ears, but the familiar words blurred.

This isn't happening. They're going to work it out. They always fight. This isn't that different. Well, other than the fact the *D* word had never been dropped before.

The ding of a text rang over the rap music flooding her ears.

NESS <3: Hey.

Well, it seemed she wasn't the only one having a tough go. Her fingers flew over the keyboard.

LACEY: Hey girl. You okay?

Lacey chewed her lip as she stared at her phone, her back pressed to the wall. Nessie's answer was fast.

NESS <3: No.

She sighed. Nessie rarely one-worded her. The appointment must have gone bad.

LACEY: I'm sorry… Do you want to talk about it?

NESS <3: No. I just want to forget about it.

Lacey's original goal to go to Nessie's solidified with confirmation of her best friend's pain.

LACEY: I'll see you soon.

NESS <3: Lace, don't. I'll be fine.

Resolve flashed through Lacey's core. She tucked her phone in her back pocket and slid on her favorite, baggy black hoodie. She hung her headphones around her neck and in well-practiced stealth, she opened her door an inch. As she'd guessed, her parents were in their room down the hall. They wouldn't see her creep through the living room or slide open the second-story balcony door.

This day is already lost to the Underworld, so who cares?

She stole away with nothing more than her headphones and phone. As the summer night sky greeted her, she let out a shaky breath. Lacey looked back through the kitchen window to confirm no one had noticed, then clamored over the railing. Some friends were worth the trouble.

Lacey wove around the plant-covered patio of the McKenzie house and knocked. The front door swung open faster than she expected and warm light pooled on the patio.

"Lacey? Nessie didn't mention you were coming, but I can't say I'm surprised." Charity gave her a sad smile and welcomed her in. Her gray-blond hair was held up with chopsticks and she was in a matching set of pj's covered in mandalas.

Lacey brushed the back of her hand across her face in case any stray tears from her brisk walk gave her away. She hoped her face wasn't as red as it felt. In her pocket, her phone buzzed. Lacey ignored it. "Is Ness okay?"

Charity's smile fell. "I think she'll be glad to see you. Do you want a snack or anything before you head up?"

Lacey shook her head and made her way to the stairwell. "Thanks, though."

The sound of brakes and a car door slamming came from outside and a chill swept over Lacey.

How was she so fast?

Lacey backed against the nearest wall to stay out of sight as the aggressive rap of knuckles met Charity's front door.

Charity gave Lacey a questioning look.

"P-please," Lacey stammered, hating how small her voice

sounded. "I can't—not right now. Please don't make me go back there." She bit her bottom lip hard.

Charity steepled her fingers, then let out a sigh. She nodded to the stairs, and Lacey scampered away. At the top, she stopped before going to Nessie's room. She crouched down and held as still as possible.

"Hey, Renee."

Renee's cool voice echoed in the hall. "Can you send Lacey down, please?"

"You know, I think the girls could really use some time together right now."

Lacey's heart pulsed as Charity stood fast against her tyrant mother.

"I think I know what's best for my daughter. Don't you think they should be studying? Getting a good night's rest before their last final of the year?"

"Of course, but I'm sure they can manage that here. Renee, the girls are growing up. They don't need constant supervision to get things done."

"Maybe Nessie doesn't, but Lacey—"

"Lacey is perfectly capable. Besides…" Charity's voice softened and Lacey leaned closer to still hear. "I get the impression your house hasn't been the most peaceful studying place anyway. Lacey was pretty upset when she arrived."

Lacey's cheeks flushed anew at her mother's silence.

"And it's okay. I don't mind keeping an eye on her. I'll make sure they have a nutritious breakfast and get to the test on time. But really, Renee, I have to ask. Are you okay?"

"I'm fine. We're fine. Everything is fine."

"Okay. I just wanted you to know that if you ever needed someone to talk to, I could be that person for you."

"I'm good, Charity. Thanks, though."

Light spilled out behind Lacey as Nessie opened her bedroom door. Her blond hair crimped where her pony had held it back and her steel-gray eyes were bloodshot. They flashed over Lacey's crouched posture. Lacey held a finger to her lips as she waited.

"You shouldn't be so hard on her. Don't you remember being fifteen going on sixteen? With the world at your fingertips and the endless waves of emotion?"

Nessie crept to Lacey's side.

"I do. But if she just came home, I could help her."

Charity sighed. "I don't know what to tell you, Renee. Being a mom is hard. Let me take care of the girls tonight. You look like you could use a good bubble bath and a glass of wine."

If Renee answered, Lacey didn't catch what she said. When the front door clicked closed, Lacey took Nessie's hand and they stole away into her bedroom.

Where Lacey's room was a designed mess of black fabric and concert posters, Nessie's was minimalistic. Everything was soft tones of gray and white. Her desk was cleared, with a single binder open, and her queen-size bed was made, topped with a bounty of pillows.

"You shouldn't be here." Nessie slumped on her bed.

Lacey dropped beside her and pulled her phone out of her back pocket. "I'd argue that you shouldn't be alone."

"Talk about a stupid day, hey?"

Lacey nodded. Her screen flashed, and she fought the urge to roll her eyes.

OVERLORD MOTHER: Come home NOW, missy.

Lacey's answer was quick.

LACEY: Excuse me for not wanting to be home through your pending divorce.

Lacey was sure her mom was sitting in their SUV outside. She didn't dare peek out Nessie's window. Her phone lit up again.

OVERLORD MOTHER: Lace, please come home so we can talk about this.

LACEY: Why? This is between you and Dad, and I need a break.

OVERLORD MOTHER: Lacey, I need you here.

Black venom coursed through her veins as her thumbs clicked away in a fury.

LACEY: So I can soothe your pains? I'm not a drug you can hit anytime you feel sad, Mom. You need to sort your life out and I need space. You're always going on about respect, so why not respect my boundaries for a change?

With a huff, she tossed her phone across Nessie's feather duvet.

"I wish I could just live here."

A gentle knock came at the door. Nessie rolled onto her belly and stuffed her face into her pillow. After a muffled "Come in," Charity's face peeked around the edge.

"Lacey. I hope you know you are always welcome here, but I don't appreciate it when you put me in situations like this."

Lacey sat up in a guilty slouch. "I'm sorry."

"I know we'll work through this, but I don't want to take sides. Your parents are going through a lot right now and the last thing they need is you running around and breaking their rules."

Her gaze dropped to her thumbs as they wove in circles.

"Next time, maybe call me before you come. I can talk to your mom, and we can take you in for a weekend if you need a break."

As if there's anything anyone could say to change my mom's mind. But Lacey nodded and let Charity believe she could have.

"Now, I would love it if you two studied before bed, but if rest is what you need, I can understand that. There will be no late-night whispering and I expect both your phones on the kitchen counter at eight o'clock. Agreed?"

Nessie moaned something that sounded like a yes into her pillow and Lacey nodded. When Charity left, Lacey flopped back down and wrapped an arm around Nessie. She felt her best friend's body tremble as she let out a sob into her pillow. Lacey's heart contracted in pain. She squeezed closer to Nessie, holding her tight in a cocoon of protection.

"I'm here now. It's okay. I've got you."

CHAPTER XVII

GARETH

Gareth's quads burned as he pushed himself harder down the field. He kept an eye out for a gap to sneak a pass through. Sebastian trailed behind him, but not close enough. It wasn't a tough choice between slowing the play down to wait for his team to catch up or attempting the goal on his own.

Come on, Fortuna. His silent prayer to the goddess of luck and chance rang with every one of his natural, long strides. He slipped past the last defender with ease. Without missing a step, he sank the ball in the top left corner of the net. The goalie looked pissed, which only drove Gareth's already enormous grin wider.

Sebastian's laughter filled Gareth's ears as he caught up. Despite Gareth having a good foot in height over his best friend, Sebastian nearly knocked them both to the ground with his celebratory hug as the match turned in their favor. Gareth's compass did its usual flutter whenever he and Sebastian were close. He covered a cough and pulled the edge of his white compression sleeve down farther, wary of anyone seeing his compass acting up. A few other teammates slapped his back but were soon cut off by the chiming of phone alarms, signaling the end of the friendly park game. Grins plastered their faces as they claimed the one-goal win.

Once on the sidelines, Sebastian tumbled to his side and made a grab for Gareth's water bottle, having conveniently forgotten his own, as always. Gareth laughed as he spritzed what was left from his bottle into his best friend's face, but his smile faded as familiar callous laughter came from behind him.

"Williams! Does your mum force you to take your boots off at the pitch to air out how dreadful you smell before you get home? Doesn't she know you can't air out your kind of stench?" Damien's sneer ground against Gareth's nerves as his rival sauntered up the sideline with a pair of girls from school. Damien offered a lazy grin as he threw his arms over their shoulders, winking before whispering to his posse. Both girls broke out in fits of high-pitched laughter.

Damien Diaz had always been a hot topic among the girls of the school. They swooned over his long tousled black-brown hair, and his famous lazy grin that framed white movie-star teeth. Sebastian joked Damien was a Spanish vampire because his skin was too smooth to be human, and said Damien probably had to wear makeup to keep himself from sparkling in the sun.

"I don't know why those girls would let him touch them. I swear I could smell him across the field," Sebastian remarked under his breath. Gareth's heart warmed. He was grateful that his best friend wasn't one to pick fights even when challenged. Sebastian was a perfect match for Gareth. He gave Gareth enough space to be his loud and goofy self, while always having his back. Sebastian was a reliable friend in a world of fakes. Quiet yet always there to make comments under his breath and up for playing endless hours of *Call of Duty* or kicking a football around.

"You would think since he has a claimed soulmate, girls would stop flocking to him," Gareth muttered as he pried off his brand-new apple-red trainers that didn't smell whatsoever.

The corner of Sebastian's mouth perked up. "Or that they would realize he's not even a good player. I mean, how many games have they come to now? I can't remember the last time he scored a goal. Now, perfect top corners, that's something to be proud of." He elbowed Gareth's ribs. "It's a wonder you don't have your own flock of drooling fools."

As it often did when Sebastian complimented him, the needle of Gareth's compass shifted. It made his stomach knot when it did that, though he didn't know what to do about it. It wasn't like he could walk up to Sebastian and be like, '*Hey, I know this is random, but sometimes my compass points at you. I swear I love you like a best friend and it doesn't have to be weird. I can't explain it, but thought you should know.*'

High-pitched laughter echoed down the field. They both looked up to see Damien carrying Alva over his shoulder, her face bright red and in an ear-to-ear grin.

"I really don't understand what Alva sees in that bloodsucker. Let alone why you would waste your time having a crush on someone who isn't your soulmate. It's one thing to admire someone who's good-looking and all, but it's not like it's going to actually work out."

Gareth changed into his worn trainers and picked up the rest of his equipment. Sebastian followed suit and they started toward the nearest underground station.

"I don't know. Maybe she thinks by spending time with Damien, it'll help her mature and make her compass appear sooner? Or maybe she thinks that she'll be able to change his compass. Not that I think anyone should want to be soulmates with that smelly arse."

Sebastian responded with his usual gratuitous laughter and Gareth smiled to himself. He loved how freely Sebastian expressed his emotions. Though he might not be as loud and boisterous as Gareth's family, Sebastian always responded exactly as he felt.

The Tube pulled up and the boys' laughter settled into a steady silence as they both found their seats and became distracted by their own thoughts.

"You don't think getting your compass changes you, do you? I mean, I get when you meet your soulmate and you get all gushy and stuff. But like, you're still you—right?" Sebastian leaned back into his chair, glancing down the aisle as he spoke. As he often did,

Sebastian's hand traced the corner of his right eyebrow where his scars crested, narrowly missing the outside edge of his eye. Gareth was surprised to hear his best friend bring up compasses, but he followed Sebastian's nonchalance.

"Course not, mate. I mean, I'm still the same, aren't I? Sure, Damien got more annoying, but puberty was bound to only make him worse." Serious talk about compasses was a rare topic between them. This was partially because Gareth didn't want to brag about getting his before his best friend, but mostly because he didn't want to have to explain how peculiar his compass was.

"I don't know… I mean, you do smell worse lately." Sebastian's sea-green eyes glittered and Gareth gave him a swift shove into the window. He started laughing again. "But at least you don't smell as bad as Damien!" The boys grinned together in their shared animosity.

As the Tube slowed at a stop, Gareth leaned forward with the momentum. "How are you feeling about the football club exchange?"

Sebastian rested his head on the window. "I can't believe it's less than two weeks away."

Gareth nodded. Even though they'd signed up ages ago, time was flying. "Are you worried at all?"

Sebastian shook his head. "No. I mean, I pray the team we're swapping with is good, but really, it's Canada."

Gareth chuckled. "The kids coming here are going to get destroyed."

"And you'll probably destroy the teams there." Sebastian grinned. "It's almost unfair to the other team. I mean, five London boys going to play football on a Toronto team? We're going to thrash the competition!"

When the Tube pulled up to their stop, the two boys made their way up the stairs to the setting sun. Gareth let out a deep sigh. "I just wish Damien wasn't coming with us. I feel like he's going to ruin everything. I don't know why... I just have a bad feeling. And I swear, if we have to sit by his sweaty arse on the plane, I'm going to jump off in the middle of the ocean."

"In the middle of the ocean, hey? Not turn around and leave before the flight takes off?" Sebastian teased.

"No, I swear. I would rather die than sit beside him." Gareth shuddered at the thought of a seven-hour flight beside his worst enemy. *Fortuna, don't let that be the case.*

Sebastian didn't seem to carry Gareth's worries. "At least we get to miss the last two weeks of school!"

"To live in Canada for a whole month. I can't believe my parents went for it."

"I think I'd be doing my parents a favor if I wasn't being replaced by another kid," Sebastian scoffed.

"I'm not sure which of our exchange partners has it worse. Yours having to live with psycho Vee, or mine having to survive Addi and Emmet attacks for a whole month."

"They're both going to die."

Gareth and Sebastian broke out in laughter.

"Hopefully they don't think the same thing for us." Gareth turned down the street where their paths split. "See you online in the morning?"

"You know it! Hopefully our exchange families have Call of Duty or we'll both suck when we get back." Sebastian smiled as he turned down his lane.

Gareth continued the last block of his walk pondering the trip. Canada seemed so far away. Everyone reassured him it was a friendly country filled with wonderful people, but he still worried. What if his exchange family was super awkward? He'd received the information packet a month ago and reread every minuscule detail. The person he was trading lives with was named Dakota. He was also sixteen years old, and he had two twin sisters named Dyani and Tamala. Gareth had stared at the single sheet of paper for so long the details felt ingrained in his brain.

His coach had assured the boys that they would all be matched with the family that was best suited for them, but Gareth wasn't sure what those criteria were. On a deeper level, he couldn't help but worry that if Dakota turned out to be some angel child, when Gareth came home his parents would expect more out of him.

He turned his key and entered his small but cozy home. It was uncommonly quiet with both the younger boys already sent to their shared bedroom. Dinner had already been made and cleaned up after, but as always, his mother had left him a plate wrapped up to the side.

As Gareth devoured his cold pasta, his dad came into the kitchen.

"How was your match today, son?"

Gareth smiled up at his dad. "Good. I got a perfect top corner."

Kenyon ruffled the top of Gareth's cropped curls.

"And how are you feeling about your trip?"

"It should be good." Gareth shrugged as he shoved the last bite into his mouth.

"Son, this trip isn't cheap. Not only do we have to pay to fly you to another country, but we also have to house another boy for four weeks." His dad cleared his throat. "You know money doesn't grow on trees. If you don't actually want to go, speak up now before it's too late."

"Dad, of course I want to go! And I'm excited." Gareth panicked at the thought of his parents pulling him out of the exchange. "I'm just a bit nervous is all."

"Your mum and I have agreed this will be a great experience for you to have, but I don't want you thinking that everything is free. And if you are having second thoughts, I'm happy to cancel it."

Having a career in accounting made Kenyon borderline obsessive about saving money and investing. It was a miracle his free-spirited mother had convinced him to let their son go on this trip. Gareth was sometimes a little surprised his parents were soulmates. Elise was so carefree about money and schedules, where Kenyon liked to run a tight ship. It seemed like every week they had opposing opinions about how they should do things.

Gareth considered himself somewhere between the two. Frugal in most expenses, but yearning for adventure. His new boots were one of the most extravagant purchases he had ever made with his allowance savings. Though his father had scoffed at the cost, his mother had beamed and encouraged him to buy them if they brought him joy.

Because of his dad's frugality, Gareth never brought up how much he wanted to see a specialist about his compass. Compasses weren't considered medical, they fell under their own private sector, and Gareth was sure the charges would be insane. His mother would insist on paying for it, while his father would glower at the cost. So Gareth did his best to accept Elise's mentality that his compass was an adventure waiting to unravel, while in secret he saved every pound he could so that one day he could have it looked at by a professional.

"I swear I want to go and that I'm excited. If anything, *you* should be nervous." Gareth grinned. "I mean, what if Dakota is an absolute terror and eats even more than I do?"

Gareth laughed as Kenyon's brow furrowed, and he bumped his father's shoulder as he made his way up to his room. He knew he shouldn't tease him, but it was too easy. Gareth slipped in to kiss his mum goodnight before hitting his overdue shower. While washing his arms, he couldn't help but scrub his compass a little harder.

Sebastian's comment about Alva and Damien lingered in an uncomfortable way. *Could it be possible someone could change another's compass? And could Sebastian be changing his?* Gareth leaned into the running water, letting it stream down the back of his neck.

Down the hall, Gareth's dad yelled about wasting water. Gareth sighed before quickly rinsing the soap off and casting away the questions he had no one to ask.

CHAPTER XVIII

JAYLYNN

"**What do you** think it means to hold space?" River's voice carried through the crisp morning woods. Jaylynn peeked her chilled nose out of her blanket scarf as they walked back toward the cabin. They carried woven baskets full of flowers; the sweet-scented, soft pink and white Magnolia petals were a sure sign that spring had arrived.

Jaylynn still found herself baffled at River's unwavering beauty. Even at seven in the morning, her loveliness radiated from her core. Her mentor danced around shrubs and ran her hands through the leaves of trees with such tenderness, Jaylynn struggled not to stare.

"I'm not sure. You say it all the time, but I don't know how to articulate it. I guess, just being there for the person?"

Weeks had turned to months since Jaylynn had made her way

out to River's cabin. All winter, River had Jaylynn practice seemingly random exercises. From grinding hallucinatory herbs for hours to bathing in the freezing winter waters and chanting under the moon, her weekends and evenings at the cabin were always interesting. The small cot had become a welcome landing place after their long days. No matter how many times River offered her bedroom in trade for the single cot, Jaylynn always refused—happy to snuggle in the incense-perfumed, handmade quilts.

Nylah had made more than one teasing remark about Jaylynn's extracurricular activities. Hiding them from their parents was getting harder and harder the more time she spent at the cabin. She'd told them she made a new friend, but she couldn't admit her compass had linked her to a woman. Not when she didn't fully understand it herself.

Her mentor continued to walk with ease, her slender, bare feet apparently unaffected by the brisk temperature. "So, is holding space physical to you?"

Jaylynn racked her brain, trying to figure out the answer River wanted to hear. "Well, yes, but also in attention."

River didn't give any clues as to if she thought that answer was right. "So physical and mental, then. Are there any other ways you think someone can hold space?"

Jaylynn huffed to herself. She could tell she was losing the game they were playing, though River had the distinct advantage of knowing what the game was. "I mean, I guess you could be there for them emotionally too?"

River nodded as she leaned to check on a nearby bird feeder, the cabin now in sight. A flurry of blue cast over the tree and Jaylynn couldn't mask her frown as she realized it was a blue jay. "Yes, I would agree. But there is one more element you're missing, and that is energetically holding space. Extending your life force out and creating a safe container for someone to open up. Physical, mental, and emotional openness help, but the energetic container is equally important."

Jaylynn opened the cabin door, grateful for the warm wave of air.

"I think I get it… Is that what you were doing the first night I came here?"

River nodded gravely. "There was much space that needed to be held that night."

Jaylynn dropped her basket on the counter and grabbed the kettle, eager to brush off every trace of the cool spring morning. "Any particular tea you would like today?"

River smiled as she pruned the petals into a glass jar. "What do you think I want?"

Jaylynn looked over the canisters of loose tea. Though she yearned for something peppy and fresh, her eyes lingered on the lavender can. Jaylynn pulled the can out and started prepping the calming tea without asking if she'd guessed right.

When they finally settled on the cushions in front of the fire, River gestured for Jaylynn to face her in a cross-legged sit. Jaylynn obliged, though she would have preferred to relax in front of the hearth a while longer before being serious again.

"I'd like to ask you a question," River hummed, a smile spreading across her face, "and for you to answer without overthinking." She sat with perfect posture, her rich, dark hair cascading down her shoulders. Jaylynn wondered when she would be able to sit with the same stillness and composure.

"Okay."

"Gaze into my left eye. The left eye is the window to the soul, whereas the right is the window to the mind. Take a deep breath and clear your thoughts." River paused, waiting for Jaylynn to settle further. "Now, tell me who you are."

"Who I am? I don't know." She let out a soft laugh, relaxing from the unnatural posture. She pushed her auburn waves out of her face. "I suppose I'm Jaylynn Clare. I'm a daughter and a sister; an animal lover and a failed philosophy student. I had a soulmate, and he died." Jaylynn took a sharp breath. "I don't know what else you want me to say."

"Thank you," River responded. River always maintained intense eye contact, but in this moment her attention on Jaylynn felt magnified. It was like River was staring into her soul.

"Um, you're welcome?" Jaylynn said, wringing her hands.

"You don't need to respond when I say thank you. What I mean is, thank you for your truth."

"Oh, okay." Jaylynn wasn't sure she understood, but rolling with it had gotten her this far.

"Now you ask me. And when you ask me, try to hold the space while you listen. When you think you've heard me out completely, say thank you."

Jaylynn took a deep breath and tried to take on River's persona, sitting taller. Gazing deep into River's left eye, she repeated the statement: "Tell me who you are."

River took a deep breath. "Ah, I missed these conversations. The contact, the depth, the opportunity for truth. My soul has yearned for too many years to be seen in its fullness."

After an extended silence, Jaylynn realized River wasn't going to say more. "Oh, umm, thank you?"

"Jaylynn, you must embrace yourself. If you constantly doubt what you're saying, how am I to believe you're telling the truth? Though a soft voice can be a special melody, an unsure one is like a broken keyboard. Either you heard me, or you didn't." Her arctic blue eyes stared back at Jaylynn, sharp as an eagle.

"I heard you, I just feel like you didn't answer the question," Jaylynn responded. She was frustrated at being reprimanded and once again losing a game she didn't understand.

"This exercise is not for the brain but the heart, and why you must listen with every tool you have. The fullest communications come through more than words. They come in expressions and body language. Tone and pace of speech. The energy around the person and how it changes as they speak their truth." River talked as if her methods were common sense.

Jaylynn shook her head. "But what if I don't understand what you've said? Why would I say thank you?"

"Because listening is not a synonym for understanding, as conversations between hearts are not the same as between minds. Now take another breath." River resettled herself and continued gazing into Jaylynn's left eye. "Tell me who you are."

Jaylynn took a brief pause, considering the question. *What does my heart want to say without my brain's filter?*

"I—" She broke the eye contact. She dug deeper into the question and how she felt in her heart. "I suppose I am confused. I don't understand why I was drawn here or what I'm supposed to be learning right now. My life path has never felt less clear, and it scares me."

"Thank you," River responded in her maintained composure.

Jaylynn sighed before returning the question. "Tell me who you are."

River closed her eyes and let out a heavy sigh. "I am ever-expansive love and longing."

Jaylynn waited for her to say more, but River didn't go on. The way she answered had such strength and finality to it that Jaylynn had no reason to believe it wasn't true.

"Thank you," she responded as confidently as she could, even though once again River had avoided the question. More than anything, Jaylynn wanted to learn more about her mentor and her past, but she suspected she would never know more than River wanted her to.

"Tell me who you are," River said.

Jaylynn's mind balked at the repetition, but she took a breath. She grappled for the depth she assumed River wanted. *What do I keep buried in my heart?* The answer bubbled up and before she could think twice, she let the words flow out.

"No matter how hard I try, I can never shake this feeling of not belonging. The only time I felt like I belonged on Terra Mater was with Elias and—" Jaylynn choked as she cut off the fresh, searing emotion. Her chin dropped. "Even though I survived his death, half of me died that day. Sometimes, in my darkest moments, I wish all of me did."

"Thank you," River hummed. A long silence stretched as Jaylynn struggled to recompose herself. River rested a hand on Jaylynn's knee. "You can expect that we will come back to these exercises often. I know it may seem redundant, but I promise you're learning and healing more than you know."

River offered Jaylynn a soft bow before getting up. Jaylynn leaned back on to her elbows as shame bloomed bright red in her blood. It flushed her cheeks and brimmed her eyes with tears. Admitting her pain did not make it better. Now River knew exactly how deeply she was broken, and Jaylynn couldn't take it back.

CHAPTER XIX

BLAKE

Blake stared down at the machinery and the grapefruit in dismay. She did her best to pay attention as Sal explained the dos and don'ts of working with the tattoo gun. She hadn't realized how much extra work went into being a tattoo artist, but she was grateful to be moving up in her apprenticeship. Until recently, her days at the tattoo parlor had been filled with greeting customers, cleaning, learning anatomy, and drawing. So much drawing.

Sal had recommended that she practice at least three hours a day, which seemed excessive. Juggling that with her job at the diner made the days fly by. Though she had a bit of natural talent, he would go over her drawings every week. He would tell her where her lines could have been straighter and criticize how long different pieces took her. This week her drawings had to be in cartoon style. Though she didn't mind the bubbly effects, Sal had heavily criticized her color choices. Some days, she couldn't understand why he'd taken her on. But at the end of every night, he would give her a new project to tackle.

She let out a huff of breath as she tried not to manhandle the grapefruit to pulp. Juice mixed with ink ran down the sides of her hand as she tried to hold her subject steady and draw out her initials. The *J.B.* looked more like an *I* followed by a pitiful blob of ink.

Sal smiled. "Try to relax, J.B. You're going to crush the fruit to death." He rested his hand on her shoulder and reached into the cabinet above her to grab a towel, then handed it to her. Though she hated when people touched her, she let it slide. Blake was determined to be as good of an apprentice as possible. She couldn't afford to lose this opportunity.

He went to step out of the room, but at the last second, he looked back at her. "Ya know, kid, I appreciate your enthusiasm. Keep practicing and before you know it, you'll be off and running."

She beamed at the compliment as he left. She went back to her mangled grapefruit with fresh determination. As soon as she could master the grapefruit, she would get to start with small tattoos on real people, which filled her with a mix of ecstasy and terror. Her grip tightened again at the thought of the current blob of ink being on a real person. *He won't let you do it until you're good enough.* Blake was confident that even if she did mess up, Sal would have her back. It surprised her how easily she relaxed into trusting him.

Sal was good to her, in a familial way. He did his best to teach her and was by far the best male role model she'd found to date. He told her when she did things wrong, but was always gentle when he spoke to her. She wondered if in some ways he considered her more like a daughter than an apprentice. A warm hum ran over her body at the thought.

After another hour passed as she mauled her project, Blake called it a night. She peeked into the room Sal was working in. He was busy sketching a new project.

"Hey, Sal, I'm off for the night. Is there anything you need me to do before I come back on Wednesday?"

He leaned back in his chair and wiped the smudged graphite off his rugged hands with a towel. Sal looked tough enough that anyone would take a second glance before messing with him. But Blake knew from the hours he had spent on her arm tattoo that he had a soft heart and gentle hands—the touch of a real artist.

"J.B. Before you leave, I wanted to give you something."

He got up and handed her the black cloth covered in gray skulls that had been lying on the counter. A gothic pattern covered the soft, dark cotton.

"It's a wrist sleeve. If we're going to have you around the shop more and more, we can't have customers seeing that garbage cover-up. Most people will assume it's to hide your compass, but it'll be better for business if people don't see that paint disaster."

He took the little sleeve and pried it open. He held the fabric tight for her to slide her arm inside. It had a cutout for her thumb, and it reached up her arm toward her elbow. The cotton was tight enough that it didn't slide back down her wrist, and the dark skulls blended nicely with the rest of her arm tattoos. Blake glowed at the beautiful gift to cover up her monstrosity.

"Sal, it's lovely. Thank you so much!" She tried not to sound overeager, but she was so touched. No one had ever gotten her such a thoughtful gift.

"Ha." He nudged her shoulder. "It's more of a gift for me not to have to see that mess anymore." He chuckled as he drew back. "Maybe don't wear it when you're practicing with the grapefruits, though. It's not going to last very long if they keep turning out like today's customer did."

Blake smiled at the joke, praying her future fruits looked nothing like today's did.

"Can do. See ya Wednesday?" She adjusted her backpack on her shoulders and turned to the door.

"See ya Wednesday." He grinned back.

As Blake stepped out into the street, she tugged at her new adornment. She couldn't remember the last time she'd gotten a gift from someone, let alone something so beautiful as well as useful. It was much nicer to look at than her compass cover-up. She hummed to herself as she made the walk back to her community center, dreaming of what tattoo she would get to try first.

CHAPTER XX

LACEY

Saturday morning, the day after her math exam, Lacey rolled over to see Nessie's long blond hair strung across her face. Lacey groaned. She didn't want to face the day, even if it was the first day of her summer vacation. Sunlight danced through the curtains and eventually Lacey rummaged through the bedding to find her phone. Nessie rolled toward her, her silver-gray eyes puffy and red.

"Morning," Lacey groaned.

"Hmph." Nessie pulled the gray comforter up to her neck then paused, her eyes widening in shock. She shot up, throwing her hands over her mouth. "Holy Minerva, Lacey!"

Nessie pointed with a look of horror. Lacey turned to see what the problem could be, when it hit her. *For the love of Cupid, not now.*

Please no. Not in front of Ness.

Lacey's brand-new silver tattoo shone above her left wrist and she held it to her chest as she searched Nessie's pale face. "Oh, Ness, I'm so sorry. This is actually the worst timing ever." She reached out to take Nessie's hand, unsure of what to say.

"It's okay, Lace." Nessie's eyes dropped. "It's not like you can control it."

Lacey's sweaty hand tightened in Nessie's. "I'm still sorry."

Nessie shrugged and brushed her face with her sleeve. "Like I said, Lace, it's no biggie. At least if my compass is botched, you might still have a chance at love."

Lacey shuffled over and crushed her best friend in a hug. "I love you, and I will always love you. Compass or not, I swear it to the stars."

Nessie nodded, then excused herself to the bathroom. Lacey flopped back into the fluffy pillows.

Getting her compass was supposed to be a moment of celebration. She had finally matured enough to be linked to her soulmate! She could leave her parents and start a new life, one where she could show them how soulmates were supposed to be. But as happy as she wanted to be, she couldn't shake her guilt.

Ness is going to hate me for this.

On cue, Nessie came back into the bedroom with a scowl on her face.

"You know what? You don't deserve this."

Lacey shrank farther back into her fluffy pillow.

Nessie planted her arms on the hips Lacey had often been jealous of. "Screw the Fates and screw my compass. We should be celebrating. You need to get up and get dressed. We have a soulmate to find." Determination burned in her best friend's silver-gray eyes.

Lacey's heart skipped a beat. "You—you mean it?"

"Yes. I have no interest in sitting around feeling sorry for myself all summer. Now, let's dress you up like the bombshell you are." Nessie strode to her walk-in closet and started pulling dresses out. Most probably wouldn't flatter Lacey the same way they hugged Nessie's curves, but her best friend flipped through hangers with determination. "I'm positive we can find one of my outfits that you'll look stunning in."

Lacey stared at her best friend with wide eyes as fabrics catapulted onto the bed.

"Up to it, Lace. Your hair isn't going to curl itself."

Lacey's eyes blurred with the cusp of tears as she clamored out of bed to the bathroom. "You're sure we don't have time to get clothes from my house?" she called back.

"And risk your mom interfering?" Nessie scoffed. "Not a chance. We don't have that much longer before she kidnaps you back. We were lucky enough to get two nights together back-to-back." She held up a powder-blue dress. "We need to make the best of every spare hour we have before she knows. How about this one?"

Lacey shook her head. "We both know I can't pull off pastels like you. I also want something less formal and more me. Accidentally beautiful. Like, I didn't see him coming, but I just happen to look cute." She took Nessie's brush and started tearing through her flat, crumpled black hair.

Jupiter Almighty, I can't believe this is happening.

"We also need to be quick. Who's to say your soulmate isn't already on their way?" Nessie asked, thumbing over a simple black dress with a white collared under-shirt. "This neckline would look adorable on you."

Lacey paused, realizing she hadn't even checked the time she was supposed to meet her soulmate. Taking her first real glance at her compass, she was blown away.

This is actually happening.

She turned in a slow circle to make her clock hands reveal themselves from underneath Cupid's bow and arrow. In the elegant lines of the roman numerals, her destiny glittered.

12:09.

CHAPTER XXI

NESSIE

Nessie slumped her head into her hands.

"Well, that was a waste of time." Lacey's hair hung over her face. "My soulmate has to be farther. Maybe we should go up to Richmond Hill and Markham? You can't get much more northeast in the GTA."

Nessie's feet ached in protest at the thought of doing any more walking. They'd already made their way by train from Mississauga to Toronto, but it was clear Lacey's soulmate was farther east. "I need a break, and I need to think."

"What we really need is caffeine," Lacey said. With a firm tug, Nessie let Lacey haul her up from the bench. "Let's find the nearest coffee shop and reset."

Nessie scoured Google until she found a caffeine source tucked down a side road in the heart of York, Toronto. It was a short, busy walk. The sidewalks were cluttered with the Saturday lunch crowd. Bells chimed as they entered the shop, and both girls sighed in relief as the AC kissed their skin.

They were greeted by a short, hipster barista with choppy red bangs and wide round glasses. Marker glistened on the white name tag and read *Nylah* in small cursive above the bold THEY/THEM scrawled across the bottom. Nessie took care of the order with a grateful smile, then sank into one of the heavily padded sofa chairs.

Lacey looked equally defeated in her leather pool of cushions. "I thought—never mind."

Nessie leaned forward and blew the steam off her double espresso vanilla latte. "What's on your mind?"

"Everyone says that before you find your soulmate, your compass feels like a magnet that pulls harder the closer you get. I thought..." Lacey looked over the nearby shelf of used books. "I don't know. I keep thinking that my soulmate will meet me halfway, but it's already almost noon and I don't feel much different."

Nessie set her cup down and reached across the narrow tabletop to take Lacey's hand. "Maybe they are coming, they're just farther away than we'd guessed. I mean, it's only the first day of having your compass. You have nothing to compare distance with yet."

Lacey pulled away from the contact and huddled around her own steaming mug. "I just thought this would be easier."

C'mon, Ness, you can make this right. Nessie's brain turned through information, trying to come up with a plan to save the day, but all she came to was obstacles. "I hate to say it, but your mom's compass has probably been driving her crazy all morning. The farther we go, the more likely she is to come hunt us down. We can justify downtown Toronto with an impromptu shopping trip, but I really don't think we should go much farther." Lacey let out a huff of disapproval and Nessie clamored to recover. "But not all hope is lost. Let's look over some online maps and coordinates. I'm positive we'll figure this out."

Lacey sighed. "Yeah, okay."

I will figure this out. Nessie pulled up her phone map again.

"Ness, are you sure you're okay with this?"

She didn't look up from the maps. "With what?"

"You know, searching for my soulmate."

Nessie paused. "Listen, Lace. I'm not going to pretend I'm not crushed about my compass, but at least helping with yours is something I can control. It's something I can do to take my mind off it."

Lacey's eyes filled with worry. "I just—"

"Stop." Nessie interrupted. "Just stop. The most helpful thing you could do for me right now is to keep me distracted. I don't want to think about my compass, and I don't want to talk about it. Can we just pretend I never got it and move on?" Her tone was sharper than she'd intended. She buried herself back in the system of maps, her cheeks hot.

She studied the direction of Lacey's compass against the map, then she finally broke into a faint smile. "You know what else falls perfectly northeast and is even farther than Toronto or the Greater Toronto Area?"

Lacey chewed at her raspberry-tinted lips. "What?"

"Montreal." Nessie grinned as her brain connected dots faster than she could explain. "You're going to be soulmates with a French boy!"

A dash of light returned to Lacey's hazel eyes, quickly followed by a frown. "Ness, how are we going to get to Montreal? It's, like, five hours away."

Nessie's mind raced with the new challenge. "Well, unless we can miraculously sneak away just the two of us all the way to Montreal, your mom needs to come with us."

"What?" Lacey leaned forward so fast that if her cup hadn't had a lid on it, it would have spilled. "No. My mom is not coming with us to find my soulmate."

"No, no, no. Hear me out." Nessie put her own drink down. She held out her hands to dramatize her idea pitch. "Girls' trip. We plan to go on a vacation with our moms. Then, when we get close and your compass pulls harder, we'll come up with an excuse to separate. We'll go shopping or something." Nessie emphasized the word *shopping* with air quotes and her lips set in a mischievous smile.

Lacey drummed her fingers on the lid of her cup. "What if she catches on?"

"She won't. We just need a plausible reason to spend one-on-one time. With any luck, your soulmate will be close and there won't be any need for any crazy schemes."

"What if he feels me getting close, then comes to meet me and it happens in front of my mom?" Lacey shuddered and leaned back into the cushions.

"All the better," Nessie said, her smile creeping wider. "Then we can play dumb and be like, 'Oh, what are the chances?'" Nessie draped her arm over her head dramatically.

"Ugh, I pray that's not how it goes." Lacey started chewing her lip again.

"Stop that."

Lacey stuck her lip out in a pout.

Nessie looked around the café. In line, a mother held a child in her arms and rocked her back and forth. "Really, the only question we need to figure out is if you should tell your mom about your compass or not."

"I'm not sure I could keep it a secret... I mean, I could try—"

Nessie cut in. "No, you're right. Renee will be suspicious if she thinks you're keeping secrets. We'll just have to hope that she doesn't associate you getting your compass with us spontaneously wanting to go to Montreal."

Lacey scoffed. "How exactly are we going to convince our moms to go to Montreal?"

Nessie's eyes twinkled, and the final piece fell into place in her mind like a solved puzzle. "Do you know what next weekend is?"

"Umm, the first weekend of July?" Lacey was slow to put it together. Nessie waved her hand for her to go on.

Lacey's eyes lit up as she put the dots together.

"Canada Day!"

CHAPTER XXII

JAYLYNN

Jaylynn wiped the dust off her knees as she got up from cleaning the last kennel. Though it wasn't her favorite part of the job, empty crates meant more pets were finding their forever homes. That and there would be space for new rescues, which always warmed her heart. She looked down at her new, dirty denim overalls as she blew a loose curl out of her face. All her clothes were covered in pet hair most days. It was the labor of love.

She moved to the cat room next. She made a point of giving the blue-eyed tabby some extra ear scratches. He pawed at the gap in her overalls. She smiled as she made the gap a little bigger, inviting him in to investigate the newfound shelter. He poked his head in the hole and she giggled as he burrowed against her white undershirt.

The front door chimed, and her curious cat lurched back at the noise. She adjusted her straps and tucked the tabby back into his home. She made her way up to the front, where she found a middle-aged man shuffling from foot to foot, gazing out the window.

"Hello, welcome to Paws on York," she said with a smile. His wedding ring glinted in the early-summer sunlight. "Are you here looking to bring home a new love to your family?"

The man paled as he made eye contact with her, then looked back toward the door. Jaylynn took a breath as she turned her attention inward. Her gut felt confident and strong, reassuring her she was safe. Though the man had a lot of anxious energy coming off him, the air still felt light. He seemed drawn to the door, yet afraid to leave. Almost ungrounded or lost. She was thankful for River's more recent lessons on reading energies. Jaylynn took a deep breath and did her best to dissipate the tension in the room.

"To be honest, I… I don't even know why I'm here." The man's voice was low and quiet. He was at least a head taller than her, but she was used to being towered over. She admired his light green dress shirt that brought out his eyes, paired with fitted gray business pants. Everything other than his energy seemed so composed and put together. In almost every way, this man was the exact opposite of her own casual attire and unruly hair.

Jaylynn offered him a smile and took a chance. "Well then, I suppose I know exactly what you're here for. Follow me." She forewent the usual paperwork and turned to reopen the door leading back to the pens. He trailed behind her. Though her hands were clean, she pumped the hand sanitizer as she passed it, trusting he would follow her lead. She opened the employees-only door and held out a hand to gesture him inside. She almost laughed at the look on his face. It wasn't like she was going to kill him.

"Go on," she nudged.

Jaylynn followed and closed the door behind them. In the middle of the room was a large plastic kennel surrounded with blankets. Momma Rosabella lay nearby, tail flapping against the crate as she saw the people come in. Tiny puppies nuzzled at her tummy and around her legs. Jaylynn opened the pen wide. She picked up the wandering puppies with extra care and returned them to their momma's tummy. She sat cross-legged beside Rosabella's head and pet her beautiful red coat. Jaylynn's smile grew as the dog's long tongue licked her forearm.

The man standing at the door stepped toward the litter, his face pale. Jaylynn had hoped the puppies would help ground him and dissipate whatever was going on with him. Now she wondered if she'd made the wrong call. *Everyone loved puppies, though—how could it be the wrong call?*

The man came to his knees beside them. Momma Rosa sat up and gave him a good sniff, checking to see if he could be cleared to touch her babies. He stayed still as she inspected him and the puppies cried at the loss of their mother's milk and warmth. She approved with a quick flick of her tongue and lay back down. Puppies clamored over one another to re-latch and snuggle against her belly. Momma Rosa rested her head in Jaylynn's hands and her tail wagged.

Jaylynn tried to break the awkward silence. "They're about seven weeks old. We think they're some kind of Irish setter mix. They're still too young to be up for adoption, so we have to keep them back in the staff room until they get a little older. Momma Rosa here was rescued from a puppy mill. These dogs can go for a lot of money and I'm sure the owners were infuriated when they lost their pregnant cash load. Even with the strenuous life she must have lived, though, Momma still seems happy to get pets. I think she will be even happier to not have any more babies. Isn't that right, Rosabella?" She drew her face down to the dog's. Rosabella licked her cheek.

Jaylynn smiled and looked up at the man and was surprised to see tears running down his face. She wasn't sure why he was so shaken. She took another deep breath and imagined she could hold his emotional energy up for him as more tears slipped down his face. The man unbuttoned his sleeves and Jaylynn tried not to shift around. Her own nerves grew as she tried to stay still and breathe. In the back of her mind, she hoped the front door didn't chime at that moment.

Then, he turned his left forearm upward, exposing his compass to the soft lighting in the back room. He took a second, then with great care picked up the smallest pup from the litter wrestling between her momma's legs. The ruby-colored pup with a few white spots on her face and back yawned and squirmed as the man held her up. He placed her in his lap and then he started crying even harder. Rosabella perked back up at the man's increased emotion holding her pup. She moved her upper body toward him and rested her chin on his knee.

Jaylynn could see the man's compass and noticed it was physically glowing. "Oh!" She started putting the pieces together in her head. "Oh…" She had never heard of someone's compass leading them to an animal before, and yet it didn't seem that odd to her. She loved some of these animals so much she was surprised her own compass hadn't attached to every single one of them.

"Does… does this puppy have a name?" the man asked. He sniffled back his tears and wiped his face on his sleeve.

"Well, technically she hasn't been named yet, but I've been calling her Lady, short for Ladybug. Of the litter, she's the runt. Always eager to cuddle and never pushy to eat. She'll probably be small when she's full-grown, but I expect she'll be an absolute sweetheart," Jaylynn replied in awe. She was witnessing magic firsthand! And it wasn't her own this time! "Do you mind me asking your name?"

The man cleared his throat and made genuine eye contact with her for the first time since he'd entered the shelter. He had such lovely deep green eyes. Where they had at first been filled with fear and anxiety, they now glowed with pure joy. "Kade. My name is Kade."

CHAPTER XXIII

NYLAH

"Really, Jazz, do you not find any of this ominous?" Nylah shrank as they walked by the colossal statues of Jupiter, Juno, and Minerva that lined the front of the church. Each stood tall and mighty and stared down the rows of empty pews. Though the church was open, Nylah got the distinctive feeling they weren't supposed to be there. An involuntary shiver made Nylah move closer to Jazz. Nylah hadn't been in a Roman church in over a decade and they weren't thrilled to be back.

"You'll get used to it," he replied with a steady smile. He held a hand out and led them through a doorway tucked in the deepest corner. "This isn't even the dark part." He winked. The room was lined with damp gray stone walls. The shallow roof threatened to suffocate the air from Nylah's lungs as the first door swung closed behind them.

Jazz knocked against a second thick wooden door. He bounced on the balls of his feet and gave Nylah's hand a squeeze. Whether it was supposed to be comforting for him or them, Nylah wasn't sure.

I should have had a drink before coming. Nylah pushed their wide-rimmed glasses up their nose. A bead of sweat trickled down beneath their striped vintage sweater and scarlet coveralls.

"If I had known this was going to be in a church, I would have reconsidered my outfit."

In a surprising contrast to Nylah's casual vintage style, Jazz was sporting a fitted black suit. The collar of his white undershirt gleamed against his deep redwood-brown skin.

"First timers always come dressed casual. You have nothing to worry about."

Sure. Nothing to worry about. Other than that we're in a creepy backroom of a church late at night, and you look perfectly composed while I'm a sweaty mess.

The oak door opened a crack and Jazz's face split into a smile. He offered a shallow bow to the person on the other side.

"Who is the guest?"

Jazz shot Nylah a look. "They're a good friend. Faithful to our cause, looking for help."

The door opened wide to a priest in crimson robes. Nylah's gaze dropped out of respect, staring at their dirty black boots. *I'm definitely underdressed.*

"The Fates serve all souls—especially those who wander and those who are lost."

The priest turned and made his way down the stairs previously hidden by his billowing robes.

Great. Dark room, down some even darker stairs, following creepy preachers. Talk about a wild Wednesday night. Jazz released Nylah's hand to walk into the narrow stairwell, and childhood claustrophobia crept up Nylah's neck. As the stairway twisted deeper under the church, Nylah wished the lanterns weren't spread so far apart. Nylah's nails imprinted half-moons into their palms. They forced the muggy air in and out of their lungs as slowly as possible.

When at last the priest opened another wooden door, Nylah was relieved to see tall ceilings and pools of light in the vaulted basement. Old chandeliers hung from the ceiling beams and a sour smell danced on the humid stone. Jazz led a transfixed Nylah to the middle of the room, where more priests and common folk gathered around a large, centered structure. Many of the people in the room wore formal black clothing, though a good number of crimson robes milled through the crowd. The black-and-crimson tide swam around Nylah, each person in their own hushed conversations, sneaking glances in their direction.

A different priest caught Nylah's attention as the crowd parted for him. The heavyset man wore black robes, but what differed from his crimson-garbed followers was that his sleeves had thick, golden cuffs. Where the crimson robes appeared light and barely grazed the ground, the master priest's robes hung heavy, dragging like a cloak of velvet on the ground behind him.

The people gravitated to the heavy-robed priest. Jazz chose a small opening in the loose circle. Behind the man was a life-size marble statue of three women. They sat in a row, leaning against one another, dressed in stone-colored fabric that clung to their clay breasts and parted their legs. The statue was both sensual and disturbing.

Nylah leaned over and whispered into Jazz's ear. "Why don't they have heads or arms?"

He coughed and leaned back, his deep voice an even quieter whisper. "They were vandalized decades ago in the Roman Empire's war. Lots of statues were defaced, but the Fates got the worst of it. After that, they were rescued by a British museum before the Fates' Priests took over their care. Now they move the statue between multiple hideaways around the world, where the priests honor them to keep the world safe."

Nylah stared at the sabotaged women, curious how such a statue came to Canada. Technically, the UK and Canada allied with the Roman Empire. With nothing more than a channel of water to defend their border, the British country was the first to negotiate a truce with the imperial force. They could run their own affairs as long as they contributed to defending the Roman Empire—

primarily against the ongoing stalemate with their northern enemy, Russia.

Nylah knew all of this from their required history lessons in primary school. Everyone had to understand their country's allegiance to the eastern superpower.

Maybe they figured an entire ocean would be better at keeping the relic safe?

The headless statue offered no insight. As the gathered people amalgamated, Nylah brushed closer to Jazz. He stood tall with his broad shoulders pulled back in pride and cast a large shadow Nylah happily hid behind.

This was such a mistake. Why did I think coming here was a good idea? How did Jazz even end up here?

The leader priest cleared his throat, interrupting Nylah's thoughts. All murmuring quieted.

"Welcome, humble humans. Tonight we gather to pay our respects to those who see all. To repent for the sins of our fathers, and to right our own fates." His robes swept the ground as he circled the headless Fates. He carried a large golden bowl with both hands. He stopped before a crimson-robed woman and held it out to her. Instead of taking it, she turned her tongue in her mouth before leaning forward and spitting into the bowl.

Nasty. Nylah tried to manage the grimace that crept onto their freckled face.

"To Nona, she who gives us life. She who births us. The goddess mocked by Terra Mater, who claims to be the beginning of time.

Then is mocked again by Juno, who claims to be the mother of the gods. Birthing the beginning of Fate itself, Nona, to you our lives will always be in debt." The heavy-robed priest continued around the circle, stopping before each of the guests. He offered the bowl to each of them.

Oh, Jazz, what have you gotten me into?

"To Decuma, she who determines the length and misery of our fates. The all-powerful deity mocked by Jupiter, the king of the gods. May you deliver with justice each of our destinies and see us honoring you instead of the fake king."

Nylah nibbled at the chipped black nail polish that decorated their stubby nails. The spit bowl moved closer. *We're not going to have to drink back out of that, are we?* Nylah suppressed a gag. The tiny red hairs on their neck rose as the cesspool moved closer.

"And lastly to Morta, she who blesses us each in life's ending. May her power be remembered as superior to Pluto, the god of the Underworld. To the one and only goddess of death. May she see our faith, our sacrifices, and our truth as she chooses our timely passing."

The discolored puddle of yellow and gray mucus came under Nylah's nose alarmingly fast. The sour smell wafted up, stronger than ever. Jazz nodded in encouragement, so with a turn of a tongue, Nylah added their own saliva to the coagulation. Jazz followed and offered a bow to the master priest.

"May we only serve the Fates, and may they judge each of us accordingly." He took the bowl of germs to the centered statues.

"And may the other gods learn their place in the hierarchy." He dipped his chubby finger into the spit wad, stirring it briefly with his head bowed. *They're insane. Jazz has gone crazy, and his friends are psychos.* Nylah couldn't help as their nose scrunched up in disgust.

The serious priest drew his spit-covered finger out of the gleaming bowl. He licked it clean and then spit once more into the bowl. Then he grabbed an unmarked glass bottle and topped off the saliva with a clear fluid. He poured the contents of the bowl out at the feet of the Fates. Nylah leaned forward and saw that the ground around the Fates was made of engraved plaques. They didn't recognize all the faces, but the Capitoline Triad were easy to make out. Jupiter, Juno, Minerva—faces in panels that had once filled their childhood home laid flat under the Fates.

The gold cuffed priest procured a match from his robe. In a flash of orange embers, he dropped the stick onto the liquid-covered plaques. "May the false gods burn." Fire pranced up at the Fates' feet, lighting their marble bodies in an ominous glow.

I've gone from one end of religious extremist group to the other. Nylah stepped back as the heat ate away at the faces of the Roman gods. When the ceremony came to a close, Nylah stayed close to Jazz, anxious in the unfamiliar crowd. A renewed murmuring started again.

"I know the opening ceremony can seem gross at first, but at least it's not blood." Jazz offered a shining smile as he took Nylah's arm. He pulled them away from the gathering to a quiet corner.

"Why isn't everyone in crimson robes? Why didn't you tell me to wear black?"

Jazz shrugged. "Newbies always wear street clothes. Once you take the pledge, you commit to wearing black, and once you make the sacrifice, you get the crimson robes."

Nylah choked. "Sacrifice?"

"I assume it's goats. I haven't gotten that far myself, hence the black. Romans were crazy about that stuff." Jazz led Nylah to a tapestry hanging on a large stone column. "It's really not that high of a price to pay for a chance to get right with the Fates."

Nylah's nails found their way back to their mouth. "And you really believe in all this stuff? That you can actually influence the Fates? And that you can trust these people? What if by doing this you get on the bad side of all the other Roman gods?" Though Nylah had given up on praying to anyone other than Cupid decades ago, it still seemed wrong to openly disrespect the other gods.

"I'd rather risk angering them than the Fates. You think it's Juno that decides when you meet your soulmate? Minerva that decides how hard of a life you live? Jupiter who decides when you die? Society got it wrong. The Fates are the ones calling the shots and anyone who doesn't believe that is blind."

Jazz stuffed his hands into his dress pants and turned to face Nylah's apprehensive frown. "Listen, I know this is hard to swallow but sit with it. I think you'll come to see, as I did, that this really makes sense compared to everything else."

Nylah nodded and glanced back at the group clad in black and

167

crimson. *One more visit. That's all I promised. Then we'll both be off across the ocean away from these psychos and I'll make him see sense.*

Nylah turned back to Jazz and gave their best attempt at a normal smile. "What's next?"

CHAPTER XXIV

BLAKE

Blake crumpled up another piece of paper and threw it across the room. *New York, the city where dreams are crushed, over and over.* She glared at the growing pile of failed sketches as if it was their fault her dreams were slipping through her fingers. Following a grueling dinner shift, Blake had returned to the tattoo parlor, hoping to get a couple extra hours in on her new impossible project. She wiped off the excess eraser bits from the upholstered tattoo bed she'd taken over as her makeshift desk.

Sal's project this week was cruel. Draw Cupid's Compass, he had said. She almost laughed in his face. Unfortunately, he was serious. He believed being able to draw the enchanted compass was the ultimate test. It would prove not only that she could work on projects against her own values, but also that she was skilled at dimensional shading and intricate line work. She thought it was a complete waste of her time. Sal swore he once met a man who never got his compass tattoo and had come in to ask for a fake one. Not that it would have magical properties, but to help him feel less ostracized.

Blake was infuriated because she didn't even have her own compass to use as a reference. She spent hours on the internet searching for photos, but was dismayed to realize every image of a compass came out a little blurred. It was as if compasses themselves didn't want to be recorded.

She tried researching sketches of compasses, but everything she found was bad, or again had a blurred quality to it. The project was eating away at her. The insides of her knuckles where she held her pencil felt raw, and the outside of her hand was covered in graphite. She drew out a fresh sheet of paper and set off again, trying to capture the stupid object.

The back door banged open and Blake looked up. She hadn't been expecting anyone at the studio so late. She got up and peeked down the hall, surprised to see Sal leaning against the back wall. His body sagged as he tried to balance himself. How many times had she seen her own mother in a state like this after her father left? Blake pushed away the memories, reassuring herself that she could handle this. Sal squinted toward her as he stumbled to stand straight.

"Blake? Whad-re you doin' 'ere so late?" His words slurred

together as he moved toward her.

"Hey. I wasn't expecting you," she said. She felt bad being at the shop so late herself. She didn't want him to think she was using the shop as a place to sleep, or for anything not apprentice related. Sal had given her keys to come as she pleased, but it still felt weird to be caught alone. "Sorry I'm here so late. I've been struggling with your latest project, but I was about to leave." Blake hastened to gather up her bag, stuffing her belongings inside. "I'll see you soon?"

"Na! Don' apologize. Show me wha' you got. Maybe I can h'lp."

Blake took a critical look at her mentor. Though he didn't seem to be in any position to teach, she felt bad saying no to him. He had brought her so much happiness these past few months, and it was clear he was struggling through something. The least she could do was support him after all he had done for her, even if he was so intoxicated that he could hardly stand.

"Well, I can guarantee they're all terrible," she said with a laugh, "but if you insist." She led him back into her drawing room and grabbed a couple of pieces from the crumpled-up pile on the floor. Sal stumbled before settling in the chair. Seated, his intoxication was gratefully less obvious. Through squinted eyes, he looked at the crumpled pages.

"Ah. I see. Ya know, Blake, I really want you to do good. It's jus' that ya got no magic, nothin' that sets you apart. You don't belong here." He looked down as he let the sketches fall to the floor. Tears pooled in the corners of his bloodshot eyes.

"Wait, what?" Blake responded, stunned at his assessment.

"You're a beautiful girl, is jus' not enough," he wallowed.

"Please, Sal. These are only my first few sketches. I can do better. Give me more time. I swear I can do this." Panic fluttered in Blake's chest as the seams of her future unwound before her eyes. Her drunk mentor crumpled one paper up and threw it to the ground.

"Ya know, I haven' always been like this. I once had a wife. Marley. She was a spitfire. She loved motorcycles and drinkin' and partyin' too. When I found her, I couldn' a picked a better half meself."

Blake pushed down the roaring emotions in her gut as she watched her mentor lean his head back to tell his story. She would listen and be polite, and then make him understand. He was drunk and wasn't thinking straight. He couldn't leave her hanging like this.

"But she changed," he droned on. "All a sudden she wantin' to have babies and buy a big fancy house. Tha's not the girl I married. Den her momma started g'tting' in 'er head and she don' left. I couldn' believe it. Now all tha's left is me and my ol' shop. Can you believe her? Up 'n leavin' like that?"

Sal's teary eyes looked up at Blake's from across the room. She moved to the table and sat on the edge. As she took his hands in her own, he bowed his head and started to cry.

"Is jus' not fair, ya know? E'rey day my stupid compass calls me back to 'er, but she jus' gon'... Off findin' love wif someone else."

"I'm sorry, Sal. I'm sorry your wife left you." Blake tried to speak with all the compassion she could muster, though her own frustration roared on inside. She stared at his giant hands in her own. "And I'm sorry you're sad. I'm sorry if I've let you down, but please don't make me go. I need this more than you know."

"Please don' leave. I know wha' I said, but it's not true." He clasped her hands tight in his and strained his bloodshot eyes at her. "You are magic. You make me so happy. I'm jus' too hard on you…" He trailed off as his mumbling became incomprehensible.

Blake felt her own eyes water. The similarities to her mother's breakdowns were too parallel. The sharp truths, the guilty confessions, the tearful apologies. Sal was more like her family than she had realized. "Maybe you should lie down for a bit. We can talk about this more tomorrow when your head is clear." She moved to get up, but his hands stayed clasped tight.

"Please don' leave me. Not like this. Not all alone." He stood up, still holding her hands in his. Blake felt her heart rate increase as the drunken man stumbled into her. She knew and trusted this man, but warning signs flared in her mind. A familiar urge to escape crept up her spine as she tried to pull away.

"It's okay, Sal. I'll be back tomorrow. You can give me some more pointers on how to draw a compass better, and we'll figure out what to do from there. You just need some rest." She did her best to appear soft and comforting. The urgency in her gut pressed on. She needed to leave.

"Oh, darlin', why you gots to be so beautiful but always be leavin'?" He held one hand up to her face. Tears still ran down his own. "You know I loves ya, right?"

Blake shifted into full panic. She pushed his hand off her face, and fear chilled her to the bone as she stared up at her large, drunken mentor. He let go of her wrist and stumbled back against the wall. He closed his eyes. Blake stepped back farther into the room to grab her bag up off the floor. Without taking her eyes off him, she circled around the tattoo bed and crept her way to the door.

She came within a few steps of the door when he moved with a sudden quickness that startled her into a scream. He brought his hand over her mouth and pushed her against the wall. Every part of her mind screamed to kick, run, or fight, but her whole body froze. What could she do when the man doubled her in size?

I know this man. He won't hurt me.

He held her pinned against the wall with his body. One hand covered her mouth, even though she had gone dead quiet.

He cares about me. He's just drunk.

The other he ran through her deep blue hair, moving from her face down the back of her neck. The hairs on her arms stood up as her skin crawled. He didn't make eye contact with her anymore as he caressed her hair over and over, trailing down to her shoulder.

He's just drunk.

His hand lingered over her collarbone, and she shuddered. Her heart pounded wildly.

"Oh, Marley. It didn' 'ave to be like this. We coulda made it. I jus' need you to keep lovin' me. Can you do tha' for me? Can you keep lovin' me?" He rested his head on the wall above her own. His hand pushed her shoulder hard against the wall. Blake's body came alive, feeling more trapped than before. She threw her hands against his torso, desperate to push his weight off her body. She twisted her head from side to side, trying to escape the hand clamped over her mouth.

"Now, now, baby. Is gon' be okay. We're gon' be okay," he whispered into her ear. Even though he was drunk, it didn't seem like any of her struggles fazed him. He stood upright and steadfast against her. Terror coursed through her blood as he pushed his stiff pelvis against hers. His hand moved from her shoulder and grasped her tender breast hard.

She cried out as he pushed his knee between her legs, prying them open and leaving her feeling exposed. Tears welled in her vision as she smelled the beer and whiskey and sweat that seeped off his body. No matter how hard she tried to pry his hands off her, he didn't move. He was so much bigger than her.

"Now, now, kitten. Hush. This'll be quick, I swear it. Shh…" He moved his hand from aggressively groping her breast to the button of her jeans. Her fear peaked even higher, and she screamed as loud as she could into his hand. He took a step back as he moved to pull her jeans down. She took the partial freedom and sent her knee as hard as she could into his crotch. Sal doubled over in pain. His hand over her mouth slipped and pinned her chest to the wall. She took the extra space and drew her knee up again. She drove it into his stomach. He cried out in pain, and she spun out from under his arm and made a beeline for the door.

Sal was fast, though. He grabbed her hair as she moved to flee and yanked her back into the room to face him. Hot angry tears streamed down both of their faces as she glared up at him. She bit down on his forearm with all the strength she could muster. His grip on her hair released, and she ran.

She ran like she had never run before. Out the back door and down the alleyway. She ran until she was out of breath and then kept running. Her legs and lungs burned. She ran blocks and blocks, moving toward the busier streets but never stopping. She didn't think, she couldn't bring herself to. Blake just kept running the only way that made sense, the only way that brought her any relief. And she didn't let herself stop.

CHAPTER XXV

Sebastian pushed the mushy carrots around his plate. As usual, his parents fawned over one other, unconscious of the food going cold in front of them. Vee chattered on about her day, unfazed by their enamored parents' lack of attention. He was convinced that most of the time she talked just to hear her own voice. His older sister had always been like that—thinking the world revolved around her, but never paying attention to see if it actually did. It was no wonder Sebastian had gotten his compass before her, despite being younger. She lacked any maturity to be in love with someone other than herself.

Vee gabbed on about the classes she had finished with honors and daydreamed out loud about what college would be like. Their parents continued gazing at one another, holding hands. They refused to sit at opposite ends of the table because they would be too far apart to reach one another.

His mum cooed a quick "That's great," to Vee, without taking her attention off their father.

Usually, Sebastian would be happy to eat his meals in silence and be quick to slip away with the excuse of chores or homework. Today he wasn't so fortunate. Dinner would be the best time to talk to them. Afterward, they would cuddle up on the couch watching their favorite crime show, not to be interrupted.

Sebastian cleared his throat. "So, only a few more days till I leave." Vee looked over as if shocked to see him sitting at the table with them. "I was wondering, Mum, if you could dig up my passport. And if you guys have decided who's driving me to the airport?"

"Of course, darling," she replied.

"Maybe you can catch a ride with Gareth to the airport," his dad suggested. "We shouldn't all have to be there that early when it's a workday." Neither of them so much as looked his way.

"Um, okay. I thought you'd want to see me off is all." Sebastian's jaw tensed. He coaxed the overcooked carrots around his plate. "But I guess it'd be easier than going to Heathrow twice in a day."

"Maybe Gareth's parents could bring your exchange partner back too, seeing as it's only a few hours later."

Heat blazed in Sebastian's cheeks. "You don't think that would be awkward or a big ask?"

"Oh, I'm sure it'll be fine. He could probably stay with Gareth's family until we're off work. What was his name again? Regardless, I'm sure Elise and Kenyon would understand." His mum's eyes stayed trained on her husband, not sparing either of her children more than a glimmer of her attention.

"Liam. His name is Liam and that's not exactly a welcoming arrival." Sebastian's frustration grew on his exchange partner's behalf. It was one thing if his parents didn't care about his own flight, but a protective anger boiled on behalf of the exchange partner he'd never met.

Maybe I was selfish agreeing to this trip. He's going to hate it here.

"Well, we're not about to drop our entire lives for a stranger. We have to go to work, so it's settled. He'll stay with the Williams family until we get home," Sebastian's dad said with finality.

Vee seemed satisfied. "It'll be so fun having a new brother." She sneered. "We'll get to take him on all the city tours, show him Buckingham Palace. Oh! Maybe we can take him on a Jack the Ripper tour. I mean, it's an excuse to pretend to be tourists on vacation for a whole month!" Her eyes glowered with excitement touched with malice.

"You don't like castles and you hated that tour. You didn't want to take the Tube or walk down back alleys for two weeks after," Sebastian retorted.

"I was ten!" she snapped. "It was perfectly reasonable for me to be afraid. Besides, it would be fun to take someone who's never seen it before. Then we'll find out quickly if he's a prat."

Sebastian couldn't bring himself to eat another bite. His family comprised the most inconsiderate people he'd ever known. He picked up his dishes, eager to excuse himself. As he cleaned up, he made a mental list of all the things he would have to do the next couple days. Because their flight was due to leave so early, Sebastian resolved it would be better to stay at Gareth's the night before. Then he could leave the new kid clean bedding, which he was sure his parents wouldn't have thought of.

Though he still had plenty of time, he hauled the luggage set from the cupboard. He went up to his room and started packing, double-checking that he had all his football equipment and essentials. He wondered if bringing his favorite ball as a good luck charm was a good idea. Setting it to the side, he decided to wait and see how much room he had. Then he cleaned the rest of his room.

Vee often teased him about how bare he kept his bedroom. She insisted it reflected his dull personality, but he liked keeping it clean and simple. The only decor he had was on his dresser. Football medals hung around the mirror, and his favorite picture of him and Gareth after a winning tourney was stuck in the frame. Gareth's mum had it printed for him a few birthdays back, and Sebastian often picked it up smiling. It reminded him of easier days. Days before compasses, the pressure of school, and trying to pick a career. Back when winning tournaments was all he cared about, and he didn't have to practice all the time to stay at the top of the team.

After taking a few empty glasses down to the sink, he settled on his bed and shot Gareth a text.

SEBASTIAN: Yo. My parents were hoping I could carpool with you to the airport this week. Cool?

He stared up at the ceiling while he waited for a reply.

GARETH: Course, mate. Both my brothers are coming though, so be prepared for a cozy ride.

Sebastian didn't mind.

SEBASTIAN: Your mum cool with bringing my partner back too? My mum is hoping to pick him up after work.

He worried it might change the response. There was a long pause before the reply, and Sebastian eventually got up and turned off the lights. After a few minutes, his phone buzzed again.

GARETH: Yeah, mum says it's fine.

Sebastian put his phone on his dresser and let himself daydream about the upcoming trip. He prayed it would be the escape he needed. Though he should have been nervous about meeting his exchange family, he felt worse for Liam. He wondered how the skinny Asian boy from the portfolio file would manage with his lovesick parents and self-absorbed sister.

CHAPTER XXVI

RENEE

Renee tried to focus on preparing supper, but it was obvious that Lacey wanted her attention. She sat across the kitchen counter and swung her feet from the barstool in a steady beat, her phone set aside.

"So, uh, Mom. There's something I wanted to talk to you about. Ness and I had a fun idea, if you would be open to hearing about it."

Here we go.

Renee had already showered and pulled her long brown hair back in a braid. Her day had been long, but even when she came home, there was endless work to be done. She continued preparing their meal, making a mental note to change over the laundry when she was done.

"Of course you do. Can it not wait until your father is home? I mean, he said tonight he wanted to have a family meeting."

"Well, like, it could... I guess. But I'd like to run it by you first. Then you can mull it over and we can talk about it with Dad too."

Renee weighed her options. Lacey's mood had brightened considerably the past few days since her sneaking away stunt and getting her compass. She'd come home from Charity's an angel child, no longer talking back and doing her chores without being prompted. Usually, her daughter's good moods were like shooting stars. Stunning to see, but quick to burn out. Renee wondered if she was building up to asking for something, though she couldn't guess what.

Possibly something for her birthday? Though it was a month away, she would turn sixteen this summer. Renee wouldn't be surprised if Lacey wanted to throw some wild birthday party. She decided there was likely little harm in hearing her daughter out, though she worried the conversation could plummet Lacey's mood. If that were the case, how would it affect the mystery family meeting?

All day, she had worried about why Kade wanted to have a formal talk. Was it finally time? Did he want to finalize their divorce? She had a hard time keeping her mind from wandering to dark places. Lacey seemed to have other things on her mind, though, and was a welcome distraction. Renee resolved her daughter couldn't have anything worse to say than Kade might.

"Well, as long as you can maintain this spectacular mood you've been in lately, I'm up for hearing you out. All I ask is that you don't go storming away if I can't give you an answer right away," Renee said. Her eyes watered as she cut up the onion.

"I swear I won't. Just please consider the idea before jumping to an automatic no. It would mean a lot to me," Lacey pleaded.

Renee chuckled. It wasn't very often she heard Lacey beg. "Alrighty then. What is it you would like me to consider?"

Lacey took a deep breath. "Ness and I were thinking the four of us could go to Montreal for the Canada Day long weekend. We could leave Dad at home and have a girls' trip!"

Renee watched Lacey chew at her lip as she pitched her idea.

"Stop chewing your lip. You know that's a bad habit and only makes them crack more. And Montreal? Why do you girls want to go to Montreal? The Canada Day parade and fireworks will be way better in Toronto."

"We've seen the Toronto ones so many times! And they're always *so* busy. We thought it would be fun to go somewhere else. Canada Day actually falls on the long weekend this year, so it feels like the perfect opportunity! You wouldn't even have to take time off work. It would be like the ultimate mother/daughter/best friend bonding trip! It would be so fun."

Lacey was spewing words out so fast it almost made Renee laugh.

"All right, all right. Calm down. There's no need to get worked up. I haven't said no. I just wanted to know why. Montreal is going to be busy too, you know?"

"I know, Mom. But going to Toronto for a weekend doesn't feel like a trip. We do that all the time. Montreal would be special. We could go get pedicures and go shopping. When we were looking at things to do in Montreal, there was even this vineyard that came up! If you and Charity wanted to go wine tasting or something one afternoon."

Renee couldn't hold back her laughter this time. "Ha. You *accidentally* found a vineyard? If I didn't know any better, Lacey, I would think you were up to something." Renee put the salad on the table and looked back at her daughter with her hands on her hips.

"I swear we're not up to anything! We thought it would be a cool trip. I mean, finding the vineyard wasn't a complete accident... We thought it would be nice for me and Ness to have a few hours one-on-one, and we figured you'd both like some bonding time too. It'll help keep the mood of the trip light. You and Charity can do adult stuff, and me and Ness can do teenage stuff."

Lacey started nibbling at her lip again. Renee sighed, turning to set the table. She didn't want to ruin her mood, but it was a pretty big ask.

"Please, Mom, don't say no yet. Talk to Dad. Talk to Charity. I think it would be an amazing way to kick off the summer together."

Renee walked up to her daughter and kissed the top of her head. "I'll talk with your dad and Charity, and I'll look into my workload for the week. Your exam results will also play into this, though. I expect you to let me know as soon as they're online."

Lacey let out a deep breath, her vibrating mood settling. Clearly, she had hoped for a better answer, but seemed okay with taking the maybe.

"Yeah, of course. Thanks, Mom. I love you." Lacey went to hop off the stool and head to her room when the front door opened into the apartment. Renee turned toward the ruckus as Kade stumbled into the kitchen, looking sheepish. His arms were overflowing with bags and at the end of a white leash stood a small ruby-colored puppy. She had long, wavy ears and a few white freckles. Her tiny tail tucked between her legs as she backed into Kade.

"Sweet Venus! Dad!" Lacey shrieked as she launched up at the sight of the puppy. "Did you get us a dog?!"

Renee dropped the utensils she had been holding. Kade knelt and placed the bags on the floor to pick up the frightened puppy. He cleared his throat as he turned to face the family.

"So, uh… family meeting?" Kade went scarlet as he carried the tiny puppy to the living room.

Lacey pranced along and plopped down beside him on the ground, eager to pet the small red dog. Renee gathered herself and washed her hands before walking in a trance to the living room, unsure of what to make of the scene.

"Kade, what is this? I know you've wanted a dog for a while, but I thought we agreed with the apartment—"

"Look, Renee, I didn't have a choice."

ASHLEY WEISS

She scoffed. "You didn't have a choice? I get that she's adorable, but surely—"

When he turned to face her, his expression was serious. "I didn't have a choice." The way he sounded out each syllable with finality confused her.

He held out his arm and whatever air Renee's lungs held disappeared. She staggered back to lean against the wall, then slowly slid down, sitting with her knees tucked tight to her chest. Kade's face softened. He turned to untangle the puppy from her leash.

Is this my punishment for wanting to end things?

Lacey's smile was as bright as when she'd shown them her compass, but Renee couldn't look away from her husband. From her vantage point, she could see clearly that his compass arrow pointed down his wrist, not to her.

When did this happen? Why didn't I notice?

The puppy leaped up to kiss his face and her husband's rare laugh echoed off the roof. *Beaming* wasn't a strong enough word to describe Kade; he was literally glowing. Light ebbed off his skin, and Renee sat still and watched as he handled the puppy. She couldn't look away from the way he held her with such care and tenderness.

Lacey happily took over the role of puppy cuddler when Kade shuffled across the floor and reached out to Renee.

She looked up into his forest-green eyes. "I don't understand," she whispered.

Lacey acted like she wasn't paying attention as she played with the puppy, but Renee was sure she was listening to every word.

"I know, I didn't either at first. But, Renee, I finally get it. I finally understand how you can have more than one soulmate. I… I'm sorry I didn't warn you before I brought her home. I needed you to see it for yourself." He stared into her eyes with vigor, as if he could press the truth into every word. She stared back at him, then gazed down at his compass.

"How long ago did it change?"

Kade gave an awkward shrug and glanced back at the puppy. He ran his hand through his hair.

"I guess when she was born." He no longer met her eyes. Renee watched him and felt a great sadness settle over her heart. Again, she had failed as a lover. The puppy must have been eight weeks old if it was separated from its mother. In all that time, she had never once glanced at her husband's compass. She had noticed his moods shifting, but lately their entire house was a roller coaster of emotions. Tears pooled in Renee's eyes.

"Oh, Renee. Please, sweetheart, don't cry. I'm sorry. I should have said something sooner. This is all new to me, and I can see I screwed this up too. I didn't mean to hurt you or go behind your back." He took her in his arms as the floodgates of her own emotions opened.

Renee buried her head in her husband's arms. "I'm so sorry." She choked back a sob. "I've been a terrible wife, and a horrible soulmate. I can't believe I didn't notice your compass changed." She gasped for breath as the apologies poured out. "I'm sorry I couldn't love you enough. I'm sorry I made your compass change. I'm sorry I couldn't be enough for you, Kade."

Kade lifted her chin and brushed the tears running down her cheeks. "Sweetheart, please stop crying. And stop apologizing. It should be me who should apologize. I shouldn't have hidden my compass from you when it changed. And I'm sorry I never truly understood. I can see it now. I can see how you can have more than one love in your life."

Renee didn't know what to say.

Kade brushed a strand of her hair from her face. "You have been an incredible wife and mother. Through thick and thin, you've held this family together and loved us through all our temper tantrums. Please forgive me. You deserve so much more than I've given you, and I will spend the rest of our days making it up to you." Kade stared into her eyes with the devotion she had been missing for years.

Renee couldn't remember the last time he looked so vulnerable. He spoke with such deep passion and yearning. How long had she waited for this? Waited for him to really look at her and love her again? She took his face in her hands and kissed him. Tears flowed down both of their faces as he kissed her back, their longing souls desperate to hold one another tight.

When they broke apart, Kade crushed her in a hug and they both continued to cry. Renee glanced toward Lacey and was surprised to see that she was crying too.

"Oh, Lacey. Get in here," she said. She pulled their daughter into their hug. The three of them held each other tight, their emotions a flurry of relief. The puppy jumped up against their embrace, barking as if she wanted to be included too.

Kade's laughter broke through as he let go to pick up the puppy. He held her up on her hind legs, touching their noses together.

"What's her name?" Lacey asked through a sniffle.

"Lady, short for Ladybug," Kade replied. The skin around his eyes creased in fondness.

Lacey smiled as she reached out to pet the puppy's soft face. "Ladybug, hey? Well, it's very nice to meet you. Welcome to the family."

Lady jumped up to lick the tears off Lacey's face, and she laughed. Renee's heart sang in relief and happiness. For the first time, her family felt whole.

CHAPTER XXVII

BLAKE

When had she stopped walking? Why had she stopped at all? Blake fought through the fog that had settled on her mind as she tried to make out her surroundings. She stood rigid on the unfamiliar street, unsure of where she was supposed to be going. She grappled with her thoughts, trying to process where she was. Too soon, she remembered why she was running at all.

She slipped back to the safety of the fog and let her feet guide her. Her body limped forward, and Blake closed her eyes against the burning lights. No, not just lights. A neon sign, bright in the late-night sky: *Hotel Janus—rest stop of crossroads.*

How many days had it been since she'd rested somewhere other than on the cold, hard ground? Two? Maybe three? Her thoughts were sluggish, but she knew better than to try and clear them this time. She let her feet drag her through the hotel doors, and all at once she was met with a new reality. People. People she would have to talk to. She slunk her backpack off and pulled it tight to her chest. It was undeniably heavier, though she had no memory of stopping at the community center for clothes or her cash stash.

The artificial heat blasted against her sensitive skin and Blake's eyes watered as they adjusted to the fluorescent white lights. Behind the counter, a heavy woman smiled with crooked, yellow teeth. She welcomed Blake as she walked through the door. Blake couldn't bring herself to smile back. She couldn't bring herself to feel anything other than terror as the walls closed in around her. *This is a trap. He'll find you here.*

Blake swallowed a lump down her aching throat and choked out the few words she could manage. "Single room, one night."

The woman's face soured. She held out a room key and explained the Wi-Fi password. Blake didn't listen. All she could hear was the amplified sound of the fan whooshing above. *Run, run, run…*

Her hand shook as she took the room key then made her way down the hall. When she finally found the matching number, she slammed the door shut harder than necessary. She couldn't slide the lock into place fast enough. Her heart hammered so hard it made her light-headed. She sank to the floor and clutched her backpack in her lap. *He's going to find you.*

Get it together.

She forced herself to put her backpack down and went to work pulling off her worn combat boots. Her feet ached and her socks were filthy and wet. She braced herself on the wall and made her way to the bathroom, careful to keep her mind as empty as possible. Blake collapsed over the sink. Her hands shook as she turned on the tap. She swallowed as much of the cool running water as she could before her stomach objected. For the first time in what had to be two days, she looked at herself.

Her cheekbones were more prominent than ever. Dark purple circles hung heavy beneath her wide, bloodshot eyes. The on-again, off-again rain hadn't been kind on her hair. It gathered in dark blue knots that accented the bruises that lined her lower jaw. Blake stared at the stranger in the mirror—a stray with nowhere to go. *This isn't me.* For the first time since the day she refused to acknowledge, she felt a desire to do more than walk or run.

She carefully stripped off her muggy clothing and tossed the pieces in the bathtub. Even with the door locked, she felt more exposed and vulnerable than ever. She peeled off her forearm sleeve and held it out like it was a cursed object, then dropped it into the garbage can. She wished she could burn it away with every memory that threatened to surface.

Blake showered on top of her filthy and crumpled clothes. She grasped the bar on the wall as she braced against the scalding hot water. Her hands trembled as she scrubbed her naked, pale skin until it was flushed a deep burgundy. Then, she pulled on the white starched bathrobe and went to work on getting the mud out of her black jeans. She methodically cleaned each of her garments with the shampoo and soap provided, then hung them to dry.

She poured out the contents of her backpack, grateful to find all her basic necessities. Blake started the slow and painful process of working out the million and one knots that had taken over her scalp. Once finished, she pulled the bed's fluffy pillows around herself and untucked the blankets. When she turned off the bedside lamp, her heart rate rose once again. The starched bathrobe chafed against her skin as she tried to sink deeper into the overly fluffy pillows. All motivation and fresh energy that had returned to her heart were snuffed out by the tiny, dark room.

The next morning, Blake woke to a furious stomach. She scrambled out of bed, surprised she'd got even an hour of sleep in. She was delighted to slide back into her own clothes. Though the waistband of her jeans was still damp, it was refreshing. She took some extra time to wrangle her long, dark blue hair into a bun and then tackled the next issue.

Food. A deep ache constricted her belly and demanded attention. She dug into the bottom of her backpack and found a couple wallets buried deep. It seemed as much as her feet had been keeping her busy, so had her slippery hands. Fear twinged in her gut.

What if I had been caught?

She swallowed against the imagery of concrete floors and metal bars. Blake pulled the cash out of the wallets and tossed their remains into the garbage.

She dug up her small makeup bag next. She did her best to cover her haunting complexion and bring a bit of color to her cheeks. Soon enough, Blake looked human enough to make it through a meal. She was still careful to keep her mind empty.

As she checked out, the plump lady regarded her with surprise. "Well, don't you freshen up nicely. When you came in last night, I could have sworn you were a ghost. That rat's nest hid that pretty face of yours."

Blake said nothing. Weeks ago, she would have retaliated against the backhanded comment, but she wasn't the same person anymore. Instead, she made her way to the hotel restaurant. She picked a table as far back as possible and faced the door, watching every customer with suspicion. Blake ate as much of the tasteless food as she could stomach before fleeing the confining walls. When she walked out, her eyes glazed over a wall of maps in the connected gift shop, but she shook her head.

It's not like it matters anyway. She dismissed the idea of trying to make a plan. A nearby sign told her enough, as it advertised the nearby tourist sight, Mt. Pocono. She'd made it to Pennsylvania. But she wasn't about to stop.

She wasn't *going* anywhere. She was going *anywhere*.

CHAPTER XXVIII

JAYLYNN

Jaylynn waded through the cool water of the creek by River's cabin, keeping her eye out for a heart-shaped rock. How searching for a rock would be useful she wasn't sure, but Jaylynn had learned months ago that questioning River's ways was pointless. River was like the wind; she bent and curved any which way she wanted, and didn't need to justify her ways or existence to anyone.

"Jaylynn. Tell me why you are here." River was a little farther up the stream, but Jaylynn heard her clear as day.

Jaylynn's eyebrows shot up at the new question. She'd grown used to answering "Tell me who you are" day in and day out during their nature excursions. A smile crept across her face as she closed her eyes to reflect on the new question, a sign she must have passed some unseen test.

Why was she here?

"Hmmm. I suppose I'm here because my compass led me here. Which I know isn't a good enough answer for you, it's far too literal. Umm. I'm here because I'm fated to be?" She opened her eyes knowing full well all she would receive was a thank-you back.

River gazed back at her with ever-knowing eyes. "Thank you. Tell me why you are here." Jaylynn's bare feet skidded for an instant before she gained her footing in the rocky creek bed.

"Oh, uhm. I'm surprised I don't get to ask you back. I thought part of my practices was to learn to listen, as well as contemplation." Jaylynn nibbled at her lip. She knew she was breaking the structure, but she felt cheated not getting to listen. River continued walking through the water, ignoring her. Jaylynn let out an annoyed breath at the unanswered question. *Why was she here?*

"I'm here to learn that which I don't understand."

"Thank you. Tell me why you are here." River's voice was steady and carried on the current.

Jaylynn sighed, but knew the exercise would only end when River decided. She let herself settle into the new question, determined to get the answer right. She abandoned her search for the heart-shaped rock.

"I am here to become the greatest version of myself and to learn what can't be taught in philosophy classes. I'm here not because I have nowhere to go, but because this is exactly where I'm meant to be." Jaylynn finished her communication with confidence, looking back at her teacher.

"Thank you. Tell me why you are here."

Jaylynn took a deep breath and closed her eyes. It wasn't as much fun when she didn't get a turn to listen. How was she supposed to piece together River's backstory when she wasn't giving her anything new to work with?

Jaylynn dug through her mind, trying to think of other reasons why she was here, but none came to her. She decided to reflect on the question differently. *Why was she here in this body, in this life?*

She dug deep in her mind once again. Wasn't this the ultimate question of philosophy? She regretted not continuing past her first semester as she tried to come up with another deep truth as to why she was alive. She stood in silence for quite some time before finally letting go of the contemplation.

"I don't know. Nothing is coming to me. Tell me why you are here," she answered. She felt daring knowing she was challenging River. She hoped her teacher would relent and offer some kind of insight as to how she was supposed to contemplate this question.

"Thank you. Tell me why you are here," was all River responded.

Jaylynn crossed her arms. At least asking who she was had so many facets that the question had a million answers. Why she was here was simple.

"Just because. Because it was the way of the cosmos. There is no known reason for me to be here, but I am. I can't pretend to know the answer the greatest philosophers seek. All I can do is live my life and trust that I'm here for some purpose. I trust that even when I don't know what that purpose is, I'm always moving toward it. That even when it feels like all of this is chaos and nothing makes sense, someone out there has a plan for me. Be it the Fates or the stars or the gods. And if it so happens there isn't some divine higher force and I have no purpose, then I suppose I'm here simply because not existing isn't the choice I want to make anymore."

Jaylynn's heart throbbed at the last piece of truth smoldering in her chest like burning coals. She took a deep breath, willing the charged energy to leave her body. She imagined she was breathing in life force, cooling and calming her nerves that were fired up at the thought of her existence being inconsequential.

River maintained her composure as she turned to face Jaylynn. "Thank you."

River leaned forward and plucked a rock from the water. It was a dark gray, with splotches of purples and blues dancing on its wet surface—and low and behold, it was the heart shape they had been searching for. She placed the rock in the bag slung from her shoulder and started back toward the cabin. Jaylynn dutifully followed, wrestling down her irritation. They walked in silence all the way back, until River's hand was resting on the cabin door. She looked back at Jaylynn, speaking in her usual husky voice.

"The wind has changed. We will soon have to hold greater space and step into harder truths. Jaylynn, you have come far. These next few steps will be some of the hardest you may take. If I worried you couldn't manage it, I wouldn't ask you to, but I also want to give you the choice I never had. Leave now and take these teachings for what you will. Live out your life as you have been. Ever searching for that which is not seen."

Jaylynn stood perplexed, the weight of the moment taking on a sudden new significance.

"Or stay with me. Stand by me as I push you further down the rabbit hole. I can't guarantee what will come of you; in this, the cards are shy to speak. Take the time to make a conscious decision. Listen to your mind, your heart, and your soul. They should all have a choice in this decision. And if one isn't on board, take the time to find out why. This is the cliff edge you have always stood on. It's up to you to look into its depths now, instead of carrying on without listening first."

Jaylynn stared at River. She had many questions, but she knew she wouldn't get any answers out of her teacher today. She understood she was being excused, even if she wasn't sure why.

"I will think about it and get back to you," she said. Jaylynn wiped the dirt from her feet before sliding them back into her Converse.

"Do not only think, child. Feel. Listen. And don't come back if the answer you come up with is a no."

Jaylynn's hands paused as she held her laces. She looked up in time to see the cabin door close. Part of her immediately wanted to agree to whatever unforeseen darkness was coming, but she took a deep breath instead. If this was a test, she planned on passing it.

She wasn't prepared to give up her new life, but she would do as River suggested.

She turned toward her truck, battling with the deep sense of longing and fear contracting in her chest. Fear of losing River. Fear of losing the only genuine companion she'd had in years. It was like her compass knew she might not come back, and it pulled harder as she drove away. Tears spilled over her freckled face until she had to pull over.

Jaylynn cried hard. She cried out for all her fears of being alone again; for not knowing what she was supposed to do; for not knowing what her purpose was or why she'd come. The vast majority of her tears, though, came with knowing that the only things waiting for her at home were vacant stares, ears filled with cotton, and people expecting her to fit into a mold that she no longer fit.

Minutes passed before her tears slowed and she could take a deep breath again. She put her truck back into Drive and made her way back to Toronto. Home to her loving parents and her familiar childhood house, where everything was simple and no one asked her why she was alive.

CHAPTER XXIX

CHARITY

Charity heaved the luggage into the trunk of Renee's tall, black SUV. No amount of daily yoga would have prepared her for the weight of the suitcase. It toppled back toward her. *Ness, what in Cupid's name did you pack?* To Charity's relief, Kade appeared beside her with a relaxed smile. He lifted the oversized bag up and into the vehicle.

She blew a stray graying hair out of her face. "Who knew four girls could pack so much for one weekend trip?" she joked. The back of Renee's vehicle was remarkably full.

Kade chuckled. "You'd think you guys were going to Paris, not Montreal."

Lacey swooped around the car in a fit of giggles. Her cheeks were flushed with youth and her eyes twinkled with excitement. In her arms, a red puppy wriggled as it tried to lick her face.

Wait, they got a puppy?

Charity considered the recent conversations she'd had with the Baker family, wondering if they'd mentioned it. The last couple of weeks she'd thought her memory had improved. She'd had less night terrors, she made it to work on time, her thoughts were less scattered. Charity thought she was getting better.

Lacey looked at Kade. "Wait, was Paris an option? Because I would happily reschedule this whole trip, if that's a thing."

"Wait, what! We're going to Paris?" Nessie's voice chimed in from the other side of the vehicle.

"I'm pretty sure your mom just said we are." Lacey grinned.

Charity's eyes were fixed on the squirming puddle of fur in Lacey's arms. *I wouldn't forget that... right?*

Charity closed her eyes. She tried to listen for the whisper on the wind that once followed her everywhere. But where the echo of her name had been, now all she heard was the buzz of a neighbor's lawn mower. It should have been peaceful not hearing Luke calling for her anymore. She should be relieved.

Charity shook herself and resolved she must not have been told. "You guys got a puppy?" she asked. Lacey handed over the dog without blinking an eye and turned to Nessie.

"Ugh, could you imagine how romantic Paris would be?"

Nessie coughed. "Not that girls' trip should be romantic." Her daughter flashed a smile Charity knew to be fake. "Unless you consider sharing a hotel, getting manicures, and bathing suit shopping couple-y."

Oh, Minerva, does she know? Charity dropped her gaze back to the squirming creature intent on licking the sharp edges of her jawline.

"What's the puppy's name?" Charity asked, changing the direction of the conversation. She traced her fingers over the pup's velveteen, wavy ears.

Kade turned from loading the last oversized suitcase with a smile. "Lady."

Lady squirmed hard as he came close. Charity handed her off, bemused. "I didn't know you guys had planned on getting a dog. Did I miss a memo or just forget?" Out of the corner of her eye, she saw Lacey whisper to Nessie with a scowl.

"I wouldn't say it was planned." Renee chuckled. She tossed a tote of snacks into the back seat. "But she was a timely blessing."

Kade's eyes softened. He held Lady back out to Charity. "Could you hold her again for a sec?"

Before she could object, her arms were full again and her face was being lapped up by Lady's eager tongue. She nearly dropped Lady, though, as Kade scooped Renee up and dipped her into a deep kiss. Charity looked away from the uncharacteristic PDA and caught Lacey's flushed face.

Renee staggered when she stood up again. Kade smirked and then turned back for the puppy. "Have a wonderful trip and drive safe, okay?"

The girls piled into the vehicle, eager to start their long evening drive. Renee offered a quick wave to Kade and Lady, then pulled out of the driveway.

"So, are you going to spill the beans on what changed?" Charity asked, confident now that she hadn't just forgotten.

Renee laughed. She tucked the loose strands of her chestnut hair behind her ears. "Well, I think we all knew something had to shift in our household. We needed something fresh to bring more playfulness into our lives, and Kade's compass delivered."

In the back seat, Lacey plunged her head into her hands.

"What? Like, his compass picked a dog?" Charity asked, mystified.

Renee smiled as she signaled into the traffic. "Yep. You would be amazed at how everything has changed since. Lady has been such a gift to our family!" Renee winked. "That, and things in the bedroom have never been better, if you know what I mean."

They both laughed as Lacey's cheeks burned.

"Jupiter Almighty! Mom, please stop. This is exactly the kind of conversation you're supposed to save for when you guys have one-on-one time. You're making my ears bleed, and I'm regretting this trip already."

Charity laughed as she turned back to the girls. "Oh, Lacey, don't worry. We're not going to traumatize you. Besides, it's normal to talk about sex. It is how you came to exist in this world."

Nessie stared at her mother with horror. "MOM! Please stop talking. Now."

Charity and Renee both laughed harder. Charity looked over at

Renee and took her hand. "I'm happy to hear things have shifted for you, and I'm looking forward to hearing all the juicy bits when we're alone." She turned her attention to the rearview mirror. "Speaking of one-on-one time together, what exactly are you two hoping to get up to?"

Nessie's eyes flashed the same way they had earlier, looking to Lacey for an answer.

What are you up to, Ness?

"Ness and I were thinking tomorrow we could go to the parade in the morning, try to get some cute pictures together, and just hang out. Maybe hit a mall or something for lunch, and then we could all meet up again for the rest of the weekend. Then neither of you need to get up early." Lacey twisted her long black hair around her finger. Her gaze out the window was casual. Nessie stared at her feet, guaranteeing that her friend's words were in fact lies.

"You want to go to the parade alone?" Renee asked, her brow knit tight. "In a new city, with no supervision, on Canada Day of all days?"

Charity watched Lacey's face to see if any part of her betrayed the lie she wove.

"Well, we just thought you guys wouldn't care for the parade. I mean, we're both almost sixteen, we'll have our phones, and we won't be more than a couple of blocks away."

"And that's what you really want? To get up early and go to the parade, just the two of you?" Renee stared both the girls down through the rearview mirror.

Their heads bobbed in unison.

"Well, I really wouldn't mind missing the crowds... Especially if we'll be buried in them through the fireworks tomorrow night too." Renee looked to Charity. "What do you think?"

Can she not tell when her daughter is lying? Or is she just pretending to play it out like me?

"If you're comfortable with it, I'm fine. I'm sure the girls can handle themselves." Charity glanced down at her own feet as smiles spread across Lacey's and Nessie's faces. *They aren't the only ones with secrets.*

CHAPTER XXX

BLAKE

"Anything else?" the bartender asked as she pushed the amber liquid toward Blake's impatient fingers. She was grateful for the female bartender's no-nonsense attitude, combined with scoring a server that didn't ask for ID. She was lucky most people assumed she was older than she actually was.

Blake shook her head as she gripped her much needed reprieve. The whiskey burned down her throat and warmed her chest. Her cash stash was dwindling, and stealing had gotten harder as towns grew sparse the past two days, but the alcohol had become a necessary expense. With every day that passed, she was having more memory flashes. The crumbled paper on the floor. The smell of his sweat combined with the beer on his breath. The pressure of his hand—

Blake's mind went blank.

When she came to, she wasn't sure how long she'd been sitting still, holding her empty glass to her lips. She blushed and put it down. She pushed it forward on the bar to ask for another. The whiskey would burn everything away. It would help her forget.

A memory surfaced of her mother surrounded by empty bottles, drowning her grief. *That was different.* Blake scowled as she rejected the thought of ending up like her.

Sometime between her second and third drink, the bar door opened. The hairs on the back of Blake's neck rose, but she fought the urge to turn and look. Even though it was the furthest thing from rational, her fear that she was being followed never went away. *It's not him. Don't turn around. You know it can't be—*

Blake was tired of freezing. She was tired of living in fear. She fought back a wave of frustration as the new man sat one barstool over. In the mirrors, she was surprised to see a young and gentle face. He was probably only a bit older than herself. His round cheeks didn't suit his broad shoulders, but she kind of liked it. All rough and tough, but still innocent.

"Same as usual?" the barkeep asked the new customer. He nodded, seeming as reclusive as she felt. The barkeep poured a beer, then looked up at Blake.

"Do you need a top-up too?"

Blake nodded, and the woman smiled and grabbed the bottle of

Jack Daniel's from the shelf.

"Well now, isn't this a wild night? The edges of my bar roaring with laughter, while my bar top stays quiet as a mouse. You two could be two peas in a pod." She laughed at her own joke. She grabbed a rag and moved to the tables to wipe and clear them.

Blake tried to relax her shoulders, breathe, and enjoy her drink while she waited for her food. She kept a close eye on the rambunctious dartboard men behind her, while also analyzing the stranger next to her. He hunched over his drink, not interested or affected by her presence. Finally, the whiskey started to have its effect. She could feel her shoulders soften as her racing nerves settled. She welcomed the numb feeling with open arms.

"I should've considered a tattoo. Would've saved me a lot of bullyin'," the young-faced man said.

She looked up at him, startled to hear him speak. He had a low but gentle voice, with the slightest drawl that felt out of place. At first, she wasn't sure he was talking to her. She looked to the splatter of ink that covered her own compass that he must have been referring to. She'd found a new pride in the terrible cover-up and had stopped hiding it. It looked how she felt: sabotaged, ugly, and permanently changed.

Blake offered a polite smile and continued to drink, but the man didn't so much as look at her.

"Ever heard of someone without a compass? 'Cause if you came to this town to see an anomaly, you've found it."

Blake couldn't help but peek over. The sleeves of his red plaid shirt were rolled up to his elbows. As he'd suggested, where the usual magical ink should have been, his muscular arm was bare. She tried to hide her surprise and turned her attention back to her drink.

The men in the back roared out in fresh laughter. A fresh surge of panic seized her. She took a couple deep breaths and tried to settle herself. The barkeep was behind the counter again, and Blake chose to believe this woman could manage the drunken men. She was frustrated that the numbness had worn off and wondered if she should leave.

At that very moment, one of the dartboard men started walking toward her. She felt every hair on her arms and neck rise as she held her breath, ready to smash his face with her cup and make a mad dash. His arm brushed hers as he struggled onto the stool to her other side. She couldn't help but shy away.

The man with dark, curly hair laughed. "Little skittish, doll? Don't worry. I don't mean you any harm. Eh, Sandra!" he called over to the barkeep. "Why your bar always be bringin' in the shy, depressed type? Can't you find us some people who want to have a good time? Bring in the ladies ready to drop their knickers!" His laughter boomed at his own joke as he draped his arm over Blake's shoulders.

Blake's strength fled her. Her face flushed a deep red and she bolted for the door, not pausing as the bartender called out. But even in her fear, her heart fluttered with a small triumph as the door swung shut.

I didn't freeze.

Blake broke out onto the street and welcomed the cool evening air as it hit her square in the face. She leaned over, hands on her knees for a moment, and tried to catch her breath. Her heart raced and sweat trickled between her shoulder blades. Her eyes watered as she fought down her anger at herself for fleeing. *I can do better than this. I need to do better than this.*

Blake chastised herself for leaving without paying, but she couldn't bring herself to go back in now. She squared her shoulders and turned toward the motel down the street. She hated that she'd been spooked so easy. The man probably hadn't meant her any harm, but that didn't stop her from seeing drunk rapists everywhere. Anyone could change after a few drinks. Blake shuddered.

She hadn't gotten ten feet when she heard the bar door slam open behind her. She whipped around, anxious the drunken man had followed her. Blake was flooded with relief to see the handsome, compass-less guy coming out behind her instead.

"I'm sorry." She cleared her throat. "I swear I'll come back and pay my tab in the morning." She stood frozen on the opposite street corner and watched the young man walk up to her.

"It's no biggie. I left some extra cash to cover yours too."

When she looked into his eyes, she didn't catch any judgment. Instead, a deep and familiar melancholy reflected back at her in his wide-set, amber eyes. As she had guessed in the bar, he was young—probably early twenties—but the natural seriousness of his face aged him. He held out his arm to gesture for her to walk with him, but she refused. She turned to walk herself back to the motel. He kept pace with her.

"Are you staying at the motel too?" she asked. Her fingers clenched the leather jacket slung over her arm.

"Naw. But I can't imagine you'd be staying elsewhere. I've lived here for ages and I've never seen your face. Figured I'd walk you back in case any of those guys came and hassled you any more."

Blake wasn't sure how to feel. Though it was endearing that he wanted to protect her, she was annoyed that he didn't think she could manage herself. The walk down the mountain town main street was brief. Before anything more could be said, the dusty glass of the motel doors swung before them. Blake paused, unsure how to dismiss the boy.

"Ya know…" He shifted from foot to foot. "If you wanted more Jack, I've got a bottle at my house. It's not far, and I can guarantee it'll be quieter than that old bar. Just if you wanted to stay out later. No pressure, though."

Blake looked at the aged motel. The neon vacancy sign flickered in the setting sun. She knew she wasn't drunk enough to sleep yet, and if she did, she was sure she'd have nightmares. She assumed that if this man knew where to find her, it wouldn't be hard for the drunken men to find her either. Was there such a thing as anywhere safe anymore? Blake considered the feeble amount of cash that she had left and weighed the risks. Could she afford to turn away free alcohol and the possibility of another wallet to snatch?

"Jack would be nice." Blake pressed her lips into a thin smile. This time, when the young man offered his arm, she forced herself to take it.

I am in perfect control. Just relax and he'll trust you.

She was conscious to keep a bit of added space between them.

CHAPTER XXXI

GARETH

Gareth woke with a jump as his phone alarm blared beside him. Despite being a morning person, he still found 4:00 a.m. way too early. Sebastian groaned, mumbling from his pile of blankets on the floor. Gareth squinted against the bright phone screen as he tried to hit the off button. Though it was still dark, his heart rate rose in excitement. The day had finally come. He got up, tripping over his best friend as he made his way to turn on the lights. Sebastian pulled the blankets over his head in protest.

"Come on, mate," Gareth said, nudging where he believed Sebastian's legs would be. He guessed the muttering that came next was supposed to be curses, but he wasn't too worried. He grabbed his phone charger and threw it into his prepacked bag.

"Let's go. My dad'll have a stroke if he thinks we're gonna miss the flight. And I need to get my room tidy for the new kid, which is hard to do when you're on the floor."

Sebastian groaned more, but finally started moving. As the boys folded up the extra blankets, Elise came into the bedroom.

"Oh, thank the stars you're both up. Here I was worried I would have to haul you down to the car myself. Can you take your luggage downstairs so your dad can load the car?"

"Where do you want these, Mrs. Williams?" Sebastian asked with the roughly folded blankets in his arms.

"I'll take those," she said, putting her tea down on Gareth's dresser. "Oh! You finally got your compass!"

Gareth couldn't help but pause, and Sebastian's face contorted.

Gareth's mum brushed Sebastian's cheek. "Congratulations, Seb. You must be thrilled. Now, go brush your hair or else I'll braid it back myself." She gathered the blankets up and took them downstairs.

Sebastian busied himself with his bags, so Gareth turned back to his own suitcase. Sebastian didn't seem surprised to have his compass, so he must have already known. *But why would he hide it from me? Unless—*

Gareth's mom's voice rang through the house from the kitchen. "Emmet, leave your brother alone! Has anyone seen my tea?"

Spying his mum's mug, Gareth grabbed it and his luggage and headed down, consciously giving Sebastian some space.

Downstairs, Kenyon paced around the main floor muttering as

he fingered the passports, lost in his thoughts.

"Ah, there it is." Gareth's mother swooped in for her missing tea, pecking his cheek with a quick kiss before turning back to the two grumbling boys.

"Did you make your beds like I asked?"

Addi and Emmet groaned a choir of yeses that Gareth was sure were lies.

"Honey, we don't have time to worry about their rooms. We should already be out the door." Gareth's dad looked around the room. "Where's Sebastian?"

On cue, he stumbled down the stairs, his puffy backpack in one hand and his suitcase in the other. "I'm here and I'm ready."

Gareth's mum frowned. "Not with that hair you're not."

"It's fine, Mrs. Williams. It'll get messy again anyway."

At last, they all stumbled out to the car, luggage in hand. Gareth was relieved to be on their way. The four boys all squeezed in together in the back seat, grateful the drive to the subway was short.

"Wonder how Dakota and Liam are gonna feel when they've got to get all cozy in the back with these idiots," Gareth said, nudging Sebastian. "Maybe Mum and Dad will put Addi in the trunk on the way back." Sebastian gave a half-hearted smile without looking over, while Gareth's youngest brother glared up at him.

Gareth settled back, accepting that none of his companions were nearly as thrilled as he was. He put on his headphones, happy to spend the time in his own bubble of excitement.

The express train to the airport was short, and soon they filed out and gathered their things. They made their way to the designated meeting point, watchful for their company. Their coach had committed to seeing them off as a group. Over the next quarter hour, the coach and the few other boys from their club joined with their families.

"Here I was hoping he would miss the flight," Gareth said as he spied Damien sauntering down the hall beside his father.

Gareth couldn't understand why Sebastian's parents hadn't wanted to come, but he hadn't asked. It seemed awkward that his parents wouldn't bring back Liam, let alone not come to see Sebastian off. Elise hadn't blinked an eye, though. As if he could read Gareth's mind, Sebastian turned to his Elise.

"Hey, Mrs. Williams? Would you mind maybe checking in on my exchange partner over the month? I'm sure everything will be fine... I just... He might like company is all."

Elise smiled. "Of course we can. I'm sure your parents are more than prepared to host him, but I can reach out and see if they want to do any sightseeing as a group. The new boys will probably be grateful to spend more time together."

Relief cast over Sebastian's face as he sank back down beside his suitcase.

When the time came to head through security, the team coach made a quick speech about opportunities, responsibilities, and respect that Gareth couldn't help but tune out. Then they were hustled on their way, saying hurried farewells. They crushed

Gareth and Sebastian in hugs and Elise kissed both their cheeks, reminding them to text when they landed.

In the line for security, Gareth bounced on the balls of his feet. Sebastian's hair hung in his eyes as he moped forward. When their turn came, Gareth made his way through without incident. It wasn't until he looked back and saw Sebastian arguing with an officer that he realized anything was amiss. Gareth made his way back to see what the commotion was about.

"Come on," Sebastian whined, "this is bollocks!"

The officer didn't look impressed. "Rules are rules, son. It may not be lethal, but if the air pressure dropped and it popped, it could cause alarm."

Sebastian slouched in a designated chair as the officer took his bag to security.

"You pack a bomb or something?" Gareth smirked as he sat beside him.

"Shh!" Sebastian glared at him. "Don't make this worse than it already is. We're at an airport. You can't make jokes like that."

Gareth threw his arms up in surrender. Bomb jokes probably weren't the best while they were still in security. Sebastian rubbed his temples and groaned.

"I brought my favorite ball for good luck. I didn't want to pack it in my luggage in case it got crushed or flattened. But now they want to detain it as a potential threat."

Gareth could hardly suppress his laughter. "That's what you had in that bag? Here I thought you stuffed a sleeping bag in there."

Sebastian let out a sigh. "Yeah. So instead of confiscating it, they need to deflate it."

Gareth smiled as he leaned back in the chair. They were still early enough that he wasn't worried about missing their flight. "Well, you may be daft, but I forgive you. We'll find a pump on the other side. Just don't do the same thing on the way back, okay?"

Sebastian sank his head in his hands. Gareth put his earbuds back in, indifferent about where they had to wait. This trip was going to be great, even if his best friend was miserable. He knew eventually he would cheer Sebastian up anyway.

CHAPTER XXXII

BLAKE

The scent of sawdust clung to her stranger as he led her down an unfamiliar gravel road. The fresh, woody fragrance was so different from that of the boys and girls back home, who reeked of weed and alcohol. Blake's palm inadvertently tightened around his flannel-covered bicep before she shook herself and forced herself to widen the gap again.

So he smells nice and he's got great muscles. That's no reason to lose your head. Eye on the prize.

They walked in silence until they came to a small off-white trailer. The grass was cut, but the landscape lacked any decor. There were shovels and tools leaned up against the side of the yellowing walls, and an old, dusty-blue truck parked to the side.

The man pulled out an old lawn chair, faded from the sun with a few holes in the back, then disappeared into the trailer.

He came back and handed her the large bottle that sloshed with golden liquid. When she took it and settled on the chair, he rolled over a tree stump to her side. Not too close that it made her nervous, but close enough that they could easily hand the bottle back and forth.

"Sorry I don't have any clean glasses. Hope you don't mind drinkin' from the bottle."

She didn't mind. She twisted the top off and looked out over the evergreen foothills that met the darkening sky, pretending not to notice his silhouette in her peripheral. Overall, he wasn't a man that would stand out in a crowd. But the way his tousled, brown hair curled against his summer-bronzed skin, she would have to be blind not to see his natural charm. How could someone look both so innocent, yet so worn? She felt drawn to him and she wondered if it was because he was like her. Lonely, quiet, and drifting through the world carrying an unseen weight.

"So, do you live here by yourself?" she asked.

"Yep. My parents live down the road, but this old place is mine alone," he replied, content to avoid eye contact.

Blake tried to imagine what it would be like to live in the mountains, tucked away from screeching cars, foul-smelling streets, and rat-infested subways. Despite it once being home, she knew she never wanted to go back to that city. She breathed in the crisp, clean air.

"I once heard a story of a man who got a fake compass tattoo."

His forehead scrunched together but he didn't say anything in return.

"They're the hardest kind of tattoo to draw. Capturing the tiny script around the edges and the magic is impossible. I would have loved to have seen how his turned out and compared it to my attempts."

"You've tried?" he asked. Happy she'd piqued his curiosity, a genuine smile crept onto her face.

"Yeah, back when I lived in New York I worked as an apprentice and I—"

She didn't remember when he handed her back the bottle, but when she came to, it was there, locked in her viselike grip. She knocked it back and took an extra-large mouthful of the burning reprieve. The silence felt heavy until his low voice broke it.

"Growing up without a compass was hard. I always felt like something was wrong with me. Now I'm just convinced the Fates have it out for me and destined me for the lone wolf life, just cuttin' trees and drinkin'."

She was happy he struck up the conversation again. She liked the deep hum of his voice.

"How are you sure you won't get it, eventually?"

"Ya know, there's a lot I don't know or understand about the world. But I always knew it wasn't going to come. Even when I hoped for it, it seemed pointless. It's like my gut knew what my heart didn't."

Blake leaned back in her chair and crossed her ankles. She handed the bottle back. "I always wished I could get rid of mine. I hate the idea that there's someone out there dictating my path. I don't want to be in love because some stupid tattoo told me to. This horrible cover-up was worth it."

He peeked over, curiosity bright in his soft eyes. "It can't be that bad."

She laughed and held out her arm.

"Would you mind if I touched it?"

She blushed but nodded. His thumb was soft as he traced over the surface of her massacred compass. The hairs on her forearm stood up at the gentle touch, and she had to resist the urge to pull away. He paused and looked up at her, then dropped her wrist.

"Sorry... That was probably weird. I was just curious." He shifted back onto his log and pressed the bottle of whiskey to his lips.

"It's okay. I told you it was bad." She chuckled. It was a foreign feeling after so many days of avoiding people. "Can I see where yours would have been?"

He looked back at her, surprised, then held out his left forearm for her to inspect. It was perfectly smooth. She ran her hand over where the metallic brand should have been and marveled at his tanned skin. She couldn't imagine ruining it with such a stupid tattoo. As she took in the moment, she realized there was something else this man might provide her with—other than alcohol and eventually his wallet.

"Honestly, I like it. It's refreshing. It's like you're free of the games the stars play with us. You're able to make your destiny anything you'd like." She spoke softly and drew the tips of her fingers away from his arm slowly. She looked up and let her gaze linger on his full lips.

"I've never heard someone put it that way before." His low voice was quieter than before, his eyes hooded as he mirrored her gaze.

She knew at that moment he wanted to kiss her. He reached his hand toward her face and shuffled closer.

This is it. The perfect opportunity to test the waters. Blake tightened her grip on the creaky chair as she leaned in to meet his kiss. All at once, the scent of mixed beer and whiskey crept through her nostrils and her throat tightened in response. Against her will, Blake froze.

He must have heard her sudden intake of breath because the centimeters between his lips and hers didn't close. His dark eyelashes blinked up at her and he met her gaze with speculation. He promptly leaned back. "I... I'm sorry. I swear that's not why I brought you back here. I just... I shouldn't have assumed..." His cheeks flushed a deep scarlet as he brought the bottle of Jack back to his mouth.

Blake's nails clawed at the arms of her chair. She was so tired of feeling out of control. Taking a deep breath, she reached out to his face with soft hands. She forced herself through her instinct to run and felt him freeze under her touch. He didn't meet her eyes but let her guide his chin back to face her. Blake held her breath. She leaned in and let her sunburned lips graze his, the flare of pain bright beside her instinct to run. His firm, bowed lips softened in response. He leaned closer.

The bottle of whiskey toppled to the ground. Her chair groaned as she leaned against the plastic arm between them. She ignored the threatening scents as his lips parted and she sank into his kiss. She put all of her attention on the moment and his softness which beaconed to her like a lighthouse. A safe haven from her own darkness. *I've got this.* Blake left her unreliable chair for his lap and his arm wrapped around her waist.

Blake's head spun at the rush as the kisses deepened. The burn and rush were much more gratifying than the whiskey. He kept his lips pressed against hers as he scooped up her legs and carried her to the trailer. How he opened the door and fit them both through at the same time was beyond her, but at the moment she couldn't care less. Her heart rate was erratic and for every moment that she won over the urge to run, she felt unstoppable. He carried her in the dark and set her on his bed. She shrugged her jacket off to the floor. His hand grasped her hair, and she inadvertently flinched.

He paused and pulled back.

"Only whatever you want, okay? I meant what I said, and I'm not going to push you if you're not into this."

Blake breathed out in relief, grateful for the moment to recompose herself. She drew his face back to hers, desire and adrenaline hot in her veins. She traced her hands down his muscle-bound back, over the waistband of his jeans, and her fingers met the flat edge of his back pocket. *Right. Wallet. Remember what we came for.* His shoulders softened, and he leaned in to kiss her again. Blake sighed. *Yeah, I'll deal with that later.* Gravity tugged their bodies to the bed as their kisses grew fevered. He relaxed his sturdy weight over the length of her body. Again, Blake froze.

"Is this okay? What do you need?" His voice brought her back. He moved up and away from her. "I mean it. If you don't want anything more than this, we can stop. Honestly, even just kissing you is a gift."

Blake closed her eyes and pressed her forehead against his, her fingertips gentle on his cheek.

"I'm sorry," she whispered. She willed her heart to slow. "I don't know what's going on. At least, I don't know how to explain." Blake's mind grasped in vain as she tried to put words to her inexplicable fear. "I really want this. It's just, I don't want to feel trapped. Would you… Could I actually be on top?" Her gaze leveled with his warm eyes for an instant, then dropped to her bony fingers in his hands. "I just feel like if I was in control, I'd be able to relax."

His warm hands closed around her own. "Are you sure you want this?"

She nodded, letting her eyes flash up to him with her honest desire. "I can't tell you how much I need this."

He smiled and scooped her up onto his lap. Her knees sank into the bed on either side of his hips and Blake sat up tall. Nothing would ruin this moment. Her dark blue hair parted in two sheets of curtains as she tilted her chin back down to meet him.

The heat in her belly rose. Her hands carved over his chest, and he met every one of her kisses with a deep-seated hunger. She peeled off her shirt, and his red plaid one found its way to the floor beside hers. They pulled their bodies tight together in the darkness. Blake's breath hitched in anticipation when he shifted to the clasp of her bra.

He slowed instantly. "Is this okay?"

She murmured a soft *mm-hmm* into his neck. She was determined to have more. Blake couldn't remember the last time she felt more alive. It took him several attempts to undo the clasp. First, he tried with one hand, and then with both. She let him struggle for a moment before she reached behind her own back and undid her bra. She tried not to smirk.

Blake stretched out flush beside him and relished in the warmth of his torso against hers. His calloused but gentle hand traced down the side of her ribs, then along the edge of her waistband to the button. All at once, the reins of control and power slid through her hands. Before she could still his hand as it neared her zipper, Blake shuddered and was swallowed into a blackness like never before.

CHAPTER XXXIII

NESSIE

Nessie carefully powdered soft pink glitter on the crests of Lacey's cheekbones.

"A bit of shimmer everywhere the sun would kiss, if there was any sun today…" She trailed off and leaned back. Nessie assessed her workmanship, then her face split into a satisfied grin. Lacey sat still and tall on the hotel bathroom counter and waited for the judgment. Her black hair hung in long satin sheets, and her wide, liner-traced eyes sparkled with hope.

"You look as stunning as Venus," Nessie sang, her dimples sharp as she smiled. "Okay, finishing touches." She traced her fingers over the cosmetics that spilled over the counter. "I'm thinking we skip any lipstick, you're lucky to have naturally dark lips anyway, and pick something sweet instead. Then you won't need to worry about staining your soulmate in poison."

"You're the boss. If I had to put on my own makeup today, it'd be a mess." Lacey wrung her hands in her lap.

"Stop fidgeting." Nessie puckered her own lips in a wordless command for Lacey to do the same, then dabbed Lacey's lips with cherry-flavored lip chap. She stepped back and took one last look over her work. "And voilà!"

Lacey turned to the mirror and broke into a grin. "Aww, Ness. It's the perfect balance of 'I tried to look hot today' and 'low-key cute.' What would I do without you?"

Nessie beamed and handed the lip gloss to Lacey, then did a quick once-over of herself. She hadn't put nearly as much effort into her own look today. Lacey looking hot was the undeniable priority. Nessie swept her limp blond hair into a ponytail, then added a red headband as a subtle Canada Day touch. She rarely wore red, convinced it only highlighted her skin's flaws.

A quiet knock on the bathroom door turned both their heads, and Renee peeked around the door-frame. "I can't believe you're both ready to go already. On the best of days, I can't get Lacey out of bed before eleven, let alone ready and out the door."

Renee's brown hair lay flat on one side, ruffled in waves on the other, and she held a steaming cup to her chest.

"The parade starts at eleven and we didn't want to miss it," Lacey explained. Nessie busied herself and packed a to-go bag of makeup for touch-ups. *Straight face, Ness. Just keep busy.*

"I can't remember the last time I went to a parade," Renee hummed.

Lacey unleashed a torrent of hairspray. "Think of how nice your guys' morning is going to be, though. You don't have to go out in the rain. You won't have to fight through crowds of people. And you didn't have to be up and ready by eleven."

What I would give to look calm and collected under pressure. In Nessie's peripheral, Lacey leaned over and gave Renee a quick peck on the cheek. "I love you, Mom."

The expression on Renee's face was unreadable, but Nessie didn't try to figure it out. She'd made it this far without giving away the lie. Now they just had to get out the door. She followed Lacey out of the bathroom and spied her own mom still curled up in the pristine white hotel blankets.

Charity peeked up from her book. "You two sure you're good to go alone? You're not worried you'll get lost?"

Lacey gave her famous winning smile. "We'll be fine. Worst case, we all know my mom can find me."

Nessie offered an encouraging smile, opting not to speak and possibly ruin everything when they were so close to pulling it off.

"I promise we'll be safe." Lacey grabbed for her purse.

"And that you'll be back by one o'clock?" Renee added. An edge of sharpness hovered over the warning.

"Yes, Mom." Lacey glanced over to Nessie as she stuffed her feet into her ankle-high boots. Lacey met her eyes with a clear stare of, *let's get out of here before they change their minds.*

"One o'clock sharp, the hotel room, back right after lunch," Nessie rattled off the rules as she slid her faded jean jacket on. She pulled her ponytail from the collar and tried to look relaxed.

Renee's face fell into a frown. Lacey rushed over and crushed her in a hug. "Mom, it's cool. This isn't some kidnapping movie plot. We're going to go check out the parade, go for lunch, and then we'll be back. We'll be gone for two hours tops."

"I'm not sure how I'm supposed to relax and enjoy the morning when you're both off wandering a new city."

Charity chimed in. "Renee, it'll be fine. Let the girls go. Besides, there's something I've been wanting to talk to you about."

Nessie tilted her chin, suddenly interested and less eager to leave. What could her mom want to talk about in private? They never kept secrets from one another. If Lacey noticed, she didn't act like it. She beelined for the door before Renee could change her mind and looped her arm in Nessie's.

"I know you'll always know where to find me. I love you and you're the best," she called out as she hauled Nessie out the door.

"Love you and see you soon!" Nessie called before the heavy hotel door slammed shut. Lacey's face broke into a wild grin as they skipped off to meet the Montreal streets.

The girls waded into the Friday-morning crowd arm in arm, excited to get a better look at the French city's allure. Despite the morning dew and impending rain, lots of people milled around the patios that stretched into the street. Nearby, a busker's low and melancholy voice hummed a cover of a familiar song that Nessie couldn't place. His rich voice echoed off the cobblestones of the beautiful, aged street. She sighed; the hardest part of the trip was finally over.

As easy as it would have been, Nessie didn't let herself settle into the gentle buzz of the city. There was still work to do. She opened up her phone map to coordinate it with Lacey's compass. It still pointed east, subtly tipping north. Nessie was sure the direction should have changed by now, but Lacey seemed confident they were closer than before. So Nessie committed to her role of precious navigator and cross-referenced the parade route with Lacey's compass.

"Okay. If the parade starts at eleven, and your compass-clock is 12:09, we have some time to kill. We can go toward the end of the parade and hang out there until the time is right. Then you'll meet, you two can schmooze and have lunch, I'll lie low, and then we'll all go back together."

Lacey pulled Nessie's arm tight to her own. "You really don't mind? I feel bad."

Nessie waved her hand. "Oh. I'll be fine. I just expect a trophy afterward that says, *Best wing woman of life*, and your promise not to outright abandon me when all your life dreams start coming true."

Lacey stopped and took both of Nessie's hands, her lips in a wide smile. "Done and done."

Nessie squeezed back, then spun Lacey out in a twirl. Lacey laughed, her excitement and happiness undeniable. Arm in arm, they continued their walk down the cobblestone streets.

The walk to where the parade would end was only a few blocks, but Nessie was sure it felt even longer for Lacey. They wove through the growing crowd and dodged the children that scampered over their feet. Lacey frequently shot disapproving looks up at the sky.

Nessie smirked. "Don't worry about the rain. It's all going to work out. You could be wearing a paper bag, drenched, barefoot, and covered in mud, and your soulmate would still be obsessed with you."

Lacey dropped her gaze from the sky. "Sometimes you're like Jimmy Cricket, reading my mind. You always know what to say."

"Don't you mean Jiminy?" Nessie laughed.

Lacey's forehead creased. "What? I thought it was for sure Jimmy."

"Yeah, no. Definitely Ji-mi-ny." Nessie laughed. "Good try, though. Besides, someone has to be your conscience. Who knows what trouble you would get in without me?"

"You will forever be the logic to my wild side, and I, the chaos to your plans." Lacey's eyes twinkled in promised mischief, and Nessie couldn't help but laugh louder.

Soon enough, the parade caught up to them, but Lacey showed no signs of wanting to watch. They pressed on behind the spectators and made their way off Ste.-Catherine toward Place du Canada. Any wishes they had that the rain would hold off were soon squandered. The crowd started popping up umbrellas left and right as the sky let its first drops loose. When the rain started to fall a little harder, the girls both ducked under a nearby patio awning. They were close to the end of the designated parade area, and Lacey confirmed that her compass still pointed in the same direction.

"Why don't we hang out here until the end of the parade? Then we can continue on if they don't show up themselves," Nessie suggested. Her mind scrounged to come up with a way this was going to work out as the clock ticked closer to noon.

Lacey bit her lip and gazed out at the wet floats against the lush green park backdrop. "Okay."

She clearly didn't like the idea, but Nessie assumed she didn't want to risk getting more wet than necessary. They settled at a table and ordered some fresh pastries. Lacey ordered a coffee that Nessie was sure would only add to her fidgeting, but she didn't say anything. Instead, she melted over her chocolate-almond croissant. She savored the buttery chocolate goodness as it coated her tongue. *I could stay here and eat croissants forever.*

After the parade ended, time ground to a halt. Every minute dragged on, and multiple times Lacey opened her mouth but closed it without sharing whatever thoughts plagued her mind.

Nessie checked the time on her phone for what seemed like the thousandth time. Noon ticked by and the rain slowed. The pastry shop was getting busy as the lunch hour drew on, so the girls bailed into the mist of rain.

"Okay. I've got less than ten minutes until my life changes forever. Any last words of wisdom, Jimmy?"

Nessie smiled at the intentional mistake as she fretted with Lacey's hair. "Don't say anything stupid. Try not to look disappointed if he isn't hot, and don't eat all your lip gloss off before you see him."

Lacey immediately stopped chewing her lip. "Mmkay. I've got this."

They crossed the street toward the park. Nessie scoured her phone map, trying to figure out where Lacey's soulmate might be. Bonaventure train station stood bright on the map and drew Nessie's attention.

"Lace. How close does your soulmate feel?"

Lacey glanced her way, a touch of accusation in her eyes. "Closer all the time. Why?"

"Why don't we head to the train station? It's public, safe, and it'll be easy for him to find you if he's meeting you halfway. He could literally be on the train, on his way to you now."

Lacey nodded, though Nessie could see she wanted to keep walking. The waiting was killing her. They trekked a little off track to the train station and Nessie did her best to reassure her that train stations were romantic too.

"It's out of the rain. Huge bonus!"

Lacey didn't respond. Nessie fell into a mirrored silence and they found a wall to lean on. People rushed around them, and the only view of interest was a large map of the railway lines. When the clock finally ticked past 12:09, Lacey's mood tanked.

"I knew we shouldn't have come here. We should have kept

walking." She crossed her arms tight. Her lips fell into a pout as she glared at the cement floor.

"Lace, that's not true." Nessie frowned. "Your clock says 12:09. That means you're at least twelve hours away from meeting him now again. No matter how far we walked, it wouldn't have been enough."

Lacey sighed theatrically, but Nessie knew she couldn't argue with her logic. Nessie tightened her ponytail and listened to the hum of French people milling around them. *I should have learned French.*

"Well. If it's at least twelve hours, I know what we have to do." Lacey struck off toward the map and ticket booth. Nessie felt a surge of panic as she jolted after her.

"What do you mean?"

"If he's twelve hours away, we'll make it easy and close the gap. We'll keep heading east."

"I thought you said he was close?"

Lacey waved her hand in the air in an unconcerned gesture. "He is close, just not close enough. We're heading in the right direction and that's all that matters." Lacey paused at the map.

Nessie took Lacey's wrist in her palm to slow her from buying the ticket. "Lacey, think. He's twelve hours away. So, we get on a train and head there. You think our moms are going to be okay with us running off? It would be midnight before he might, and I emphasize *might*, meet us."

"Midnight on Canada Day would be the most romantic scenario.

Montreal, Quebec—what's the difference?" Lacey's finger traced over the map. Nessie understood immediately that Lacey would do anything to make this happen.

"Lace, listen to yourself. We can't get on that train. We have next to no money, no clothes, no chargers, no plan, nowhere to stay." But every rational reason that Nessie could find crumpled at the force field of Lacey's will.

"So, what? I'm supposed to wait for him to come to me?"

Nessie reached for Lacey's hands, but she pulled away. "No. Well, maybe. Or maybe we plan another trip for another weekend. We know Montreal isn't far enough now, but we're already here. Why don't we enjoy the weekend while we can? Find some wild reason to try Quebec City another time." Nessie had hardly needed to look at the map to know that was the next northeastern city, which Lacey had clearly figured out too.

"How am I supposed to enjoy this weekend? It's raining. It's cold. We're stuck with our moms. What part of this is fun to you?"

Nessie paused. Was this really not fun to her? Swallowing against the growing lump in her throat, she tried another stream of logic. "What's going to happen if you do find your soulmate tonight? You'll be grounded for the rest of summer. You know your mom is going to lose it if you leave."

"You?" she asked.

"What?"

"You said 'you.' Like you're not coming with me." Lacey's mood went from angry to deadly in a second.

"Lace. You can't seriously think I'm getting on that train with you, let alone letting you get on. You never think things through."

"Well, neither do you!" she spat. "You think you're so smart and that you think of everything, but have you ever thought of what's going to happen to you when I find my soulmate? When I have someone to spend time with other than you?"

Nessie froze.

"Nothing. That's what's going to happen. You're probably going to be all alone, just like your mom."

Nessie's eyes swam as she tried to catch her breath. "You don't mean that."

"Tell me I'm wrong," Lacey challenged. "Tell me you haven't thought about it yourself. You're a loner, Ness, just like I was. But I refuse to go back to that life. I have a soulmate out there and my happiness is waiting for me. If you were a real friend, you wouldn't be holding me back."

Lacey jabbed the computer screen with her thumb. Nessie grappled for a response, but her mind spun as Lacey's words brought her subconscious fears to light.

The ticket printed, and Lacey flipped her long black hair over her shoulder. "I don't even know why I brought you along. I should have known you would only hold me back."

CHAPTER XXXIV

BLAKE

When Blake came to, she was in the fetal position. She blinked, not quite registering what had happened. When had she been crying? Her face was feverish and damp with tears. In the dark, the young-faced man sat beside her. His eyes were hooded with concern. Tears filled her eyes again as she crossed her arms over her bare chest. It was one thing to disappear for a moment, but she could tell this episode had been much longer and different from her pauses before. The stranger shifted to lie in front of her and mirrored her position without bringing up his knees. He pushed the pillows back and took her hands.

"I… I'm so sorry," she whispered.

"No, no. Please don't apologize. I'm sorry. I didn't know…" His apology seeped with guilt. He held her hands tight and kept his eyes cast down.

"You shouldn't be the one apologizing." Blake tried to swallow through the phlegm. "I feel humiliated. If I had known this would happen I would have never…" She trailed off, her breaths sharp and rapid.

"It's okay. Really. You don't need to apologize. I just wish I noticed and stopped before we got that far. I should have known better. I'm sorry I pushed you into it." He leaned in and pressed soft kisses on her knuckles. It had only been a moment since she'd gotten her tears under control, but now they pooled anew. She moved to fill the space between them, desperate to feel less exposed. She buried her head against the soft curls of his chest hair as she cried, and he wrapped his arms around her head and upper body, his grip grounded and tight. There in the dark, held in a stranger's arms, Blake cried herself to sleep.

When she woke a few hours later, she was shocked she had slept. It could have been a dream turned nightmare, but she didn't have to open her eyes to feel his arms still around her. The morning dusk trickled light into the unfamiliar bedroom. She unraveled herself from her snoring protector, careful not to wake him. She wrestled her shirt over her head, then peeked back. The man lay on his stomach. His bare back rose and fell steadily with his breath, and there on a platter before her, his wallet peeked out of his back pocket.

For once, Blake hesitated. *It's just a wallet.* But for whatever reason, she couldn't bring herself to take it. She didn't even know his name, and yet he had seen almost every part of her: the scared, the brave, the weak. She forced herself to leave the bedroom before she could change her mind.

Blake made her way through the trailer, the morning sun giving her the first glimmer of her surroundings. The trailer wasn't outright dirty, but it was well lived-in. Countertops were lined with empty beer cans ready to be taken out, and the sink was filled with dishes. A basket of clothes sat on the couch, and traces of crumbs flecked the table.

Blake found the bathroom on the opposite end of the trailer. As she stared at her puffy and swollen eyes in the speckled mirror, memories of the night played over in her head. His lips on her, his brawny arms as they carried her in, the muscles of his bare chest under her nails. Her cheeks flushed, and she turned away from her reflection. Besides a razor, deodorant, and men's body wash, the bathroom was remarkably bare.

Blake cranked the shower faucet and cringed at the noise it made as the water sputtered on. She locked the door, stripped down, and showered as fast as she could. She dried off with the only towel in the room, then combed her fingers through her limp and knotted blue hair.

Why am I doing this? It's not like it matters. Blake abandoned the damp mess and pulled her clothes back on. She braced herself for the awkwardness that was bound to come. *Too bad there's no whiskey now.*

Blake came out of the bathroom to the smell of coffee. The crumbs on the table had been wiped up, the laundry basket gone. He'd clearly tried to clean up in the limited window she'd given him. The young man turned to her with a lopsided smile she hadn't seen before, and she felt her insides do a miniature swoon. *Stop that. He's not some knight in shining armor. So what if he rocks the dark and brooding type but is also infinitely kind and handsome... That's not what we came here for. Get your head together.*

"Coffee?" he asked.

She didn't have to fake her smile. "Please."

She sat at the kitchen table, sliding down the bench until she was beside the window. He handed her a cup then sat opposite to her. They slipped into a surprisingly comfortable silence. She liked that he was okay with the quiet; it made it easier for her to relax. Her eyes traced around the room. *A carved walking stick? That'd be helpful, but tricky to get away with. That hunting knife, though...*

"You know, my dad had PTSD from his time with the army," he said, distracting her from her mental inventory. He stared into his cup, his face a set of serious lines once again.

"I, um—what?" she asked.

"He used to have flashes back to the fighting. It took a while to figure out what was happening. Gunshots were a fast and obvious problem, then thunderstorms and fireworks. But it seemed no matter how careful we were about making loud noises, he'd still have episodes. Sometimes it'd be a joke someone said, other times just a dog barking. Sometimes we'd find him staring off into space, holding a hose and watering the dirt, as if he forgot he was watering anything at all."

Blake didn't know what to say. She watched the crest of his lips while he talked and cherished the hum of his low voice.

"Momma fought with him for years to see a shrink, but he lost himself to the bottle every night instead. I often wonder how different my life would have been if he had gotten help." His hands wrung his coffee cup.

Blake considered his story and pictured his childhood life. A father prone to breakdowns and spacing out. Isolated, alone in the mountains. The clash of parents and alcohol and shrinks. She knew that part too well. She could only imagine there was more to the story than he shared, but she chose not to push him. Instead, she took another sip of her coffee.

"You think I have PTSD?" she questioned, unsure if she'd interpreted the story right.

"Well, I'm no doctor, but I see the way you stare sometimes. Drop off midsentence, freeze in the middle of a move. Like you lose yourself and don't know how to come back. Reminds me of my dad is all." He peeked over at her before looking out the window. "It's not a bad thing. I just wanted to say something so you knew I understood. It's 'cause of that I feel like last night was my fault. I should've known better than to push you. I was so wrapped up and…" His cheeks flushed.

Blake reached across the table and took one of his hands. "Listen. Last night wasn't your fault. Neither of us could have known. It came on so fast. I... I didn't actually know what was happening to me. I've never had an attack that bad before." She thought back to the moments she'd frozen before. Though awkward, they'd all been relatively short. Last night, she felt like she'd disappeared somewhere far darker and deeper than before.

"I'm just sorry I was the one to cause it. Maybe this is why I don't have a compass. I can't even make love right."

Blake clenched her fist. She put her cup down and crossed over to his side of the bench. She took his face in her hands so he couldn't look away. His amber eyes stared wide into hers.

"You are not a bad lover, okay?" She held his face tighter when he tried to drop his gaze. "You are generous and kind. You are respectful and every bit of a gentleman. Don't let my issues make you think poorly of yourself." She realized how tight she was holding him and softened her hands. "You're one of the most wonderful people I've ever met and to be honest, I can't imagine what it would have been like if it had happened with anyone other than you."

Before she could overthink it, she leaned in and kissed his forehead. His forehead creased and he risked a glance up. He moved slowly, drawing her into his arms, and his warm mouth found hers again. The intensity from the night before wasn't there. Instead the kiss was soft, a blend of apologies and thank-yous, graceful and not urgent.

When he pulled away, his cheeks were flushed. "I noticed you already showered. You don't mind if I step away and do the same for a few minutes, do you?"

"Go ahead." Her heart rattled in her rib cage.

He grinned and pressed a soft kiss to her forehead, then disappeared into the bathroom.

As soon as she heard the water kick on, she put her cup down. She was not staying. She couldn't. She'd already been here too long. Under the sink, she found a grocery bag filled with other plastic bags. As quietly but quickly as possible, she ransacked the fridge first, packing the bag full of what deli meat and cheeses he had. She plopped a whole loaf of bread in after. Scrambling through the cabinets, she found some granola bars and took those too.

Honestly, this is probably even better than his wallet.

She retrieved her black leather jacket from the bedroom floor and then headed to the door. She considered the walking stick resting against the corner. Her fingers lingered on the knotted wood, then left it. Instead, she grabbed the pocketknife she'd spied earlier. She wondered if she should leave a note but couldn't bring herself to. Who knew how much time she had left, and she needed to get as far away from here as possible before he finished. She swung the trailer door shut behind her and gazed out at the rising sun. The plastic bags hung heavy in her hands as she made her way back to the motel to get the things she'd left there. With a new spring in her step, Blake took off and didn't look back.

CHAPTER XXXV

Jaylynn sat in familiar silence at her parents' dinner table. She prodded at the stew with her spoon, her mind miles away. It had been days since she'd last been at the cabin, and her options weighed heavily on her heart.

If your answer is a no, don't come back. River's sharp last words haunted her. Even with the company of her parents and the pets at the shelter, Jaylynn felt lonelier than she had in ages. A vacant space throbbed in her chest, and the pull of her compass was persistent and impossible to ignore.

How many months had she been encouraged to say exactly how she felt? Given every opportunity to tell the truth and her story? Conversations of depth and actual eye contact, things Jaylynn had never realized she needed, ripped away in an instant. River had never turned her away before, no matter how ugly her stories or emotions were. And then, right when Jaylynn had finally grasped what she was supposed to be learning, she'd been excused.

Jaylynn knew that her heart wanted to go back, but she wasn't sure it was the right choice. Was the reason she wanted to go back because her compass pulled her? Or desperation to end her loneliness? And how was she supposed to go back when there was an obvious risk but she had no clue what it was?

She looked up at her parents. They both sat in their usual places, eating their stew in a habitual mindless trance. Their house had always been quiet, especially after Nylah had moved out. Recently Jaylynn noticed the constant eerie silence that loomed over their home in a way she hadn't before—the blanketed air that discouraged conversation of depth or reality. She'd thought she was lucky to grow up in a house without yelling parents; her little family was always so cool and collected. Now she saw the truth of her home. She grew up in a house of secrets, with unsaid words swept under a rug of politeness.

Jaylynn put her spoon down.

"Mom. Why do you think we're alive?" Her voice echoed in the vast silence. The wallpaper tried to swallow the sound, but River had taught Jaylynn to speak clearly. Her question would not be ignored.

"Oh." Natalie paled. "My dear… you're not having another episode, are you? I thought when you stopped seeing your therapist back in the fall that things were finally straightened out for you?" Her mother's reply was genuine, but Jaylynn wanted to roll her eyes.

Couldn't she tell she was fine? She felt nothing like she had in those days. She took a breath, conscious she would now have to do everything to convince her mother otherwise.

"No, Mom. I'm fine. Whatever existential dread has overcome me, it hasn't brought me to those lows again. I won't ever be that low again." She gave her mother a gentle smile, filled with promise.

"Well, dear, we can always schedule you more appointments," she replied. The message was clear: case closed, move on.

"Mom…"

Jaylynn reached across her place mat. Her mother's spoon clattered on the bowl in surprise. Jaylynn looked deep into her mother's wide-eyed gaze. How had she never noticed the fatigue and fragility that freckled those pale blue irises? Jaylynn searched for the depth that she craved and believed her mother needed as much as she did. She asked again. "Tell me why we are here."

Natalie's discomfort was palpable. She pulled her hand away and stared down at her dish. "Now, Jaylynn. I know a lot has changed for you since you started spending time with that…" She paused as she searched for the word. "… woman in the woods, but this isn't appropriate dinner conversation. Let alone general conversation. You can't walk around the normal world expecting people to bare their souls to you."

Richard cleared his throat. "Jaylynn, your mother and I are

worried about you. We think it would be best if you stopped going out into the bush. This woman has gotten in your head. You've started speaking strangely, and frankly, you're making our home uncomfortable. I would strongly urge you to stop your gallivanting and return to regular therapy before this gets any worse."

"Father! How can you say such things?" Jaylynn exclaimed, upset at her parents' agreement. *How can they think these changes are bad? Can't they see how much happier I am?*

"Your father is right, you know. You've made our home awkward, and even family friends have commented on your recent behavior. When you were low before, it was fine because you stayed home and were safe. But now… now, dear, you're out and about in the world, acting as if you have this extra sight. Frankly, it's disturbing. I stand by your father. I would like you to stay home from now on. Perhaps you can find a job you can do remotely, instead of going downtown to the shelter all the time too."

The mood in the room darkened, and the walls crept closer like a pack of coyotes on their prey. The patterned wallpaper hovered over Jaylynn's shoulder, prepared to wrap her in a box and pack her away. Another problem under the rug. She'd become something embarrassing that they needed to manage, and they'd already agreed on the solution.

"I'm sure your therapist will have a new prescription to help you feel more like yourself. We can set up an appointment this week for you. We just want what's best for you, darling." Richard's tone sounded caring, but she could hear the undertones. His offer was not negotiable.

Jaylynn's spirit fluttered against the glass coffin that threatened to seal her future in this house. This wasn't how it was supposed to be. She knew her parents loved her and that they were trying to do their best, but they couldn't see, not to the same depth she could now. Jaylynn knew they would never understand her newfound life. They would only continue to question her intuition as magic or voodoo.

Years of her future played out in her mind. Her parents would keep her from functions for fear of being embarrassed. She would be heavily medicated to keep her relaxed. And she would be alone— dreadfully alone. She felt her eyes tear up as the final piece of her decision fell into place.

Her biggest fear had been leaving her family. She had a sense that if she went back to River, she wouldn't be returning. At least, not as the same person. Jaylynn was afraid of their grief, that they would feel she had wronged them. She never wanted to take advantage of their hospitality, but now she could see that they no longer served each other. Being the quiet and polite daughter was a coat that no longer fit. The time had come. She needed to move on, just as Nylah had.

The chair's legs ground against the patterned rug as Jaylynn stood. "Mother. Father. I love you dearly. I see that I have made you uncomfortable and for that I apologize." Both their shoulders dropped. Welcome smiles spread across their faces, ready to accept their dutiful daughter back. But Jaylynn wasn't finished. "I am grateful for all that you have done and all that you have provided for me. I will set an intention that we will all be able to move through this transition with grace. Do not fret about me while I am away. I assure you, I will be exactly where I'm meant to be."

She left her parents at the table with jaws open wide in disbelief, and darted up the staircase to her childhood bedroom. Doodles of stars and constellations cluttered the walls, and her pile of philosophy textbooks was in its usual corner stack, never sold despite her best intentions. Dream catchers hung from the ceiling, and every piece of her childhood shone in the streetlight. The entire room was a diorama of the introverted, magic-dreaming child she had been—a skin she was finally ready to shed.

Jaylynn dressed in a pair of brown leggings and a green tunic, then pulled her favorite black cloak over her shoulders. She picked up her engagement ring from her nightstand. Her therapist had encouraged her to stop wearing it after Elias had passed, but she could never bring herself to part with it. Now, she slid it on her right ring finger. Elias was a foundation to who she was, now and forever. She wouldn't leave him behind.

When she went back down with a bag slung over her shoulder, her parents stood in the foyer. Her mother spoke first.

"Please, Jaylynn, don't go. You are clearly not well. Sleep tonight and we can start fresh in the morning."

Jaylynn pulled out her phone and placed it in Natalie's trembling hands. She knew if she kept it that they would call her nonstop and beg her to come back. She squeezed past her mother's frail figure and her truck keys chimed freedom as she picked them out of the bowl. Her father stood tall and rigid with his hand on the door.

"Jaylynn. You know this isn't right. We can't let you go off wandering to who knows where. It's not safe."

Jaylynn could see that he was at a tipping point. She stood up on her tiptoes and kissed his cheek. She took his hand in hers.

"I love you, Dad, but I need you to let me go. Take care of Mom, okay?" She ran her hand over his flushed cheek. His bottom lip trembled. She squeezed around him and walked out the front door. Her time had come.

CHAPTER XXXVI

SEBASTIAN

Sebastian's knee vibrated as he waited for their turn to board the plane. Though they were traveling with three other boys on the team, they sat on opposite sides of the boarding gate. Gareth and Sebastian had expected as much. Damien rarely went anywhere without some kind of posse, and being divided suited them. It made the trip feel like a best friend adventure instead of a team trip with the people they liked least. They'd see the other boys at games, but if they were lucky, that would be it.

"How long is the flight again?" Sebastian asked. In a steady, quick repetition, he bounced on the ball of his foot, vibrating the sequence of seats.

"Nervous?" Gareth nudged with a wicked grin.

"About flying?" Sebastian waved him off and forced his legs to be still. "Of course not."

Gareth smirked but let it drop.

Sebastian had only been on a plane once before and he couldn't get over the idea that if the plane crashed in the ocean, they wouldn't die immediately. They would probably be injured in the impact, then either freeze, or drown, or be eaten by sharks. He couldn't decide which was the worst of the options but prayed that if it had to be any of the three, it would be to drown to death. He'd seen the *Titanic* movie. Freezing didn't look enjoyable, and drowning would be fast and far better than being eaten alive.

He heard Gareth mutter under his breath, and Sebastian looked up to see Damien and his posse heading their way.

"Hey, lovebirds. Enjoying your little bromance vacation already?" Damien sneered, the two other teammates sniggering. "Make sure you don't forget to buy lube once we land, boys. I'd hate to make a poor impression on the new team if neither of you can walk, let alone play."

Sebastian's cheeks burned as the boys all *oohed* at the insult.

"Piss off, Damien," Gareth said through clenched teeth, his fists balled at his sides.

"Oh, getting a wee protective over your lover, Williams?" Damien smiled his famous lazy smile, reveling in the tension. "You two should be celebrating. I hear in Canada gays are celebrated and paraded through the streets like war heroes."

Sebastian couldn't bring himself to say anything. He wanted to rip Damien's head off.

"I said. Piss. Off." Gareth's voice was stern, and he glared at the group with hatred.

"No need to get sensitive." Damien threw his hands up in the air, taking a casual step back. "I mean, if my compass pointed to my best friend, I'd probably be defensive about it too." Gareth shot up, fists balled tight, ready to strike. Damien laughed, backing up farther. "Now, now, Williams, no need to get angry. Seriously, it's fine. It's not like they're going to kick you off the team for being gay."

Sebastian stood, grabbing Gareth's shoulders. "He's not worth it," he whispered. His voice came out calmer than he felt, and he sank his thumbs in deep to pull Gareth's attention away. People were looking up from their phones to watch the impending showdown. "Listen, Gareth, he's just goading us. He probably wants to see you get tackled by a security officer or kicked off the plane. Let him go. He's a bloody wanker and not worth it." He could feel the tension rolling off Gareth as he tried to coax him away from the potential fight.

"That's right." Damien smirked. "Listen to your lover. Best you just enjoy your little honeymoon while it lasts." Damien and his followers sauntered off. Sebastian could feel Gareth's fury pulsing next to his own.

"It's okay, mate. Breathe. He's a dickhead. That's nothing new. We'll take him out on the field like we always do, okay?"

Gareth pulled away, avoiding eye contact. "I'm going to go use the loo before we take off. Watch my stuff?"

As Gareth walked away, Sebastian considered what Damien had said. Was it possible Gareth's compass pointed to him? He'd never seen Gareth's compass himself, least of all paid any attention to it. He resolved Damien had to be lying. It would be weird if his best friend was in love with him, especially when his own compass didn't point back. He didn't care if his best friend was gay. But if it were true...

Sebastian chided himself for letting Damien get to him. He had kept his compass from Gareth; his best friend had every right to the same privacy. The boarding announcement chimed over the intercom, so he gathered up both of their bags. A burning desire to run back toward security thrummed inside him, but he took their place in line and did his best to smother the growing fear. When Gareth rejoined him, Sebastian handed him his bag and they settled into a patient silence.

Sebastian let his mind shift back to worrying about flying over the ocean, praying if they did crash that he would drown fast.

CHAPTER XXXVII

The Quebec City platform was less busy than Montreal's had been. The railway's brick walls stretched up high to a beautiful skylight, and stained glass decorated the vast ceiling. Lacey shuffled between passengers. A clock at the peak of an archway sat with its hands splayed up and down. It was almost six o'clock, a solid six hours away from meeting her soulmate yet. *Just think of how romantic it will be to meet him under the midnight fireworks.*

Lacey's stomach growled, and she wondered how she would spend the rest of her evening. As they did most days since getting her compass a week ago, her fingers traced over the tattoo's edges. She reached into the pocket of her still-damp and crumpled sweater. Her heart skipped a beat. Where was her phone? With frantic energy, she patted down her sweater. She ran her hands over her leggings. She patted her chest to check that she hadn't put it in her bra. Then she tore open her purse as wide as it would go. It was gone.

Lacey turned back toward the train, just in time to see it pull away. She couldn't be sure if it had been stolen, or if it had fallen out of her sweater pocket. She thought of how furious her parents would be, but chose not to dwell on it. If she ever got back home, the phone would be the least of her concerns.

Lacey sat down on a bench and restudied her compass. *If Nessie was here, she'd know what to do next.* She shook herself. *But she isn't here, is she? Get yourself together. You've got a compass and an arrow to guide you. You don't need maps or anyone.*

She stood up and pushed herself out into the streets bustling with the Canada Day patrons. Sunlight peeked through clouds. *At least I don't need to worry about the rain here.* Restaurants bore red flags, and bars had French signs covered with giant red maple leaves. Lacey felt her own resolve build again, like an ocean that rose to devour the evening beach. She turned a corner and came to an abrupt stop, shocked. Her heart pounded as her emotions exploded in a fresh fury.

"Mom? What are you doing here?"

Relief was plastered on Renee's face, despite the hatred Lacey glared back at her with.

"Oh, Lacey. Ness came back to the hotel and told us everything. I came as fast as I could." She moved to touch Lacey's face, but

Lacey shoved her hand away. How could she dare to show up here?

"Are you kidding me?" Lacey's core tightened. "Why do you insist on following me everywhere, all the time? Why can't you move on with your life?"

Renee's face fell. "Lacey, you didn't really think I'd let you travel across the country by yourself, did you? What kind of mother would that make me?"

"You think you can stop me?" Lacey raised her voice. She didn't care if she made a scene in the crowded street. *Let them see.* "I may be your daughter, but you don't own me! No matter what your compass might make you feel, I am my own person, Mom. You need to let me go." The sharpness of her words rolled off her tongue with ease.

Renee didn't seem shaken, though. "Lacey. You're *my* daughter. I know you better than anyone and I can see that you're scared. Stop pushing everyone away when all we want to do is love you." Renee reached out again.

Lacey stepped back. *No. I will not continue this stupid game.*

"Don't pretend you understand me! You're tricked by your compass to think you know me better than anyone, but in case you've forgotten, *my compass doesn't point to you.*" Venom laced her every word. "I don't need you. I don't need Ness. I don't need anyone. Now, get out of my way." Sweet victory blossomed in her chest as she drew the boundary she'd craved her entire life. She pivoted on the heel of her boot, her intention set. Before she could take a step, a cold hand grasped her wrist.

"I will not let you destroy everything good in your life!" Renee's voice rose from her prior calm. "And I refuse to let you destroy yourself. You say hateful things, and you try to cut me down. But you forget, *I am your mother.* Though your compass may not point to me, mine points to you. And though all you seem to have in your heart for me is hate and fury, mine is only filled with love and longing for you to be happy." She grabbed both of Lacey's arms, forcing her to face her. "Lacey. Anger like this doesn't serve you. It might feel good to unleash it, but the highs will come with lows. I know you mean it now, but tomorrow or next week you will feel different."

Lacey wrenched her arms free and turned to walk away. Her mother would never see reason.

"Lacey, stop. You know I won't leave you, but I don't have to be a burden."

A few people had stopped to stare at the spectacle on the street, pausing by the nearby water fountain that crashed against its concrete foundation.

"Please let me help you."

"How? Huh?" Lacey whipped around. "Want to take me home and keep me locked up like a prisoner, like some Rapunzel trash? I can't keep living under your watchful eye! For the love of Cupid, I'm almost sixteen! Let me go!" She felt everyone watching her, but she didn't care. She wanted the world to see her mother burn in the same shame and embarrassment she had made her feel so many times before. The world needed to see her mother for the villain she was.

"I didn't come to bring you home, Lacey." Renee cast her eyes down. Her voice dropped. "I came to help you on your adventure. Meeting your dad was the greatest moment of my life, and I was lucky enough to get that experience twice. I came to help you find yours."

Lacey stared in disbelief. *No, no way.* "I don't believe you."

Renee's head hung in defeat. "I know you don't want me here."

"You're right. I don't want you here. I don't want you in my life at all."

"Lacey, so help me. If you want to burn the entire world down, so be it. If you want to hate me, fine. I accept the challenge of loving you through this." Renee looked up with a fresh intensity. "But I'll be damned if I sit here and let you treat me like a whipped dog any longer. If you want to accept my help, you can come find me, but I won't chase you anymore." She turned and walked back the way she came.

Lacey stood on the street bend, flabbergasted. All at once, her anger deflated. The rage that had fueled her burned out as fast as it had ignited. She should have felt like she'd won, but everything inside her stilled. *Could it be true?*

"You... you actually came to help me?" She had been so sure her mother would do anything to stop her.

Renee paused, her back still to her daughter. Her voice was soft, but Lacey heard every word. "Lacey, one day you're going to wake up and realize that the entire world isn't against you. I can't be your friend because I have to be your mother, but it's never been my intention to hurt you or make you feel trapped."

Lacey's cheeks flushed as a woman ushered her kids away from their fight. She looked around and saw people shaking their heads. Lacey took a step toward her mom and stood close enough to touch the back of her long jacket.

"All I ever wanted was for you to love me in a normal way," Lacey said quietly. "Not to smother me. Not to dictate every move I make in my life. How can I believe you're here to help me, and not because your compass ached from me leaving you?"

Renee turned. "There is nothing I can say that will change your mind if it's already set, Lacey. I know your willpower. You have the choice here." Her eyes brimmed with tears. "Believe me when I say I came to help you or continue painting me as the monster you see fit, but you have to decide right now." Renee stepped back. "Because I will not spend my life chasing you and continually being burned. I will love you from afar if I have to, but I will no longer be tolerant of your hateful words. Now. I'm going to step into this café and get a coffee. You have until I leave to decide which it's going to be."

CHAPTER XXXVIII

NYLAH

"**Well, cheers!** I guess that makes us both fine disappointments of the Clare family." Nylah laughed and red wine sloshed toward the rim of their glass.

Boots purred in a black-and-white puddle of fur as if she was in the Elysium fields. She stretched out across Jaylynn's lap, her fluffy tail flicking back and forth. It'd been a year since Jaylynn begged Nylah to rescue the overly affectionate kitten. *"Your apartment is too empty, and how can you say no to this adorable face?"*

The split-faced cat now ruled Nylah's home with undisputed authority.

Jaylynn giggled as she popped the cork out of the second bottle. Nylah considered how much she'd changed in the last year since her compass had come back alive. Jaylynn had always been wound so tight before. Seeing the smile stretching their sister's face made Nylah's heart sing.

"Cheers," Jaylynn toasted with her newly filled glass, "to growing into yourself, no matter what your parents think."

Nylah grinned and clinked their glasses. "And to continually sticking together, no matter what storms we have to weather." The rich wine was smooth in Nylah's mouth, their appreciative sips turning into easy mouthfuls. A familiar glittering jewel caught Nylah's attention.

"When did you start wearing Elias's ring again?" The question was out before Nylah could think twice.

Jaylynn waved the question away. "I decided I didn't want to leave it in case Mom got rid of it when she purges my room. That's beside the point, though. Tell me what's new. I feel like we haven't talked in ages."

Nylah let the engagement ring slide with a suspicious squint. "Hmmm, let me think. I'm pretty sure my boss wants to fire me. Mom's still pretending I don't exist, so that's not really new. I convinced Jazz to come to the UK and the Roman Empire next month with me... Oh, and I joined a cult."

Jaylynn choked on her wine. "I'm sorry, what?"

Nylah laughed, happy to have gotten the reaction they were going for. "Not actually. Jazz has got me going to these meetings. It's our trade-off for him to come backpacking with me."

Jaylynn's face creased with worry. "Cult meetings? Why is Jazz in a cult now?"

Nylah shrugged. "He thinks it's going to help him find his soulmate."

"And how is it going to do that?"

"Apparently, once you've moved up in the group, the priests facilitate trips to help you find your one true love. There's some fine print, like you have to attend a certain number of meetings first and have a certain ranking. Then when you go on your trip, you have to do a few hours at whatever ceremonies they hold there. But basically, it's a free trip with the perk of hopefully finding your soulmate!"

Jaylynn frowned. "And they're prepared to take you anywhere your compass points?"

"Yeah! Isn't that crazy? Here I thought Fates' Followers were a small Canadian thing, but it turns out they're huge back in the Roman Empire." Nylah licked the rim of their glass as a drop sought refuge toward the stem.

"You're going to join them, aren't you?"

"Why do you say it like that?"

"I don't know. After everything with Mom and Dad... I just thought religion was over for you. And with your whole soulmate situation..." Jaylynn trailed off, not having to say more.

Nylah sighed. "This is different. I'm not joining them because I believe what they're selling. It's just a means to an end. And I mean, it's been such a long time… What if my soulmate is waiting for me to come to them?"

"I thought that was what the Roman Empire trip was supposed to be about?" Jaylynn countered.

"Well, yes. But no. Crossing the ocean isn't going to guarantee I'll find them. I guess I'm hoping by going to the Roman Empire, if my compass-link pulls harder, maybe it'll spark my person into wanting to find me sooner?"

"So why join the cult at all? Are you doing this for Jazz? I know things have always been… *interesting* between you two…"

Nylah flushed at the implication.

"No, I wouldn't go if Jazz wasn't there. But I feel like he needs someone looking out for him. Sometimes he gets himself in positions—"

"—you mean like you?" Jaylynn smirked.

Nylah laughed. "Okay. I get it. I'm not innocent either, and trouble suits us both. Don't pretend like you're not joining the trouble bandwagon, though."

Jaylynn held her hands up in surrender. "Trust me. I know I boarded the crazy train. I'm just making sure you know what you're getting into."

Nylah reached for Jaylynn's hand. "I promise my head is on straight. This is just a backup plan in case my trip falls through. I'm keeping an eye on Jazz more than anything."

Before Nylah could say anything more, Jaylynn pulled them into a hug. "Minerva knows I'm going to miss you."

"Miss me? I'll be gone for a month, max. Even if my soulmate lives on the other side of the world, I promise I'll come back and visit."

"I'm not talking about you leaving."

"What do you mean? Are you going somewhere?"

Jaylynn pursed her lips.

Nylah rolled their eyes. "So, you're going to go stay with River. Jay, it's an hour away. We're still going to see each other."

"I know, it's just... something's changed." Jaylynn swirled the wine in her glass, avoiding Nylah's gaze.

"What changed? Did you tell Mom and Dad that your compass led you to a woman? Because you know I'll support you through whatever complicated love stuff you've got going on."

Jaylynn let out a small huff of laughter. "I know you'll support me regardless, and I already told you River's compass doesn't point to me. No, this is something different. Something I can't explain. I just feel like things are about to really change for me and I don't know where I'm going to end up."

Nylah placed their glass on the secondhand coffee table they'd rescued from the café dumpster. "No matter where you go, even if you get lost in the woods and become the Wicked Witch of the East, you know I'll still love you and be here for you, right?"

Jaylynn smiled. "I know. Just as I'll always love and be here for you. I don't know why I said anything at all. It's probably nothing."

Nylah smiled and reached to top up their wine glasses.

Something more had changed for Jaylynn, but Nylah couldn't put their finger on what it was.

"Well," Nylah said, choosing to take the mood back to the lighthearted night they'd originally imagined, "you're here now. Let's make the best of the time we have before your life mysteriously changes forever. Are we doing Disney sing-alongs tonight, or painting our nails?"

Nylah's own black chipping nail polish really needed a do-over, but Jaylynn's soft blue eyes twinkled at *Disney*.

"Disney it is."

CHAPTER XXXIX

CHARITY

Charity flicked the electric kettle button on and massaged her temple with her free hand. A familiar headache nagged behind her eyes, worse than usual. Across the room, Nessie sprawled on her stomach and watched from the crumpled hotel bed, her face swollen with red blotches.

Charity moved to her daughter's side and gave her a gentle nudge. "You know, this isn't necessarily a bad thing."

"How is this not a bad thing in your mind, Mom?" Nessie grabbed the nearest pillow and smothered her face with it.

"Well, it's only Friday and now we have an entire weekend together." Despite all the emotional turmoil caused by Lacey's stunt, Charity had relaxed for the first time since they'd left. A weekend with Nessie was even better than she'd hoped for.

Apparently, Nessie didn't share her optimistic lens. Her daughter dragged the pillow off her face, her smoky-quartz eyes still puffy from crying. "How are you able to find a silver lining right now? My supposed best friend literally ditched me and her mom hightailed after her. Now we're stranded in a city hours away from home with nothing more than our luggage, and we're spending Canada Day in Montreal, of all places."

Charity frowned. "I thought you wanted to be in Montreal for the Canada Day fireworks?"

Nessie groaned and rolled on-to her stomach. "That was just an excuse to come this far east for Lacey's compass. In what world could Montreal's fireworks be better than Toronto's? If I wanted a light show, I would have said that we should go to Ottawa."

Charity ran her fingers through Nessie's clean, damp hair. "If you had the choice, how would you like to spend the rest of the weekend?"

Nessie lay still. Her arms trapped the oversized pillow to her chest. "I just want to go home."

Charity considered the five hours they'd driven here last night and sighed at the thought of heading back so soon. "Is that really what you want?"

"Yes, but it's not like we could anyway. Renee took the stupid car and now we're stranded."

The kettle hissed, and Charity rose to make some tea. "You know, we could always train home."

Nessie peeked over her trapped pillow. "Really?"

"Sure, why not? I mean, if you're going to be miserable if we stay, let's leave. Go with the flow. If Lacey can take off on an adventure, why can't we? Maybe we could even go to Ottawa for their amazing fireworks show. We could still make it, you know. It's early enough in the day."

Nessie wasn't one to bail on itineraries or to go on spontaneous trips, but Charity could see that she'd tempted her. Charity poured the orange pekoe tea into two cups and sat back beside her daughter. "Come on, Ness. This weekend was supposed to be fun. If you can't make the best of it here, let's go somewhere else."

"But what about all the money we spent?"

"Don't worry about it. We'll figure it out. I'll work some extra hours at the greenhouse."

Nessie sat up and wrapped her hands around the cup of tea. "I don't think Ottawa is a good idea. Let's not waste any more money than we have to. If going home is an option, I would love that."

Nessie with her undying logic.

"Let's go home, then. How about you look up the train schedule and I'll figure out checking out of the hotel after tea?"

Charity's shoulders protested as she hauled her suitcase into the train car. Within the hour, they'd started their improvised trek home, and as luck would have it, they found two seats tucked in a quiet corner. Nessie sulked as she settled in, her chin tucked and head hung low. Even the ponytail that was usually pulled tight to her scalp hung limp and lacked its usual luster and shine.

Charity rubbed her temples and willed the edge of her headache to go away. She knew it would be gone in a couple of hours, but hoped it wouldn't get worse before then. How had this weekend gone so sideways? And could the timing possibly be any worse?

The train lurched forward. Charity sighed at the reality she faced as the car's momentum increased.

I need to tell her.

I can't tell her. She'll be crushed.

I can't keep lying to her, though.

She'll understand. She's a smart girl. She's going to figure it out eventually.

"Mom?"

Charity looked at her daughter.

Nessie met her gaze with heavy eyebrows and scrutinizing eyes. "Are you okay? You're doing that thing where you get all spacey on me again. I thought you were doing good and that your nightmares were getting better?"

Trust Nessie to be in a crisis and tally if everyone else is okay.

It was true, Charity's recurring night terrors were getting better. Though Nessie knew her dreams were always about Luke, what she didn't know was how graphic they were. How so many times Charity wrapped her arms around him to shelter him from the blast. How every time, his body was torn apart in her arms, while she herself remained whole. How she would sink through the ground, to a dark place where she could hear him calling to her. No, not calling. Crying, borderline screaming for her. His screams would tear her heart to shreds as she tried to find him, her frail nails clawing through endless obsidian clouds.

Nessie was right, though; her night terrors had been getting better. Now when she dreamed of Luke, his voice was a far-off echo instead. *Please. Release me.*

Charity shuddered. She'd spent the past four years trying to release him. She'd buried a thousand coins in hopes he could take them, but of course he couldn't. That was by far the worst part. Because the military hadn't been able to find Luke's body, no one could guarantee he'd been buried with a coin to pass into the Underworld. Charity had no doubt in her mind that her husband floated through purgatory, begging to cross the river Styx to the Fields of Elysium. That's where his soul should have been, in peace as a proper hero.

It seemed so long as Luke couldn't have peace, neither could she. She begged the army to send her to the incident site, but they insisted it wasn't safe. Charity tried therapy. She spent hours in Savasana at the yoga studio. Her summers were dedicated to the local greenhouse, where she was intent on nurturing Terra Mater and all her fruits. Yet, peace always evaded her.

Charity smiled at her daughter, grateful she didn't experience her father's death the same way. "My nightmares have gotten better."

275

She'd told Nessie it was because of some new remedy she'd been trying, but that wasn't the truth. If only it was that simple.

"But you're not actually better, are you?" Nessie's voice was hushed but direct.

Tell her. The train lurched and Charity resettled herself. "The nightmares have been better, but you're right. I'm not feeling entirely myself. I thought going away for the weekend would help, but…" She shrugged. Her headache began to fade, proof that being away had only made it worse.

"We could have stayed, Mom. I didn't know—"

"No, honey. Trust me. It's good that we're going home."

Nessie wasn't fooled. "What aren't you saying?"

Charity wished she could have kept her secret longer. She wished she could wait until things with Lacey's soulmate and Nessie's broken compass had blown over, but of course it couldn't wait any longer. *You're the queen of 'go with the flow'. Do it now.*

"I… I have something to tell you. A secret, if you will. I wasn't sure and—"

"Mom, stop rambling. Spit it out." Nessie's arms were crossed over her chest. Charity couldn't find the words as her mind scrambled to figure out when her daughter had become such a strong and mature woman. So sure of herself, so clear in her intentions. So direct. *So opposite to me…*

Charity sighed in defeat and pulled up the sleeve of her cream cardigan.

"Holy Minerva…" Nessie's lips parted as her arms fell into her lap. "Mom. What? When? How?"

"I don't know. All I know is it came a few weeks ago."

"That's why your nightmares went away."

Please don't let her be mad. "I thought it had to be a mistake. I kept waiting for it to disappear, but..." She turned her palm upward. "I'm sorry I didn't tell you. The timing didn't feel right and—"

"Mom. Stop." Nessie pulled her in for a hug. "The timing would have never been right." Her voice was soft in Charity's ear. "I'm happy for you."

Warmth rushed to Charity's cheeks as she registered her daughter's reaction. She blinked back tears.

"What have you figured out so far?"

Charity tilted her head back. "Not much, really. I'm pretty sure he's in Toronto, though. My headaches get better when I'm there, and they have only gotten worse since we left."

"And they're getting better now, aren't they?" Nessie's big eyes stared back at her, certainty flecked like glimmers of silver.

She nodded.

"What time?"

Charity looked down at the fresh compass that glittered where her faded gray one had once sat. "Just before eleven. Say, ten fifty-seven?"

"Do you—do you think it could be soon? I mean... Our train technically stops in Toronto and it is on our way home." Nessie mused as she fiddled with her faded blue denim collar.

"No. Not a chance. This weekend was already hijacked by one person intent on finding their soulmate. I will not put us through that again."

You. I will not put you through that again.

"Listen, Mom. If it's not meant to happen, it won't. But I understand if you're not ready…" Nessie trailed off and Charity caught her subtle glance at her own broken compass.

Charity's heart faltered. *Here I am with a second soulmate, when my daughter doesn't even have one.* "Ness, I'm sorry—"

"You don't need to apologize, Mom. The question is, do you need me to listen and support you, or do you want advice?"

Charity laughed out loud. How many times had she asked her daughter that same question? "Advice, I suppose, if you have any."

Nessie smirked. "Take your own. Go with the flow."

The corners of Charity's eyes creased as she pulled her daughter in for a second hug. *How did I get so lucky?*

CHAPTER XL

BLAKE

Blake coughed against the lump growing in her throat. The officer in front of her looked over her license, then went through her meager possessions. He pulled the Swiss Army knife out of its sleeve and it glistened in the morning light.

"Where are you headed?" His voice was gruff and hung heavy with a French accent.

Blake swallowed and thought back to her basic rules of lying. *Rule number one: just enough truth to make it believable.* She twirled a strand of her hair on her finger to appear less threatening. "I'm, uh, kind of embarrassed to say." Her left fingers curled over the hem of her jacket sleeve. She dropped her eyes and tapped her toes together. "I'm looking for my soulmate."

Not a runaway. Not a thief. Just an innocent girl.

She wasn't sure her charade would pass. What kind of innocent girl spent the last six days limping down highways, being scorched by the sun, and hardly sleeping? And that was hardly considering her last twenty-four hours in Buffalo City. How many pockets had her fingers brushed, hoping to get more cash? Somehow the officer didn't find the stack of bills suspicious, though.

Instead, he smirked at her excuse, and Blake didn't have to pretend to blush. Her cheeks burned. It was bad enough that she had to pretend to be ditzy. But what was worse was that she actually was following her compass. She hadn't put it together until yesterday. Her hunger pangs were gentler. She'd assumed it was because of how much easier it was to steal food in bigger cities again. But then, she noticed her sunburn didn't hurt as bad. Her toes squirmed in pools of sticky blood, but they ached less. When she realized it was because she was getting closer to her soulmate, she'd puked over a bridge banister.

She didn't need to read her botched compass to know she was getting closer and going in the exact direction of her soulmate. The one person she had successfully avoided for three years.

"So no need to ask if you're visiting on business or pleasure, then, I suppose, eh?" The guard winked.

Blake didn't answer. She had no intention of finding her soulmate in the flesh. *I'm going to cross the border and find somewhere to lie low. Then pray they don't come to find me.*

"Do you have any food, drugs, or weapons to claim?"

Blake stared at the beautiful wooden knife. *Please don't let him take it.*

"Just the knife."

"Knives are considered tools, not weapons. Are you carrying anything else, such as pepper spray?"

Blake shook her head and sighed in relief when he handed the knife back to her. Her thumb slid over the smooth, rich wood, which was engraved with a single word.

Brooks.

Blake wondered if it was her mountain man's name or the brand of the knife. *What kind of girl sleeps with a man and doesn't even know his name?* Blake was. No attachments, nothing to look back to. She couldn't go back even if she did miss his sure and steady presence.

The guard handed her license and backpack back. "Then you're all set. You should know, you can cross the border into Canada without a passport, but you'll have a hard time getting back without one."

"Don't worry. I have no intentions of coming back."

The guard smirked his greasy smile once more, then waved her through the gate. Blake made her way across the massive bridge that spanned the water border. Niagara Falls crashed down in an impressive display on her left. The thundering water showered mist on the two glowing cities that framed it.

Blake walked through the crowd of morning tourists that lingered between the comical, brightly colored tourist traps. Her shoulders grew taut, and she tightened her hands around the straps of her backpack. *I hate this. I need to get out of these stupid, busy cities.*

She was making her way up a hill past a restaurant when a hand suddenly cupped her bicep and a body stumbled into her. A gasp of breath sounded close to her ear. Blake didn't think twice. The knife was in her hand and the blade flashed out in an instant. She whirled around and slashed out blind. Her ears flooded with pounding blood and she was met with a satisfying cry as the switchblade met its mark like a fist.

Blake thought back to the border patrol for half a second. *Whoever claimed a knife wasn't a weapon was stupid.* In her peripheral, she saw her victim. A college-aged boy grasped the sleeve of his football jacket in shock. She turned with the momentum of her swing and ran, not sparing a moment for the silhouette that strung out curse words behind her.

Blake's thoughts sang in triumph as her feet pounded across the pavement.

Look who can protect herself after all.

Adrenaline coursed through her veins, and a wild smile plastered her face. Her blue hair whipped back and forth as Blake fled the scene. She ran until her lungs gave out, and then she slowed to a walk. A woman walked toward her with a teddy bear of a dog. Blake did her best to look approachable.

"Excuse me! I'm so sorry. I'm visiting and I seem to have gotten all turned around. Could you point me to the nearest transit stop?"

The woman smiled in a knowing way. "Of course."

Twenty minutes later, Blake boarded a bus with the only destination she recognized as her choice: Toronto. Blake sank into the tall, cushioned seat with her backpack in her lap. Relieved to be off her feet for a couple of hours, she stared out the window, anxious to be on her way as the last passengers boarded. Though it had taken most of her Buffalo City cash to pay for the ticket, she knew it would be worth it. She had to get out of Niagara fast, and now that she had a border between her and NYC, she couldn't help as a smile crept up the corner of her mouth.

She was free.

CHAPTER XLI

RENEE

I can't believe we're doing this. The SUV was too warm and dried out Renee's eyes as she strained to see the winding road in the late-evening darkness. The farther they traveled, the taller the trees got, broken up only occasionally by glimmers of water. Lacey had asked if she could drive, but Renee had given her a hard no. These weren't roads for learners. *Let alone fearless teenagers following their compasses into the unknown.*

Renee shivered at the thought of what Lacey would have done if she hadn't shown up. She pictured her daughter walking down the secluded highway, thumb high and a sweet smile, waiting to be picked up by some stranger.

Lacey's voice broke Renee out of her nightmare. "Mom, are you mad Dad loves a dog more than you? Or even as much as you?"

Renee laughed as she flexed her hands over the steering wheel. "It doesn't work that way. That would be like comparing my love for him to my love for you. It's impossible. What if I asked you who you love more: your father or Nessie?"

"Nessie." Lacey's answer was instantaneous. "Well, most days. Not today. I guess today it's Dad."

Lacey's mascara was smudged down to her cheeks from the earlier rain and tears, but now her hazel eyes shone with fierce determination.

Renee smiled. "Okay, then. Who do you love more: Lady or coffee?"

Lacey crossed her arms. "Those are wildly different things, Mom. Coffee isn't a person."

"And would it not eat you up if you had to decide which one to have and which one to give up? Never to have coffee again, or to watch your father lose his best friend?"

Lacey stuck her lip out in a pout and gazed back out at the darkening forest.

"Life isn't as black-and-white as you may want it to be, Lace. We can love more than one person and we don't have to be bound by a tattoo. Love is one of the most expansive languages in the world. To claim that you have only one dedicated person would mean to choose to love nothing else. There are friends, animals, places, and all kinds of things that can and should also be cherished. You can't let yourself be blinded by the idea of 'one true love.' You'll end up isolating yourself."

Lacey stared ahead at the endless highway. "Why would you need anyone else? Your soulmate is the person who can provide everything you need in a way no one else can."

"And are you prepared to fill their every need? That thinking breeds codependency. You can't have a healthy life if every moment of every day you only live to serve another's needs."

"I don't think that sounds bad."

Oh, Lacey. You're more like your father than you know. Renee sighed. "Even soulmates need space to exist outside of their relationship. To work, to make money, to build a community. I know one true love sounds romantic, but imagine how much more love you could have in your life if you opened up to it coming from everywhere. Do you imagine that when you find your soulmate that you'll stop needing your family? Your friends? Money or food to eat?"

"You don't need anyone else to be happy. It's the way of Fate."

Renee wanted to batter her head on the steering wheel. Or maybe Lacey's. *Breathe. You once thought the same thing.* She relaxed her grip.

"You're being optimistic. Media and society have clouded your vision to believe your soulmate is your happily ever after, but that's not the truth. It's amazing, but it doesn't guarantee the rest of your life to be painless. I mean, you grew up in a home where you can see that isn't true."

"Yeah, that's because we're an anomaly."

Renee scowled. "What about Charity? Is she an anomaly?"

"No… I don't think she's an anomaly." Lacey twirled a piece of her hair. "She's just unlucky."

"Can you imagine relying entirely on one person, and then one day they disappear? What if Charity had no friends or family to turn to in that time of grief? That's what I'm talking about. Love someone and love them with all of your might, but don't forget others in your life can serve you in ways your partner sometimes just can't."

Renee spied the bag of snacks in the back seat. Lacey followed her gaze and took charge of being the food coordinator. *Thank Jupiter I thought to stop for groceries before we left Quebec City.* The gas gauge ticked closer to empty and Renee fought down the urge to turn around. *Do it for Lacey. She needs this.*

Lacey dug through the tote bag. "Okay, so in the worst-case scenario where my soulmate spontaneously dies, I see what you're saying. But that's so unlikely. Why else would I need other people? What didn't you get from Dad?"

"Ha." Renee laughed as every fight between her and Kade flashed through her mind. The endless days she yelled at him for not helping around the house. The nights he begged her to have another child, and she refused. The endless arguments about couples therapy and whether they needed it. Every time Kade left her to be the bad guy in parenting decisions. But Lacey couldn't understand that. None of that would make her see why she needed other relationships in her life. *What don't I get from Kade?*

"I guess help making decisions. There's lots of things that I choose to get advice about from other people before him."

"Like what?"

"Career choices. Decorating the house. Getting my tubes tied. I mean, some stuff he had opinions about, but most of the time he was too supportive. He'd tell me I could do anything I wanted, so I would turn to my family and friends for advice instead."

Lacey tilted the open bag of salt-and-vinegar chips toward her. Renee smiled and dug her hand in.

"You got your tubes tied?"

"No. We decided for your dad to get the surgery instead. It was less invasive and easily reversible. He was pretty set on having the choice to have more kids, even though I was sure after you I didn't want any more."

"Because your compass points to me?"

"I never wanted my children to feel like I had a favorite, so it seemed easier to stop."

"Do you ever wonder if you guys weren't actually soulmates? I mean, everyone swears love is easy, but it seems like you guys just always fight."

"I know your father is still my soulmate. Lacey, I know you want it to be easy, and I hope for you it is. All I ask is that you don't abandon all your relationships for a boy. Don't isolate yourself. Set yourself up with a healthy and strong support system. Then, if for some reason things aren't easy, you won't be entirely alone."

"I guess I could do that."

Renee couldn't remember the last time she'd had a genuine conversation with Lacey that hadn't ended with slamming doors. Her heart swelled at the bonding opportunity this trip had provided.

"So, what was it like for you? When you met Dad. Was it like all the magazines say? An insane high, and the best moment of your life?"

"Hmmm." Renee contemplated. "I suppose in a lot of ways it was. It was exhilarating, and yet simultaneously peaceful. Like all the tension and turmoil leading to that moment dissolved off my shoulders. Even after all this time and all the changes, I can still feel our compass-link deep inside my heart. I have never once stopped loving your father, as much as he or you may have doubted. I don't think I'll ever stop loving him. As sure as I am that Charity will never stop loving Luke, and I will never stop loving you."

Renee sighed in relief when the next curve in the road revealed an isolated gas station.

"We'll stop here quickly, then we can keep following your compass. I'd like to call your dad too and update him while we're stopped. Have you talked to Nessie at all since you left?"

Lacey's entire demeanor shifted as her relaxed smile fell.

"Lacey, you should call her. If not, at least text her. I don't think you know how much you hurt her when you left."

Lacey mumbled something under her breath.

"Speak up."

"I said I would if I could," Lacey said as she clasped her hands tight.

"What do you mean?"

"I might have maybe, accidentally, kind of, sort of lost my phone." Lacey bit her lip.

Are you kidding me? Renee's chest constricted. "Well. If you think we'll be buying you a new one, you're going to be disappointed, but we can talk about that when we get home to your father. You can call Nessie from my phone while I gas up and then we can figure out what the plan is from here."

Renee started a mental list of phone calls and apologies she had to make. *Charity, Kade, work. I'll call them all and explain.* She handed her phone to Lacey and got out of the car, desperate for fresh air.

From the pump, Renee watched as Lacey set the phone back in the center console, then sunk her head in her hands. *You and me both, girl.*

When Renee got back in the car, she swallowed before delivering the bad news. "Well, apparently the next jaunt is a long one. If you need to pee, you should go now. It's over one hundred kilometers to the next stop."

Renee had already done the math in her head. Basically, either Lacey's soulmate was going to be in the middle of nowhere or they had a long night of driving ahead of them. Lacey opted to use the bathroom and stretch her legs before they continued on. Renee picked up her phone and wished she could leave it in the console like Lacey had. *Why was the price of repairing her relationship with Lacey so high?* She dialed Kade's number first.

CHAPTER XLII

BLAKE

A loud car horn brought Blake's attention back to the gravel path in front of her. A whole day had slid by as she wandered out of the bustling Toronto streets into rural country. Her defaced compass tugged her along with growing insistence as she battled with how close she was getting to her soulmate. *I'll just get close enough to keep the pain at bay. Then I'll find somewhere to settle and hide until I come up with a better plan.*

The memory of Tatiana's tear-stricken face crossed her mind. *"Don't lie to me, J.B. You're going after your soulmate and we both know it. You can't avoid your Fate no matter how much you claim to love me."* But that was a lie. Blake hadn't loved Tatiana; she'd just appreciated having someone else to fight the world by her side.

That was, until her partner in arms became more of a thorn in her side. Tatiana would roll her eyes if she could see Blake now.

But I still control my Fate. I don't need anyone else.

Blake's hand slid over the smooth wooden handle of her knife. The blade was proof that she was in control—ready to fight and done with running.

The sky dimmed as another day slipped away. Blake sized up the trees in the wilderness that surrounded her. As she searched for a secluded and safe spot to rest, a small wood cabin came into sight. Blake came to an abrupt stop. She could feel her compass as it throbbed through its mess of black ink. She struggled to swallow against her constricted, parched throat.

Before she could move, the door opened. A woman with tanned skin and rich black hair stepped out of the cabin into the evening air. She stopped when she saw Blake. The woman's yellow dress had a delicate flower pattern and tightened at the waist to show off her hourglass figure. Blake flushed at the woman's full breasts and delicate bare feet in the grass. In comparison, she was a dirt-covered, bloodied disaster standing next to this sun-kissed goddess.

The woman smiled a perfect smile, her bright eyes more radiant than stars, and extended her hand in an unspoken invitation. Blake didn't move. The woman shrugged, then grabbed a basket leaning against the small home. She spoke with a warm and husky voice.

"I was just heading to collect some fresh berries for my evening tea. Join me if you'd like." Her skirts wrapped around her hips with her graceful turn.

This can't be real.

Blake didn't know what to do. The trees swayed above her, and with every step the lady took away from her, Blake's lungs tightened.

It's not too late. Turn around. Go back to where you came from.

But she had nowhere to go back to. She took a step toward the yellow dress sashaying away from her, and then another. Step after step, she followed the woman who hummed her way down the root-covered path.

When they came to a stream, Blake relaxed her attention from the strange beauty. She couldn't remember the last time she had clean drinking water. She knelt on the side of the bank and splashed water up into her face. The cold shock cleared her fuzzy mind, and the trance she'd slipped into faded.

Get it together. What's your plan?

Blake's compass pulsed hard enough that she almost fell face-first into the stream. She sat back on the bank and observed the woman. Though Blake had never felt partial to men or women, she couldn't see how she was meant to be with someone so incredibly beautiful. *I don't belong here. I should go.*

Instead, she waited.

Blake's breathing got easier, and her anxiety lessened when the stranger started back her way. The woman smiled at her, then headed back up the path, basket in hand. Blake was slow to follow. When she got up to the cabin, she was surprised that the door had been left wide open. She paused on the doorstep to peer in. It was a small and humble cabin, filled with all manners of herbs and books. The black-haired beauty stood over the stove, tending to a pot.

"The bathroom is in the corner and I've laid out a towel for you. You're welcome to wash up if you'd like, and then join me for tea when you're finished." The woman didn't turn around. Instead, she continued to crush the wild berries, their deep violet juices dripping down her long, delicate fingers. Blake hesitated for a moment on the threshold of the door.

You can do this. It's not like you have anywhere better to go.

She stepped into the cabin. Most of the furniture looked well worn and the rugs were covered in a thin sheen of dirt. Blake was grateful that the woman was also barefoot, making her own messiness seem inconsequential to the earthy space. She almost laughed at the stark contrast this home had to the boy's trailer. Both were small and only for one dweller, but where the trailer was evidently lived in by a man, the cabin overflowed in womanly love. The smells of flowers permeated the air and hand-knit blankets covered many of the surfaces.

Blake slid the bathroom door closed between them and let out a shaky breath. The woman was humming again, and it echoed through the slats. Blake turned in the small confines and with one look in the mirror, her suspicions were confirmed. She was a mess. Her blue hair was ratty from the rain and struggles with bushes. Her gray shirt was covered in dirt, and mud caked the bottoms of her black jeans. Only her leather jacket seemed reasonable.

"Feel free to use as much hot water as you need." The woman's rich voice rang through the door, and Blake turned to the tin tub.

The loud, clear blue water ricocheted off the silver basin. When she ran her hand through the current, she was relieved by its warmth. She stripped down and braced herself for the swell of anxiety that usually came when she was naked, but nothing happened. *It's probably because of how close she is. It's just the compass magic. And probably that she's a woman.* Blake let out a sigh and then reached for the soap bar.

When she was sure she couldn't get any cleaner, she grabbed the towel folded on a shelf and dried herself. Then she looked around the tiny room for something to manage her soaked blue hair. In a basket, she spied a wide-toothed comb along with a few other odds and ends. Her fingers danced over a package of matches beside a candle. *I'll grab them later. I'll leave within the hour.* She did her best to dust her clothes off into the basin and wished she had something else to change into. She left her destroyed combat boots on the bathroom floor as an excuse to come back for the matches.

Well, what are you going to do now? She resolved there was nowhere to go but out to meet her host. Her supposed soulmate. Blake swallowed.

CHAPTER XLIII

JAYLYNN

Jaylynn leaned against a tree as the crowd jostled around her. What she was waiting for, she couldn't have explained. It had been two days since she left her parents. Two days of getting her ducks in a row and wondering if she was crazy. The day before, she gave her keys back to the pet shelter, kissed Rosabella goodbye, and gave her tabby friend some extra ear scratches. Her boss was dismayed by the abrupt departure but wished her the best.

She'd spent both nights with Nylah, grateful for the opportunity to have somewhere else to stay while she covered her bases. At her sibling's insistence, Jaylynn bought a burner phone just in case. Now it was Friday and her last night in the hectic city. Her truck was gassed up, her backpack was stocked with essentials, and all her errands were finished. Nylah had given her a tight hug and made Jaylynn swear she'd be safe, and then she had been on her way. Now, as she leaned against the park tree in the evening breeze, she closed her eyes to say a wordless goodbye to the vibrant energy of her home city.

She could have left for River's hours ago, but she had convinced herself to stay for the day. Not out of cold feet, but something felt—

"Excuse me?"

Jaylynn looked up, surprised to be acknowledged. The pair of people in front of her were clearly related. Blond hair and curious eyes shone back at her, and anticipation danced on the energy between them. The woman with the natural aging silver in her wispy hair had a tangible edge of nervousness, oddly reminding Jaylynn of the man who had come for Ladybug. She was the one who spoke, her hands wrung together tight.

"This may seem a little unorthodox. In fact, I'm not really sure why I'm here. Let alone what to say..." She stumbled over her words, and blood rushed to her cheeks. The younger, full-figured girl rested a reassuring hand on her companion's shoulder.

Jaylynn noticed that the woman wasn't actually wringing her hands, but her wrist. Her delicate, pale wrist, which shone with a beautiful etched compass that glowed against the night sky.

At a loss for words herself, Jaylynn raised her own left hand, palm faceup to the sky. Her metallic compass hadn't changed from its pull back to River. The crow's feet that spanned from the woman's eyes creased with sadness when she realized their compasses weren't glowing equally. Her brow furrowed, but Jaylynn understood what was happening. She closed the gap between their fingers, gently resting the tips of her fingers on the woman's skin. A wave of energy pulsed out from the touch and beat through her core. The world around them became sharper, and Jaylynn's senses flared as her body processed the shift.

No one in the busy park seemed to notice the interaction or the burst of magic. Children chanted for the fireworks to start, as parents wrestled them to stillness. They all looked to the sky, oblivious to the light show and magic in front of them.

Jaylynn smiled at her newfound companion. "You. You're the reason I haven't left yet. All day I thought I was procrastinating, and I wasn't sure why. But I was waiting for you."

The woman blushed deeper, though now her eyes glittered, fresh with magic and adrenaline. "But your compass doesn't point to me."

Jaylynn laughed. "Would you believe me if I told you I had the same experience? My compass points to someone whose doesn't point to me either. I was actually headed back to her now."

The woman's gentle eyes widened. "How is this possible?" she asked.

"I've always believed that magic is like love. It isn't meant to be understood; it's meant to be felt."

Explosions sounded in the sky, but the crackling fireworks couldn't shake the foundation of their bond. Jaylynn gestured for the pair to follow her away from the noisy park. They walked a block or two through the dense crowds, toward the parking lot where her truck sat prepped for her adventure. The sound of the fireworks crackled in the background, but they would be able to hear one another here. Jaylynn turned back to her companions.

"I know this is crazy, but I'm confident that you found me today for a reason. I was about to leave town to join my friend at her cabin, and I would love it if you joined me. Which I realize sounds wild—"

The woman with the glowing compass smiled. "You don't need to explain, and you don't need to ask. In light of some good advice I recently received, I'm happy to go with the flow." She winked at the younger girl.

Jaylynn sighed in relief. *They're just as crazy as I am. They're going to fit in fine with River.* "Once we get out there, if you want to come back, you'd be welcome to take my truck. Gertrude may be old, but she's reliable." Jaylynn patted the hood with pride.

The girl laughed. "Your truck's name is Gertrude?"

Jaylynn smiled. "Yep. And now that I think of it, I don't think we exchanged names. My name is Jaylynn."

The girl with dimples smiled and extended her hand. "Nessie, but most of my friends call me Ness."

"Pleasure to meet you." She smiled back, before turning to her other companion.

The woman extended her hand. Another rolling wave of energy raced through Jaylynn's body once again as they connected. "Charity. Ness is my daughter."

"You almost look like you could be sisters."

Charity laughed. "You're too kind." She turned to Nessie. "You know, you don't have to come. I can't explain it, but every part of me feels like I *need* to follow this path. I'd hate to leave you on your own, but—"

Nessie cut her off. "Of course I'm coming. Don't be ridiculous." Light danced in her eyes as she took her mom's hands. "I love you, Mom, and I trust you. Even if you want to pull a Lacey and go on a wild escapade, I'll stay by your side. At least this adventure won't result in me being grounded or starving."

The pair laughed at their inside joke, and Charity crushed her daughter in a hug. Jaylynn unlocked her truck and hopped up on the old leather seat. Gertrude rumbled to life with a turn of a key, and the girls slid onto the bench seat through the passenger door.

"Well, we've got a good hour's trek to get acquainted before we get to the cabin. I can't wait to introduce you to River. Until then, I'd love to hear your story of how you came to be in Toronto tonight."

Nessie smirked, and Charity laughed. "Well, if you want to hear a story about two girls who lied through their teeth to follow some diabolical plan that went haywire, then we've got the story for you."

CHAPTER XLIV

BLAKE

Blake emerged back into the open cabin and made her way to a worn, round emerald cushion on the ground next to an old bronze table. The dark-haired woman sat next to her and offered a dark, steaming mug.

"For the pain," she said.

Blake's black-and-blue toes curled against the rug. It was nice to be free of her bloodied, falling-apart combat boots, but she hated displaying her injuries. *Like you can hide sunburned and split, swollen lips, a limp, and the fact your entire body is withering away like a lily in a desert.* Blake shifted in silence.

"Water alone is an excellent healer, but I always say there's nothing quite like herbal tea. Don't you think?" The woman's dazzling arctic eyes connected with Blake's. She didn't know what to say, so she raised the mug to her lips. The tea smelled wonderful, hot raspberries laid over mint.

Blake wondered if she should tell the cabin woman about her compass, or if she already knew. She seemed like the type that would know things before anyone told her.

"Ah. I suspect that is the rest of our company."

Blake followed the woman's gaze out the window. Sure enough, she could hear a vehicle's rumble as it made its way toward them. Blake's right hand dropped to her lap, inches away from her knife. *Alone in the woods, with a model and a knife, in early hours of the night. I should have known my life would end like a horror movie.*

The loud, white truck came around the bend and parked close. The warm lights of the cabin painted the scene as a petite redheaded lady stepped out. Two long French braids pulled her lively hair back. A pair of blonds followed next, one with a bun at the nape of her neck, the other with a high ponytail that hung straight down her back. Both were at least a head taller than the redhead. They walked to the cabin, their voices and laughter sharp in the evening canopy of trees.

The redhead let herself in. A bright smile spread on her delicate, freckled face. The cabin woman rose to greet the new guests. Blake shrank back. *Okay, this is getting weirder by the moment.* With one hand, she held her small cup of tea for strength; with the other her fingers wrapped around the familiar wooden edges of her security blade as bodies clumped around the only exit. *I should have never*

303

followed my compass here. This was a mistake.

"Ah, Jaylynn." The dark-haired beauty held her hands covered in rings out in greeting. "I started to wonder. The cards insisted everything was coming together, but I am ashamed to admit I worried otherwise. I see that you have found our missing pieces. I knew you would, even if you didn't know what you were looking for." They clasped their hands tight between their chests and held one another as if they were friends who went way back. They stood hardly a foot apart and stared into each other's eyes in an unspoken conversation.

The youngest girl shifted from foot to foot. *At least I'm not the only one who looks uncomfortable.* Blake guessed she was close to her own age, and based on the matching heart-shaped face, likely the oldest woman's daughter. The girl's speculative eyes searched the cabin and her hands clutched her faded denim jacket around her hourglass waist.

"I'm sorry I couldn't come sooner," Jaylynn replied after their extended staring contest. "I had to make sure everything was in place. Though now that I'm here, I can say I wish I hadn't dallied. Being so far from you makes my heart ache unbearably. I don't know how we're going to house the guests, but something told me I had to bring them with me."

It shocked Blake when she noticed Jaylynn's compass also pointed at the cabin woman. Blake swallowed. *Of course, my stupid compass would bring me to someone who's already claimed. I should have known better than to trust the Fates.* A flash of heat pressed through her limbs, and Blake's pale skin went blotchy. *I need to find a way out of here. Now.*

"Not to worry. I have manifested a guest of my own." The black-haired lady smiled back at Blake. She sat rigid in the attention. "We will figure out how to share our space."

Don't worry. You won't need to make space for me. As Blake went to stand, Jaylynn pranced over. She folded her slender limbs on top of the cushion between Blake and the door, her lips stretched in a wide smile. Blake leaned back as Jaylynn plucked up the cabin woman's mug and inhaled the steam.

"Valerian root? You must have really been fretting about my return."

The cabin woman smirked as Jaylynn teased her, then turned to greet the other new women. Jaylynn's attention turned like a spotlight and froze Blake in place.

"You can call me Jaylynn." She extended her hand, but Blake didn't take it. The cabin walls shrank around her. Her head felt light and the details of the room blurred. *Focus.* Her fingers trembled back to her closed blade. She stared at Jaylynn's thin lips, desperate not to disappear in the fog that threatened to settle around her.

"Do you have a name you prefer to go by?"

Blake flashed a furtive glance up to Jaylynn's eyes. "What?" *Keep your answers short. The less they know the better. You're leaving anyway.* Blake looked back at the cabin woman. Her silky black hair bounced on her sun-kissed shoulders as she tossed her head back.

"I mean, River is a great example." Jaylynn waved toward the cabin woman. "She chose her name. Though now that I think about it, she never has told me what her name was before. Regardless, I believe it's a polite question. You get to decide from this moment on who you want to be to me, and a name can shape that."

River. The name twirled in Blake's head like a satin ribbon that curled in a summer breeze. Across the room, her possible soulmate's laughter was rich and easy. Blake's compass ached to close the gap. She'd come so close before the others had shown up, but she still hadn't sealed the connection. On a physical level, she wanted to close the gap more than anything. On every other plane, she wanted to run for the hills.

River's rich laughter filled the room again as she wrapped the two newcomers in a hug.

"Did you choose Jaylynn?" Blake asked. *Rule number two for lying: whenever possible, ask questions instead of answering them.*

"No. My parents chose it. I've never found a name I liked better, so for now I choose to keep it." Her smile was genuine. Blake wondered how someone could seem so happy and carefree. *This lady has probably never had a hard day in her whole life.* Blake could feel her resentment for her competition growing.

Most of her life, Blake's family and friends had called her J.B. Well, other than her mother, but that was unavoidable. But since she'd left New York, the nickname carried a grime that she wasn't sure would ever wash off. J.B. wasn't someone who was tough or resilient. J.B. was a girl who was left in the dust. A child that slept on benches and surfed friend's couches. A nobody. No, she didn't want to be J.B. anymore.

"Blake." Her last name felt odd in her mouth, sharp and unfamiliar from lack of use. As soon as she'd spoken it, she wished she could reel it back in. A piece of truth that could tie her here, to River, to Jaylynn.

Jaylynn smiled in her carefree way. "It's nice to meet you, Blake. We're happy to have you." Her lips wrapped around Blake's name with ease.

Good luck, lady. Be as nice as you want, but I am not sticking around. How could she? Not only could she never deserve the dark-haired beauty's attention, but with Jaylynn around, she was a star being muted out by the rising sun. Blake could never describe herself as kind or gentle, or even happy. They couldn't be greater opposites, and River was bound to see that. Blake stood and took a step back to retrieve her belongings.

"Your compass brought you here, didn't it?" Jaylynn asked.

Blake stopped. She nodded her head.

"Mine did too. Though I suppose it was hardly over a year ago, it feels like it's been ages."

"You don't think it's weird that both of our compasses point to her?"

"Not at all. River has a special way of drawing people to her. When I first met her, she told me we were kindred spirits. Like a family that had been torn apart over generations that was slowly knitting itself back together."

Blake couldn't imagine considering Jaylynn, let alone anyone, as family. She'd had enough experiences of family gone wrong. She wasn't dumb enough to make that mistake again.

"So, you're not like, romantically involved?" Blake's arms wrapped around her torso. Jaylynn's laugh was soft and pleasant, like a wind chime. *She probably couldn't laugh ugly if she tried.*

"Of course not. I suppose that is what most people expect when they follow their compass. River may be gorgeous, but I'm pretty positive her heart is reserved for someone else. Compasses are a strange thing. I'll have you know," she said, lowering her voice to a whisper, "I once met a man whose compass led him to a dog."

Blake couldn't help as her eyebrows shot up in surprise, and Jaylynn burst out in her chiming laughter.

"Not romantic at all, I swear. He just found a life companion in the sweetest little ruby-colored pup. Compasses really are wild." Jaylynn tapered off as River approached with the other two women. Blake kicked herself for letting Jaylynn reel her back in.

River grabbed pillows from the couch and spread them around the table. She settled onto her own faded deep blue cushion then encouraged the others to do the same. Blake let out a sigh before she sat back down. River's bright eyes were enchanting, and Blake's compass pulsed harder. *At least another hour. It would only be polite. I did only just get here. I can leave tonight when the others fall asleep.*

"I understand this may seem confusing, but I ask that you trust me. Each of you is here for a reason, with a gift or skill that no other can provide, and it will all become clear in time."

Blake wondered if being so close to River helped negate her fear of being trapped. The room was clear once again, and Blake's heart rate was smooth despite being inches away from her soulmate. *Is she even your soulmate if she's in love with someone else, like Jaylynn said?* Blake's face fell as she realized yet again, Fate had thwarted her. *Stupid gods and stupid stars and stupid gorgeous women, with their perfect smiles.*

River made eye contact, and Blake's heart skipped. *Okay, maybe she doesn't keep me as steady as I thought.* She took a breath and tried to return a feeble smile. Her lips cracked in protest.

"Let us begin."

CHAPTER XLV

RIVER

After the formal introductions and learning one another's names, the five women settled into a circle and River took a deep belly breath. How could she be sure this was going to go well? What if the women didn't get along? What if she was wrong in thinking she could lead them? As each fearful thought surfaced, she acknowledged it and then let it go. She couldn't afford to live in fear—not now. River looked to Jaylynn, hopeful the girl was ready, and cleared her throat.

"Jaylynn. Will you be my second hand? Help me help these women grow, as I have with you?" Jaylynn nodded without hesitation and River's shoulders softened with relief. At least she wouldn't be alone. She sat tall in her cross-legged position, her thick hair heavy and hot on her neckline. The new, nervous energies vibrated off the wooden beams, full of life and promise. She took a turn to gaze into each of her new guest's eyes before she continued.

"If you each wouldn't mind, I would like to start us off with some agreements. A pact of sorts, to strengthen our bond."

After a few shifting gazes, they nodded. Jaylynn beamed back at her. River smiled as she took Jaylynn's hand, conscious of the usual soft and calming vibration as their skin connected. Then she offered Blake her left hand. The minute their hands met, the blue-haired girl's compass surged, rushing energy through River's body. The vibration of the connection was fierce with strength and resilience, and it filled the cabin with even more power than it had the moment before. River noticed that as opposite as her two companions were, they both had the same effect. They steadied her.

Blake's body relaxed as what River guessed to be a long-overdue wave of peace washed over her body. A twinge of guilt tugged at River's core. If she had taken the time to notice, she could have relieved the girl's pain already. *And I gave her herbal tea when the power of the gods rested in my very hands.* Her smile wove with her apology, but Blake's eyes weren't open to see it.

Two compasses were now bound to her, and River's arms surged with love, connection, and magic. Charity's compass still glittered fresh from hours earlier. To have two alight compasses in the same room? If that wasn't a sign from the stars, River wasn't sure what was.

She smiled as Charity and Jaylynn joined hands, causing more magic to rush through her veins. When Nessie and Blake closed the circle, the momentary head rush that had stolen River's breath released. The buzz in the air stilled.

"When I speak, I will speak only with truth. I will tell no lies, and I will speak no harm against another." River's voice dropped in depth as she delivered the first agreement. One by one each of the women nodded.

Jaylynn added, "I agree," which prompted everyone else to do the same.

"When I listen, I will listen with intention and will not interrupt another's truth."

The energy in the room shifted. The unspoken questions brought another layer to the tension in the room. Even so, each woman agreed.

"No matter what is to come, I will keep an open mind and an open heart."

Blake's hand was slick in hers. River gave a gentle squeeze to reassure her. The women agreed, Blake's frail voice last, but there.

"Last but not least. I understand I am here of my own volition. If I should choose to leave, I agree to keep what has happened here confidential from those who haven't said the agreements."

"I agree," they replied in unison.

"Let us begin."

How lucky was she to have so many brave souls led here? Without doubt, the stars had aligned to deliver her this gift. *No, not just the stars.* River took a moment to enjoy the hum of curiosity in the air before taking the next step.

"I have a question for each of you. You can take as long as you would like to answer, though we will not leave the circle until each of you do. When you receive a fellow member's share, at the end I ask that you reply with a thank-you. It is our way of saying 'I have heard you and understand what you've said.' Try not to fret about when your turn will arrive. Listen to the other shares and contemplate your answers only on your own time."

River hoped they would forgive her for going straight for each of their hearts. *They'll learn fast or they'll leave fast.* And then she would know what she had to work with.

"Jaylynn," River said. "Would you mind going first?"

Jaylynn smiled. "Not at all."

River gazed into Jaylynn's familiar soft blue eyes, then settled into her listening mind.

"Tell us something about your relationship with your compass."

Jaylynn took a deep breath and relaxed into her cross-legged seat as she closed her eyes. They all sat for minutes, hands clasped, their quiet breaths filling the room. When Jaylynn finally opened her eyes, she sat up tall again and made intentional eye contact with River.

"My relationship with my compass is complicated. As a child, I loved it. I loved the magic of it, the wonder. The proof of the gods' power. But then I grew to fear it."

River pressed her tongue to the roof of her mouth. The memory of Jaylynn's tarot card reading swirled anew, but River excused it from the forefront of her mind. She knew this story well enough, but it was important the others heard it.

"When it brought me to Elias—well, I suppose when his compass brought him to me—I was shocked. Of course, Cupid knew exactly which soul would compliment my own. I experienced boundless love, safety, and happiness like never before. Elias's warmth melted away my every fear and insecurity, and I began to believe—well, it didn't matter what I thought. We had less than a year together before the Fates' claws ripped my heart out and dragged my soulmate to the Underworld."

The energy in the room took the noticeable dive that River expected. She knew Jaylynn's share would be emotional and deep, which was why she'd chosen her to go first. She wanted the women to bond, and nothing bonded people like trauma and vulnerability. Charity stifled a sob. River kept her attention on Jaylynn as best she could.

"When the metallic silver of my compass settled into the faded gray, and I knew nothing would ever be the same again, I grew to hate it. Honestly, I'm not even sure *hate* is a strong enough word. It reminded me every single day of the happiness I had lost—a scar I could never heal."

Charity no longer held her sobs back. Tears trickled down Jaylynn's cheeks and her pale blue eyes shimmered. "When my compass came alive again, I followed it to River with enormous superstition. It seemed too good to be true, and to be honest, I was terrified of being broken twice over. Though it's been a blessing, I'll admit I am still afraid. I'm scared that because I have found love once again, it means I could lose a loved one again. And that kind of pain, I don't think I could survive a second time around."

"Thank you." As usual, River was humbled by Jaylynn's depth and honesty. She turned her attention to the rest of the group as they echoed her thank-you. Charity's tears spilled over her cheeks, her hands clenched tight in Nessie's and Jaylynn's.

"Charity, would you mind going next?" River asked.

She nodded and took a ragged breath as she composed herself.

"Tell us something about your relationship with your compass."

Charity followed what Jaylynn had done and closed her eyes and contemplated the question. River could tell before she spoke that her share would be equally powerful in pulling the group together. She returned River's gaze.

"I suppose my relationship with my compass has been one of grief and pain. When I met Luke, I thought I was the luckiest person in the world. Where I was unsure, he was confident. Where I was afraid, he was brave. He was my strong and steady. He yearned for family, and soon we brought Nessie into the world." Her eye contact flitted to her daughter, paired with a quick smile.

"I was lying in bed late one night when my compass went dark. To know the exact moment the greatest love of your life dies, it was... well, my soul split in half in the same beat. I knew all at once that I would never know warmth again; I would never feel peace again; and I would never know a love like that ever again." Tears burned down her cheeks. Jaylynn's fingers tightened in River's clasp.

"First, I lost the imprinted clock hands that sat at seven thirteen, the perfect Tuesday morning that Luke wandered into my life. I spilled scalding tea down my dress pants in the middle of a train. I probably looked like a clumsy wreck, but he stared at me like I was a shooting star in a clear night's sky." Charity choked back a cough. "Of course, the Fates are not known for kindness. For years my clock hands glittered at their seven thirteen time. Then, for the last four years, my compass marked his exact time of death: two thirty-five. What a cruel but suiting detail from the god of love—a permanent reminder of lost love etched in the skin.

"But then I lost even that. My tattoo revived with fresh brilliance and a new time: ten fifty-seven. The time I would meet Jaylynn. Without Ness, I'm not sure I would have had the strength to follow it. I was so afraid… But now I'm here. This is the closest thing I've had to peace in years, and to be honest, I'm not sure what's harder: feeling broken, or losing my last link to Luke."

Nessie squeezed her mom's hand. River and Jaylynn replied with their thank-yous. Blake chimed in a touch late. The tension in the room was high, exactly as River had expected. She turned her attention to the next heart she wanted to open.

"Nessie," River said. The girl's gray eyes shifted back and forth, unsettled. "Tell us something about your relationship with your compass."

Nessie didn't need time to consider her answer.

"I was fourteen when my compass appeared, the first of many of my friends, and I thought I was lucky." Nessie scoffed. "Instead, it turns out I'm cursed with a frozen compass. So while all my friends seek their future soulmates, all I can do is watch them find their partners and leave me in the dust.

"I've tried not to be jealous, but I can't help the anger that bubbles up in me. It hurts that everyone else seems to get a happily ever after except me, when I've done nothing wrong. It's like no matter how hard I try to be good and kind and patient and sweet, my sentence of solitude stays stamped on my soul. I don't know what I did to deserve this. So to answer your question, River, I hate my compass. I hate it with every cell in my body, and I wish I could rip it off."

Nessie's steel-gray eyes flashed with defiance and River tilted her chin in approval. It was a terrible but honest share. The women in the room replied with a chime of thank-yous and River suppressed the temptation to examine Nessie's compass immediately. Concern creased in the folds that spanned Charity's eyes, and River wondered if this was the first time she'd seen this glimmer of her daughter's truth.

River turned toward her newest link and took stock of the fear in her companion's eyes. She offered a smile that she hoped would be reassuring.

"My friend. Tell us something about your relationship with your compass."

River remained patient as she waited while Blake sat frozen. She opened her mouth, then closed it again. River was confident that she was as integral of a piece as the others had been, so she waited while Blake sifted through her thoughts.

"I think that faith in compasses and linked soulmates is idiotic, and the gods can rot in the Underworld for all I care." She took a quick breath. "And I know mine led me here, but it doesn't mean anything. There's no such thing as happy ever afters, and anyone who thinks there is, is in for a harsh wake-up call."

Blake held her chin high as her share came to an abrupt end. The women all replied with their thank-yous. Blake's thin frame clenched tight.

Is she worried we will kick her out? River smiled and traced her thumb over the back of Blake's hand in reassurance. For a heartbeat, River caught a flash of the girl under the tattoos. The girl who was used to being trampled over for her brave ideas. The girl who had to grow thick skin to protect herself.

River's gratitude for each of their truths beat deep in her heart as she took it all in. The purity; the honesty; the fear; the hurt. Despite that, there was love. The compassion that filled every breath was tangible as each woman's heart reached out to the others.

Jaylynn spoke up before River could, a sly smile on her face. "River, tell us something about your relationship with your compass."

River felt a wave of emotions course through her as she faced the question. Of course Jaylynn would go there. When had anything stopped her curiosity before? As much as River felt reluctant to share, she knew her contribution was necessary. She took a breath and closed her eyes. The group sat in silence for the longest stretch yet as she battled internally with the truth. How much could she share with this ragtag group of women? Finally, River looked up and returned the intense gaze back to Jaylynn.

"I know my compass was a blessing, but in commitment to our pledge of honesty, it's been a gift laced with poison. It is a vicious reminder of the devotion we all crave but don't deserve. It is a broken promise—"

River cut herself off. Even the small truth was painful to admit. Every time she reflected on her own compass, years of grief came rushing back, threatening to drown her in guilt. She pushed the bubbling emotions back down and smothered them back in the darkness where they belonged. No, she didn't want to go back there. Her short share would have to be enough.

Thank-yous filled the room for the last time. River released the hands she'd been holding and raised hers into a prayer position. She offered a bow to the group and closed the practice off. "Thank you. The truth in me sees and honors the truth in you."

CHAPTER XLVI

GARETH

Gareth shifted in his seat as the second movie of the flight ended. His high energy and long legs weren't made to be cramped up like this. Though the movies helped pass the time, he still felt antsy with another hour to endure. The old man who sat in the window seat beside him had fallen asleep, but Sebastian was wide awake. Since they'd boarded, he'd sat alert, worry plastered on his face. Gareth was convinced he had almost bailed as the plane had prepared to take off. Gareth was glad he didn't. He couldn't imagine what it would be like to be on this trip alone.

"Hey, Seb?" He nudged Sebastian's arm. Sebastian pulled out both his headphones and turned to give his fullest attention. Gareth always appreciated the way he listened. At school, so many kids would continue to scroll on their phone with an earphone hanging out of one ear, half committed to the conversation.

"What's up, mate?"

"I don't want to start this trip off weird. I know we don't talk about love and compasses usually, but I don't like feeling like we're keeping things from each other."

Sebastian nodded in agreement, his eyes flashing in an unspoken emotion before dropping.

"I'm sorry I didn't tell you I got my compass," he replied. His shoulders slumped. "I didn't know when to bring it up, and then the longer I waited, the more it felt weird to say anything." Sebastian spoke in a hushed tone to keep from disturbing their sleeping neighbor. "I also don't want things to be weird or to come between us now that we both have compasses. I just can't help but worry that when we find our soulmates, we'll grow apart." He gathered his thoughts. "I thought that maybe if we didn't talk about them, then maybe it didn't have to be true."

Gareth smiled. "Mate. No girl or guy, soulmate or otherwise, is going to come between our friendship."

"But what if we get distracted and so lovey-dovey that we don't have time for each other anymore? What if I end up like my parents?" Sebastian's thumb traced over his scars in a slow pattern.

Gareth leaned forward. "You don't have to be like your parents. I mean, mine turned out fairly normal, and they still love each other. Besides, I'll kick your butt if you think you disappear when you meet your soulmate. That's what best friends are for."

Gratitude shone in Sebastian's eyes. "I'm sorry I didn't tell you sooner. I know I made the morning awkward and I'm sorry."

"Don't worry, mate. It's cool." His knee vibrated as he stole the courage to bring up what he had meant to talk about. "That whole thing with Damien…" He trailed off, unsure of how to say what he wanted to.

Sebastian scoffed. "Damien's a dickhead and we both know it. We are not letting him ruin this trip for us."

"He is a dickhead… But what he said was true." He took a deep breath to steady himself. Was he about to ruin this trip? "It's just… I don't know how to say this. The reason I think compasses are weird between us is because I feel weird about mine." Sebastian waited for him to go on, adding no comment. Gareth could feel the anticipation hanging in the air. "I thought I did a good job of hiding it, but—it's broken, mate. My compass has been broken for as long as I've had it."

Sebastian's eyes darted down to his covered forearm before looking back at him. "What do you mean?"

"I mean, it changes all the time. It's bloody all over the place. Every time I think it's settled, it changes again." Sebastian didn't move to interrupt him, so Gareth continued on. "And I mean, that's not even the weirdest part. It points at all kinds of people. Dudes, chicks, friends—but they never seem to notice. Even when they're standing right next to me and it's humming so loud, I swear someone will think I have a damn vibrator in my pocket." He took a breath, reminding himself to keep his voice down. Gareth couldn't read his best friend's expression.

"So, Damien…?"

Gareth sighed and leaned back in his seat. "I don't know how or when he noticed. But yeah, he was telling the truth. Sometimes my compass points at you. Which is exactly why I've kept it hidden and avoided talking with you about it. I feel weird. I swear I'm not into you, but it's like it has a mind of its own." Gareth felt his face burn with shame as he vocalized the secret he'd held for so long.

"Gareth. It's cool. I'm sorry you didn't feel you could tell me sooner. If you swear you don't want in my pants, I believe you. But like, if you did, I wouldn't blame you." Sebastian winked as he grinned at his best friend. Gareth couldn't help but laugh as the tension dispersed.

"You're really not upset?" Gareth asked. He'd spent months playing this scenario out in his head, and every time he'd imagined Sebastian being uncomfortable and walking away. But he didn't leave. He didn't even look away.

"Honest, mate. We'll figure this out together. It's what best friends do."

Gareth sighed in relief as his knee finally stopped shaking. He hadn't realized how much tension and fear he'd been carrying until this moment. He smiled and moved to grab his headphones but stopped when Sebastian started talking again.

"While we're on the subject, there's something else you should know." It was as if Sebastian had taken on all the nervous energy that had escaped Gareth's body.

"My compass is changing, man. Like not directionally, but I can feel it. The pull is getting stronger, and I swear it's getting warmer by the hour. I... I think my person might... I don't know, live in Canada?"

Gareth's jaw dropped. "You're telling me we might actually meet your soulmate on this trip?" His voice was loud and startled the old man awake beside him. Sebastian turned bright red as he threw his hands over his mouth to hush him.

"C'mon, mate. Let's not tell the whole world. The last thing I need is Damien looming over me to potentially spoil this. And maybe I won't meet them on this trip, but at least now I know they don't live on the same continent."

Gareth's knee started to vibrate again, but this time with excitement instead of anxiety. "Who's to say it can't be this trip? You know my mum would tell you to follow it. But I agree, we need to keep the other guys out of this. Once we land and figure out our schedules, we'll have to find ways to casually follow it." Gareth's eyes twinkled.

"I don't know..." Sebastian said. He looked down at his arm as he pulled his sleeve back. "I'm not sure I'm ready for a soulmate. Least of all one that lives all the way across the world."

"C'mon. It would make my trip if we at least gave following yours a shot."

Sebastian looked up at his friend skeptically. "We'll see. If it seems like everything is falling into place, we'll follow it. But if it's going to be complicated or risk our exchange, we bail. Okay?"

Gareth nodded eagerly. It was the closest to a yes that he was going to get for the moment, so he took it. He smiled as the day's mood took a significant turn. He breathed in relief as all their secrets were aired, and he found himself settling into their trip, excited for all the new possibilities.

CHAPTER XLVII

NESSIE

Saturday morning, Nessie woke with a groan. The smell of incense lingered on the heavy yellow quilt that threatened to smother her. She tossed it aside and rolled on the rigid wood floor, the bite of her impromptu sleeping arrangement bright against her shoulder. Sunbeams trickled in, and her mom lay beside her on the ground, her jaw slack and her arm draped over her head.

Ten years of nightmares and now she sleeps on the ground like it's the Fields of Elysium.

Jaylynn snored softly on the couch and Blake could barely be made out on the cot, surrounded by a fortress of blankets. River stood by the stove top and swayed, quiet in her dance as she prepared her morning tea. Today River wore a dress covered in sunflowers that cut off below her knees, its small straps thin and delicate on her tanned shoulders. When Nessie sat up, River smiled and held out a cup in a silent offering. Nessie took it with a polite nod, conscious to maintain the silence, and excused herself outside, desperate to escape the sauna. The dew of the morning clung to the blades of grass, and the green canopy rang with birdsong.

She eased herself onto the cabin-front bench and relished the moment to herself. Though Nessie didn't mind spending the weekend in the woods, her mind whirled in protest. *Am I going to sleep on the floor every night? How many nights will we stay? Is Mom going to want to stay longer now that Jaylynn is in the picture? What are they going to be to each other? Did I just become a third wheel?* She tried to only consider the questions she might have control over, but there was one that trickled through that stumped her most of all. *Did Lacey find her soulmate?*

A wave of grief threatened to surface, as hot and angry bubbles rose from her abdomen to her chest. She wrestled the emotions back down. Nessie kicked the dirt under her white sneakers as her brain ran through how everything had changed. How Lacey had changed. How her mom would change.

As if she'd read her mind, the cabin door swung open again and Charity stepped out, a big smile plastered on her face. She sat on the bench and wrapped her arm around Nessie's shoulders.

"Crazy weekend, eh?" Nessie said, her eyes trained on the steam of her cup that curled in the cool morning air.

"Ha! That's an understatement. Who could have guessed what an adventure this would turn out to be?"

Nessie chuckled and kicked her shoes through the dirt.

"Ness, thank you for being here with me. I know this is all weird and new for both of us, and to be honest, I have absolutely no idea what we're doing…"

"It's cool, Mom. If you want to stay here for a few more days, I'm sure we can figure it out. Eventually we're going to have to talk logistics, though. This can't be sustainable." Nessie tried not to come off as pessimistic as she broached the subject. "As much as River seems happy to host us, we didn't bring a lot to contribute. I mean, the clothes we packed were for a city weekend away, not a middle-of-the-bush trip." She looked down at her own torn-up jeans and white T-shirt, then at her mom's lace embroidered Buddha shirt and leggings.

Charity took her daughter's hands. "I hear what you're saying. I've already thought the same myself. Would you be okay if we continued playing this by ear? I can't explain this feeling I have, but I'm confident we're meant to be here."

"Of course, Mom. I'm all in. I just have a hard time turning off my brain sometimes. You know me." Nessie smiled and tried to appear more enthusiastic than she felt.

Charity beamed back at her. The cabin door swung open again. River came out carrying the pot of tea and a handful of mugs. Jaylynn followed, her red braids wild, with a large wooden bowl of berries. Blake trailed behind with a large blanket, her face pinched against the sunlight. They set up the simple picnic between them as all five women settled onto the blanket around the breakfast.

Blake wore a soft blue jumper today, with billowing pants that came mid-calf. Nessie guessed Jaylynn must have lent it to her, as it was a stark contrast to the black leather jacket she'd worn the night before. The outfit showcased the tattoos that crawled up her arms to her neck, and Nessie was surprised at how the combination could be both feminine and regal at the same time.

River cleared her throat. Though they didn't sit in the same formal circle they had yesterday, they all listened with eagerness.

"Through the years I have learned many unique practices. Some may call it sorcery, but I like to think of it as honing natural intuition. As my gift to you, I would love to share some of these skills. I thought this morning we could spend some time learning to read energies. With so many fresh compasses, our space is overrun with magic and there will never be a better opportunity to learn."

From sorority circles to voodoo training. This should be great. Nessie looked down at her own dead compass. Despite her immediate resistance, she resolved to be a good sport for her mom's sake.

"I think we should start with Charity," River offered. "Your magic is incredibly vibrant and will be the easiest to learn with. Would you mind holding out your compass?"

Charity nodded with a smile.

"The compass should feel unique and like an energy of its own." River demonstrated bringing her hand from a close hover over

Charity's compass to farther away. "When I listen, her energy feels powerful to me. Protective. Not aggressive, but clear and assertive." She moved her hand between Charity's compass and where Jaylynn sat. "When I move my hand here, I can feel the energy pushing through me and shoving me away. It's a very passionate feeling. I would say Charity's love for Jaylynn is similar to Jaylynn's for me. Storge—a bond of kinship and a familial love."

Yep. Definitely voodoo. Nessie tapped her toes together in a quiet, rhythmic beat.

Jaylynn and Charity beamed at one another. Jaylynn moved forward and held her hand out as River had.

River leaned forward, watching. "Feel how the air is like a magnet. Because you're bonded, it might pull you in, whereas it pushed me away."

Jaylynn smiled. "It feels like a cool breeze welcoming my palm." River nodded at the statement, then looked at Nessie.

"Come see, dear."

Nessie took a breath and moved toward her mother. *Fake it till you make it.* Nessie knelt in front of her mother, then held her hand over the compass. The air did feel cooler, and she wondered if it was her imagination. Nessie pulled back, opting not to comment on the experience. River then encouraged Blake to try as well. She didn't look eager but did as she was asked. She didn't offer any commentary either when she pulled back.

River smiled. "Now, to compare, I want you each to hover over Jaylynn's compass and see if you notice a difference."

They each took a turn. Nessie was surprised when her turn came as she felt physically pushed away. *It's got to be in my head.* Charity's brow furrowed as she made her first attempt at feeling Jaylynn's compass. Soon each of the women settled back to their spots, the overall mood quiet and curious.

"Blake, would you mind holding yours out next?"

Blake squirmed at first, then thrust her arm out with her eyes cast down.

Holy Minerva... Nessie tried to keep her features relaxed and not surprised by the ruined compass before her. River didn't break her stride for a moment.

"Ah, yes. There's the magnetic pull. Your energy pulls me the same way Jaylynn's does. Where hers is like a soft melody, yours feels like strength. Resilience. While hers pulses with love and compassion for me, yours feels more grounding. Like you will hold me tight and bear the fiercest storms in my name." Blake flushed at the explanation, but Nessie found it intriguing. *How could she pick that up?*

When Nessie's turn came to hold her hand over Blake's covered-up compass, she tried to feel what River had described. It felt like more pressure than Jaylynn's and her mom's had, but she couldn't understand how River read the emotions.

When Jaylynn took her turn at Blake's compass, she frowned. "I... I don't know if I'm feeling this right. It feels like—" She cut herself off.

"What?" Blake asked bluntly. "You're not going to hurt my feelings."

Jaylynn blushed. "Nothing."

Blake pursed her lips but dropped it. She sat back and looked at Nessie with a please-take-the-attention kind of look. Nessie's stomach knotted. She both wanted her compass read and didn't. What would River see that she couldn't? She held out her arm without being asked and held her breath.

Jaylynn reached out with a hovering hand first. She said nothing, but looked up into Nessie's eyes after. Nessie tried not to squirm. Next, her mother held her hand out over her compass.

"I would say it feels peaceful. I'm not pulled or pushed away. It's like putting my hand in a warm stream. Less assertive than Blake's and not as bubbly as Jaylynn's. I can see what you mean, that they can all be different."

Nessie wasn't sure if her mom was making things up to make her feel included, but she let it go. When Blake put her hand over her forearm, she said nothing, happy again to keep her observations to herself. Then River sat across from her.

I'm not ready for this.

River closed her eyes and held her hand steady, hardly an inch above Nessie's skin.

"Ah, my dear. Now, this is something I haven't seen in ages." She opened her eyes and smiled at her. Her bright blue eyes bore into hers and Nessie mustered her courage to sit tall through her sentence.

"Have you ever heard of the love of Philautia?" River asked.

Nessie shook her head. She held her thumbs tight in clammy fists.

"I have a wonderful book I think you would enjoy. Philautia means love for oneself. Your compass is alive, and actively pointing to you. Your greatest love and companionship in this lifetime will come from within." River beamed at the reading as Nessie stared down at her arm. The arrow had always pointed straight up her arm.

Jaylynn chimed in. "I think River's reading is spot on. I couldn't explain it when I felt it, but now that you put words to it, that makes sense."

"But," Nessie started, "how can that be right? Does that mean I'll never get married? That I'll never have kids? Am I going to be a loner my whole life? Why would I have a compass at all?" Her mind raced as she tried to process the possibilities.

River cleared her throat. "Don't fret, dear. You will likely have great love, and a family if you wish it. All your compass is saying is that your relationship with yourself is the most important in this lifetime."

"Lucky," Blake muttered under her breath. When she realized everyone had heard her, her cheeks turned pink. "Not that I don't want my compass to point to River. I just think you're fortunate that Fate didn't make your choice for you."

Nessie scowled. "How am I lucky? If every person on Terra Mater has a compass, I'm never going to have a person to be matched with. This is basically a life sentence of loneliness, unless I find someone with a dead soulmate."

Jaylynn and Charity both cringed. Nessie coughed and her cheeks burned. "Holy Minerva, I'm sorry. I didn't mean it like that. I—"

"It's fine, Ness," her mother replied. "You're just processing. At least this is more than Dr. Cavanagh could explain."

"I guess." She pulled some grass from the ground and picked it apart.

"Loving yourself can be a very rewarding journey," Jaylynn said. "Maybe your compass will change after you fully accept your self-love."

"Where does someone even start with loving themselves? Do I need to look in the mirror every day and tell myself I'm beautiful?" Nessie laughed, but her heart wasn't in the joke.

"I think for some people it might start like that," Jaylynn answered. "It can also be doing favors for yourself. Like completing projects early instead of waiting until the last minute and being stressed. Or buying yourself a sweater that makes you feel amazing. Like every relationship, I think it takes effort and intentional care."

Nessie threw her grass pieces aside. "Okay, okay. So I've got to figure out how to love myself. I hear you. Can we move on to River now?"

River looked surprised as she shook her head. "I don't think—"

Jaylynn cut her off before she could make an excuse. "Come now, River. There's no better way for us to learn." Nessie could swear

Jaylynn was pushing River's boundaries, but the woman gave in after a moment and held out her arm.

Each of the girls took a turn at feeling the energy around her compass. When Nessie got her chance, the first thing she saw was that the clock hands on River's compass both pointed to noon—exactly like her own. Nessie closed her eyes and tried to pay close attention. Though she didn't offer her commentary to the rest of the group, she could have sworn that the compass made her palm ache, if not even burn a little. When she pulled back, the sensation went away.

Of everyone, Blake was the only one to speak. "It feels so sad compared to everyone else's." Jaylynn and Charity nodded in agreement.

River coughed and stood abruptly. "Nessie, I'll go grab you that book that I mentioned." She walked away without an invitation to join her.

CHAPTER XLVIII

LACEY

The glare of the Happy Valley Goose Bay gas station danced across the Saturday evening sky, and Lacey slumped back into her seat as her mom scrolled over her phone maps.

"Hey, Lacey. I know you were really hoping for today, but honestly, it's not looking good." Renee's eyelids drooped. "It looks like when midnight hits, we'll be in the middle of nowhere again. I know you want to keep pushing, but we need to get a hotel tonight. My back is aching, and I could use a meal that isn't convenience store garbage."

"It's okay, Mom. I know it's not your fault. With every day, we get a little closer. Besides, it'll be a treat to get a real meal and bed." With a dry smile, Lacey bumped Renee's shoulder. "Who would have thought we'd be spending Canada Day weekend in such a random place just you and I, eh?"

Renee smiled back. "Who would have thought? We don't need to stop long, just a few hours."

Lacey nodded, her attention on the distant horizon and the glinting lake.

It's just a quick stop, nothing to fret over. I am going to meet my soulmate tomorrow, and everything will finally be right.

"Mom, I haven't properly thanked you. I would have never made it this far without you. I'm sorry for the things I said back in Quebec, and I'm sorry I've been such a terrible daughter lately."

"I know that your father and I haven't made it any easier on you."

"So, with Ladybug now, does that mean you guys won't be getting divorced?" Even as Lacey said the word, it caught in her throat.

Renee reached out and squeezed her hand. "We're not getting divorced. I'm sorry you had to hear that fight at all."

"I'm sorry I ran away and hid at Nessie's. I was just so angry and…" *And I needed to get away. It was too much.*

"I get it, Lacey, and I forgive you. I'm glad you had somewhere safe to go that was nearby, even though I was furious at the time. You know, you're really lucky to have Ness."

Lacey's mouth went dry. "Yeah, I know." She eyed her mother's phone and wondered if she should reach out. Renee had hardly heard from Charity since she'd left, only a quick message that they'd headed home early by train. Lacey ground her bottom lip between her teeth. *I'll reach out later when the service is better. I don't want to start a conversation I can't finish. Besides, it'll be better if my apology is in person.* Nessie's tear-stricken eyes in the train station came back to her.

"I love you."

"I love you too, Mom."

Despite the ridiculously early hour, Sunday morning, Lacey and Renee had made it back on the road with wide smiles and overtired giggles. Even as the rain fell harder and the winds grew more aggressive, Lacey smiled out her window, confident today was the day she'd finally connect with her soulmate. The humming on her arm was definitely different, and now that the needle was less north and more east again, she had no reason to doubt otherwise.

Hours later, when they finally pulled into Mary's Harbour, the coastline city of Newfoundland and Labrador, Lacey was practically vibrating. The clock on the dash flashed to 12:07. This was it.

Renee planted a kiss on the top of Lacey's head. "Be safe and come back soon. I'll get a table in the motel restaurant and wait for you. I love you."

"Thanks, Mom." Lacey hugged her over the console and turned to face the heavy rain. She pulled the hood of her gray sweater up and stepped out of the SUV, ignorant of everything other than the moment and her compass. The clock was right. Her compass was right. The place was right.

The cold rain hit her face hard. She blinked away the frigid raindrops intent on ruining her moment as she crossed the street. She had waited far too long to meet her soulmate for the weather to have any say over how magical this would be. Lacey looked down at her beautiful compass. It continued to point east, adamant in its direction.

Gasping for breath against the furious wind, she crested a hill of large rocks. Her heart raced as she took step after step, stumbling over the jagged stones. She had traveled so far, believing that at any moment it would happen, and it was finally time. She wiped her hands off on her soaked jeans as she cleared the last crest. The expanse of the beach opened before her. Her feet sunk into the damp sand.

Fool. Her gut turned as she took in the scene in front of her. The tumultuous ocean, the raging winds, the sharp, biting rain—and not a soul in sight. She should have known no one else would be foolish enough to be out in this blasted storm. She looked back down to check her unwavering arrow. Her mind tried to rationalize that her soulmate could be on a boat, but that thought died as quickly as it surfaced. Her pulse shuddered as she came to terms with the reality of her situation, something she had refused to believe. Her soulmate wasn't here. They weren't on a boat. They weren't even on the same stupid continent.

Reality struck her as Jupiter's thunder rumbled deep in the sky. She sank to her knees and pain tore through her chest, a blade of dispassionate truth, sharp and cruel. Hot tears contrasted the cold rain on her face. Her fingertips clawed deep through the sand. As she bowed down to the roaring storm, she thought of everything it had taken to get here. The lies and manipulation. The fight with Nessie, then the fight with her mom. Driving for days and nights across the country. She cried for all the pain she'd endured and all the pain she'd caused. Above all, though, she cried knowing the entire ocean stood between her and her soulmate.

Neptune, I know I've never prayed directly to you, but if you're out there, I could really use a hand.

But the god of the ocean who once allowed his waters to part for Moses didn't respond. Her fingers clawed into the sand and her core spasmed in pain. Curling forward, she let her forehead rest on the ground.

So, this is it.

Suddenly, warm hands grasped her shoulders. They were soft as they pulled her up and wiped the sand away, then moved to push her clinging hair out of her face. Lacey looked up in the pouring rain at her mother. Renee, the woman who was always there, even when things got ugly. Lacey burrowed into her mom's loving arms and sobbed.

CHAPTER XLVIX

BLAKE

"Where are you going?"

The voice echoed in the darkness, and Blake froze. Her fingers tightened around the straps of her backpack. Blake had been sure that forcing herself over the threshold of River's cabin door would be the hardest part of tonight. Well, other than going back to the unknown, in the darkness, in a foreign country, all by herself. She turned slowly, her palms slick despite the cool breeze weaving through the night's trees.

"Out for a walk."

As the figure stepped closer, the glimmer of moonlight outlined the girl's curvy silhouette.

"With your backpack?"

Blake shrugged. The weight rested heavily on her low back, and her heart rate rose. It had been hard enough to convince herself to steal things from River, and now she was caught red-handed.

"You know I don't want to be here either, right?" Nessie's face was now close enough that Blake could make out her dimples and the thick, ashy-blond arches of her eyebrows.

"Why are you out here?" Blake retorted. *I just need to turn and leave. She's young. She won't follow me for long.*

Nessie played with the cuffs of her denim jacket. "I couldn't sleep. Believe it or not, sleeping on a cabin floor isn't exactly my dream vacation."

Blake nodded, unsure of what to say or how to excuse herself from the unnecessary conversation. Wind whispered through the canopy above their heads and the darkness loomed heavy behind her.

"Why are you leaving?" Nessie's question was simple compared to the ones River had challenged her with that day.

What does love mean to you? Do you think it's possible to repair the relationship you have with your compass? Share with the group how you came to be here. The entire twenty-four hours since Blake arrived had been an absolute nightmare of therapy questions that she wasn't ready to face. No matter how much physical relief it brought her to be near River, she'd decided it wasn't worth it. She couldn't say that to Nessie, though.

"I don't belong here," Blake said. *The best kinds of lies are the truth.*

Nessie huffed. "And you think I do? At least your compass led you here. I'm pretty sure I'm the only one not divinely fated to be in this group."

Blake considered that every woman had a compass that brought them to the cabin, except for Nessie. She'd only come because she was with her mom when they'd found Jaylynn.

What do I care? The only person who should matter to me in the group is River, and the stars know I don't deserve her.

Blake took a casual step back to the hovering darkness. Her eyes flicked to the trees then back to Nessie's inquisitive eyes. Blake had rarely been one to notice eye color before, but with River's intense eye contact rules, even in the dark she could see Nessie's stormy-gray irises. *Odd how we spent all day basically in therapy, but I still barely know this girl.*

"How old are you?" Blake asked.

"Fifteen, but I'll be sixteen in September. How old are you?"

"Nineteen."

"Huh, you look older."

Blake shrugged and clasped her forearm. "You act older."

Nessie smirked and leaned against a tree trunk. "Can I ask you something? Something more serious?"

"Will it be easier or harder than answering River's soul-searching questions?"

"Probably harder."

The wall that usually shot up whenever someone asked her something personal didn't, so Blake gave a small nod.

One question, then I'm going.

"When we're doing River's exercises, it always feels like you're holding something back. Something bad. Is that why you're leaving?" Nessie stared out into the darkness as she asked, her thumbs hooked in the pockets of her jacket.

Blake sighed. "Maybe. Yes, and no." The darkness provided a welcome relief from Nessie's inquisitive eyes, and the girl's patient silence made it easier to talk. "Something bad did happen."

"With your compass?"

"Kind of, not really."

Nessie didn't move as she waited. Blake rolled her neck from side to side. "After I wrecked my compass, I met someone. Someone I trusted a lot. They took me in and gave me a home. A job. A chance."

Why am I even telling her this? The trees rustled, but Nessie made no move to leave.

"Did he hurt you?"

"Yeah, he did. I thought he—well, I don't know what I thought. He didn't think the same, though."

"Were you in love?"

Blake sputtered a cough. "What? No. It wasn't like that. He was like a father figure to me."

"Oh."

"Yeah."

"What… Can I ask what he did? Or didn't do?"

Even in the safety of the darkness, Blake's shoulders stiffened. She couldn't bring herself to answer. The scent of whiskey mixed with beer hung like a rotted perfume in the air. Blake swallowed as a black pit opened at her feet, a chance to slip away. Nessie's voice drew her back.

"Is that why you don't like being touched?"

Blake frowned. It was weird how much Nessie noticed. Blake couldn't bring herself to answer, but she nodded.

"Did he... did he hurt you?" When she didn't answer, Nessie dropped her voice. "Blake. Did this man—did he rape you?"

Blake dashed a tear off her hollow cheek. "No." Her voice was coarse, and she tried to clear it. "Nothing that bad. It was stupid. He was drunk. It was nothing."

Dammit, why did I agree to one question when I knew she wouldn't stop? Blake pushed off the nearest tree and coughed against the phlegm building in her throat. "Other girls have way worse things that happen to them. It's not a big deal. I'm fine, see?"

She held out her arms in a display of bravado. Nessie met her gaze.

"You know, just because it wasn't rape doesn't mean it was okay or something to write off as not a big deal."

Blake's stare hardened.

Nessie met her intensity and stood to her full height. "The guy sounds like he belongs in the pits of the Underworld."

"Yeah, he does."

Nessie glanced back toward the cabin. "You know, you don't have to tell everyone that story. And truly, I'm glad you shared it with me. But I can guarantee these people don't want to hurt you."

"I know."

A coyote's howl broke the night air. Nessie shivered and nodded in the direction Blake had been heading. "Do you know where you would go?"

"Not really."

"You're not worried you'll be eaten by wolves or bears or something?"

Blake coughed against a low chuckle. "I hadn't really considered it, to be honest."

"You seem like the type to do a lot of things without thinking." Nessie's remark was cool, but it didn't shake Blake.

"And you seem like the type who overthinks everything."

To Blake's surprise, Nessie smirked. "You're not wrong. Listen, if you want to leave, I get it." She rubbed her arms against the chill of the night. "But I think you should stay. I know all these stupid things River makes us do are awkward, but... I don't know. It just wouldn't feel the same without you here. Everyone else feels so, I don't know, old and wise and timeless?"

Blake let out a huff of laughter in agreement.

"There's no pressure, but I would like it if you stayed."

It was like clips of a movie flashed in bright color through Blake's mind. Her mom as she leaned over the kitchen sink. *"Well, if you're so fed up with me, why don't you leave me, just like your father did!"* Tatiana, wrapped in a bedsheet, with tears streaming down her cheeks. *"We both know you're leaving, so why are we even playing this game? Just go, J.B. I don't want you here anymore."* Sal, drunk with her crumpled drawings in his hands. *"You don't belong here."*

But here was Nessie, cool and calm and serious Nessie. *"I would like it if you stayed."* No one had ever asked Blake to stay before.

Nessie smiled and turned back toward the cabin. Her blond ponytail swung in the moonlight until it was out of sight. A fresh coyote cry sang in the night, closer than before. It wasn't Blake's fear of the wildlife that uprooted her feet toward Nessie's retreating silhouette, though. It was the shock that maybe, for the first time in her life, someone wanted her to stay.

CHAPTER L

CHARITY

Charity stoked the fire as the sky grew dark Monday night. The earlier rain had left the air fragrant, and she smiled as the group settled around the warm coals. It had been another long day of mental exercises and if Nessie was upset about them staying past the weekend, she hadn't said anything yet. *She looks exhausted. Why is it now that I've finally found my peace, my daughter is the one who pays the price?*

Charity wrapped her arm around Nessie and kissed her on the side of the head. Jaylynn came and sat on her other side with a blanket in tow. Charity's heart did a little skip when they brushed hands. She wasn't sure she'd ever get used to the new bond, or what to make of it, but she would never complain. Her headaches, brain fog, and nightmares were gone. The only thing about being near Jaylynn that was hard was the eerie silence on the wind where Luke's voice once called to her.

Maybe he found peace too. Maybe his restlessness was because he'd left me on my own. But Charity could remember his invisible whispers. They had been begging her for help. She shuddered and was grateful when River came back to break her train of thought.

River brought her nighttime tea blend to the gathering and offered cups to everyone. They all settled in the darkness, prepared to wind down with the cooling coals.

"Tell me where you believe compasses come from." River's warm voice filled the sleepy silence.

Nessie was the first to respond. "I mean, everyone grew up on the story of Cupid and Psyche. He blessed her with the original compass."

"If we were to accept that legend, then why would the compasses appear on anyone other than Psyche herself?" River asked.

"Isn't that the beauty of magic?" Jaylynn chimed in. "It doesn't need to explain itself to exist; it just does."

Charity considered her own compass, which hummed happily with Jaylynn's proximity. *Does magic like this need to be explained?*

River continued. "If we all agree that magic exists independent of natural laws, then what is stopping it from disappearing as mysteriously as it came?"

The group fell silent. The fire embers crackled. Jaylynn seemed to be the only one with enough wits to respond.

"River, it's late. We're all tired. I'm sure you've got a point to your mind exploration, but for tonight can we skip contemplating life and its existence?"

Charity sighed in relief. *How is it she always knows what to say? It's like she can hear the group thinking.*

River smiled. "Fair enough. Let me instead tell you a story to waken your spirits. Nessie, you speak of the story of Cupid and Psyche. Unfortunately, many of the stories children are told at bedtime are diluted. I will tell you the tale of Psyche and Cupid as I know it, and then we can come back to this."

River took a long pause as she sipped her tea. In a silent gesture, Jaylynn offered Charity part of her blanket. Charity smiled and shuffled closer. Nessie shook her head at the extended offer. She opted to lean back on her own blanket, within whispering distance to Blake.

I hope Nessie knows what she's doing befriending that girl. Charity chose to trust Blake because Jaylynn did, but she remained skeptical.

River cleared her throat. "You all know of Venus, the goddess of love and beauty, and her jealousy of Psyche's beauty. All the stories start the same. When the goddess of love's temples grew sparse and those who worshipped her stopped coming, she grew immeasurably angry. She lost her mind and called for her son to be brought to her.

"When Cupid came, Venus begged him to vanquish Psyche. 'Use your power,' she said, 'and make that despicable woman fall madly in love with the vilest and most despicable creature there is in the whole world.' Cupid was eager to please his mother, and so he flew down to the mortal realm to end his mother's torment. This is the beginning of where the stories differ. He never shot himself with one of his own arrows, as the stories nowadays like to say. He genuinely fell in love with Psyche at first glance. Though, the stories are true in the following passage. He took her to a secluded and magical temple, hiding her away from the world and his mother. He only visited her at night and did his best to hide his identity. And more than anything else, he loved her endlessly.

"It was Psyche's horrid curiosity that drove a stake into the heart of their love story. As her days passed, her curiosity of her lover's face grew to madness, and her loneliness resulted in horrible thoughts: nightmares that she could be in love with a monster; fears that it was a demon who trapped her so far from her family and everyone else that she loved. One night Psyche decided she could not bear the mystery any longer. She pretended to fall asleep in her secret lover's arms and when his own breathing settled, she imagined a lit match in her hands. Her temple of endless gifts obeyed, providing her with the immediate light she desired.

"As the small flame lit the space between them, she recognized the god of love and was immediately overwhelmed by his immortal beauty. Cupid's rosy cheeks and perfect skin glittered against the flame, and in the shadows his innocence shone like a lighthouse in a midnight storm. As he stirred and awoke, Cupid was shocked to see Psyche staring at him in awe. His surprise quickly shifted to fury. He promptly shot up to the clouds, the beating of his magnificent wings snuffing out her match. Cupid flew away without saying a word, leaving Psyche in the darkness.

"When Cupid returned to the sky, he went to the only place he knew to go—his mother's arms. In his pain, he couldn't have foreseen the consequences of telling his mother the truth. Despite being the goddess of love, the betrayal drove Venus over the edge, and any compassion she might have once been able to spare for the lovers evaporated in a mist of outrage. Without hesitation, she caged Cupid to the stars, locking him away for his treachery and for breaking her heart. Then she tethered Psyche's soul to Terra Mater, cursing her to never be able to reach Cupid."

Charity's grip tightened on her cooling mug, the evening tea forgotten with River's fireside story.

"Psyche wallowed in shame in her mountaintop temple. She watched the skies day and night, desperate for her lover to return and distraught that her wretched curiosity had driven him away. She was ashamed that she had ever worried her lover could be a villain. For weeks she waited for Cupid to return, for an opportunity to plead forgiveness. She burned blessing after blessing for him, praying for him to come back to her. When she resolved she couldn't bear the silence anymore, she left her sacred mountaintop, desperate to find another way to him.

"Cupid was equally distraught as he fought against his prison in the stars and watched over Psyche's fruitless travels. His heart ached from their distance and his brash departure. He wished he could tell her he still loved her, that he forgave her, and that he needed her more than ever. His loneliness and his anger with his mother grew with every passing day.

"One night as Psyche traveled the land, she collapsed and gazed at the constellations with tear-filled eyes. Cupid couldn't bear it anymore. He reached through his prison bars up to the surrounding stars and began creating a beautiful gift of love, magic, and stardust. Then he tethered it to an arrow and shot it down at her. Despite the cage that held his essence tight, the arrow flew strong and true. As Psyche watched the shooting star grow brighter and brighter, she held up her arm to cover her eyes from the blinding light. The arrow struck her hard, bursting in unspoken love and longing, as a part of his magic and soul interlaced with her own. Whispers of what had happened filled her ears, and at last she knew her lover hadn't stayed away of his own free will.

"Cupid blessed Psyche with his gift, hoping one day she would free him. What he hadn't intended was the clock that manifested with the magic, foretelling the time they would one day be reunited. It was the Fates who added this blessing as they watched his arrow streak across their sky.

"Though the compass-clock was a gift, a commitment of undying love, the amount of pain it brought was inconceivable. Psyche would forever know her love waited for her to come and free him, but she was cursed by Venus never to be able to—tethered to Terra Mater, watched over by the skies. And despite Fates' clock hands promising they would one day be reunited, Venus's wrath isolated the lovers from each other for all of time."

Crickets sung in the darkness as a hush fell at River's last words. Nessie was the first to speak. "Surely Venus couldn't be so cruel."

River sighed. "So she would like everyone to think."

Jaylynn sat rigid beside Charity, her face set in contemplation.

"River…" Jaylynn seemed to choose her words carefully. "If the gods existed, where do you think they went?"

"I would guess another world. Somewhere they can be free of the trials and faithlessness of mortals—a parallel universe of sorts. Abandoning ours to live in one of their own volition, whilst we try to rationalize what we are left with."

If only there were a parallel universe where I could have kept Luke but also met Jaylynn.

Jaylynn stood, leaving Charity with the bulk of the blanket. She walked around the fire, each step slow and intentional.

"The stories often talk about Psyche and her beauty. What was Cupid like?"

River smiled for the first time since telling the tragic story. "He was the god of love. He had both the innocence of a child and the beauty of an angel. His hair was soft as feathers and his cheeks were flushed rose, like a rising sun kissing the sky. Youth, captured in the prime of adolescence—a pure and shining light."

Charity watched Jaylynn pace.

"Ever longing…" Jaylynn pondered out loud. "If we accept gods are real and still exist today, just through a veil, what happened to Psyche?"

That's a good question… Why is she so good at asking all the right questions?

"She would have died? I mean, she was mortal," Blake answered.

Jaylynn crossed her arms, her pacing settling in an unconvinced stance.

Charity tried to think creatively. She sipped her now-cold tea. "Maybe she reincarnated through the generations?"

"Or she never died," Jaylynn answered. Her stare at River was flat and relentless. "You've been so careful, hiding your past. None of us have any idea where you came from or why you changed your name. You never talk about your compass or how you know so much about them."

Charity watched River's smile fade as a new energy danced around the fire.

Jaylynn looked much taller as the fire's light danced on her short frame, projecting her shadow out onto the trees. "You know the ways of nature like the back of your hand. You tell stories of the gods and their wrath as if you've seen them firsthand. Tell me I'm wrong about what I'm thinking, River."

River bowed her head, not venturing to speak. Charity could barely wrap her head around the accusation.

"Tell me who you are." Jaylynn stared down at her mentor. A chill crept up Charity's spine.

River seemed more shaken than Charity could have imagined. The firelight danced on the features of her sorrow-filled face. "I am exactly what you accuse me of being. Ever longing. Blessed and cursed by the same compass as you. I once had a beloved, and like you, he was stolen from me."

Jaylynn didn't reply with the expected thank-you they'd been taught over the past couple of days. Her voice was taut. "Say your name out loud."

"The name I was born to was Psyche."

Wait, what? Charity's mind tried to process the information, but the pieces lagged as she tried to understand what she was witnessing. Could it all be real? The truth echoed in the quiet night sky, repeating over in Charity's thoughts.

Nessie was the one who broke the extended silence that followed River's admission. "Well, there's no crawling our way out of this rabbit hole now. Psyche, tell us why we're here."

CHAPTER LI

JAYLYNN

Jaylynn made a new batch of tea, no longer wanting the nighttime blend. Lavender to soothe the soul. Vanilla to open the heart. Citrus to sharpen the mind. Much like the tea she had the first time she'd come to the cabin. She tried to process everything that had unfolded. How was it possible for everything to make sense, yet be so baffling? How was she okay with believing her compass had led her to a woman who was over two thousand years old? Questions swarmed her mind as she tried to integrate her new knowledge.

Charity and Nessie appeared quizzical. They seemed committed to seeing this through, whatever *this* was. Blake seemed the least fazed of everyone, though Jaylynn wasn't sure if she'd know otherwise. That girl had a fortress of walls built around her that boggled Jaylynn.

Last, she considered River. Psyche. Whoever her mentor was or wasn't. Every single wall that woman had held came tumbling down, and Jaylynn could now see her with unnerving clarity. It was as if finally admitting her truth had made her beauty shine even brighter. Psyche's eyes were wide open and vulnerable in a way Jaylynn had never seen. She seemed both more real and more out of this world with every passing moment.

Nessie had taken to interrogating her on how she'd lived through the ages. Psyche explained that when her soul had been tethered to Terra Mater, she had stopped aging as well. She believed it was part of her curse, another way for Venus to cause her agony.

The moon was high in the sky now, its shining light peeking through the canopy of leaves. Jaylynn made her way back to the fire. Despite the late hour, no one appeared tired anymore. They all sat attentively, eyes wide, listening to Psyche's story.

Nessie's hair was pulled up in a tight ponytail and her face was set in hard concentration. Jaylynn smiled at her poise. Even though Nessie seemed to believe the story, the girl had a lot of questions.

"So, if you've been alive for thousands of years, how is it you haven't found a way to free Cupid yet?"

Psyche's brow creased. "For centuries I've searched for ways to get to my love. I sought fortune tellers, psychics and sorceresses. I've tried to learn every mystical art I could. I've traveled the globe seeking answers, but with every decade that the gods have been gone, truths have grown scarcer."

Blake listened attentively, sitting close to Psyche but not quite touching. Jaylynn considered sitting on Psyche's other side, but she couldn't help the way her heart shielded itself against her presence. Jaylynn went back to Charity's side, grateful for the soothing energy that radiated off her friend. *Ironic how over one weekend complete strangers can become friends, and deeply connected people can become strangers.*

Psyche's husky voice was filled with sadness. "I would have given anything to have a conversation with him again; to tell him how sorry I was; to tell him I would never stop searching for a way to be together again. But as time has passed, I can't help but wonder if Fate got it wrong. Maybe we aren't meant to ever be reunited again."

Jaylynn set her fresh mug on the ground, taking Charity's hand in her own. Somehow physically connecting with Charity helped— like a tether to reality as the world she thought she knew turned upside down.

Psyche continued. "More recently my life got dark. Hopelessness washed over me. I'd spent so much time searching for him without success that I gave up. I decided I was tired of giving Venus the pleasure of watching me struggle, and I tried to settle into a new life. I stopped traveling the world, choosing to settle far from the Roman Empire. I tried to make connections with friends and build a community. My heart had been stretched and empty for so long that I craved companionship."

A bat raced out over their heads, causing a momentary pause in the story. Jaylynn's heart skipped a beat, but she couldn't tear her eyes away from River's arctic-blue eyes. Not now that she was finally hearing the story she'd waited so long to hear.

"But that's the thing with living over generations. Every companion I met aged when I didn't. And when they began asking questions, I would have to leave again. Eventually, I stopped trying to make connections all together. It was then that I settled into my psychic shop and tried to find a new purpose in my life. I figured if I couldn't solve my love story, the least I could do was help others."

Charity sighed. "Oh, Psyche, I can't imagine how hard that would have been."

Of course Charity could find compassion in her heart for the story. She wasn't the one who was lied to for months. Charity wasn't the one who had received the supposedly precious love advice that had flipped Jaylynn's world upside down. No, it wasn't compassion that stirred in Jaylynn's heart. Sparks dashed into the sky as Blake threw another log on the fire.

Psyche's eyes shimmered in the growing firelight. "I think that the hardest part is seeing how many people praise the gods but are oblivious to their cruelty. Worse, even, is having to bear all the ridiculous statues depicting the love Cupid and I never got to share. Everything about our story and what we could have been has been romanticized and plastered everywhere. For years, psychological, personalized torture covered every city across Terra Mater's precious plains. I wasn't sure how I could bear to go on, then the most amazing thing happened."

Psyche's gaze met Jaylynn's across the flames. "Jaylynn came to me. It was then that I wondered if Cupid was sending me a sign. And now that all four of you are here, I am more confident than ever that he has sent you my way." Hope danced in her bright blue, starlit eyes and moonlight brushed the smile that traced her lips.

Jaylynn broke the gaze, her cheeks flush. To her side, Nessie swirled her tea, her gray eyes ever calculating. "You mentioned before the story that if magic could spontaneously appear, it could also spontaneously disappear. What did you mean by that?"

Psyche smoothed out her dress, her hands fretting with its edges.

"I think that if magic can appear, it can also disappear. It is my intention, should you be open to helping, to try something new. My plan is to reach out to Cupid and to ask him to take my compass away. If we can't be together, I can't continue to live on this way. I don't believe our love was meant to live confined by the black-and-white world of compasses, and I can't endure this torture anymore."

Jaylynn spoke before she could think otherwise. "River, you can't—I mean Psyche, sorry—you can't give up. Undoubtedly, we've been drawn here to help, but it has to be for a cause greater than getting rid of your compass."

Psyche's sorrow-filled eyes met her own. "What cause is greater than the relief of millennia of sadness and pain? What cause is greater than finding peace?"

Sweat glazed Jaylynn's hands. "What about love? Isn't love worth it? You think you're going to get rid of your compass and move on and forget about Cupid? Do you think that's even possible?"

"I think the way I mean to move on and the way you mean move on look different." Psyche cast her eyes down.

Concern flickered on Blake's face in the firelight. "Psyche, you don't mean that."

"But I do." Psyche reached out and rested her hand on Blake's knee. The girl glanced down at the gesture but didn't shy away. "Every injury that I get heals. Every illness that I get, I recover from. I've watched society grow and evolve to become this toxic, love-obsessed monster, and I know that I'm done with it. I am confident when my compass is gone, I will finally be able to move on from this world. That would be a kinder Fate than this."

First, Jaylynn had felt betrayed that Psyche had spent so long lying to her, and now she was supposed to accept that her second soulmate was about to pass on to the Underworld too?

Charity's voice was gentle compared to the vibrant fear that pranced through Jaylynn's chest. "Psyche, I hear your pain and sorrow. I'm sorry for what you've had to live through. If you can't survive without Cupid, then we will do everything to get you to him. Maybe we will be the key to freeing him. Tell us what to do—because the alternative isn't an option we want to consider."

Psyche's eyes shone with wonder.

Blake took Psyche's hand in her own. "I'm in as well. Tell me what you need us to do to get to Cupid."

Jaylynn looked at Blake. *Am I the only selfish one? Am I the only one who can't handle this?*

Nessie nodded in agreement, as if answering Jaylynn's unspoken questions. "I have seen so much hurt come from compasses, and I hate the idea that we're being treated like Venus's playthings. We should be able to live our lives for ourselves. I would revel in the opportunity to live without a compass." She hesitated for half a second. "Psyche… if we make it to Cupid, if he can take away your compass, would it be too much to ask if he can take mine too?"

Now it was Charity holding Jaylynn's hand tighter.

Psyche bowed her head. "If that is your wish."

Jaylynn nibbled at her lip. This woman had changed her entire life. She'd taught her how to see people for all that they were and helped her step into the woman she wanted to become. Jaylynn had chosen this rabbit hole almost without hesitation. Why was it now that she could finally see over the cliff's edge that she hesitated?

Jaylynn thought of being a girl, marveling over the magic in her compass. She thought of the magic moment of meeting Elias. She thought of how the magic had brought her here. Was she ready to lose another soulmate?

"I think I need some time to think." Jaylynn coughed and released Charity's hand. Before anyone could stop her, she left and made her way to the nearby clearing that River loved to meditate in. Jaylynn sank back into the blooming clovers under the watchful moon. She closed her eyes and basked in its soft beams. Crickets and frogs sang a soft harmony to Jaylynn's thoughts.

Was Terra Mater really underneath her, feeling her heart pound against her cool surface? Was Apollo up there, preparing to pull their sun into existence every day? Where did their universe end and hers begin? She thought about the world and she thought about the women she had gathered. She thought about River, and Psyche, and Cupid. She breathed it all out until her mind came to stillness.

When she made her way back to the fire, everyone had gone to the cabin to sleep, except Psyche. She sat alone, gazing into the dying embers of the night. Jaylynn sat beside her. She wished the fire gave off more heat now that her jumper was damp from the meadow.

"I would give anything to make things right." Psyche's voice was soft, careful not to disturb the peace of the night. "Jaylynn, you must know that. I can't do this without you. I would never force you into something you didn't want to do, but I can't stress enough how crucial you are to the process. We are going to need your compassion, your intuition, and your ability to stay focused while holding space. I know it's a lot to ask, but I will wait for you as I've waited for my love. I would rather have you by my side because you want to be, and not because a compass told you where to be."

Jaylynn took Psyche's hand. "I will stand with you, Psyche. I will reunite you with your love, out of my love for you. But I will ask you this. If we can't free him, if he removes your compass and you survive it, please consider living out this life a little longer. I don't want to lose you if I don't have to."

Psyche's eyes swam as she came to kneel before Jaylynn. Tears fell from her arctic-blue eyes and splattered on Jaylynn's freckled knuckles.

"Thank you," Psyche whispered, crying in her reverence.

ACT 3

MORTA

Last of her sisters, Morta reigns tall;
her shears of death, the end of all.
Cutting the thread of mortal life
her blades mark the end to human strife.
And so it is known, by both gods and man,
that the three Parcae reign ultimate command.
—The Inflexible Fate

CHAPTER LII

Tuesday, July 5
7:56 a.m.

"Nylah!"

Nylah's heart lurched, and they jolted up at Jazz's voice. Nylah rolled out of bed and stumbled over mounds of unfolded clothes to their silk cherry blossom robe. Boots mewled in protest and she resettled at the foot of the bed, also inconvenienced by the suggestion her catnap should end. The blurry alarm clock glowed green across the room.

Nylah sighed. *Four more minutes and my alarm would have gone off anyway, I suppose.*

With a groan, Nylah grabbed their glasses off then stumbled out to open the front door. Before a word could be said about his unexpected visit, Jazz's tall body lurched forward with the swinging door and Nylah had to leap forward to catch him.

Seriously? Drunk on a Tuesday morning? Nylah's hands clenched his arms to hold him steady and they gave Jazz an apprising once-over. He clutched his arms tight to his torso and his usual rich brown skin was washed-out. "Jazz, are you okay?"

Jazz said nothing as he slumped forward, his head hung low. His eyelids fluttered shut.

Nylah kicked the door closed and with the least grace possible, helped him slide down the wall to the floor. A scarlet streak smeared the wall as he settled down, and Nylah choked back a sob.

"What happened to you?"

Jazz didn't answer. Nylah's mind raced like a hamster in a wheel as they tried to figure out what to do first.

I need to stop the bleeding, but where is it even coming from?

"Jazz, I need you to talk to me. Where are you hurt?"

He doubled over, his arms tight to his torso. Nylah's heartbeat was faster than a hummingbird's wings.

"Jazz, we need to get you to a hospital."

"No." His voice was stretched thin.

Nylah tilted his chin up with a shaky hand. "What do you mean, no? Jazz, you're bleeding out on my damn floor!"

"Not… not bleeding out," he stammered, then gasped for breath.

He reached out and Nylah swallowed bile at the sight of his blood-soaked hand.

"The blood covering you and my floor suggests otherwise." Nylah took his bloody hand in their own.

He coughed. "I can't go to emerge."

"Why not?"

Jazz held out his arm. Nylah carefully rolled up the sleeve that clung to his muscular forearm and gasped at the gash below his compass. It was a straight, deep cut, and blood pulsed forth in an angry current. Nylah gagged and pushed his arm back to his torso.

"Damn you, Jazz." Nylah let out a sob. *Minerva, please. Help me. I can't do this.* Nylah hadn't prayed to any of the Capitoline Triad in years, but now the goddess of wisdom's name traced through their mind—an old, familiar melody.

"Jazz. Please tell me you didn't do this to yourself."

Jazz sputtered. "It's not what you think."

"Then tell me what to think? Because I'm about five seconds away from losing my ever-loving mind."

He tilted his head back against the blood-smeared wall. "I-I did the ceremony, Nylah."

Nylah's sticky hands froze as they took in the words.

"*They* did this to you?"

"No, I did it myself. I completed the next part of the process to move up." Jazz pulled the bottom of his shirt tight around his arm as a temporary sling.

"You mutilated yourself to get right with the Fates?" Nylah's mouth hung open.

"It was supposed to increase my soulmate's urgency to come to me." Jazz coughed. "If they don't come when their compass flares in response, then the priests take it in their own hands to bring you to them."

I knew it. I knew they were psychos.

"Jazz, do you hear how messed up that sounds?"

"Nylah, it's not a big deal—"

"Not a big deal?" Nylah's voice shook as it hit an octave high enough to rattle windows. "You're bleeding with an open wound, refusing to go to a hospital, on my floor, when I'm supposed to leave for work in half an hour, and you think it's not a big deal?"

A smile broke on Jazz's lips. He leaned forward and Nylah closed their eyes as their foreheads met.

"What were you thinking?" Nylah whispered, a stray tear breaking over their freckles.

His voice was quiet. "I'm sorry. You're mad, and you have every right to be."

"Damn right I do."

"It just felt right. I mean, it's been so long… It didn't seem like that big of a sacrifice for finally meeting my soulmate."

Nylah's chest cinched tight. They'd both waited so many years to find their soulmates. *But not this way. It shouldn't happen this way.*

"You're insane." Nylah let out a feeble laugh. "There is no way I'm going back for that second meeting now. You know that, right?" They traced Jazz's face with the tips of their fingers. *Oh, Jazz, what am I going to do with you?*

"Nylah, I haven't even told you the best part." Even pale and weak, his smile was dazzling. "It worked."

Nylah glanced down at his butchered arm, then back up to him. "What do you mean, it worked?"

"My compass is changing. I can feel it. My soulmate is coming. That's why I can't go to a hospital."

"Why? Because you don't want them to find you in the mental health ward? You don't want them to know you manipulated them into rushing to you?" Nylah's fingers clenched into wet fists.

"I just—" Jazz coughed and sagged back against the wall. "I just wanted it to be somewhere nice."

Nylah crossed their arms. "Oh, okay. Let's go for a morning stroll through the park, shall we? I'm sure no one will notice the trail of blood and the fact you can hardly stand."

Jazz chuckled. "You're only mad that now you'll have to share me."

The pool of blood under Nylah's knees crept closer to the door. "At this rate, I'm not going to have a best friend to share. Jazz, please, let me take you to the hospital."

"Nylah, it's going to be okay. I'm going to be okay. My soulmate is coming." Jazz's eyes fluttered closed as he slumped farther down the wall. "They're coming for me," he whispered.

"For the love of Cupid, so help me, Jazz! If you pass out and die on my floor—"

"Nylah, I'm fine. Really. But could you grab me a blanket? It's a little chilly in here."

Reluctant to leave Jazz, Nylah staggered up and hurried back to their bedroom. Boots meowed and leaped off the bed to weave between Nylah's legs. In the background, their phone alarm chimed with insistence.

Four minutes. How could everything go sideways in such little time? Nylah swiped the alarm away, leaving a red streak across the screen. Without a second thought, Nylah tapped the keypad to call 911. *I'll call an ambulance, then I'll call in sick. My boss is going to murder me, but that's nothing new.*

As the call went through, a new sensation swam through Nylah's body. Nylah looked down in shock, adjusting their glasses in disbelief. Their compass arrow moved for the first time ever.

You've got to be kidding me.

CHAPTER LIII

BLAKE

8:24 a.m.

Blake should have left. She should have never followed Nessie back to the cabin. She should have never heard Psyche's story. But here she was, Tuesday morning, following a scrawled note of ingredients for some special medley Psyche needed. *'To help open the mind and loosen the borders between worlds.'*

What that meant, Blake didn't know. All she knew for sure was that she and Nessie were the least qualified people to be crushing herbs and going through all of Psyche's tinctures. *If she'd labeled them, this would be ten times faster.*

"Do you think this is lavender?" Nessie asked, strands of her long hair falling out of her ponytail. Dark circles hung under her eyes.

Blake shrugged. "I guess so? I mean, it's a purple flower?"

At least Nessie was here. She was less intense than everyone else. Well, that wasn't true. She was intense in that she had startling stormy-gray eyes and asked a lot of questions, but she wasn't prepared to bare her soul to the world. Even though they were three years apart, Blake could see the potential friendship.

Blake scoffed internally. She didn't belong here. There was no long game where her and Nessie would become close. She'd already stayed too long, but the same question troubled her as the night she'd tried to leave: *Where would I go?*

Jaylynn came into the cabin, her sunset-orange curls desperate to escape her braids. Even disheveled, she looked lovely, and Blake loathed her for it.

"Have you seen Riv—I mean, Psyche?"

Both girls shook their heads.

"Is this lavender?" Nessie asked, holding out the cluster of dried flowers.

Jaylynn smiled a stupid, perfect smile. "Yes. Here, let me help you." She reached for the list. Blake's initial instinct was to clutch it to her chest. This was supposed to be *her* task. But Jaylynn waited patiently with her hand out, her smile kind and inviting.

Ugh. Blake handed it to her and watched as her sky-blue eyes skimmed over the writing. Jaylynn pulled dropper bottles down from a nearby shelf and gathered herbs from the windowsill, all with an infuriating spring in her step.

"I hope this helps. I need to get back and help Charity with the altar. Call me if you need more help."

Nessie thanked her as she left. Blake did her best not to glare at Jaylynn's graceful skip out. Both girls turned back to the ingredients now laid out simply in front of them.

"Now what?" Blake asked.

Nessie's eyes twinkled for half a second. "Now I guess we pretend we're witches."

Blake smiled and picked the list back up off the counter.

"Okay, now, which of these do you think is ginkgo?"

Laughter turned to a comfortable silence as they worked through the ingredients.

"Hey, Ness?"

"Hmmm?"

"You know, the other day you mentioned you thought you'd have to find someone with a dead soulmate to be with you."

Nessie stilled.

"I just thought you should know, there are other ways. I met a guy recently that never got a tattoo. Kind of like you, he thought he was screwed out of love."

Nessie slid her hands into the pockets of her faded jean jacket. "And was he?"

Blake chuckled. "Well, I mean. Depends on what you mean by screwed." She winked and Nessie burst out laughing.

"Holy Minerva, Blake. You slept with him?"

Blake's smile fell. "Well, not exactly. But he was kind and sweet, and I don't think you're as alone as you think you are."

Nessie's dimples sank deep with her smile. "You know, you're not alone either." She gave Blake's hand a gentle squeeze. "So are you going to tell me the details? Was he hot?"

Blake's heart swelled, and she chuckled. *Jeez, I can't remember the last time I laughed this much.* "I would say so, yeah."

"What was his name?"

"I didn't actually catch it."

"So you had an almost one-night stand with some compass-less hottie, who you didn't even catch his name, and you have no more details than that? C'mon, Blake, don't leave a desperate girl hanging!"

"Well, he would probably be a bit old for you."

Nessie shrugged, and her stormy eyes twinkled in mischief.

"What do you want to know?"

"Everything." Nessie beamed.

CHAPTER LIV

LACEY

8:49 a.m.

Lacey wasn't sure how long they'd been driving for. She had cried every bit of her strength out the first few hours following the beach, and since then she'd sat in a solitary mist, her mind eating away at how badly she'd messed up. Renee coaxed her to eat every few hours, but it made her nauseous. She could tell her mom was worried, but she couldn't do anything to assuage her fears.

Lacey thought about how her fight with Nessie had been all for nothing. She worried about how mad Charity would be when they got home days later, after outright abandoning them in Montreal. She wondered if her dad would be mad, and if she would ever be allowed a phone again.

"Mom?" Lacey asked, her voice hoarse.

"Yes, honey?"

"I love you."

The worry in Renee's face didn't disappear, but she reached over and lovingly brushed her dark hair behind her ear. "I love you too."

"I'm sorry," Lacey whispered, pushing back tears.

"I know, love." Renee's forehead creased before she turned back to the quiet road ahead.

They sat in silence as the sun rose behind them. Soft pinks contrasted the purple clouds as the sun staked its claim to the new day.

"You were right. There's more to life than finding your soulmate. I feel stupid thinking this was the solution to all my problems." Lacey could feel the weight of her new world settling on her shoulders.

"*Omnia vincit Amor: et nos cedamus Amori,*" her mother replied. Renee's gaze drifted down to her own compass. "Love conquers all, and so let us surrender ourselves to love."

Lacey saw the quote in a new light. It wasn't about surrendering everything in your life for your lover. It meant that love was something that would break you until you gave in to it. Why had she ever thought she could control meeting her soulmate? It was almost fitting that he would be across the ocean.

All her mom's talk about love being everywhere started to make sense. She had to surrender to the love that she had, whatever the source. She wished her mom would drive faster as a new sense of urgency filled her. Without her soulmate in the picture, she knew she needed to get home. She needed to see Nessie and set things right.

Lacey imagined how to make it up to Nessie. No gift could capture her remorse. She toyed with the idea of texting Nessie an apology, but resolved it would be better if she told her face-to-face. As she played it through in her mind, she couldn't help but notice that the already stuffy air in the SUV was growing more unbearable by the minute. She peeled off her sweater and rolled down the window, grateful for the crisp morning air. Renee wrapped her arms around herself and gave Lacey a curious look as the breeze entered the car.

"Sorry, Mom. I just need some fresh air."

Lacey checked to make sure her heated seat wasn't on as her core temperature continued to rise. *Do I have a fever? I swear, if all this stupid rain made me sick, I'm going to—*

That's when she felt the hum. The softest vibration, calling her attention downward. She looked at her compass and was shocked to see it moving. Not the tiny increments it had crept in the past four days. Steady in its counterclockwise movement, the arrow was slow as it turned away from the rising sun.

"Mom." A bead of sweat trickled down her forehead. "Mom, it's changing. It's actually changing." Lacey's thoughts swarmed as she tried to sort out what was happening.

Renee stole a glance over the console. "It's moving so fast."

As the beautiful arrow came to the quarter mark, both girls looked up and out of the passenger window. They searched for a car, sure one must be about to pass, but the highway was quiet with the early day. Lacey's arrow continued on its course and passed right on by.

"A plane," Renee suggested. "They must be on a plane."

Lacey almost laughed at the thought. How many days had she wasted crossing to the edge of her country for her soulmate to come when she was on her way back? She worried how much farther west he was going to go. She tried to think like Nessie might. Maybe he had felt her getting closer and was trying to bridge the gap? She had thought they were close before, but the feeling in her body now proved they hadn't been. It had barely changed as she crossed provinces. Now she could feel the buzzing and shifts in the air, as well as the hard pull, even as he distanced again.

"So. What now?" Renee asked.

Lacey took a breath, her mental apology to Nessie fresh in her mind. "Nothing yet. We need to get home. You need to get back to Dad and to work. I need to apologize to Ness. Then once everything has settled, we'll see." Newfound pride fluttered in Lacey's chest. She wasn't about to go gallivanting across the country again. Whims got people hurt. She would repair things with Nessie. Then, and only then, she would figure out what to do. With her best friend by her side, as she should have the first time.

Renee smiled and reached out to hold her hand. The sun continued its steady incline into the sky as the girls relaxed into the easier part of their drive, the last stretch beckoning them home.

CHAPTER LV

GARETH

11:07 a.m.

Gareth pulled his luggage off the conveyor belt and went to Sebastian's side. A shoulder caught his own and Gareth turned to catch Damien's vampire-like gray-green eyes. Not missing a beat, Damien smirked then shrugged and carried on his way to the sliding doors—the last thing between the boys and the new families they'd be staying with.

Wanker, Gareth thought to himself before Sebastian surged forward at the sight of his own suitcase.

"You ready?" he asked, unsure if he was ready himself. Sebastian nodded, his face covered in a light sheen of sweat.

"You more worried about the family or your soulmate?" He nudged Sebastian with his elbow, willing him to laugh along. He didn't.

"I don't know."

Gareth wrapped his arm over Sebastian's shoulders and gave him a light, jostled hug. When they cleared the sliding doors, they were met by a group of people with wide, welcoming grins. A pair of men, one Asian and the other Caucasian, clung to each other's arms as they waved vigorously, their eyes bright with excitement. Next to them, an indigenous family of four gathered close, their dark hair and tawny skin clearly marking them as related—a mother, a father, and twin daughters. Gareth had looked over the information packet so many times he practically had his exchange family memorized.

Between the hovering families, a man with a small frame stepped forward, adjusting his ball cap before extending his hand. "Gareth and Sebastian, I presume?"

The boys nodded.

"Perfect, that's it, then. Welcome to Canada, boys. My name is Trevor, but you can just call me Coach." A mouth crammed with yellowing teeth smiled at them as he shook each of their hands. "Now, if you boys want to follow me and meet your new households." He ushered the two groups together. "Which of you is Gareth?"

Gareth raised his hand, keeping it low as he already towered over the group.

"Excellent." Coach gestured to the family of four. "We figured because you came from a large family of your own that you guys

384

would be a good match."

From two brothers to two sisters? How is that a good match? Gareth tried not to let his doubt show. The sisters were a mirror image of one another. Their thick black hair was plaited back in waist-length braids, and identical mistrust cast across their faces.

Beside him, Sebastian was introduced to the beaming gay couple.

"Liam and Dakota were inseparable, and your coach suggested as much about you two." Trevor laughed as he rested his hands on their shoulders. "Here's to hoping you have as much chemistry on the field as they did. So, our first practice is this Friday. If you have any questions, this is the number you can reach me at."

Gareth couldn't help as he zoned out, a new fear battering in his chest. He'd never felt so far away from home.

When the coach finally released the boys to their families, the collective group made their way to the train station. Sebastian's new exchange parents chatted about all the sightseeing they had planned and about food preferences and lunch plans. Gareth's family politely followed along. Somehow, their steady silence ate away at his nerves. How had Sebastian gotten the extroverted family?

When the train pulled closer to downtown Toronto, Sebastian's hand grasped Gareth's wrist hard.

"Gareth, it's happening." Sebastian's voice was quiet, hardly a whisper, but Gareth caught every word.

He shoved down his excitement and tried to keep his own voice low as the parents chattered about stopping at some aquarium. "Really? Now? What are we gonna do, mate? It's not like we can just ditch our new families on day one. Maybe I could cause a distraction and you could make a run for it?"

"Don't be dense," Sebastian scoffed and rolled his eyes. He shook his hair out of his eyes. "The last thing we need is to screw up this trip on day one. Maybe we should talk to them? Or take them with us?"

"You're going to take a group of complete strangers to meet your soulmate? Seems like a solid way to kill the mood. What if they say no? What if they won't let you go?"

"What if I bail, I meet my soulmate, and then when I come back, I end up being grounded for the rest of the trip? I don't want to start things off on the wrong foot."

Gareth chuckled. "They can't ground us, mate. You just need to make a run for it. I'll say you had to use the loo or something."

"And what if my soulmate is farther away? What if I don't make it back right away? What if I can't find my way back? Listen. Canadians are supposed to be nice. I think we should tell them and pray to Cupid they agree to let us go. And if they say no, then we can go with your wild escape plan. Deal?"

Gareth grinned. "Deal."

CHAPTER LVI

RENEE

11:54 a.m.

"**Mom. I think** it's happening, and I think I might puke."

"For the love of Cupid, please do not puke in this car, missy. We've done enough damage already and your father will not be happy if we have to add a cleaning bill on top of this weekend," Renee threatened.

Lacey's round cheeks were flushed a wild-berry red. "I've never felt it pull this hard before. We're not even intentionally following it, but it's aching."

Renee tried to make sense of it in her mind. She flexed her hands over the steering wheel.

"Well, I suppose you have a decision to make, then. I would guess that he's probably looking for you now. So, what do you want to do?" She tried hard not to give her daughter any hints as to what she thought. She didn't want to have any influence over this choice.

"Mom. MOM. Pull over. Sweet Venus, please pull over."

Renee pulled out of the mainstream traffic, frantic to find somewhere safe to stop in the lunchtime rush.

"So help me, Lacey, if you puke now your breath will smell like vomit just when you might be about to meet the love of your life. Take deep breaths, and whatever you do, do not puke in this car, missy."

She pulled into an alleyway off the side street. The lack of parking spots forced Renee to stop on the narrow road. *Please don't let anyone come up behind me now.*

Lacey's seat belt was off in an instant. She pushed open her door and leaned over her knees. Her face was scarlet, and if Renee didn't know better, she would say her daughter looked feverish.

"Sweetie, tell me what you need. Do you want some water?"

She wished she could take off her own seat belt and go to Lacey's side, but her illegal stop kept her still. Renee ran through scenarios in her mind of how this was going to play out.

"Mom. I need to go. I… I need to do this. And I think I need to do it alone." Lacey straightened. Her hazel eyes were pleading when she turned back and rested her arm on the open door. "It's not that I don't love you, and it's not that I'm ditching you. I just feel like I need to do this on my own."

Renee nodded. Who wanted to meet the love of their life with their mother looming over them? She handed her daughter her own phone.

"Take my phone in case you need it for an emergency. I'm going to work my way back downtown. I'll meet you at your favorite Italian restaurant by the CN Tower at one o'clock, sharp. Don't you dare be a minute late or so help me, I might lose my marbles."

Lacey nodded, but where in the beginning of the trip excitement had danced in her eyes, now Renee saw hints of fear.

"You have an hour, Lacey. If you haven't found him by then, you come back to me. Understand? Then we'll figure it out from there." Renee put the vehicle in Park and unbuckled her seat belt. She leaned over, and Lacey sat back in the passenger seat to meet her halfway. She hugged her daughter hard.

"I love you. Stay safe. I hope he's amazing." She kissed Lacey on the forehead. Her daughter's eyes watered as she smiled back at her.

"I love you too, Mom."

Lacey got out of the car and made her way toward the busy street. Renee fought the urge to follow as her own compass pulled. She took a deep breath.

She's going to be okay. I'm going to be okay. We're all going to be okay.

But both her heart and compass ached.

CHAPTER LVII

CHARITY

11:57 a.m.

As the sun reached its peak in the sky, Charity traced over her instructions to make sure she'd covered everything. Jaylynn had been paired with Charity to prepare a ceremony site, and they had chosen the clearing of clovers near the cabin. Tall birch trees ringed the outside, their canopy reaching up to kiss the wide, blue sky. Birds chirped in afternoon song and a soft breeze ruffled Charity's hair.

Psyche had instructed them to make sure the clearing would be a space of truest love and intention. For her final task, Charity hauled a massive bag of Himalayan salts around the perimeter of the meadow, which was large enough to fit three cars inside, to set the boundary of their ritual.

Jaylynn knelt in the center of the circle beside the short, bronze table that now had tarot cards and a stem of incense burning. She was taking the time to pray and bless their sacred space, her usually soft eyes shut tight in concentration. Charity wasn't sure where Psyche herself went, but she imagined she was mentally preparing for the reality of trying to reach Cupid. When the salt boundary was complete, Charity made her way back to the cabin to gather any last items that would help set the mood of the altar.

When she stepped through the cabin doorway, she came to an unexpected sight. Blake and Nessie leaned over a counter, their shoulders knit tight together and laughter dancing off the wooden beams around them. They were covered in crumbled flowers. Nessie screamed as lemon juice sprayed out of Blake's clenched fist.

"I'm not sure what that lemon did to either of you, but I'm pretty sure murdering it wasn't in the instructions." Charity shuffled over to the brewing pot. Blake gave up the crushed lemon with a shrug and Nessie snorted.

Looking at Psyche's scrawl, Charity searched through the ingredients. "The recipe says a zest of lemon, not its whole soul." Charity spied a nearby knife and skimmed part of the lemon skin into the pot. "This is a zest of lemon."

Nessie laughed harder and Blake's face fell.

"I swear, if we have to start that whole thing over because of a stupid lemon—" Blake stopped as Psyche swooped into the room with her ever-radiant smile.

Her dark curls slipped over her shoulders as she leaned forward to assess the work. "As I thought, no harm done. I knew you were both up for the task." She pecked Blake on the cheek, who promptly turned bright red.

Psyche turned to Charity. "How close is the ceremony site to being ready?"

Charity remembered why she came back to the cabin. "I was just getting some last tokens. Ness, could we use the love handbook Psyche lent you?"

Nessie brushed her hands off on her jeans and went over to her open suitcase. Her eyes flashed before she let the leather-bound book go. "I haven't gotten through it all yet."

Psyche smiled. "You'll still have all the time in the world to read over my scribbles afterward. An excellent choice, Charity."

Afterward. Charity had a hard time wrapping her head around how this was going to play out. She grabbed the book, and at the last moment also reached for a jagged, palm-sized pink stone that sat on a windowsill. If there was any stone meant to be on an altar of love, it had to be rose quartz. She made her way back to the clearing, carefully placing the last items on the small bronze table. Jaylynn sat back as her murmured prayer came to completion, and smiled.

An altar, a boundary, and an intention. Nessie had made a joke earlier about how she thought spells were meant to be done under the cover of night, but Psyche insisted they could do it during the day. She had explained she would rather attempt under Apollo's watchful eye than under the mystery of the night.

"Darkness cannot hide us from the gods. Therefore, we shall use the ambient energy of the sun to light our path."

When Psyche revealed her compass-clock was bound to twelve o'clock, the same time as Nessie's, they'd agreed to run trials every afternoon until they found something that worked, committed to helping her have a conversation with Cupid, if nothing more.

At last, they all gathered in the clearing. The sun beat down from above. *At least doing it in the daylight makes it feel less ominous,* Charity thought to herself. They each gathered within the salt circle, following Psyche's lead to kneel. The women joined hands, following Psyche as she closed her eyes and bowed her head. Before Charity could acknowledge that they were starting, Psyche broke the silence.

Her voice was deep and reverent as she spoke. "Juno, mother of the gods, hear me now. Help me stay grounded. Help us blur the lines that keep our realms apart. Help us reach the god of love."

Charity put all her attention on holding space as they had been practicing daily. She imagined a giant bubble extending from her salt line, creating a dome over their prayer. Psyche continued to pray as the rest of the women held tight.

"Mercury, messenger of the gods. See our pleas and send word to Cupid. Help us mend that which was long-ago broken. See our call and send it on its rightful path."

Charity continued to breathe deep into her belly. The mild

breeze that had ruffled the trees earlier now fell silent. She wasn't sure if it was a good sign or not.

"Janus, god of doors, beginnings, and endings. Let us bring this cycle to a close. Send for Cupid. Give us a chance to end what was once started. Your eternal servant, I always remain."

The ground grew warm under Charity's knees. The radiant light of the sun shone hot on her eyelids. She didn't dare look up. Terra Mater could be burning around them, but she would not look. She had to hold the space. She couldn't afford to be distracted by—

"I have long awaited your call."

CHAPTER LVIII

12:02 p.m.

"Where in Jupiter's name have you been?" Nylah's manager's face was hard with contempt. "I expected you here hours ago!"

Nylah grabbed the black uniform apron and tied it behind their neck, conscious of the growing lunch-time crowd.

"You know, Nylah, I've been patient with you, but you're reaching the end of my tolerance."

"I know, I know. I swear I'm sorry!" Nylah washed their hands and stole a glance over the cups prepped with names scrawled on the sides. "It was an emergency. I had to take my friend to the hospital."

Nylah thought back to the cot they'd left Jazz on. His stitches had been sewn shut promptly, but he hadn't been allowed to leave because of the amount of blood he'd lost. Nylah hadn't wanted to go, but after a lot of angry texts from the manager and reassurance that Jazz would be under good care, they'd raced to the café.

Nylah's composure was a mess. The usual tight, red curls that danced on their neckline were pressed flat. They hadn't even had time to shower. The only thing working in Nylah's favor was that they'd managed to clean every trace of blood from their hands.

"Nylah, this isn't the first emergency that's torn you away from work and left me stranded with swarms of customers." The manager held up a steaming mug and called out the customer's name. Nylah's cheeks warmed at the memories of calling in at the last minute after the blowup with their parents, the day their grandma had passed away, and then the one morning they'd accidentally woken up three hours late with a wicked wine hangover.

"I swear it was an emergency. I'll be better."

The ground swayed under Nylah's feet. They planted their hands on the counter. The tiny clock in the corner of the ordering screen came into bright focus: 12:03.

For the love of Cupid, now? What is wrong with this day?

Nylah stole a second to assess their reflection in a stainless-steel coffee pot. Greasy fringe bangs clumped against the rim of their large glasses.

I literally couldn't look worse.

Nylah looked at the growing line of cups waiting to be filled. The manager was processing customers with a fury masked by a fake smile as Nylah's legs became jelly.

"I—" Nylah gasped for breath. The reality that their soulmate was only three minutes away pulsed like waves against their eardrums.

"Nylah, get it together."

"I think I need some fresh air, I… I don't feel so good." Please let me go. I can't do this here, now.

"Are you asking to be fired? Nylah, I swear…"

The manager's voice grew fuzzy, and soon all Nylah could hear was the steady hum that filled their ears.

Breathe.

But they couldn't.

The air in the room went still.

The bells on the door chimed.

Nylah leaned to try and see around the people that blocked the doorway.

LACEY

Lacey tried desperately not to puke as her mother's words lingered in her head. Her body burned as hot as an oven, and she couldn't take a full breath against the weight of her anticipation. She walked down the sunny Toronto street, her eyes darting from side to side. Thoughts raced through her mind. Why hadn't she brought any water? Why hadn't she fixed her makeup? Was a busy street really where she wanted to meet the love of her life?

She knew without a doubt it was about to happen and took a chance. She turned down a less busy street, relieved to see a small coffee shop off the corner. *There. Coffee shops are romantic, right?* She could touch up her makeup, grab a water, and wait there.

Bells chimed as she stepped in. A barista with red fringe bangs, large rose-gold glasses, and ear stretchers looked up and caught Lacey's eye. The air stopped moving. Her heartbeat pounded over the chattering patrons.

Sweet Venus, this is actually happening.

SEBASTIAN

Sebastian ran. He had tried walking calmly, but eventually he couldn't suppress the urgency he felt at his core. He wove between people, muttering apologies as he went. Though the crowds and the streets were unfamiliar, his compass pulsed clear directions.

He couldn't believe how cool his exchange family had been about him venturing off on his own. After a quick exchange of phone numbers, Gareth had given him a huge hug before pushing him on his way, and Sebastian hadn't stopped moving since. Sweat trickled down his back and he worried he might start to smell bad, so he slowed.

He let his run shift to a soft jog, then to a fast walk as he felt his compass pull change directions again. Checking down the street, he was pleased to see it was less crowded. He let his feet guide him forward as he tried to slow his breathing. His heart hammered in his chest. He wasn't sure that he was ready, but he also couldn't turn back. He had to know. Taking one step in front of the other, he approached his fate.

CHAPTER LIX

PSYCHE

12:04 p.m.

The voice hummed through the air, chiming with power and a beckoning presence.

Jupiter Almighty, I can't believe that worked. Psyche could barely contain her shock.

It sounded like music that had never graced her ears before. It was enticing and begged her to open her eyes. She tightened them shut, as she had instructed everyone else to do as well. She'd already learned the hard way once what the price of seeing the gods was.

Hold the space. Don't be distracted. She could feel Nessie's energy tense, so she did her best to open her heart to her companion and lend her any extra strength she had.

"You seem surprised that I came," the melodic voice sang. Not the voice Psyche swore to never forget. Instantly, she realized her mistake.

Psyche's deep voice clashed against the other as she suppressed a shudder. "Venus. What are you doing here?"

"You think you can call upon my son and I wouldn't be informed? You think that you have Terra Mater and Fortuna's favor? Again, you underestimate my power and influence. You call for a god of love, and here I am. What is it you wish to speak?"

Psyche took a second to gather her wits. She could feel the pressure that pushed against the mental bubble she'd extended around their group. She swore she could feel tendrils of air playing through her hair. Smelling her. Investigating her.

Stay focused. Just tell her what she wants to hear. You could still make this right.

"Venus, great goddess of love and beauty. We worship you above all else. Please, bear us this gift. Bring forth Cupid. It has been ages. Surely you've tired of this game by now."

The temperature spiked, and Psyche wondered if the salt boundary was literally burning around them. She could feel Blake's hand getting sweaty as their clasp started to slip.

"Punishment is not a game, Psyche, and as you well know, your centuries are nothing to me. I will not come to my knees before you with a platter of all that you crave. Even in your blessing you mock me. Should I assume you've gathered these beautiful women as a sacrifice to me? To try and gain good faith?" Venus's melodic voice grew in strength.

"What?" Psyche's voice shook. "Absolutely not! The age of human sacrifices has passed, Venus." Psyche shifted from anger to submission in a heartbeat. "Instead, my offering to you is my humbleness. I'm sorry for all the trouble I've caused you. Please, Venus. You are the mother of Love itself. Surely you want to free your son by now."

"Well," Venus continued with an air of arrogance, "I refuse your offering. I will not destroy their souls, for it would only set your own beauty further apart. I see through this trap. It is clear to me that you doubt my strength."

"I have never doubted your strength, as I have never doubted your ability for compassion." Psyche scrambled for the right words to flatter the goddess. "Please, Venus. If you cannot let us be together, could you at least consider another option? You are powerful beyond means. If you are still adamant to keep Cupid and I apart, I offer you my compass instead. Take it away. Without my compass, I swear I will stop seeking your son. I swear it to the skies and the sea. I swear it to Terra Mater and to Jupiter above. Let me be free of this, and I will never bother you again."

Bitter laughter rang loud in their clearing. "Take your compass away? That's what your next greatest wish is?"

"Surely you have the power to do so."

"Of course I do. Your offered sacrifice isn't great enough, though. To be free of the link to my son is a great ask, and so the price will be higher."

"What do you want, Venus? I'll give you anything."

Psyche was positive the surrounding clovers were actively burning as heat licked her knees and arms, but she didn't dare open her eyes. She knew that when gods took on their true form, it could blind a mortal. And it would be so like Venus to show up in her full, glorious form.

"What I want, *you* cannot give. But fret not, I will grant your wish. But know that doing so isn't to release you from punishment. It is to extend it."

Suddenly, it occurred to Psyche that her companions might be about to die. Panic rose in her chest as Jaylynn's and Blake's grips tightened simultaneously. How could she stand up against a goddess? What gifts did she have?

"For a time, I've let your compass stay, believing it would bring you greater torment. Now I see it has only bred hope, and that I refuse to allow. So may it be that my son's magic shall be ripped from the mortal realm. May your soul know despair, as you feel the last bit of his soul torn from yours. May your heart shudder as it feels the shared pain of souls across the world. And may you continue to survive, rotting in your own prison. Let us see how your beauty fares then." Venom leaked from Venus's booming voice.

Psyche clung to her boundaries. She prayed hard to keep her

container solid as she felt it melting away. A crack and a heavy crash sounded nearby, followed by a howling wind that tore through the scalding air around them. She cried out as her flesh burned, pain searing the skin of her hands. Tears rolled over her hot face as she tried desperately not to let the horror break free on the rest of the world. But she wasn't enough, even with the support of the other women.

The boundary broke, and the fierce wind blew the five women apart. Psyche slid on her back out of the ceremony circle and through the salt line. She tried to open her eyes but the heat had seared them shut. She pulled her legs to her chest and wrapped an arm over her head to hide from the ferocious white light that beat down at her.

Oh, Cupid… What have I done?

CHAPTER LX

LACEY

12:05 p.m.

Her heart tore in half in her chest. Lacey screamed as she fell to her knees, the sudden pain an unimaginable agony that ripped through her body. She curled up on the café floor and clutched her head to her chest. A wild thunderstorm crashed through her skull, roaring and lashing against the fabric of her existence.

People in the café were up in arms; some jumped from her scream, while others fell to the ground as well. Shock rippled through Lacey's body as all the oxygen was sucked out of her lungs. She rolled onto her back, clutching the neckline of her top. She couldn't tell what hurt the most: the pounding in her head, the crushing weight on her lungs, or the feeling like her heart had been torn out of her chest.

What is happening to me?

She could make out the sound of crying and people calling for help. Screaming echoed from the streets. She rolled back to her side, looking herself over to see if she'd been shot. Though her vision was blurry around the edges, she could make out enough to see the damage.

She may as well have been shot.

She noticed the clean skin immediately, her forearms perfectly pale, as if they had never been otherwise. She frantically ran her hand over where her compass had been imprinted.

It was gone. Literally, without a trace.

Lacey clutched her arm to herself, tears streaming down her face in fresh vigor as she tried to make sense of what had happened. She surveyed the room that had changed from such a soft and calming demeanor to chaos. Two people held the barista, who must have collapsed as well. They looked at Lacey with equal concern. Another couple sobbed as they held one another in a corner.

Before she could stop herself, Lacey puked on the floor.

RENEE

Renee felt the wheel slip between her fingers as her world fell apart. Car horns shrieked and tires screeched in response. In an instant, her seat belt lashed into her aching chest. Her shoulders wrapped forward and her head swung with the momentum as the nose of her vehicle hit a light post. Her heartbeat hammered in her ears, the sounds of the world a fuzzy blur. If there was screaming from the crash, Renee didn't hear it. Only one thing was clear in her mind.

Lacey.

The airbag exploded in her face and thrust her back against the seat. A thick metallic taste filled her mouth as blood pooled to her throat, hot and threatening to choke her. Waves of black washed her vision.

Jupiter Almighty, please no.

Renee couldn't lift her arms. She couldn't open her eyes. She tried to guess.

Was she hit by a car? Jumped in an alley? How—

Renee's head lulled as she passed out against the bloody airbag.

SEBASTIAN

Sebastian tripped and stumbled into a brick wall. Not a block away, he could hear a massive crash, followed by screaming. A vise clamped over his head as the unnatural ripping within his mind started. He clutched his skull as his knees buckled. He collapsed on the pavement. Invisible pressure crushed his temples and sweat coated his forehead.

A hard foot caught his ankle as bystanders ran in mindless chaos, and he grimaced as the sharp pain from his previously healed ankle swelled fresh. He struggled to push himself up and out of the stampede. That was when he noticed that his two-week-old compass had vanished.

No.

He had hardly gotten used to its presence, only now to have it unexpectedly torn away. A single tear broke free, and he wiped it away in a fury.

I will not cry about this. I won't. I can't.

Sebastian watched the world crumble around him in plumes of black smoke and piercing sirens.

KADE

Kade staggered through the front door with a lurch as a piece inside him snapped. In her crate, Lady howled and cried, her little claws ringing sharp against the metal door She whimpered as Kade clenched his fists and stumbled forward. He hurried to take the blanket that covered her kennel off, confused as his body shuddered. Lady barked a series of high-pitched yelps. He reached down and unlocked the clasp. He tried to coax her out, but the stubborn puppy wouldn't move.

"C'mon, Lady. I'm here now. It's okay." He tried to coax her out, conscious his lunch break was short. She whimpered as she curled up in the back. He sat back as a wave of nausea hit him.

Then Kade noticed his bare arm.

No. His first thought was of Renee. He fumbled until he found his phone. He pulled up her contact and hit Call. The phone rang and rang and rang.

NYLAH

Nylah struggled to their feet and wiped the tears from their eyes. Their limbs were ice cold, and they trembled as they adjusted their glasses. A ringing phone added to the cacophony of noise.

The door flung open. But where Nylah expected an officer would stand, instead stood a lean boy with ruffled hair.

"Excuse me," he gasped. The small café crowd quieted, and the phone stopped ringing. Sweat covered the boy's brow and his English accent trembled with fear. "I… I know this is crazy. But I swear I was just about to meet my soulmate." His vibrant eyes scanned over the people in the room, borderline frantic.

Sweet Venus. Nylah's legs quaked. Was it possible they'd won Fortuna's favor, even in this madness? But before Nylah could step forward, the girl with long black hair intercepted him.

LACEY

Lacey stepped forward in a haze and let go of the chair she'd been leaning on. His eyes locked on hers and she couldn't believe it. She walked until she was right in front of him. He tentatively reached out and brushed the curtain of hair that clung to her round cheeks behind her ears. There were no fireworks or crazy magical explosions. Lacey felt the excitement building in her chest all the same, though. He'd found her, even against all the odds. From being separated by an ocean and their compasses being torn away moments before they were to meet, they found each other.

She stared up into his eyes. The room filled with people around her melted away.

"You," he murmured, his rich eyes gazing into her own. "You are undeniably worth crossing oceans for."

She bit her lip and her eyes watered. *Could I be this lucky?* She was too breathless to speak. His chin tilted down to meet hers, and he wrapped his arms around her waist. Self-conscious of recently puking, she turned her face away before his lips brushed hers.

"Sorry," she said as she gasped for air. "I'm just having a hard time breathing." She coughed as she pulled back to see a forgiving smile. She leaned into his chest and welcomed his unfamiliar warmth as he held her tight, pulling all her pieces back together.

Everything will be all right now.

As people started to clap, Lacey's awareness of the café came back to startling focus. Around her, tear-filled faces brimmed with hope. The only exception was the pale-faced barista. Two men helped the employee stand, and Lacey was met with a look of absolute distress. The redheaded barista held out their hand and mouthed a wordless plea. Lacey could read the pale lips from across the room easy enough.

No.

Lacey broke eye contact and turned abruptly. She looked up at her soulmate and took him by the hand. "Can we leave this place? Please?"

"Of course," he said with an easy smile. He pulled her out onto the street. They settled side by side on the concrete step, fingers clammy but interlaced. She looked up to her soulmate, still amazed they had found each other.

"My name's Lacey," she offered. She figured it was as good of a place as any to start.

He smiled back, showing off a perfectly lopsided grin. "It's nice to meet you, Lacey. I'm Damien."

His wristwatch glinted in the sun as the time shifted from 12:05 to 12:06. But Lacey's head was swirling in euphoria. She was too fixated on Damien's startling gray-green eyes to notice that she was three minutes too early. And with her bare left forearm, there was no magic left to remind her otherwise.

THE END

Stay tuned for book two of the Soulmate Seekers Series:

VENUS'S VENGENCE

Find more information at www.ashleyweisswrites.ca and

sign up for exclusive newsletter updates!

CHARACTER APPENDIX

Addi: Gareth's younger brother

Alva: Damien's friend

Blake: Nickname J.B. | Tatiana's girlfriend, Sal's apprentice

Boots: Nylah's rescued kitten

Charity McKenzie: Nessie's mother, Luke's wife | compass-clock 7:13, 2:35

Dakota: Gareth's exchange partner

Damien Diaz: Teammate and rival of Sebastian and Gareth

Dr. Cavanagh: Compass Specialist

Elias: Vancouver university student

Elise Williams: Gareth, Emmet, and Addi's mum.

Emmet: Gareth's younger brother

Gareth Williams: Sebastian's best friend

Jaylynn Clare: Nylah's younger sister | compass-clock 7:36

Jazz: Nylah's best friend

Kade Baker: Renee's husband, Lacey's father | compass-clock 8:29

Kenyon Williams: Gareth, Emmet, and Addi's dad.

Lacey Baker: Renee and Kade's daughter, Nessie's best friend | compass-clock 12:09

Lady: Full name, Ladybug | Rescued red puppy with white spots

Liam: Sebastian's exchange partner

Marley: Sal's soulmate

Natalie Clare: Jaylynn and Nylah's mother

Nessie McKenzie: Charity's daughter, Lacey's best friend | compass-clock 12:00

Nylah Clare: Jaylynn's older sibling, Jazz's best friend | compass-clock 12:05

Renee Baker: Kade's wife, Lacey's mother | compass-clock 8:29, 9:18

Richard Clare: Jaylynn and Nylah's father

River: Toronto psychic

Rosabella: Rescued mother dog

Sal: New York City tattoo artist

Sebastian Evans: Gareth's best friend

Tatiana: Blake's girlfriend

The man at the bar: New Jersey boy | No compass-clock

Vee: Sebastian's older sister

ROMAN MYTHOLOGY APPENDIX

Apollo: God of the sun, archery, prophecy, and healing

Cupid: God of love | Psyche's soulmate

Decuma: One of the three Fates | Decides the length and quality of the thread of life

Fortuna: Goddess of chance and luck

Hekate: Goddess of magic and dark arts

Janus: God of doors, gates, and transitions

Juno: Goddess of marriage and childbirth | Queen of the gods

Jupiter: God of the sky and thunder | King of the gods

Mercury: Messenger of the gods | God of interpreters and translators

Minerva: Goddess of wisdom and defensive warfare

Morta: One of the three Fates | The one who cuts the thread of life

Neptune: God of the ocean and the seas

Nona: One of the three Fates | The one who spins and creates each thread of life

Pluto: God of the Underworld

Psyche: Cupid's soulmate

Terra Mater: Goddess of the Earth | "Mother Earth"

The Capitoline Triad: Jupiter, Juno, and Minerva

Venus: Goddess of love and beauty | Mother of Cupid

ACKNOWLEDGMENTS

The amount of time and effort that goes into writing a book borders on incomprehensible. Despite my own incalculable hours planning, writing, and editing, this book wouldn't exist without my amazing community.

First, to my enormous beta reader team. Thank you all for taking the time to read my manuscript in its various states of chaos and for answering my million questions about your reading experience. To Ashley, Sam, Alora, and Melissa, thanks for all your thoughtful feedback through the rough drafts as I figured out how to scale back the themes and intensity of certain scenes. Thank you to Kaitlyn for convincing me to commit to Roman mythology instead of a blended Greco-Roman retelling, and to Angeline for spear-heading my sensitivity readers team.

To Aleisha, I cannot thank you enough for not only heavily reviewing my first draft, but being my editor for almost every newsletter and related project since. Casia, I adored all 327 comments you left cheering on my manuscript but also gently reminding me I don't actually need a comma every time I take a breath. And I have to give a huge shout-out to Janet for printing hundreds and hundreds of pages so my local betas could have paper copies. I hope getting the sneak peek at my novel was worth it and I totally owe you.

To all the authors and writers I've connected with online, thank you for sharing your knowledge and support. To Danielle, Sabrina, and Zanne: you each revolutionized my craft in different ways with your beta feedback and I am forever grateful to finally understand what showing versus telling means. Thank you to Kathrine for double-checking all my UK characters' chapters for accuracy. To Laura for virtually holding my hand as I struggled with deciding on my publishing journey—I can't wait for more of your published works to hit the shelves. Then, of course, my biggest thank-you goes to Cathrine. I don't know what I would have done if Instagram hadn't connected us. You have been my faithful sidekick in the writing world and I couldn't have chosen a better human to spend all my creative hours with. Thank you for giving me a hard time when I needed it, for reminding me to celebrate each achievement, and for explaining so much of publishing down to the tiniest of details.

As for family, I have three specific people to thank. First, to the oldest of my brothers, Brandon. Thank you for not only beta reading for me, but meticulously pointing out my strengths and weaknesses. To my mother, Cindy, thank you for reading the first draft and drawing highlighter hearts around all your favorite paragraphs and quotes. Your endless love is reflected in every page of this book. And to my dad, Rob. Not a single other person has been more on my case about bringing this book to life than you. You helped me push through some of the hardest points of balancing writing and life and I hope even though this book is far from your preferred reading genre, that you're proud.

I have to give special thanks to my beloved life partner, Brendan. What started as a passion project when we were stuck in a one-bedroom apartment over months of quarantine, became years of me killing laptops, crying about plot holes, and ranting about publishing platforms. Your patience as I chase my author dream is a blessing. To the rest of my friends and family who ask how my writing is going even though you run the risk that I might talk forever, thank you for all your encouragement.

Next, we have my editors. Thank you to Emily Marquart for the thorough copy edits and generous feedback. Thank you to Cathrine Swift for formatting this book faster than I dreamed possible. And to Leah Mol for proofreading *Cupid's Compass* and helping me make the final product perfect.

To my book cover designer, Franziska Stern, aka @coverdungeonrabbit, words alone cannot capture how grateful I am to you. You are an incredibly talented artist of this generation, and I am honored that you took on my project. Thank you for bringing the cover of my dreams to life.

Lastly, thank you to my readers. I may have written this book with only one person in mind, but it's all of you who make all the hours and years of writing worth it. I hope you don't hate me after that ending, and I promise I know exactly how badly you want book two. Not a day goes by without these characters living rent free in my head. They have a story to tell and I'm committed to getting it out there.

About the Author

A natural storyteller with a flair for the dramatic, Ashley Weiss lives in Alberta, Canada. Her debut novel, Cupid's Compass, began as a 2020 quarantine project and grew to be an irreplaceable passion. When she isn't writing, Ashley can be found cuddling her dog or watching movies with her love.

Find her on Instagram @ashley.weiss.writes